I0823928

Trail of the Red Butterfly

TRAIL *of the* RED BUTTERFLY

Karl H. Schlesier

TEXAS TECH UNIVERSITY PRESS

This book is typeset in Bembo. The paper used in this book meets the minimum requirements of ANSI/NISO Z39.48-1992 (R1997). ♾

Designed by Lindsay Starr

Library of Congress Cataloging-in-Publication Data
Schlesier, Karl H.
Trail of the red butterfly / Karl H. Schlesier.
p. cm.
Summary: "In 1807, Whirlwind, a Cheyenne Kit Fox headman, leads a search across New Spain, hoping to recover Stone, his twin, captured in a horse-raiding expedition. From the Colorado plains to the Camino Real, the trek is rooted in the author's anthropological research and draws on Juan Pedro Walker's 1805 map"—Provided by publisher.
Includes bibliographical references and index.
ISBN-13: 978-0-89672-617-8 (alk. paper)
ISBN-10: 0-89672-617-7 (alk. paper)
I. Title.
PS3569.C5128T73 2007
813'.54—dc22

2007014349

Printed in the United States of America
07 08 09 10 11 12 13 14 15 / 9 8 7 6 5 4 3 2 1

Although this is a work of fiction, all habitation sites mentioned in the story are historical, and the land features named are accurately described. The distribution of Indian camps in the High Plains at the time of the story is historical, as are the names of the bands involved. Brief descriptions of ceremonial behavior, essential to the story, are based on published material in the anthropological literature. The characters in the story are fictional.

Texas Tech University Press
Box 41037, Lubbock, Texas 79409-1037 USA
800.832.4042 | ttup@ttu.edu | www.ttup.ttu.edu

For Sibylle,

Sedna, Ariane,

Dorian, and Gerhard

They speak of me as being

From the north they came

Against the winds they roamed

At the time of the white dawn

On the journey to the evergreen mountains

Beyond the flat lands

Did we go riding.

***The butterfly here considered is the monarch* (Danaus plexippus).** It has a wingspan of three and a half to four inches (89–102 mm). Above it is bright orange red with black veins and black margins sprinkled with white dots. The tip of the forewing is black, interrupted by larger white and orange spots. Below it is a paler, duskier orange. On the male, one black spot appears between the hindwing cell and margin. The female is darker with black veins smudged.

The monarch is the only butterfly that annually migrates both north and south as birds do, on a regular basis. But no single individual makes the entire round-trip journey. In the fall, monarchs of the north begin to congregate in large flocks and move southward. Monarchs of the Great Plains continue south all the way to the Sierra Madre of central Mexico, where they spend the winter in fir forests at high altitudes. In the spring they head north, breed along the way, and their offspring return to the starting point.

Monarchs were present in historic time throughout Cheyenne territory. In Cheyenne religious philosophy, the monarch belongs to the *maheoneveksеo* group of holy birds. Cheyennes call the monarch *maehoze,* the Red Messenger, who brings to select humans information and instruction from the spirit world.

INTRODUCTION

In the year 1800 the entire eastern part of northern New Spain, with the exception of New Mexico, was under attack by raiding parties of four different groups of mounted tribesmen of the Buffalo Plains: Apaches, Comanches, Kiowas, Gatakas.

The Apaches included groups of such diverse origin as the Palomas, Carlanas, Llaneros, Lipans, and Mescaleros. In 1800 their home ranges extended from the Pecos River west to the Rio Grande and, farther south, from the Edwards Plateau across the Rio Grande to the Bolsón de Mapimí of Coahuila. From the 1740s on, raiding parties of Lipans and Mescaleros, soon followed by their kin groups, struck throughout Coahuila, eastern Chihuahua, and southwest as far as Durango.

The Comanches, of Shoshonean origin, were newcomers to the southern Plains. Their bands had arrived around 1750 from the north after having forced Plains Apache groups, such as the Palomas, Carlanas, Llaneros, and Lipans, into Mescalero territory in eastern New Mexico and beyond, to the lower Rio Grande. Beginning in the 1760s, Comanche war bands raided through Coahuila and part of Chihuahua to Durango and Jalisco.

The Kiowas, Tanoan speakers, and their closely affiliated Apachean-speaking Gatakas or Prairie Apaches (sometimes called Kiowa Apaches), were originally peoples of the northern Plains, who followed the Comanches south. They left the Black Hills area beginning in the 1780s and, in the central Plains, made a lasting peace with the Comanche in 1790. After that date their war parties roamed deep into Spanish Mexico, even beyond Durango toward the suburbs of Mexico City.

Owing to decades of bitter warfare between them, Apache and Comanche raiding parties tried to avoid each other in Spanish territory. When they did meet, they usually fought. Kiowa-Gataka parties and Apache parties tolerated each other, mainly because the Gatakas spoke an Apachean dialect.

Plains Indians raided into northern New Spain for economic reasons, although the thrill of adventure and the lure of distant places also played important roles. The spoils were horses, plunder, and captives. The latter could either be adopted or traded for ransom at fairs in New Mexico (Taos, Pecos). Many hundreds of thousands of horses were taken and driven to Apache, Comanche, Kiowa, and Gataka camps. From there they were dispersed throughout the Plains, the Plateau, and regions east. Usually Cheyenne bands served as middlemen for Spanish horses captured by Comanches, Kiowas, and Gatakas, trading them at the Arikara Fair on the Missouri River for items of European manufacture, including muskets, powder, and lead.

Centuries of warfare, first by the Spanish against the Indian peoples of the region, a series of devastating epidemics of European diseases, especially smallpox and cholera, and later intrusions by raiders from the Plains, had made the northeastern frontier of New Spain a Tierra Despoblado, an "empty land."

The Algonkin-speaking Cheyennes were the last tribal group to join in the raids. Three of their six divisions left the Black Hills region around 1800 and moved south in the wake of the Kiowa and Gataka withdrawal. On friendly terms with both, they settled in the front range of the Rocky Mountains midway between the North Platte and the Arkansas River. Just as the Kiowas and Gatakas had learned about New Spain from the Comanches, so the Cheyennes learned from the Kiowas and Gatakas. Between 1802 and 1806, the first of the Cheyenne men, married to Kiowa and Gataka women and living in their camps, visited the Spanish lands in the south as members of war parties led by men of the latter two tribes.

Habitation sites in northern New Spain here mentioned are based on the excellent map by Juan Pedro Walker, dated 1805, and on diary notes by Lieutenant Zebulon Montgomery Pike, who traveled from Chihuahua to Monclova as a Spanish prisoner in April–May 1807. Some of these habitation sites disappeared later or, often, were renamed after successive Mexican revolutions. The description of the Laguna de Tagualita (called Lac du Cayman, Laguna de Mapimí, or Laguna de San Pedro on other early maps), the inland lake fed by the Nazas River, which disappeared when the river's run was arrested by dams, is also based on Juan Pedro Walker's map.

The original of the Walker map of 1805, entitled *Mapa geográfico que comprehende los terrenos de las Provincias de Texas, Coahuila, Nuevo Biscaya y Nuevo Mexico . . .*, is in the Henry E. Huntington Library and Art Gallery, San Marino, California. The author is grateful to Bill Frank of the Huntington, who made a copy of the map available. The author is indebted to the two anonymous readers of the manuscript and, especially, to J. M. Hayes, without whom this work would not have come into print.

MEMBERS OF THE SEARCH EXPEDITION, 1807–1808

Men

• • •

Stone, 27, *headman, Cheyenne*
Big Bow, 16, *Cheyenne, Stone's brother*
Powderface, 27, *Cheyenne*
Porcupine, 22, *Cheyenne, Powderface's brother*
Bear Tooth, 26, *Cheyenne*
Lame Bear, 19, *Cheyenne*
Yellow Eyes, 22, *Cheyenne*
Necklace, 20, *Cheyenne*
Little Bird, 26, *Cheyenne*
Red Bird, 25, *Cheyenne*
Lame Coyote, 23, *Cheyenne, She-Wolf's brother*
White River, 22, *Cheyenne, cousin of Stone*
Standing, 28, *Cheyenne*
Holy Singer, 29, *Cheyenne*
White Wolf, 30, *Cheyenne*
Daha, 25, *Gataka, Eaglenest's brother*
Däveko, 20, *Gataka, Eaglenest's brother*
Setpagoy, 24, *Kiowa, Sendehma's brother*
Set'toni, 19, *Kiowa, Sendehma's brother*

Women

• • •

Eaglenest, 22, *Gataka, Stone's wife*
Sendehma, 25, *Kiowa, Whirlwind's wife*
Bear Doctor Woman, 25, *Cheyenne, Little Bird's wife*
She-Wolf, 25, *Cheyenne, Red Bird's wife*
To'giai, 21, *Gataka, Daha's wife*
Tasenma, 18, *Kiowa, Setpagoy's wife*
Maria, 19, *Hiaqui [Yaqui]*

Children

• • •

Gondaima, 2 , *daughter of Whirlwind and Sendehma*
Walking Last, 4, *daughter of Little Bird and Bear Doctor Woman*
Manuel, 3, *Maria's son*

Set, *Gondaima's wolf dog*

Trail of the Red Butterfly

THE PARTING
April 17, 1805

He is twenty-five years old, Hohona, Stone. He stands in the tall grass in front of the Hovxnova camp and looks into his brother's eyes. Vovetas, Whirlwind, is mounted, holding the chestnut mare back. Cheyennes are shy, rarely showing emotion. Men cry only when performing in religious tribal ceremonies, in the presence of the sacred. Women cry only when they suffer a severe personal loss. Even twins do not touch in sorrow or in joy. Stone and Whirlwind do not touch. Stone is the stern, quiet one, solemn, stiff at times. Whirlwind is like his name, rotating from laughter to thoughtful introspection to laughter, always in motion, mischievous. He is prepared to leave. Behind him his new Kiowa wife, Sendehma, is fidgety, transmitting her restlessness to her horse.

Whirlwind looks at the sky. "It is a good day to ride." The early morning sun rests on his open face.

Stone nods. The two have never been separated before. He already feels a loss, feels as if something has been torn from him. "Come back in the spring. We will travel north together." He smiles. "Come earlier if you don't like the Kiowa food."

Whirlwind smiles. "Take care, brother. Don't let the Pawnees get you." One last look, deep into Stone's eyes. He knees the chestnut and touches the right side of the mare's neck with the right rawhide string of the double reins. The horse turns and moves off, followed by

Sendehma's mount. Stone watches them leave. Way down in the floodplain of the South Platte, the Ka'ta band of Kiowas has set in motion a long column of travois and riders and dogs, bunches of horses driven alongside on the march south, a colorful sight before the blue wall of the Rocky Mountains.

Whirlwind raises the lance over his head and shouts a carefree sound, the loose black hair waving as the horse gains speed. Stone watches with a strange feeling. The brown torso glistening in the sun, Sendehma in her yellow antelope gown behind him—these are the last he sees of them. He will always remember.

THE KIT FOXES

September 12, 1806

Sunrise. They ride slowly through an old streambed of the South Fork of the Republican River below the steep rise of the upland, a hundred feet high, that edges the floodplain. They ride in single file on the soft red sand. Two scouts are a few hundred paces ahead of the two headmen who lead a party of about forty Kit Fox soldiers. The headmen are Stone and Yellow Wolf. Stone is in command of the Kit Foxes of the Wotapio division, Yellow Wolf of the Heviksnipahis division. Half of the Heviksnipahis warriors, whose camp is two days of riding away on the South Platte, have joined the Wotapio men to repulse an intrusion by the Kitkahaki Pawnees. On both sides of the dead stream channel, among tall midgrasses, rise scattered groups of red cedar and, to the northwest, stands of cottonwoods and thickets of bur oak.

The noise of battle is directly to the north of the riders, but they move on east for another half mile. Stone whistles the mournful call of a kingbird, and ahead the scouts hold and look back, waiting. When the war party reaches them, Stone points northwest. He turns the horse and gestures to the men behind. The single file breaks up and the men fan out. Slowly they ride through the trees until they reach the edge of the open ground. They halt in cover.

Stone and Yellow Wolf sit their horses side by side. To their left and right the men form a skirmish line. Before them lies a rolling grassland almost a mile deep, reaching to the green curtain of cottonwoods that mask the place where the South Fork and the North Fork of the Republican come together. In the distance, in front of the dense woods, sits a tight camp circle of about eighty tipis, the Pawnee camp. Breastworks have been thrown up around it. There is no smoke from fires in the air.

Yellow Wolf points to the camp. "They have expected us."

Stone nods. He watches the battle going on to the west of the camp. In the full glare of the early morning sun, in swirling dust less than half a mile away, two lines of horsemen meet like two floods coming together, colliding in a mad churn, then flow apart again, each retreating, leaving something on the ground. The hoofbeat of many horses, wild yelling. From the camp women chant to fire up their men, and wail as well. Brown bodies shine in the sun, lances wave, shields, feathered staffs, a few war bonnets sway, sometimes the boom of a musket. As the lines fall back, showers of arrows crisscross the battleground. Then the lines halt beyond arrow range. A long pause. Single men ride out to taunt the enemy, calling for single combat. They wait. They are met. One Kitkahaki is down, one Cheyenne. Riders hurry out to retrieve them, and once again the lines surge forward, clash, and separate.

The Kit Foxes have done what they have been asked to do. They have outflanked the enemy and wait for their opportunity.

Stone looks along the line of Kit Foxes. They are members of one of the five soldier societies spread unevenly among the six Cheyenne tribal divisions. They see themselves as the bravest and most colorful of them all. It matters little that the Red Shields, Bowstrings, Elk, and Dog soldiers all boast the same for themselves.

Dressed for war, the Kit Foxes are an impressive sight. Every man, stripped to breechclout and moccasins, is painted yellow over his body excepting the forearms from the elbow down and the legs below the knees. These parts are painted black. On the chest between his braids, each wears the *hemen,* a small, black-painted piece of rawhide, crescent-shaped in the image of the early moon, both ends held by leather strings. Each wears two golden eagle feathers standing upright from the back of the head. Each carries a lance and a painted shield, a bow-and-arrow case slung over the shoulder. On each of the few who hold muskets, a powder horn and a pouch with lead balls are attached to a bandolier strapped across the chest.

Stone holds a long-barreled firearm cradled in his arm. This is a .577 Barnett trade musket, a "North West" gun, stamped 1804, which he got from English traders for a fine horse two months back at the Arikara villages. A lance is held by a loop on his left side.

He softly touches the neck of his nervous war horse, a dun mare who has come through Kiowa hands a long way from Coahuila. Around him the sound of insects, horses snorting, the swishing of tails.

While he watches a lull in the fighting, he thinks of his brother. Whirlwind should be beside him, but he is not. He did not come in the spring when the Wotapios broke camp to travel north for the tribal ceremonies held near the Black Hills, and the trading after that. He should have come. Every Cheyenne, young and old, is obligated to attend Maxhoetonstov, the ceremony of Mahoz, the sacred arrows, holiest of Cheyenne religious objects. But Whirlwind did not come. Why not? What happened? In every previous dangerous situation, the twins have watched out for each other. Not this time.

The battle in front of him resumes. With frantic yells, the two sides roll forward and clash once again. This time the Kitkahakis seem to break through and the Cheyennes give way, the enemy in pursuit. Stone and Yellow Wolf watch. The Pawnees are reckless. They press their charge and leave a wide gap between themselves and their camp. The moment of the Kit Foxes has come. "Natóeoavo," Stone shouts and pushes the dun forward.

All around him horses shoulder though the undergrowth into the open. Stone urges them into a fast run and, in the rolling grassland, they make for the now empty space between the Kitkahaki men and the camp. The Kit Foxes have been taught to fight in a close formation, and they stick to it. Cries from the camp, where the new danger has been recognized, try to alert their tribesmen. But in the heat of the chase the Kitkahakis have difficulty disengaging, and the Kit Foxes get closer. They have ridden in silence, but when they see the Pawnees turning back they burst into their shrill war cries. The enemies now stream back, but before they can band together for a defensive line their flank is hit by the Kit Foxes.

Stone shoots a warrior on a white horse through the body and dodges a lance thrust. He throws the musket over his shoulder and grabs his lance with his right hand, the shield on his left arm covering his body. Around him men mix in close combat. Horses squeal. A hatchet thrown at him misses his head. He parries another lance thrust with his shield and sees his weapon penetrate deep into a Pawnee thigh. He pulls the lance free and looks for another enemy. A horse bucks into the dun. Stone ducks under the jab of a lance and hits the enemy with the butt of his lance before he can bend to the off side of his horse. Expert riders all, men of both groups maneuver their horses for advantage. The battle is now fought in silence except for shrieks of pain from injured men and horses. The Kitkahakis desperately try to get away to their camp. Because of their greater numbers they press through the thin screen of Kit Foxes and make for their camp, leaving some warriors and a few horses in the dust. The fight is over. The Cheyennes who had run before the onslaught of the Pawnees gallop back. When they reach the Kit Foxes they stop and watch the enemies pass around and into their camp to safety. They shake their weapons and yell in triumph. They hold on the ground for a while, then turn away. Four enemies killed by the Kit Foxes have been stripped and scalped. Five of the Kit Foxes are wounded, one seriously. It is not even midmorning.

The Kit Foxes gather around the two headmen. Young men all, only three are older than Stone and Yellow Wolf. Their faces are somber, stirred by the tension of combat. Stone looks at the wounded men. Three are of his band. He feels responsible; he is the headman. If it comes to getting wounded or killed, a headman must suffer first. A Cheyenne rule. The Kitkahakis are hard and skillful enemies, though; he could not prevent some of his men getting hurt. The one more seriously wounded has a deep cut high up in his right chest. He will heal and retain an honorable scar, a reminder of this day. Stone nods. They have done what had to be done. They did well.

His eyes shaded, he glances over to the Pawnee camp. Whirlwind, brother, he thinks sadly, where are you?

The next morning scouts report that the Kitkahakis have broken camp and moved away east to their own country, leaving fourteen burial scaffolds behind on the deserted campsite.

ONE
September 16, 1807

Four riders come north across the flat, broken country of the shortgrass Plains. They are two young women and two young men. The men ride their travel horses, holding their war horses on lariats. One of the women rides ahead, alone. The second woman brings up the rear, leading two packhorses. Beadwork designs on the leather clothes and the hair ornaments of the men identify the riders as Kiowas.

This is the afternoon of the fourth day since they left the camp of the Ka'ta band of Kiowas on the Arkansas River, 140 miles to the south. A group of Heviksnipahis horse catchers, who had trapped mustangs in the little lake country between Horse Creek and Big Sandy, had visited their camp and given directions. "Wotapio, two bands," they had said. "Hovxnova band is northeast of here, on the South Fork of the Republican River. The other band, Hoohksitan, is some distance to the east, on the same river."

The four riders had moved at a good traveling pace under the mid-September sun, with a steady south wind at their backs. On the second day they had come upon a huge herd of buffalo slowly moving west. A black cloud of ravens escorted the herd from above, while wolf packs hugged the perimeter on the ground. The land, as far as the eye could see, was blanketed with shaggy brown bodies. These were a segment of the immense herds that the Pawnee, Kansa, and Omaha hunters had pushed across the Solomon and Smoky Hill rivers and driven west. Under the relentless pressure the herds had split, some going south across the Arkansas River when others turned north to cross the Platte. The herd going straight west before the four riders had been spared further attacks and was safe for a little while. But the animals were wary of the Kiowa party. Snorting and rolling their eyes, they went by, ready to stampede if threatened. But the riders had no such intentions, waiting until the bulk of the herd had passed, then moving slowly through the stragglers.

On the third and most of the fourth day, they had seen no more buffalo but glimpsed the habitual life of the Plains: bands of antelope, family herds of mustangs, elk, and mule deer feeding in the draws, burrows of black-tailed prairie dogs, a few grizzlies, including females with cubs. They see the smoke flags of the Hovxnova camp when they are still miles away.

The woman leader, Sendehma, urges her mount, a roan mare, into a lope. When they come to a part of the Cheyenne horse herd grazing on the high ground above the river valley, they slow down and ride through. Youthful guards see and recognize them and wave them on. Sendehma calls out, and one of the boys rides over. They sit their horses on the lip of the escarpment.

"I am Sendehma," the woman says. "Wife of Whirlwind, brother of Stone." She speaks Cheyenne well, with a Kiowa accent. "Is this his camp? Where is his tipi?"

The boy, a fifteen-year-old with a sharp, inquisitive face, looks over the Kiowa party with a quizzical glance, then raises his arm and points. "On the west side of the camp, see. There are four tipis together, then two, then two more. Third camp from the west—they are the tipis of Bull Rib and Stone. The tipi of Stone has a black horse tail over it. You know that."

Sendehma nods and says thanks. "Aho." The boy backs his horse away. Below them stretches the valley of the South Fork of the Republican, running west to northeast, five miles wide, framed by the edges of the tableland. Its rock walls protrude a hundred feet above the floodplain. In some places the walls have crumbled and given way to grassy slopes that slant down toward the middle of the valley. There the streambed meanders through stands of cottonwoods, poplars, and ash. Now, in mid-September, cottonwood leaves are beginning to yellow, hinting at the flaming golden canopies of fall. Beyond grazing horses, partly concealed by trees and shrubs, stand upward of forty tipis. They are grouped in family clusters, two or three or four tipis here and there, each individual camp separated from others by some space and a screen of brush and trees. The string of family camps extends for over a quarter of a mile on the valley bottom near the river.

The Hovxnova camp holds no surprises for the sharp eyes of the Kiowas measuring it. They observe that it is in an ideal location. The high walls of the tableland protect it from the fierce winds of winter to come. There is good water, plenty of firewood, and grass for the horses. Tipi sizes and the camp arrangement are much the same as among their own people. While the men quickly estimate the size of the horse herd, Sendehma thinks about the tipi she is to visit.

Now that she has arrived, she muses. She brings bad news. What will happen after she has told it? She twirls one of her long braids between the fingers of her right hand. It is time to get there. She calls out softly and knees the roan forward.

They ride through a gap in the escarpment onto the slope and slowly down through midgrasses standing two to three feet tall. Wheatgrass and needlegrass are turning russet and yellow, their waves speckled with bright yellow sunflowers and goldenrods, the deep pink of prairie roses, the white of asters. About two miles down they pass through a curtain of cottonwoods and reach the riverbed, then cross the sand flats and the stream channel, the water barely reaching the horses' fetlocks. They climb the north bank, but before they reach the two tipis standing side by side between two cottonwoods, half a dozen dogs halt them. Growling ferociously, they throw the Kiowa horses into a sudden panic. A woman's sharp voice calls from the direction of the tipis, twice, three times, and the white and gray wolflike guards fall silent and withdraw.

Sendehma rides on and approaches the tipis. They are like others in this camp and in most camps of peoples in the grasslands. Made of buffalo hides scraped white, they are smudged at the tops from fires burned inside during cold weather. Because of the warm September weather, lodge covers are raised a few feet off the ground, rolled and tied. One tipi is painted with a band of disks in red and black. The other, unpainted, has a black horse tail hanging limp from the lifting pole. A meat rack is hung with slabs and strips of meat. Two horses are tethered nearby. Behind a pile of wood in front of the tipis, a fire burns, attended by two women. One is of middle age, the other young. Both women stand and watch the Kiowa ride in.

"Naaxaoto," Sendehma says in Cheyenne, raising her right arm. "I greet you." When the women at the fireplace recognize her, the older woman, Whirlwind's mother, moves away to the painted tipi. The avoidance rule, requiring parents-in-law and their sons- and daughters-in-law to stay apart from one another, is strictly observed among Cheyennes and Kiowas. The young woman, Eaglenest, Stone's wife, steps forward when Sendehma dismounts. They embrace fondly. When they let go of each other, Eaglenest asks, "Where is Gondaima? We have not seen her for a while." Sendehma drops the reins of the roan to the ground. Eaglenest hooks her arm under the Kiowa woman's arm and leads her to the fireplace. Behind them the Kiowa dismount and stand by their horses.

"I left her with my mother in our camp on the Arkansas River," Sendehma says. "She wanted to come, but it was not good to bring her."

Two men walk around the tipis, one young, the other middle-aged. The older of the two, Bull Rib, turns and joins his wife when he sees his daughter-in-law. The young man, Stone, walks up after a quick look at the Kiowa party. He and Sendehma stretch the palms of their right hands forward, close to touching but not. It is the ancient form of greeting. He smiles.

"I have come to see you," the woman says. Stone looks closely into her eyes. "I have brought my brothers." She gestures toward the two men behind her. "You know them. Setpagoy. Set'toni. And Setpagoy's wife, Tasenma." When their names are spoken, they briefly raise their right hands.

Stone does not speak Kiowa well, so he uses sign language. "Feel at home," the signs say. He points with his chin to the tipi with the horse tail. "This is my lodge. It is yours too. You may take your gear in. Let your horses graze wherever you want." He makes a wide gesture with his hand.

• • •

They sit in a patch of shade near the gnarled trunk of a cottonwood. Buffalo robes have been spread over ground cleared of dead branches. Stone sits in a circle with Sendehma and the Kiowa men. Eaglenest and the young Kiowa woman, Tasenma, sit a few feet away. Eaglenest was born a Gataka. Beside Apachean, the Gataka tongue, she speaks Cheyenne and Kiowa fluently. Near the two women, but separate, are Stone's parents. Avoidance rules demand that they remain distant from their daughter-in-law, Eaglenest. Although Eaglenest and her mother-in-law, Owl Woman, work together in camp, the two do not speak to each other directly. Conversation between them occurs through a third person, Stone or his young brother, Big Bow.

A pitcher of water has been passed around and everyone has taken a drink. There is silence but for the crackling of the fire, the neighing of a horse, the humming of insects.

Finally Stone speaks. He asks the question everyone expects. "Where is Whirlwind?"

Sendehma looks at her brother-in-law, one of the seven headmen of the Kit Fox warrior society of the Cheyennes. Twenty-seven years old and of medium height, Stone is hard and lean, with a taut face, sharp nose, wide mouth, prominent cheekbones, and dark, keen eyes. The braids of his straight black hair hang forward on his fringed shirt. That he commands men of his society in military action or in scouting is reflected in his bearing. Sendehma is a little afraid of him.

"My husband did not come back from a raid to the Spanish land far in the south," she says, looking into those keen eyes.

There is a sudden groan of pain from behind them. Owl Woman. The sound of a soft slap when she strikes the palm of her hand against her mouth to silence herself.

Stone raises his right hand. "When was this?" he asks harshly.

Sendehma shrugs. "Perhaps two moons ago. I was told five days ago. I hurried to see you one day after that."

There is a heavy silence.

"What happened?" Stone asks.

"There was a raiding party," she says. "Eleven men." She makes signs with her hands. "Nine Kiowa men. Two of your people, my husband and Magpie." She pauses. "They left five moons ago. Our camp was on the Cimarron River at that time. The party was led by Two

Bears. They were ambushed on the way back. Magpie was killed, and my husband did not come back with the others." She pauses again.

"I fear for him. I fear he is dead." A tall, sturdy woman, she is close to tears.

"How do you know this?"

"My brother was there," Sendehma says. She points with her chin to Setpagoy who sits next to her.

"How did this happen?" Stone asks coldly.

Setpagoy understands the question but answers in Kiowa. He is twenty-four years old, one year younger than his sister, an experienced warrior with an open face and a strong build. He speaks slowly, looking straight into the headman's eyes. Sendehma translates.

"I am Setpagoy. I smoked the pipe with Two Bears to ride with him. So did my brother-in-law and Magpie. Two Bears had been in the Spanish country two times before. We had gone four moons from our Ka'ta camp. We had gone southwest through what the Spanish call the Mapimí Bolsón. We went as far as the town called Fresnillo, looking that country over. From a big rancho near there we ran off many horses. Two hundred, more." He makes signs.

He looks at Sendehma as she gropes for the Cheyenne words. He waits until she has finished.

"All had gone well," he continues. "We had two little fights with vaqueros, men who guard horses and cattle, but we threw them back. We rode north, hurrying. The many horses slowed us down, though. We were careful. We had scouts out, ahead of us and behind."

He waits for the translation, then continues. "No one followed us. Five days later we were suddenly attacked by Spanish soldiers. They were horse soldiers, lancers. They came out of nowhere. They hit us hard."

"We split up. We came together at a place called Tagualito. We had fifty horses left of the many we had taken. We asked a vaquero for the name of the place before we killed him. There is a rancho. My brother-in-law and Magpie did not come. We waited for them, but they did not come."

He listens to Sendehma's voice as she speaks the words in Cheyenne. He looks at the headman.

"We hid those horses and rode back to where they had ambushed us. We found Magpie. He had been pierced through with lances many times. His head had been cut off. We saw no sign of Whirlwind. We searched for him. There had been a fight. We found two dead soldier horses. We found Whirlwind's bloody shirt and his bow-and-arrow quiver, nothing else. We searched more, but he was gone. We buried Magpie in the ground near there. We stayed for some time. Then we rode north with the horses that were left."

He waits, lets Sendehma translate.

"That is all. I think they took him away as a prisoner. We tried to read the tracks on the ground. We think the Spanish took him."

As an afterthought, he says: "Ten of the horses we gave to our Taltoky, Keeper of a Tsaidetali bundle. The other horses were divided between Magpie's wife and my sister."

Sendehma's words of translation have fallen like rocks. There is a long silence.

Finally Stone asks his brother-in-law: "You remember the exact place of the ambush? Could you find it again?"

Setpagoy nods. "Yes."

Stone looks at the ground in front of his crossed legs. Without knowing what he is doing he bends and grabs a twig and breaks it. He looks at Setpagoy, at Sendehma. "We are the same, Whirlwind and I. I would know if he were dead."

He pauses. "He is not dead. That much I know."

He sits as if listening for something or someone. After a while he continues. "Maybe he is alone there. Maybe the Spanish took him."

"If he had escaped the Spanish, we would have found him," Setpagoy says. "We searched for him. We waited. He was not there."

Stone nods. "I believe you. I think, too, that the Spanish took him prisoner."

He pauses again. He looks into Setpagoy's eyes. "Will you take me to the place where Magpie died? I will look for my brother. I will not leave him there."

Sendehma translates. "Yes," Setpagoy answers, "I take you there."

Silence is broken by the shrill cry of a red-tailed hawk who circles above them in the arc of the sky, unseen. The call comes three times, four.

"How will you do this?" Bull Rib asks. He has gotten up and stands behind his son.

"I start from the place where the Spanish took him," Stone says.

"It is a huge country, strange to us, with strange people," Bull Rib says in sorrow. "How can you know where he is?"

"He is alive," Stone says stubbornly. "Someone knows. I will find the one or the ones who know."

"Yes," Bull Rib says with doubt in his voice. So much to think about, so much to say without knowing how.

Owl Woman speaks from behind them. "You must see old man Hump in the Heviksnipahis camp. See him first. He could hold a Mxeeom, a spirit lodge for you. He can call the spirits, ask them. They will tell you something."

So it was decided.

• • •

Before daylight on the following day the mournful howl of a dog breaks the stillness. It is quickly answered by others until all the camp dogs, well over a hundred, join in. Starting soft and low, the sound grows louder and deeper until finally it dies in a prolonged wail. The singing, inherited from the wolf, occurs three times in camps throughout the Plains: early in the evening, around midnight, and during first light. The morning song serves as a wake-up call for the people.

By the time the dogs have ended, the party is getting ready in Stone's camp. Horses from Bull Rib's and Stone's herd have been brought in to replace the Kiowa travel horses; Setpagoy and Set'toni keep their war horses, however. Men and women of the party paint their faces with red ocher. They take provisions for a two-day journey but do not wait for a morning meal. Bull Rib and Owl Woman watch silently until the riders are swallowed by the green foliage of the floodplain.

Stone leads the party north to one of the slopes that allow access to the tableland. He holds the dun war horse on a lariat. When the riders reach the shortgrass country above, Stone turns straight west. He rides ahead, alone. A short distance behind him ride Setpagoy and Set'toni. They are followed by the three women: Eaglenest, Sendehma, and Tasenma. They ride side by side. Tasenma, eighteen years old, the youngest, again leads two packhorses. In the rear Stone's brother of sixteen, Big Bow, loose-herds two good horses. They are brought, along with other gifts, for the two prominent ceremonial men in the Heviksnipahis camp: Hump, the spirit lodge man, and Black Feather, the Keeper of Mahoz.

After they have covered a few miles, the fiery rim of the sun peers through the pale bluish mist that shrouds the horizon in the east. With the sun at their back, they ride into the great stillness of the land, under the turquoise-colored sky. The carpet of short blue grama and buffalo grasses is barely stirred by the south wind. Embedded in the grass are the dried droppings of buffalo and antelope. Old trails criss-cross. Here and there gleam white bones of animals killed by teeth or claw or arrow in times past. The riders are watched by prairie dogs from the shelter of burrows and by bands of antelope browsing among sagebrush. Alternating walk and lope to preserve the strength of the horses, after thirty miles the riders reach the cut in the flats that the Arikaree River has dug on its course to the northeast. The stream channel lies empty. Stone searches for and finds one of the few natural tanks left, then calls for a rest. They water the horses, and men and women sit in a circle and eat a first meal of cold meat brought from the camp.

After stretching out for a little while, they mount again. Three miles farther west they climb the next shelf of the rising high Plains. Now they come into sand hills grown over with sand bluestem and sandsage and dwarf shrubs. It is a land with few springs and an occasional pond marked by isolated stands of trees. No stream runs through these hills. Stone now turns to the northwest. He aims for a perennial little lake on higher ground above the sand hills, about twenty-five miles away. Beyond distant hills the tops of the Rocky Mountains appear as a blue gray ridge, more an apparition than something real.

In late afternoon they climb out of the sand hills and are once again in shortgrass country. The lake, half a mile wide, lies in a depression, its shores edged by belts of reeds and groups of cottonwoods. Stone holds his horse on the rim of the depression and scans the near and distant places. There is no sound but the low moaning of the wind. Above, two red-tailed hawks drift lazily on air currents that carry them north. He counts two bands of antelope, the animals feeding undisturbed. A lone grizzly walks on the slope to the north. Stone rides down toward the lake, followed by his party. They cross series of game trails, some cut deeply into the ground. Stone chooses a campsite near the shore. There is plenty of firewood under the cottonwoods.

During the day there had been little chance for talking. Around the evening fire come questions. The Kiowa men are curious about the recent Wotapio trading on the Missouri. The women already know—Eaglenest told them. Stone describes how all horses offered to the English had been taken. Most of these were from the Guantekana band of Gatakas and the Ka'ta band of Kiowas. Goods brought back for the Gatakas are stored in a tipi next to that of One Horn, the Hovxnova chief. Goods for the Ka'tas are with the Hoohksitan band. Stone says that the Wotapios arrived on the South Fork only ten sleeps ago, after a long summer of traveling, an absence of five moons. The trade goods can be collected at any time.

When Setpagoy asks how many muskets with ammunition the Ka'tas will get, Stone answers that he thinks about seventy, the Guantekanas receiving an equal number.

The Kiowas are pleased. From their camp and that of the Gatakas, most of the trade goods, muskets, dry goods, hardware, hatchets and axes, thread, yarn, and twine, kettles made of copper, brass, and tin, and paint will be passed south to other tribal bands and to the Comanches in the southern Plains.

They break camp at first light and make for the northwest. They move through a pleasant country with many ponds and small, perennial lakes, rich in game but without a trace of buffalo at the present. The great herds that Sendehma and her brothers had seen a few days back have not yet come north. After thirty miles Stone decides to rest and have a first meal by a spring close to the dry streambed of Sand Creek. Later, downstream on the creek, they meet with a party of Heviksnipahis hunters who point them toward their camp on the south side of the South Platte, at the mouth of Badger Creek. By the time they reach the camp in early evening, Stone's group has ridden about 120 miles in two days. Upward of eighty tipis spread out in front of the dark green ribbon of trees and brush that shields the last major bend of the Platte from sight before the river starts its long run northeast toward the forks.

TWO

Among the Heviksnipahis tipis Stone is guided to Yellow Wolf's camp. This headman's lodge is also marked with a horse tail tied to the end of the lifting pole. The party is well received. After Stone tells his war mate the purpose of their coming, a tipi is raised for the visitors; they may have to stay a few days. For the evening meal they are joined by the members of the Heviksnipahis Kit Fox society. Afterward, Yellow Wolf visits Hump and returns to say that Hump has agreed to see Stone and Sendehma in the morning. At sunrise Yellow Wolf takes the two through the camp to Hump's tipi. Stone leads a good chestnut mare on a lariat. Sendehma carries a striped Hudson's Bay blanket over her arm and holds a finely quilled pipe bag. At Hump's tipi Stone ties the horse to one of the pegs that holds the lodge cover. Yellow Wolf knocks four times on the tipi pole next to the closed entrance and steps away when a voice from the inside calls, "Come in."

Stone lifts the hide cover and lets Sendehma step in, then follows her and closes the entrance behind him. A low fire burns in the center of the tipi on carefully brushed ground. Behind it, on the west side, a gray-haired old man with long braids sits on a buffalo robe. To his right lies a ceremonial bundle on a bed of male sage. Hump gestures to his right where buffalo robes have been spread out. "Sit there," he says. Stone lets Sendehma sit between himself and Hump. He makes a sign and Sendehma places the folded blanket in front of her, with the pipe bag on top.

Hump looks briefly at the two of them, then stares into the fire. Stone sits relaxed, but Sendehma sits stiffly, in awe of this strange old man said to be powerful, a man to whom the spirits talk. There are such men among the Kiowas, and she is in awe of them also, but this one is not of her own people; there is no telling what he might demand of her.

After a while Hump says in a quiet voice: "You wanted to see me. What do you want of me?"

Stone waits for a moment. "You know me," he says. "I am Stone of the Hovxnovas. This woman I brought with me is Sendehma. She is Kiowa. She is my sister-in-law. My brother, Whirlwind, is her husband. He has been living with her in her parents' band, Ka'ta, down south. They have a little girl, Gondaima."

He pauses.

"My brother went with Magpie, who lives in the Ka'ta camp, and a Kiowa war party into the Spanish lands for horses. Magpie is dead and Whirlwind is believed dead, too. I feel that he is alive. I want to search for him there and find him. I have never been there myself. I want to know where I should look for him."

While he speaks, Hump has turned his gaze first on Stone, then on Sendehma. The light from the fire gives his eyes a stark, penetrating glint. "You speak Tsistsistas?" he asks with a kind voice. When she nods he says, "Tell me what you know." The woman bends forward and moves the blanket and pipe bag toward Hump.

She begins haltingly in the Cheyenne language, with a low voice, almost a whisper. Eventually she is caught up in the story and speaks firmly. At the end she starts crying, her body rocking forward and backward, tears running down her cheeks.

The men sit motionless, respecting her grief. When she is able to control herself, the three sit looking into the fire, watching the blue flames lick around sticks of wood, the thin swirl of smoke rising toward the smoke hole.

"What do you want me to do?" Hump asks finally. He knows what they have come for, but they have to express it.

After a pause, Stone says, "We want you to hold a Mxeeom for us, ask the spirits to find Whirlwind, tell us. I want to look for him and bring him back. I would be grateful if the spirits would help us."

There is a silence.

"Yes," Hump says. "I will do that. I will try to help." He pauses. "You understand that this is not up to me. It is up to the spirits. I will ask them."

He bends forward and pulls the blanket and pipe bag toward him. He touches the earth with the fingertips of both hands. He places them on the gifts. He prays with a quiet, solemn voice. Sendehma and Stone sit stiffly erect, listening, looking to the ground in front of them.

Hump ends with a grunt. He looks toward both of them. "I need some time to prepare. I have the lodge set up. Tomorrow evening. I will call you. You live with Yellow Wolf?"

Both nod. The meeting is over.

Stone touches Sendehma and points with his head toward the door. Both get up, and Stone directs the woman to cross between the old man and the fireplace. Following her, both walk around the fireplace on the north side toward the door, go through, and close it. They hear Hump pray when they move away.

• • •

The messenger comes after dark. He is an old man wrapped in a robe and simply says, "Come." Stone and Sendehma have been sitting with Eaglenest and Big Bow, and with Yellow Wolf and his wife. The Kiowa relatives have joined them. Conversation has been hesitant, muted, and has finally died, everyone thinking, waiting.

While the messenger looks on, Stone and Sendehma gather the prepared offerings. These are two beautifully quill-decorated buffalo robes, two shawls, and other dry goods obtained in trade on the Missouri River, and a small bag of vermilion paint. The old man leads them through the camp past dying campfires. They pass through tall grass, under a sky ablaze with stars, toward a bright fire burning next to a pole set in the ground. The messenger points and the two tie their offerings to the pole. These are gifts not to the caller of spirits, Hump, but to the spirits themselves, for them to recognize and accept. On the following morning the offerings will be distributed in camp; because they have been blessed by the spirits, they have acquired protective power.

When Stone and Sendehma finish, the messenger points beyond the pole, to the east side of the fire, where half a stone's throw away a tipi stands almost hidden by a bur oak thicket. It appears to be a large tipi, made up of two regular tipis, ghostly white in the shadows. Inside, a small fire is burning out, barely giving light. The messenger walks ahead and lifts the door flap. Stone and Sendehma step inside. The old man follows and closes the door.

The air is filled with the aromatic smell of sweetgrass. In the near dark they see three figures seated in a row along the inner wall of the tipi, on the northeast side. To the left of the door sits a single figure in front of what seems to be an animal. Sendehma does not know that it is the complete skin of a badger, with quillwork around his feet in the color of the four directions. Stone knows; he has seen the sacred animal before. The old man who has brought them in tugs at Stone's arm and points to two robes laid out on the southwest side, beyond the badger and his keeper. Stone nudges Sendehma, and both walk to the place prepared for them. The old man joins the three figures and sits down.

Stone sits with crossed legs. He wears only breechclout and moccasins, no feathers or personal marks. Sendehma sits with legs stretched to one side. She is dressed in a plain leather gown and plain moccasins. When their eyes have adjusted to the dim light, Sendehma notes that she is the only woman present. The four men on the northeast side have rattles and bone whistles lying before them. The badger man has only a drum beater. All these are ceremonial men, helpers to Hump. Sendehma also sees that a line of coals extends from the near western edge of the lodge wall across the fire in the center of the tipi to the entrance on the east side. On these coals sweetgrass has been burned to purify the tipi, filling the space with fragrance.

No one speaks. In the silence of the tipi Stone sits stoically. A proven soldier, he shows no emotion, but inside he is in turmoil. Whatever the knowledge that might come through the ceremony, it will influence his and perhaps his brother's life; it might mean life or death for both of them. Sendehma shows a brave face. She hides her apprehension, trying to prepare herself for what she stands to learn, good or bad.

A soft sound comes from the outside. The door flap is lifted, and Hump steps into the tipi, closing the entrance again. Sendehma holds her breath when she sees him. His long gray hair hangs loose, covering his face and much of his torso. He wears only a breechclout; his feet are naked. His whole body is painted red. He carries a rattle and a bone whistle in his hands. He walks slowly around the fire on the south side and sits down by the lodge wall on the west side, directly in front of the line of coals. One of the men on the northeast side gets up on his knees and moves along the coals, stirring them and adding little twists of sweetgrass. Two more men get up and carry bowstrings and a buffalo robe to the motionless figure on the west side. They kneel in front of Hump and start to work on him.

Stone does not look, but Sendehma wants to burn this event into her memory. In the poor light she sees that the men tie Hump with four bowstrings, each finger of each hand separately to the next finger, the hands tied together behind his back; each toe of each foot tied separately to the next toe, the feet tied together and then securely to his bound hands. When the men finish, Hump lies bent on his left side facing east, in what seems to Sendehma an inextricable position. The men place his rattle and whistle in front of his face and cover him with a buffalo robe. Both spread their hands and walk back to their seats.

Later, Sendehma does not remember how long she sat in the stillness of the tipi. The last flames flicker and the fire dies. The red coals crust over, and the tipi becomes a black pit set aside all by itself, unearthly, belonging neither to the World Below, the Middle World, or the World Above, a weightless place drifting, perhaps drifting in the spirit world. Outside a wind moans and cuffs along the lodge skins, brushes the poles in the fork above. Are the spirits already here, she wonders. If they are here, where are they?

As she sits dreaming, four rattles sound from close by in a rhythmic, punctuated chatter. They keep going, accompanied by four soft, low voices, men giving their hearts and minds and their throats to spirit songs. These are songs without words, addressed to the unseen. They are soothing, imploring, reaching out. They seem unreal to Sendehma, belonging to a realm she has never known. In the black, closed space they seem to come from a nether world, from somewhere beyond imagination. The first song ends. Then, after a brief pause, another song follows. Sendehma cannot help swaying with the songs, moving her upper body forward and to the sides. There are four songs in all.

When the singing ends, the badger man starts, hitting the badger parfleche with the drum beater, humming with the strokes. Sendehma sees nothing. She only hears the muffled sounds of the drumming on skin, the barely audible voice. She does not know that it addresses Maa'ko, badger, one of the Listeners Under the Ground, urging the spirit to hear, to get ready to make himself available.

And it ends. In the tipi the still air is oppressive. Sendehma finds it hard to breathe. Then another voice. It comes from the place where Hump, tied up, lies under the robe. It is a clear voice despite the heavy cover. Sendehma hears the words of a song but does not understand. The words are in the secret language of the Cheyenne Zemaheon-evessos, the Mysterious Ones, the ones who accomplish extraordinary feats with the help of their *nisimon,* spirit allies. The song is short and ends with a wail.

Suddenly the large tipi shakes as if hit by a sudden gale. The poles creak under its force; the lodge is compressed inward and billows out again in a series of assaults from outside. The conical, firm structure of the tipi is in danger of being ripped apart. Sendehma is in shock. She leans heavily against Stone as if to seek protection. She hides her head behind his shoulder. Then something enters the tipi from above, and the pounding from outside ends. There is a noise in the forks when a rattle pushes through and bounces wildly inside the tipi, ricocheting among the walls, leaping, the clacking sounds springing back and forth. A bone whistle enters and slips down, letting loose the fierce, shrill cry of an eagle, terrifying in this small space. The whistle arches within the bounds of the lodge walls, fluttering up and down. A second rattle comes in and adds to the din. Sendehma thinks she hears animal voices, the long-drawn cry of the puma, like a woman's desperate cry, the grunting of a bear. She feels something brushing her shoulder, her face, something furry and soft like a paw.

The noise made by the rattles and the whistle comes to an end. Now strange voices speak in the secret language asking questions. Hump answers and another voice speaks. Sendehma is so scared she does not want to hear. A new voice seems to come from below the ground as something, or someone, perhaps badger, moves up and comes into the tipi from out of the earth. Strange voices all, though sometimes Hump's recognizable voice speaks.

Sendehma has passed out or fallen into a trance. She will remember, as from a great distance, Hump singing. Later, she is told that it was his parting song releasing the nisimon. Then comes a final, violent shaking of the tipi, and silence. When Sendehma comes to, she sees someone blow into the coals of the fireplace through a pipestem. The coals turn red. Carefully kindling wood is piled on. First a blue sheen licks around the wood sticks, then comes the burst of a small yellow flame, and with more wood the fire starts again, lighting the tipi.

Looking past Stone, who sits unmoved, Sendehma sees that Hump is sitting with crossed legs. The buffalo robe, which had covered him, lies folded by his side with what appear to be four bowstrings rolled up on top, next to his rattle and bone whistle. The moment comes that she has feared but which she and her brother-in-law have waited for. Into the stillness charged with emotion, Hump speaks slowly and clearly.

"The spirits have told me that Whirlwind is alive." He pauses. "He is a prisoner. He is moved from place to place. He is wounded in his right arm. He cannot use this arm. There is a woman in that country who cares for him. She is a prisoner from one of the tribes there."

He pauses again.

"At this time he is in a large, yellow stone lodge with horns. The lodge is by a small river that flows north into a swampy lake. This is far, far away. There is a single mountain close by that has the form of a great hat, a hat like the ones we have seen the English wear on their heads."

Another pause.

"This is all."

He looks toward Stone and Sendehma as the woman bursts into tears. Stone muses: large stone lodge, yellow, with horns, a mountain shaped like a great hat. He bows to Hump. "Aho." He and the woman rise slowly. Hump comes over and brushes them off with a bundle of male sage, starting above their heads, moving the bundle along their bodies, along both sides to the ground, praying. The two have been in the presence of the spirits. Now they are allowed to leave the Mxeeom lodge and go back to the visible world.

• • •

The howling of the dogs brings the Heviksnipahis camp to life at first light. Everywhere door flaps are lifted and lodge covers raised and tied. Smoke from new fires hangs lazily in the morning air. In Yellow Wolf's camp the women put meat on spits and arrange them around the fireplace. Stone explains what has happened in the spirit lodge. Everyone knows that he will try to rescue his brother. The women talk with muted voices, but the men sit in silence. There is one other thing Stone must see to before they leave for the camp on the Republican.

After they have eaten, the two men rise. Stone takes the second horse brought as a gift. Yellow Wolf takes the lead. The Maheoneom, the tipi of Mahoz, the sacred arrows, stands apart on the northeast edge of the Heviksnipahis camp. It is marked on the lodge cover by four triangles in the four directions: southeast, southwest, northwest, northeast. Two of the triangles are painted red, two painted black. They symbolize the four sacred mountains in the four corners of the universe. The Mahoz bundle, encased in a fringed rawhide cover almost four feet long, is lashed to the lodge in a horizontal position above the open door. The bushy tail of a male gray wolf, whose body serves as the quiver for Mahoz, protrudes from the south end of the rawhide cover. Because the tipi faces east, the bundle points north and south.

The Arrow Keeper's wife, an elderly woman with long braids, her face painted with red ocher, is feeding two grandchildren by the fireplace. Black Feather sits on a log off to the side. He is hunched over, working on something. When they come near, Stone sees that he is running an unfinished arrow shaft through a shaft straightener. A bunch of green shafts lies at his feet. He is a noted arrowmaker, and is absorbed in his work. He looks up when Stone brings the horse up, a fine bay mare, and lets the halter drop. When Yellow Wolf walks discreetly away, Stone says, "Old Man, I have come to see you." He uses the honorary term befitting an elderly man of distinction.

Black Feather, his old, wrinkled, friendly face, painted like his wife's with red ocher, looks up at the young headman. He recognizes him and smiles. He asks almost the same question Hump asked. "What is it you want?"

"I have brought a horse as a gift for Mahoz," Stone says.

Black Feather nods. He gets up slowly and calls out to his wife. The woman goes into the tipi and brings out a plain rawhide pipe bag. She hands it to him and gathers the children at the fireplace and takes them away. The Arrow Keeper points to the fireplace. He sits down on the west side, the tipi door and the bundle behind him. He gestures to Stone to sit on his right. He hands him a short prayer stick. In silence Black Feather opens the pipe bag and takes out an old tubular pipe, cut from pale red catlinite. He slowly fills the bowl with ceremonial tobacco and, with his prayer stick, places both in front of his feet.

They sit motionless, looking into the fire. Stone is aware that he sits next to the highest-ranking priest of the Cheyenne tribe, and that Mahoz behind them hear everything that will be said. Then Black Feather asks once more, "Grandson, why have you come to Mahoz and me?"

Stone explains about his brother and what the spirits have told Hump. He finishes, saying, "I am going south to find him and bring him back. I ask Mahoz to let me find him and let no harm come to us and to the ones who go with me. I ask for protection, for a safe journey." He pauses. "I bring a horse as a gift to Mahoz."

The priest nods. "It is good. Mahoz have heard you. I now pray for you and your brother and for those who ride with you." He prays with closed eyes in the ancient language of the Zemaheonevessos, a language Stone, a soldier headman, not a ceremonial man, does not understand. He hears his and his brother's names. He listens with closed eyes. Black Feather concludes his prayer. He bends forward and moves an ember from the fire with his prayer stick and, resting on an elbow, puts the pipe bowl against the ember. He sucks on the pipe and the tobacco is lit. He gets back to a sitting position and draws on the pipe, making sure that the tobacco burns properly. Next he makes four formal puffs, blowing the smoke forward, then lifts the mouthpiece to the ceremonial directions. He passes the pipe to Stone, who also makes four puffs.

The pipe passes between them, tamped down twice with the Arrow Keeper's prayer stick until the tobacco has burned out. The priest empties the bowl and makes Stone kneel in front of him. He touches him with the empty pipe on both shoulders, twice on each side, praying. On the ground he wipes the ashes away and looks at the headman. "It is good," he says. "Thank you for the horse."

"Aho," Stone says. "I thank you." He glances toward the Mahoz bundle. A monarch butterfly has settled on the rawhide cover, folds its orange red, finely veined wings and closes them, again, again. Stone points with his chin, and the Arrow Keeper turns and looks. His wrinkled face is lit with a soft smile.

"Yes," he says, "maehoze, the Red Messenger of the spirits." He nods. "This one has also heard what you said. "Watch for him and his kind. They might take you where you are supposed to go."

The butterfly lifts itself from the bundle and sails away. Stone puts the palm of his right hand toward the priest's raised hand without touching. He gets up and stands, his usually solemn face relaxed, shining with emotion. He bows his head and leaves without looking back. Black Feather stands up when he is gone. He goes to the horse. He prays, touching the ground and the horse's neck, accepting the gift for the sacred arrows.

In Yellow Wolf's camp three men wait for him. They are Kit Fox soldiers: Holy Singer, Standing, and White Wolf. Stone knows them. They were with him for the battle with the Kitkahakis a year earlier, and the Skiri Pawnees three years before. Standing is a broad-shouldered man twenty-eight years old, two years younger than White Wolf, who is tall, lean. Holy Singer, aged twenty-nine, medium-sized, with a strong face, is both a Kit Fox and a Zemaheonevsz.

The trio sits with Stone. Holy Singer acts as speaker for the other two. He does not waste words. "We heard that you take a search party into Spanish country for your brother. We want to ride with you. We want to learn about all that country. We want to smoke the pipe with you."

Stone looks at them. Serious, intelligent faces—reliable men who have proven themselves many times. They are good to have with him. That Holy Singer wants to come is a blessing; he is a traveler in the spirit world like Hump.

Before he can speak, Sendehma comes up from behind. Her two brothers are with her. She says simply, "Brother-in-law, Setpagoy and Set'toni have asked me to speak for them. They want to smoke the pipe with you. They want to join you on the long ride."

Stone is not surprised. He gestures for the two men to sit with the others. Of the two Kiowas, Setpagoy is a member of a Kiowa soldier society, and he has been in the place where Whirlwind was lost. He already promised to take Stone there. The younger brother, Set'toni, is not yet experienced but will walk in his brother's tracks. Stone is pleased. These are five good men regardless of tribe. Once they smoke the pipe with him, they accept his leadership. A pipe bearer on an expedition is granted real authority, more than to a band chief or even a tribal chief.

He has to warn them though. "This will be a long trail," he says. "Six moons. Maybe more. We may have to fight. I will do everything I know, but some of us might not come back." He looks from one to another.

"Yes, we know," Holy Singer says. Standing and White Wolf nod in agreement. Setpagoy moves his hand in sign language. "Yes, it is good." His brother does the same.

Stone makes the sign for good. "Pewe." He does not have to call for Eaglenest. When she brings the pipe bag from his pack, she briefly touches his shoulder, shyly, happy for his being.

THREE

At sunrise Stone's party is ready to leave the camp. Standing, Holy Singer, and White Wolf are there, each with his traveling horse and his war mount. They have said farewell to their wives and children in their own camps. Their families will be taken care of by relatives and fellow Kit Foxes during their absence. Each of the three has brought clothing and necessary items for the journey. Additional bows and packages with new arrows are attached to their travel horses. Two, Standing and White Wolf, carry sheathed trade muskets; powder horns and bags with lead balls are attached to their bandoliers. The women of the party have been supplied with fresh meat for the ride to the Hovxnova camp.

Stone thanks his hosts for their hospitality and the food and moves out. He does not look back when he knees his travel horse into an easy lope and passes through the floodplain of the South Platte dotted with cottonwoods and through part of the Heviksnipahis horse herd before gaining higher ground and the sand hills along Badger Creek. He rides point with his young brother, Big Bow, at his side. Behind him the party has formed up. The three Kit Foxes ride next, followed by the two Kiowa warriors. The women, Eaglenest, Sendehma, and Tasenma, bring up the rear. Now the relentless south wind stands in their faces. They ride into the sun on a southeastern course. It is an easy ride, and, but for a scattering of antelopes, it seems that they are all alone under the vast tent of the sky. Stone calls for a halt at a spring by the sandy emptiness of Sand Creek. They have a first meal and rest and let the horses graze, then move on and make the little lake by early evening. They camp on the same site as on the ride in.

During the night the wind shifts and brings a cloudy day and a steady rain. They ride in the same formation as on the day before, now wrapped in robes with the hair side in. The men have covered up firearms and bow cases. Halfway between the lake and the Hovxnova camp they rest under a cottonwood by a natural tank on the Arikaree. The women build a fire and roast meat. Eager to get home, Stone calls for the party to leave after they have eaten. The rain turns into a thin drizzle and peters out when the wind shifts again. They reach the camp in the early evening.

Word of the party's return spreads rapidly. A small crowd converges on Stone's and Bull Rib's camp. Relatives of Magpie and Stone come, and many others, the eleven Kit Foxes of the Hovxnovas, and the band chief, One Horn. Also present are two Kiowa men married to Cheyenne women. They sit tightly packed on robes spread over the wet ground. Talk ends when Stone gets up.

He stands, a lean, composed man lit by the fire in the gathering dark. In his hand he holds the short prayer stick the Arrow Keeper had given him. He points with it, singling out or giving emphasis when he speaks. He points to Sendehma, who sits with Eaglenest and Tasenma. He explains briefly what news she has brought, although those present have already been informed during his absence. He tells of what the two of them learned in the spirit lodge. A rustle runs through the crowd: sighs, a muttering, utterances of surprise, satisfaction. He waits for silence and says that he is leaving after two sleeps. He adds that he is not riding alone. He points to the five men who have smoked with him. He says that he wants to take a few more men, only a few. There is a stirring among the men in the crowd. He says that those who come with him should come to this place in the morning. Some questions are asked and answered.

One Horn speaks, the gray-haired band chief, giving his blessing to the search party. The crowd disperses. Stone does not mention his visit to the Arrow Keeper. He himself should not talk about that in public. But those who were with him in the Heviksnipahis camp know, and because this was a good and right thing to do, they will tell the others.

At sunrise about three dozen men gather by Stone's fireplace and sit down in a circle. The women, who have just started a fire, step away. Stone comes back from the river where he has washed himself. He faces them. These are experienced men, but he cannot take them all.

He selects four of his Kit Fox warriors who are still unmarried but have served with him in the Kitkahaki fight and in a skirmish with Crows on the Belle Fourche River, north of the Black Hills, during the past summer. Lame Bear is the youngest, nineteen years old. The others are Necklace, twenty, and Porcupine and Yellow Eyes, both twenty-two. Six more men chosen are related either to Magpie or to himself. They are Bear Tooth, twenty-six, another Kit Fox but married, and four members of the Red Shield soldier society: Lame Coyote, twenty-three, White River, twenty-two, Red Bird, twenty-five, and his brother, Little Bird, twenty-six. Of the latter, only Lame Coyote and White River are unmarried.

One other man, a cousin of Magpie, insists and is accepted. He is Powderface, twenty-seven, a priest of the Oxheheom ceremony. He is not a member of a soldier society but has been on two war expeditions against the Crows.

"These are all," Stone says. Reluctantly the men not chosen get up and leave. They know the rules. It is an expedition leader's right to pick the men of his party; to refuse an individual is not an insult. Still, some might harbor a grudge for some time.

The chosen men smoke with Stone and leave to prepare for the journey.

He stays alone by the fireplace, thinking. He thinks of the vast country far away with places and peoples he has never seen. Somewhere there is Whirlwind, a captive moved from place to place. A woman from a tribe there, a captive too, cares for him. What does Sendehma think? She heard what the spirits told Hump. Is she grateful? Jealous? How can he find him? He begins to feel the burden pressing on him. So many now depend on him on a journey into the unknown. He is responsible for them all. He stares into the shifting flames. But no image emerges. He sees nothing. He closes his eyes. He sees Whirlwind in his mind's eye as he was when he rode away with his new wife, so exuberant. How does he look now? He cannot use his right arm, the spirits said.

Stone hears a soft sound and looks up. It takes a moment before he recognizes his young brother. Big Bow stands across from the fireplace. He looks serious.

"I want to go with you," he says.

A slim youngster. A bright face, sensitive eyes.

"You are not a warrior," Stone says reluctantly.

Big Bow nods. "Yes. I will be one by the time we are back."

"Why do you want to come?"

"He is my brother, too," Big Bow says. "If it were you who were down there and Whirlwind would go for you, I would do the same."

Stone searches Big Bow's face. "Did you talk with our parents? They need you here when I'm gone."

"I talked with them. They understand. I can be of help to you, do things. I can take care of horses, do camp work. I won't be in your way. I will do anything you want me to do."

Stubborn, Stone thinks. Like me, like Whirlwind. He is right, he is Whirlwind's brother, too. He hears himself say, "Yes. Thank you. I want you to come."

• • •

Later that day, when Bull Rib and Stone sit together, five women approach led by Eaglenest. Bull Rib gets up and leaves when he recognizes his daughter-in-law. The women group themselves around Stone.

He looks at them. He is surprised but does not show it. There is Eaglenest, lithe, vibrant, twenty-two years old. Sendehma, twenty-five, robust, strong-willed. Tasenma, eighteen, married for only a few months, polite, always trying to please, slim, a small figure. Bear Doctor Woman, a Náe, healer, twenty-six, wife of Little Bird. A sharp face, penetrating, often melancholy eyes, a thoughtful person with a slender but strong body. And She-Wolf, twenty-five, wife of Red Bird, younger brother of Little Bird. She is a quiet, often withdrawn person, but devoted to her husband who is opposite in behavior. All of them are competent women with minds of their own.

"You want something," Stone says cautiously.

Eaglenest's eyes sparkle. "Yes. We talked about something. We want to go with you."

Stone looks from face to face. He shakes his head. "This is not a hunting party."

Eaglenest nods. "This is not a war party either. We have to hunt on the way to stay alive."

"True," Stone says. "But we are going where danger waits. How can I protect you?"

"You protect us when you protect our husbands," Bear Doctor Woman says. "Our husbands protect us. And we protect ourselves. We will not be a burden on you."

A pause.

"You are going for my husband," Sendehma says quietly. "I want to look for him too. Together we will look for him."

"This is not a war party," Eaglenest repeats. "You are not going against men like the Pawnees or Crows. That would be different."

Stone shakes his head again. "Where we are going it is unknown country. We don't know much about people there. Some will be enemies."

"It is not that unknown," Sendehma says. "My brother has been there. Parties of my people, parties of Gatakas, have been there many times."

"Yes," Stone says. "But we don't know how far this one has to go, perhaps farther than the others have gone." After a pause, he adds, "Did these other parties take women with them?"

Sendehma nods. "Many times. Women take care of the horses and the camps. These parties have hideouts in the mountains when the men raid for horses."

Stone looks composed. The appeal of the women is unusual and unexpected. Their arguments are plausible, but their presence on the journey might cause friction.

"We could be useful in other ways," Eaglenest says. "Between us we speak Kiowa and Gataka and some Comanche. We can talk to the Apache people of the mountains who know that country. They could help us."

"Did you talk this over with your husbands?" Stone asks.

"Not yet," Eaglenest says, smiling.

"We have," Bear Doctor Woman says. Tasenma and She-Wolf nod in agreement.

Stone sits thinking. This is unheard of among Cheyennes. Never are women brought along on a war party. But then, this one is not entirely a war party either. There is sense in what the women say. They could be an advantage on this journey. He looks from face to face, fiercely, demanding attention.

"Your husbands took the pipe with me," he says. "I am responsible for them. Your husbands are responsible for you. I am not. But you must also accept my rules. Should any of you quarrel or make trouble, I'll send you back however far we have gone. You understand?"

He looks at Eaglenest. His wife nods and smiles. Around her the other women nod and make the sign for "good." They leave. Eaglenest sits down next to her husband. She touches his arm. "All will be good," she says.

• • •

Stone's party leaves the camp at sunrise. The riders pass through the valley in single file and climb the southern rim of the uplands. On the flat ground above they form into loose groups, heading southwest. Stone waves over his brother-in-law, Setpagoy, and the two take the lead.

Behind them ride the five Kit Foxes of the Hovxnovas and the three Kit Foxes of the Heviksnipahis, followed by the four Hovxnova Red Shield warriors. Next come Big Bow and Set'toni. Each of the men leads his war horse on a lariat. Big Bow, not a warrior yet, brings two spare horses along on halters. The five women are at the rear. Eaglenest, Sendehma, and Tasenma ride together. Bear Doctor Woman and She-Wolf end the column. Eaglenest and the two Hovxnova women each lead two packhorses loaded with camp equipment and food and, for the men, bundles of arrows, a few extra bows. Bear Doctor Woman takes her four-year-old daughter, Walking Last, with her. Her husband, Little Bird, insisted that she come; he said he did not want to be without her. The child rides on the flat saddle in front of her mother.

This spontaneous positioning becomes the order of march until they reach hostile territory. When crossing coulees and deep cuts in the surface of the land, the column merges into single file. Stone aims for three perennial lakes that sit side by side above the North Fork of the Smoky Hill River, forty-eight miles away. After a brief rest at midday, they reach the lakes in early evening and make camp for the night. The women jointly cook the evening meal for all the men, not favoring husbands. One other pattern is set that first night: the women sleep in a group separate from the men. It is understood that on an expedition such as this, as in war, men abstain from any sexual contact. This unquestioned rule is expected to hold for the duration of the journey.

They break camp at first light, saddle up, and continue southwest in the same order as on the day before. Now they have come into country considered the hunting ground of northern Kiowa and Gataka bands. The core area of Kiowa and Gataka tribal divisions lies from the Arkansas River south; the land to the north, including the headwaters of the Republican and Smoky Hill rivers, are areas of Kiowa and Gataka secondary use. This land they share without friction with the two Cheyenne divisions, the Heviksnipahis and Wotapios, who came south from the Black Hills region only a decade before.

They ride in a gray mist and surprise a huge male grizzly in a draw. The bear stands, paws raised to his chest, fearless and still, and watches humans and horses pass. When the golden ball of the sun rises behind them, they have covered fifteen miles of rising ground. At midday they rest and eat and let the horses drink and graze. When they ride on, Setpagoy, who knows this country better than Stone, changes direction to a point farther west, where two lakes lie near Rush Creek. In late afternoon they cross the sand flats east of the Big Sandy and, after moving through the dry creekbed and reaching a low rise, have before them a wide, grassy bowl with the lakes in its center five miles away. Stone raises his right arm and the column comes to a halt. Then the riders move forward and form a line looking down.

The two lakes lie next to each other surrounded by stands of cottonwoods and belts of reeds. The larger one is about three quarters of a mile long, the other less than half that size. Both lakes are covered by a dark mass of buffalo. Animals slowly move through the shallow lakes, pushed on by thirsty, tightly packed ranks following. And behind them, trotting up from the south, still more buffalo flood over the rim of the bowl; among the dark bodies here and there are the reddish furs of spring calves as they run beside their mothers. Wolf packs and ravens, which usually accompany the herds, are missing.

The party watching knows that until the stirred-up mud settles, the water is undrinkable. "No wolves and ravens," Stone says to Powderface, who holds next to him. "Down south someone killed buffalo." Powderface grunts in agreement.

Stone turns to Setpagoy. In sign language he asks, "Where do we get water?"

Setpagoy points to the southeast. "In the creek we passed," he answers in Kiowa, supplementing the words with signs. "Southeast of here a little ways. There are some waterholes. One or the other should have water."

The party turns back and, upon reaching Big Sandy Creek, follows the empty streambed south until a tank is found that holds water. They camp for the night. Again they push on at first light, continuing southwest toward the Arkansas River.

Twenty-five miles farther on, around noon, after climbing the tongue of a plateau, they halt on the western lip of the high ground and view a wide plain dotted with small lakes. Before them they see the aftermath of a great buffalo hunt. The carcasses of animals are dispersed over a distance of perhaps ten miles. Hundreds of wolves and a restless crowd of ravens feed on the remains of buffalo that have been skinned and butchered on this day and the day before. Between the scavengers a few groups of women and some men dress animals and load horses and travois with hides and meat. Wolves and ravens are oblivious to the close presence of humans. To the south, heavily loaded pack trains are seen being led away.

Eaglenest edges her horse to Stone's side. She fixes her gaze upon the people in the distance still working on the kill site. "I think they are my people, Gataka," she says, excited.

Stone looks at her and nods. He clicks his tongue and knees the horse forward. They come down the rough, barren slope in a whirl of dust. Stone makes for the first group of people well over half a mile away. They walk the horses past carcasses where gray-, white-, and black-colored wolves noisily tear at flesh, rip, growl, struggle with coils of intestines, crack bones. And ravens feed around and between the wolves, winging upward and sliding down, cawing, pulling morsels with shiny beaks. Wolves and ravens pay no attention to the riders who circle around them and hold nervous horses under tight control. There is an ancient cooperation between the two species of predators. And there is an ancient bond between these and the human hunters who leave part of their kill so that wolves and ravens, prominent in tribal mythologies and stories, will eat too.

Down where people have been dressing buffalo, work has stopped. Women stand by their horses. Men have gathered and ride forward, forming a protective screen, not knowing yet what to make of Stone's party—enemy Utes or friends. Eaglenest rides ahead, pushing her horse into a lope. She shouts in the Gataka language. While the party follows slowly, she reaches the men. They gather around her. Stone counts nine hunters. There is laughter and talk when Stone and the companions arrive. Stone greets the Gatakas solemnly. Eaglenest translates. She explains briefly where Stone's party is going. She asks about her parents, her brothers. She turns to her husband. "The Guantekana camp of my people is southwest on the big river." She points. "The Ka'ta camp is near it, straight south of here."

Stone gestures with his right hand. "Good. Tell them that the goods we brought for the Guantekanas from the white traders are in our camp. They should send people to get them."

After some small talk, Stone calls out softly and the column moves on. With Setpagoy beside him, they ride south in the direction of the Kiowa camp. Stone notices that one of the Gataka men is riding swiftly away to the southwest, probably to inform his camp. The column passes over the killing ground for another eight miles. They see that a few grizzlies and flocks of turkey buzzards have joined wolves and ravens. Once Setpagoy points to a broken arrow on the ground. "Kiowa." It seems that Kiowa hunters got to the herd before the Gatakas did. Stone decides to have a brief rest by a tributary of the Arkansas River. Later, riding on, they see smoke from the Ka'ta evening fires from a distance, then parts of the horse herd, and, finally, the first cream-colored tipis in the green shield of the cottonwoods of the Big Timbers that cover broad sections of the floodplain on both sides of the river.

FOUR

Stone wakes up at first light. He comes out of a dream he does not remember and lies still for a moment, thinking. He becomes aware that Eaglenest is not next to him. Then he remembers where he is. He is in his brother's and Sendehma's tipi. He looks up to where the tipi poles cross. The smoke holes are open. He half raises himself and looks around. A pale bluish haze steals through the partly open door. Sendehma made his bed last night on the southeast side. His brother, Big Bow, lies on the opposite side, on the northeast, bundled up, asleep. Sendehma's bed is on the west side beneath the tipi wall. Her little daughter, Gondaima, two years old, has half slipped out from under the covering robe and lies with her head on the floor, the hair a black tousle. Mother and daughter still sleep. Beside them is where Eaglenest would be if she were here. Last night her brothers, Daha and Däveko, came over from the Guantekana camp, seven miles to the west, and took her away for a visit to her parents. She has not seen her family for over a year.

He pushes the robe away and gets up. He looks for his weapons; finds them on the ground beside his bed. He puts on the breechclout and moves the door flap and steps soundlessly outside. He looks around. Two tipis sit close by. One is that of Sendehma's parents where Set'toni lives. The other belongs to Setpagoy and Tasenma. Four of Stone's Kit Fox men are sleeping there. Setpagoy is a member of the

Kiowa Tokogo, the Black Legs Society. The remainder of Stone's party has been distributed among the tipis of men of Setpagoy's society. Three Kiowa horses are tied up nearby. The horses of Stone's party were taken away last night by Black Legs, who volunteered to care for them.

Barefoot, Stone strolls to the river. He passes a few dogs curled up in the grass. They raise their heads and watch him quietly, then slip their muzzles back under their tails. He walks under a canopy formed by the tops of black willows and cottonwoods and across a few open spaces high in grass. Fresh buffalo hides are staked out everywhere, and meat racks are heavy with meat. He reaches the sandbars through which the Arkansas River hurries on its way from the Rockies to the lowlands in the east. He gazes south across the river to the green curtain of trees on the other side, half a mile away. Horses graze here and there; the Ka'tas are known to be rich in horses. He walks to the streambed and removes the breechclout. He enters the cold current and urinates. He washes himself and drinks deeply and lies down in a nook, the water up to his chin. From the west come splashing sounds, and, looking there, he sees a rider hurry through the river, perhaps a guard coming in. And behind him rises the chorus of the camp dogs greeting the new day.

He gets out of the river and stands for a time on a sandbar, naked, praying, facing east. He dresses and walks away following the shore. All along the river's edge adults and children arrive to wash themselves, some rolling in the water or taking a dip. Women walk out to where the current reaches their thighs and fill containers with water for drinking and cooking. Stone makes for a group of red cedars and sits down in front of them facing the river, his back to the tangle of forest and the camp beyond. He sits with legs crossed, bent forward, scratching signs in the sand with the point of a twig, not thinking, thinking. In his mind's eye he sees two boys running. Both on their father's stallion, he behind his brother, holding on to him on a wild ride, yelling, laughing. Shooting jackrabbits with small bows, missing, hitting, taking a catch proudly back to camp. He sees a face brightened by a smile, a man's face, intent, yet with a twinkle in his eyes. Somewhere beyond this river and many rivers . . . where will I find you?

A voice. Stone looks up slowly. Sendehma. She sits bareback on a horse in front of him. "Come, brother-in-law," she says with an inquiring look. "I have searched for you. Come and eat. We have been waiting for you."

He nods and gets up. He walks beside the horse when she leads him back to her camp. "I must tell you something," Sendehma says. She pauses. "Last night I sent a message to Zebatai. He is Taltoky, Keeper. He lives with the Tsaidetali bundle. I want to ask him to pray for us, to ask the spirit to help us find the father of my daughter."

She pauses. "He has sent a message back. He wants us to come when the sun is up there." She points to the sky, indicating a time near midmorning. "You have to come too, you and Gondaima."

She looks down at him from the horse, her dark eyes determined. "You are our leader. The Taltoky must see you."

Stone looks up. His eyes probe hers. "Yes," he says quietly.

They reach Sendehma's camp. They sit around the fireplace, Sendehma's parents and Set'toni, Setpagoy and Tasenma, Big Bow and the four Kit Foxes. Gondaima sits on her grandmother's lap. The little girl's dark eyes, wide open, serious, inquisitive, watch Stone. Food has been served on wooden plates, roasted buffalo meat and Mexican bread. Sendehma dismounts and points to a place next to her, and Stone sits down. Everyone waits.

Sendehma's mother, Tso'giado, takes a piece of meat and a piece of bread from her plate and holds both pieces up. She prays. She speaks in Kiowa, and although the Cheyennes present do not catch every word, they understand what the prayer and the food offering mean; Cheyennes have the same ritual. "Honde dâky," Tso'giado says softly, "spirits, whoever you are, here I give you this food. My children, when they eat of it, let them have long life! Those present who eat of it, let them be safe! Let no sickness come to us. This food, you have given to us."

All have listened with bowed heads. Tso'giado gets up and, her grandchild on her arm, walks behind the tipis and places the food on the ground. When she returns she says, "Go and eat," pointing to the plates, a gesture that is the same in any culture.

• • •

The sun has risen half the distance to midday. Stone sits and watches Sendehma as she paints herself. A tall, handsome woman, she is dressed in a long, soft antelope skin gown and boot moccasins. Gondaima sits next to her, her eyes on her mother.

From a little buckskin bag she puts a pinch of yellow ocher into her left hand and, with her right hand, mixes the paint with water. She rubs both hands over her face. She opens another small bag and sticks her right index finger inside. The tip of the finger is daubed with red paint. She smears the paint over the yellow on each cheekbone, drawing a red disk. Next, she parts her hair with a little pointed stick and applies yellow pigment to the parting. She lets her hair hang loose.

She is aware that Stone watches her. She lets him look but says nothing. Kiowa women paint differently from Cheyenne women, she knows. Cheyenne women do not paint their faces yellow but do paint red disks on their cheekbones. Thinking about this, she paints Gondaima as she has painted herself. When she is finished she looks up and says to Stone, "We go now."

Stone stands up. He is wearing breechclout and leggings and an unadorned buckskin shirt, plain moccasins. He has not painted himself but wears the hemen, the black crescent mark of the Kit Fox soldiers, on his chest.

They walk past Sendehma's tipi to where two horses are tied up. These are two of the ten horses given to Sendehma by the raiding party into Spanish lands from which Whirlwind did not return. She lifts Gondaima up and sets her on the bare back of one of the horses. The little girl is alarmed when Stone steps to her side. She looks at the strange man and to her mother and starts to sob. But Sendehma talks to her, trying to put her at ease. She takes Gondaima's hand and places it in Stone's sturdy hand. He looks at his brother's child in as friendly a fashion as he can, saying reassuring words in Cheyenne. Sendehma grabs the halters and leads the horses away, Stone walking beside the girl, holding her hand. She looks at him with large, serious eyes, looks again to her mother, back to Stone.

They are on their way to the Keeper of one of the Kiowa sacred tribal bundles in the Ka'ta band. They walk slowly as is proper on a mission such as theirs. Stone looks around with experienced eyes as they pass through the Kiowa camp. Everywhere women flesh staked-out buffalo hides or slice meat into long, thin sheets to hang on lines of buckskin to dry. They barely look up when Sendehma and Stone pass. Children play outside tipis. Horses and dogs. The smell of smoke. Travois frames are stacked up against trees. Men sit by smoldering fires, working on something on their laps, or two or three sit together talking. Riders come and go. A Kiowa camp, but it is very much like a Cheyenne camp, Stone observes. Tipis are of about the same size, a few are painted. He estimates the number of Ka'ta lodges to be around sixty or a few more.

Sendehma leads him through the floodplain forest beyond the western edge of the camp. There, away from the bustle of activities, stands a single tipi in an opening surrounded by willows and brush. Sixteen lodge poles, excepting the smoke-hole poles, Stone notices. The tipi is undecorated, the typical lodge of an important religious bundle. By a fireplace on the east side sits a middle-aged couple. Both the man and the woman wear their hair loose. Stone sees that the woman is painted the same way as Sendehma and Gondaima. The man's paint is more elaborate. On the yellow ocher face he has a little vertical zigzag in blue under each eye, in addition to a line of paint under each eye close to the lid, and a little crescent in black on the cheekbones. Tied above the open door of the tipi, facing east, is a fringed buckskin bundle. To Stone it looks similar in shape to a shield cover. It appears that a number of scalps are attached to it. The Taltoky and his wife arise. The Keeper notices the black hemen on Stone's chest, his eyes searching the Cheyenne's face, glancing along his body. He looks at Sendehma.

"We have come to make a gift to Tsaidetali," she says in Kiowa. "I am asking Tsaidetali for help to find my husband, for protection for this man, Stone, who is my husband's brother and a Cheyenne headman, who leads us, and for all of us who ride with him." She repeats part of her words in Cheyenne so Stone knows what she said.

The Keeper's wife walks away from the fireplace. The Keeper nods. His shirt, leggings, breechclout, and moccasins are plain leather without any embellishment. He points to a pole set away from the tipi. Sendehma steps forward and ties the horses to the pole. She lifts Gondaima off the horse's back and sets her on the ground. "You know my daughter," she says. "Gondaima." She pauses. "She longs for her father."

The Keeper smiles and stretches out both arms, speaking softly. The little girl walks up to the man without hesitation, and he bends and raises her in his arms. He hugs her and strokes her hair with his gritty hands, talking to her. He is everyone's grandfather, Stone muses, a real Keeper of sacred things. He watches as the man walks to the tipi door and places Gondaima's hands for a moment on the bundle. He turns and says something in Kiowa, and Sendehma goes and touches the bundle with the fingertips of both hands. The Keeper nods and points to the east side of the fireplace. He hands the girl back to her mother and fetches a pipe bag in the tipi. They sit.

There is a long silence. Some sounds come from the distant camp. The horses shift from foot to foot, lift and duck their heads. The buzzing of insects, a bird's cry over the tree line. The Keeper, who has gazed into the fire, looks up. Quietly he addresses Sendehma, but his eyes focus on the headman, taking in what he sees, feeling his way into Stone's soul. Stone meets these probing eyes without reluctance. He hides nothing. He projects his mind into the Keeper's, and the two, one Kiowa, one Cheyenne, meet in a place beyond language. Finally the Keeper nods and shifts his eyes to Sendehma.

She speaks demurely. Stone knows what she explains without understanding the words. Sendehma ends, crying softly. The Keeper opens the pipe bag and brings out the long stem and the red bowl of an elbow pipe. He slowly fits the bowl to the stem and fills the bowl with ceremonial tobacco. Bending forward he pulls a coal from the fire close with his finger and places the mouth of the bowl over it. He sucks on the stem. After the tobacco burns, he makes a few puffs before blowing smoke in the ceremonial directions. Finally he points the mouthpiece toward Tali, the spirit in the Tsaidetali bundle, and begins to pray.

Stone listens with closed eyes. It was like this when he sat with the Arrow Keeper in the Heviksnipahis camp. The Taltoky ends, and Stone opens his eyes. The Keeper finishes smoking the pipe and empties the bowl according to ritual. He separates the bowl from the stem and places both on the ground beside him.

It is over. "Aho," meaning "good," says the Keeper. It is a term used in both languages.

• • •

Eaglenest rides into camp at noon. With her come her two older brothers, Daha and Däveko, and Daha's wife, To'giai. They dismount in Sendehma's camp, and, Eaglenest and To'giai standing back, her brothers approach Stone with big smiles on their faces. They extend the flats of their right hands forward without touching. They are fond of each other. Brother-in-law teasing, like sister-in-law teasing, is normal behavior among Cheyennes, Kiowas, and Gatakas.

"It's good to see you here," Daha says. "You can't stay north and fight the Pawnees and Crows all the time. What about us?" He is a burly man of twenty-five with a broad friendly face. He laughs.

Däveko only smiles but says nothing. He is twenty-three, with a sharp, sensitive face and strong eyes. Both men are experienced members of the Gataka Manatidie warrior society.

They speak in the Gataka Apache dialect. Stone understands much of it and speaks it quite well owing to his wife's efforts. Still, when he talks to Gataka speakers, such as her brothers, he and they accentuate points of speech with sign language for clarity.

Daha points with his chin to To'giai, a pretty, shy, slender woman of twenty-one with loose, long hair. "My wife," he says, "To'giai. You have not met her yet." Eaglenest puts her arm around her as Stone nods to her.

"Sit with me," Stone says. As the two women walk toward the place where Sendehma stands with her mother, in front of Sendehma's tipi, Daha and Däveko join Stone at the fireplace.

They sit in silence for a few moments, gathering their thoughts. Then Daha speaks with a serious face. "We heard from Eaglenest where you are going. You can use us. We have been down south. We want to go with you." He pauses. "We talked about it. We want to smoke with you." His hands flutter in sign language for emphasis.

His brother nods. "Yes. You can't leave us out."

Stone looks at them. This is unexpected. But it is good. They are dependable men, good to have with him. Also, they know some of the country where the party is going. "Yes," he hears himself say. "I want you to come." He turns around to look for Eaglenest, but she already stands with his pipe bag in her hands.

He slowly opens the strings that close the top of the buckskin bag. He tips the bag sideways and removes the long pipestem, the elbow bowl of black stone, a tobacco pouch, and a short wooden tamper.

Daha and Däveko watch as he blows through the stem and the bowl, making sure that both are free of residue. He fits the bowl to the stem and slowly fills it with tobacco. He places the pipe on the ground in front of his crossed legs.

He looks into the faces before him. "Tell me again what you want."

Daha clears his throat. "I want to ride with you to find your brother. It will be a long ride. I will stay with you to the end. You are our leader on this raid. I will do as you say." He looks at his brother.

"The same with me," Däveko says. "You lead on this ride. I will stay to the end." He throws signs with his hands.

Stone nods. He digs with the tamper in the coals of the cold fireplace and isolates one that is still glowing faintly. He moves it close and, with thumb and index finger, places it on the bowl. He sucks on the stem. The tobacco starts to burn, and he wipes the coal off with the tamper. He makes a few puffs to keep the tobacco burning, then, after a moment of reflection, makes four puffs, deeply inhaling the smoke. Now he turns the mouthpiece toward the six ceremonial directions. After this he offers the pipe to Daha, who, after four puffs, passes it to Däveko. After he has smoked, he hands the pipe back to Stone. The pipe circulates among them until it is burned out. Stone empties the ashes on the ground before him and wipes them away. He removes the bowl from the stem and, after blowing through both to remove remaining particles, places them back into the buckskin bag.

"Aho," he says. He makes the sign for good.

"Aho," Daha and Däveko repeat. They sit and look at each other.

After a brief silence Stone asks the question that has bothered him for some time. "Do you speak the language of the white people and the mixed people down there? Spanish?"

Daha shrugs. "No. None of us do. We know some words, that is all."

"Do you know anyone who does?"

"We never needed to know their language," Däveko says. "We ride there for horses. Sometimes we take captives, young women or small boys. Whoever takes them keeps them or trades them to the Comanches or the Spanish after a while."

Stone shakes his head. "Not this time. Horses we will take after this is over. No women. We have to find my brother first." He pauses. "How can we talk to people there to get information? We don't understand them, and they don't understand us."

There is a silence. Daha nods. "We have three young women captives and two young boys from down there in our camp. The boys are too small for this. Perhaps the women speak Spanish and our language well enough to help us."

"How do they live in your camp?"

"They live with men of our camp. I do not know whether they would let them go."

"Can we trade for one of them?"

"I don't know." Daha shrugs. "I will find out when I get back to our camp."

They sit in silence thinking about this. "We know something else, though," Däveko says. His hands move fast. "Southeast of the pueblo of Pecos, on the headwaters of the river that runs south into the big river of the west, there are some small settlements. Placitas, the Spanish call them. We have been there. We have traded with them. The people there are called *genizaros.* They are halfbreeds, part Spanish, part Indian."

He pauses.

"Some of the people there used to be Comanche, or Kiowa, or Gataka, or even Ute and Jicarilla. The Spanish do not treat them as Spanish. They treat them as a separate people."

He pauses again.

"We should find someone there who would go with us who speaks both languages. These genizaro places are called San José del Bado and San Miguel del Bado." He has difficulties with the pronunciation. He laughs. "The largest is San Miguel. We were there a winter ago when they built a large stone house, a church, that is what they call their place of worship."

There is a silence.

"My brother is right," Daha says. "We will find someone there." He pauses. "These settlements are already in the Spanish lands."

Once again he pauses. "We know the fastest trail there. There is a pass in the mountains to the south of us. We use it when we go to the pueblos, Taos or Picuris. We will win two days going over the pass."

There is a brief silence. "Good," Stone says finally. "You take us there." He looks to where the women wait. "We ride from here in the morning. We will come by your camp after sunrise and you take us through the mountains and to the genizaros."

FIVE

In the evening, Magpie's widow, Koima, comes to Sendehma's camp. After the raiding party's return twenty days ago, when she learned about her husband's death, stricken with grief, she cut off her hair, the tip of the little finger on her left hand, and cut her arms with horizontal slashes. The wounds are healing; the cuts on her arms are covered with scabs. She cries, reaching out to Stone. With Sendehma translating, she implores Stone to avenge her husband, to kill some enemies in that faraway land for her husband, for her. Upon Stone's promise to do so she becomes silent, her eyes wild, searching the headman's somber eyes. He nods, making a sign with his right hand. A pledge to be kept. Koima is led away by her mother, who has stayed back.

The party moves out at sunrise, later than Stone had planned. But Sendehma's parents and Setpagoy's fellow society members had insisted that they should have a good meal before leaving the Ka'ta camp. While they were eating, the Ka'ta band chief came over and talked with Stone about the summer trading of the Wotapio Cheyennes in the Arikara Villages on the Missouri. They finally got away after food supplies for about eight days had been loaded on packhorses.

They have crossed the Arkansas River and now ride west along the edge of Big Timbers, Stone in the lead with Setpagoy beside him.

The column behind follows them in the order adopted on the first day of the march: first the Hovxnova Kit Foxes, then the Heviksnipahis Kit Foxes, then the Hovxnova Red Shields, Set'toni and Big Bow, and the women bringing up the rear, leading packhorses. From her own small herd Sendehma has added four horses to the column, one for her husband, she said, the others for emergencies. Two of them are added to Big Bow's two extra horses; the other two are handled by her brother, Set'toni.

New are the additions of Gondaima and her favorite dog, a male the size and shape of a wolf. While the brave little girl will shift from riding on her mother's saddle to resting on her breasts in a soft skin looped around Sendehma's neck, the dog, named Set, "bear," stays close to the party, circling, sniffing, watching, but always returning to Gondaima's side. During the journey Tasenma and Eaglenest will share in the care of the child as She-Wolf will share in the care of four-year-old Walking Last, daughter of her sister-in-law, Bear Doctor Woman. The women on the party are close-knit, and the children of two are the children of all.

At first Stone denied the wish to take Set along, but then reconsidered. He measured the dog carefully. With his coarse reddish coat, the outer hairs tipped with black, the buff throat, and whitish underparts, Set, to Cheyenne eyes, looks like a relative of the rare, solitary red wolf of the grasslands, a mysterious male called Xaenone in Cheyenne. He is regarded as a manifestation of the protector spirit of wolves and as a servant of Nonoma, the thunder spirit. Xaenone figures prominently in one of the Cheyenne ceremonies. Set certainly is not Xaenone, but the dog's bearing, his apparent intelligence, and his unusual color hint at something special. A good omen, perhaps, Stone thinks. And a dog such as this one could be helpful once they are in enemy lands.

They ride with a cool wind out of the north, below drifting clouds. The women wear fringed elk or antelope skin gowns that reach below the knee, moccasin boots. The men are dressed in breechclouts, fringed shirts and fringed leggings, and low-top moccasins. The men ride their travel horses and lead war mounts. To the war mounts are attached lances and bow-and-arrow cases. Bows are unstrung because the party is still in Kiowa and Gataka territory. The seven

Cheyenne men who have "North West" trade muskets in addition to bows—Stone, Powderface, Bear Tooth, Yellow Eyes, Standing, White Wolf, and Little Bird—carry the muskets across their backs in fringed cases. Both men and women carry belt knives. A few men have trade hatchets with iron heads in their belts. None of the men show feathers.

All are painted; paints are mixed with buffalo kidney fat to keep them soft and pliable. Cheyenne women, including four-year-old Walking Last, wear a disk of red ocher on their cheekbones, while Cheyenne men show a line of red ocher extending from the corner of the eye across the temple. Eaglenest, although of Gataka ancestry, paints as a Cheyenne woman. Kiowa women, including little Gondaima, wear disks of red ocher on their cheekbones over a thin yellow face paint. The two Kiowa men are painted more elaborately: on a yellow ocher face a little zigzag in blue is drawn under each eye, a small black crescent on each cheekbone. The Kiowa black crescent in male paint, like the hemen, the black crescent rawhide piece every Cheyenne Kit Fox warrior wears, is associated with the moon, the "night sun," and the red-shafted flicker, a mystery bird whose plumage displays a black crescent moon on its breast and red war paint on its cheeks.

Stone suddenly realizes that fall has come to the Big Timbers. The green of the cottonwoods is transforming itself into golden canopies. Some of the trees stand with flaming leaves, while others still mix the gold with green. With the morning sun full on the wide, dense stand of forest, treetops glisten like golden torches in the rustling wind.

The camp of the Guantekana band of Gatakas is located in the floodplain forest on the south side of the Arkansas. A few miles east of the camp Stone's party sees the first of the Guantekana horses. They graze on the long grassy slopes rising toward mesas in the south. A few young herders guard them. They watch the riders pass. Stone assumes that the Gatakas keep their herds east of the camp in the direction of the Kiowas, attempting to protect them from Ute raiding parties that sometimes come out of the Rocky Mountains.

Half a mile outside the Guantekana camp they meet with Daha, Däveko, and To'giai. The three sit on the ground, their horses grazing around them. When Stone and Setpagoy ride up, they slowly rise. Stone observes that their faces are painted with blue color, the men with short vertical lines below their eyes, the woman with a blue disk on each cheekbone. It is not the usual Gataka facial paint. But Stone remembers that the Gataka sacred color for the cardinal direction south is blue, and perhaps the three painted with this color because it is the direction in which the party travels.

"You are late," Daha says with a broad smile. "You could not get away from all that Kiowa food." He makes the proper signs with his hands.

Stone signals back. "I waited so you could sleep longer. We know how much you like to sleep."

The column has halted. Eaglenest comes up from the rear and guides her horse to Stone's side.

"What did you find out?" Stone asks, suddenly serious. Eaglenest translates. "Could you get any of the Spanish captives to come with us?"

Daha shakes his head. "No. None of them was let go." He pauses. "We have to try in the genizaro villages."

Stone nods. He surveys the Gataka horses. Three travel horses, two war horses, two packhorses. "You are ready to leave?"

Daha signals "yes." The three Gatakas mount. "You two ride ahead and take us through the pass you talked about yesterday," Stone says. The two men hand the lariats of their war mounts to To'giai, who holds the packhorses. While the woman waits to join the rear of the column with Eaglenest, the two warriors take the lead. Stone notices that Daha carries a sheathed musket on his back, Däveko the bow-and-arrow case with a strung bow.

They pass the camp. Only a few tipis are visible in the gold and green tangle of cottonwoods. Two horsemen watch them ride by. Eight miles west of the camp the Big Timbers thins out, and a few miles farther trees are gone. Above the Arkansas lies a sandsage and bluestem prairie with shrubs and cedars. Another few miles and the two Gataka guides turn south and disappear into the valley of the Purgatoire River, five miles above its mouth.

"Tso'p'a," Setpagoy says to Stone, "Rock River," giving the Kiowa name for the Purgatoire.

Now they move away from the golden valley of the Arkansas and ride parallel to the distant blue wall of the Rocky Mountains. Some of the peaks are speckled white with snow.

For Stone and his Cheyenne companions it is the entrance into a new world, into lands they have heard about but not yet seen.

• • •

For two days they travel on a seldom used trail toward the heights of the Raton Ridge looming in the distance. The two guides, Daha and Däveko, ride two bowshots in front of the column, scouting ahead, sometimes in sight, sometimes swallowed by a ravine or a sudden rise of cliffs. The trail meanders through the Purgatoire Valley strewn with rocks and climbs to mesas above until a coulee forces a diversion. This is broken country still covered with grasses and low shrubs, but the ground becomes more and more rocky and dry. This is not buffalo country, but there are old and fresh tracks of deer and bighorn and elk and grizzly and coyote, occasionally a puma's. They make the first night camp by a small lake next to the river about thirty miles up from the river's mouth.

On the second day, climbing steadily, the range has changed to a juniper and piñon woodland, open groves of evergreen trees with yuccas and admixtures of shrubs and herbaceous plants. The Raton Ridge, covered with dark green pine and Douglas fir, is an impressive sight up to the south, and their second night camp is made by a tank in the riverbed a few miles below the edge of the forest. Däveko has shot two elk cows with the bow near the campsite, and the party feasts on fresh meat that evening.

On the next day the trail enters the thick forest of pines and firs; it is often blocked by debris and fallen trees. Stone and the others are reminded of parts of the Black Hills. Progress is slow through the dense green growth, and at noon the party rests in a glade by one of the headwaters of the Cimarron River near a small brook flowing east. In the afternoon they pass the Alps west of Devoys Peak and move through the gap west of Emery Peak, 7,350 feet high, hidden from sight, and ride up the narrow course of the Dry Cimarron and come out of the forest and gaze at Capulin Mountain and the high plateau to the south past Sierra Grande. They make camp for the night there, at the edge of the world the Spanish consider theirs, eager to move on in the morning. Before first light, wolf packs call from the southwest and southeast, familiar sounds to which Set raises his articulate voice in camp, answering.

In the cool morning they ride on toward the gap between Capulin Mountain in the west and Sierra Grande in the east. There is no water source on their trail for the next twenty-five miles until they reach Carrizo Creek, so they filled water bags before leaving. The wind is from the north. They ride again in the open, high country woodland of piñon and juniper, and in midmorning they hear the voices of the messengers of the cold season. Above, under drifting clouds, suddenly the first wings glide and flap south, formations of sandhill cranes impelled onward by the rasping calls of leading birds, trumpeting calls responding to the formations of whooping cranes heading the same way. The great annual fall bird migration has begun.

Since morning the three Heviksnipahis Kit Foxes have formed a rear guard behind the women. This is land often visited by Ute hunting parties, and if they met with one there might be a fight. At midday the party reaches the knee of Carrizo Creek east of pine-clad Laughlin Peak, 8,820 feet high, and Stone calls for a rest. They do not build a fire, making do with cold food. The streambed is empty. Kiowas and Gatakas are experienced in finding water in dry places, more so than the Cheyennes. Daha walks the streambed to gauge the location of hidden water sources, and finding a promising spot he starts digging in the sand. The first hole produces nothing, but a second hole, dug to a depth of almost two feet, has water seeping in from the bottom. After it is extended in width and depth, it slowly accumulates liquid that is lifted out with a skin. It is a slow process and takes time, but the horses need water and time to graze in order to remain in good condition for the long journey.

They move on in a southwestern direction and after ten miles leave the open woodland behind and once again enter rolling hills covered with grama and buffalo grass. They pass the remains of an antelope pound, wide wings of brush converging on a drop into a ravine that holds a corral built of brush strengthened by a system of vertical poles. A cluster of tipi rings is off to the side. Later they come upon an old, solitary buffalo bull, and suddenly there are bands of buffalo in every direction, each containing a few hundred animals, brown, shaggy bodies on the yellow grass, feeding, moving slowly east. A short time later Daha and Däveko halt and let the party ride up. They point to the west. All watch.

There, slowly coming over a rise, a column of riders appears, approaching in their direction. The others have seen them and halt. There is a flurry of activity in the distance as riders gather in front of the column. Warriors, Stone knows. Lances rise upward.

"Kiowas," Setpagoy says. "Kiowas."

He drops the reins of his travel horse and mounts the war horse. He pushes the animal forward into a lope and rides toward the strangers. Stone watches as he reaches the screen of men and halts. He is surrounded by a half circle of men. There seems to be a talk, and then Setpagoy turns his horse and, with two men beside him, rides back toward Stone's party, the column behind them starting up again. As the three riders come close, Stone sees that one of them is a young man, probably a headman, the other an older man. Only the young man rides a war horse and is fully armed with lance and shield and a bow-and-arrow quiver. Tied horizontally to his long hair is a single eagle feather. The older man is unarmed; he shows no feathers but wears a buffalo skin belt around his waist, the fur on the outside. The belt marks him as a ceremonial man. Behind them are about twenty men and five women with packhorses. Stone rides a few paces forward. He raises his right hand, and the two Kiowa leaders do the same. They survey each other. They seem to be pleased by what they see. Their stolid faces give in to smiles.

In sign language the ceremonial man explains. "I am Sun Boy, Ko'nep band, Big Shields." He points with his chin to the young man next to him. "Stone Calf. Ko'nep band. Soldier headman."

Stone signals his name. The three leaders nod to each other. "Where do you come from?" Stone signals. "Where are you going?"

The ceremonial man points to the northwest. "We went over the mountains to the pueblo to trade. Taos. We are returning to our camp three rides this way." He points east.

Setpagoy signals quickly. "I told them who you are and where we are going," he says. Stone nods.

The Kiowa headman speaks. "There is a party that went to Dokanitakai, Coahuila. Fifteen warriors, three women. They left one moon ago. They are from our Kogui band, the Elks." He pauses. "They will make trouble for the Ätakais, the Spanish, there." He laughs. Then serious again, he says, "You may meet with them. Perhaps they can help you."

Stone makes the sign for "good."

The Kiowa headman signals again. "Down there is a camp of buffalo hunters." He points southwest in the direction Stone's party is heading. "We met some of their men back there." He points west. "They are from across the mountains, from Picuris Pueblo." He pauses. "They are like the Taos people. They speak a tongue similar to Kiowa."

Stone nods. "How far to their camp?"

"Only a little way," the Kiowa signals.

While they talk, Set has circled the Kiowa column in his swift, floating running style. The Kiowas crane their necks to watch the red wolf. Their horses are nervous, jerking their heads, and have to be held tightly. Set sits and stares at them for a moment before drawing away when Gondaima calls him. He puts his front paws on Sendehma's horse and licks the child's face. She tries to brush him off, and he drops to all fours and lopes away.

Stone makes the sign for "thank you." Then, "We leave now." He backs the horse away and once again raises his right hand. He makes the sign for a safe trail. The two Kiowa leaders do the same. Stone turns the horse and leads his party away, quickly joined by Setpagoy. The Kiowa's column lets them pass, the people of both groups looking at each other. Nods, a shy waving of a hand, guarded smiles, a shout from Set'toni answered by laughter.

Three buffalo herds give way before them and then the wide plain is empty. They ride a few miles. In the sky, in the distance, below the noisy wings of cranes soaring south, sharp eyes see a dark mass of vultures circling. A buffalo kill, Stone knows. It should be near the camp of the Picuris hunters. Another ten miles, and coming over a low ridge, they see the killing ground, a stretch of land dotted with a hundred buffalo carcasses. Beyond, a few miles farther, the *cibolero* camp is pitched under cottonwoods by a small lake on Chico Creek. Smoke from fires is driven away low by the north wind.

Stone rides on. "These are friends," Setpagoy says and makes the sign. "We know them."

They ride across the killing ground. A host of animals is working on the carcasses: a few grizzlies, packs of wolves, coyotes, kit foxes, ravens and magpies and vultures. A feast left behind by skinners and packers. As they approach the camp, men armed with lances gather in front of it. Dogs begin to howl. Eighteen arbors covered with brush and skins are set near the lake shore. Wagons are stationed around them. A body of mules is bunched in a provisional holding pen; some horses are held in another pen, others are tethered by the arbors. Lengthy lines of ropes held by poles hang with long thin slabs of meat to dry in the sun. Women flesh buffalo skins pegged to the ground.

Stone sends Setpagoy forward as he halts the party a few hundred paces from the camp. The Kiowa approaches the men. They talk, gesture. It goes on for a while. When Setpagoy returns, Eaglenest has ridden to her husband's side to translate.

"These are the people from Picuris," Setpagoy says. "They make this hunt for buffalo meat and skins every fall. They say there is a camp of people from two other pueblos east of here. These are from Santa Clara and San Ildefonso. Other parties from over there," he points west, "are coming soon. That is what they say."

He pauses as Eaglenest translates.

"There is a big party of Spanish settlers southwest of here, they say. They are from two villages in the mountains, Cordova and Truchas." He stumbles in the pronunciation of the Spanish words. Stone smiles. Setpagoy continues. "These have come to hunt buffalo too. These Spanish fear *norteños*." He shrugs. "This means people of the north, us, Kiowa, Gataka, and you, Cheyenne." He pauses again. "Because they are afraid of us, they are hostile to us. We have to watch for them, the Picuris say."

Stone nods as Eaglenest translates.

"The Picuris know that we are at peace with them." Setpagoy makes a movement with his hand. "They say we are welcome to camp next to their camp or anywhere around the lake. They will give us buffalo meat."

Stone thinks for a moment. "I accept their invitation. I thank them." He sends Setpagoy back to inform the Picuris and takes his party to a good campsite by the lake two bowshots south of the Pueblo camp, under golden cottonwoods. After they have unpacked, watered the horses, and started two fires, a delegation of Picuris men and women arrives with a packhorse loaded with meat. They also bring two loaves of the hard brown bread baked in Pueblo *hornos,* considered a delicacy among the grasslands tribes. As a return gift the visitors receive a beautiful buffalo hide with an ornate quill-work design and two packages of vermilion paint traded from the English at the Arikara Fair.

In the evening there is visiting from camp to camp. The Cheyennes, new to the country and its different ethnic populations, observe intently and memorize everything they see. The Pueblo women are fascinated by the children in Stone's group: Bear Doctor Woman's daughter, Walking Last, and Gondaima, Sendehma's child. Especially Gondaima. The little one is passed fondly from one woman to another as Set sits close by, concerned, vigilant. Like the Kiowas earlier, the Picuris regard the huge red dog with awe and some apprehension. Set has already circled the Pueblo camp and learned all he was curious to know. During the cool night coyotes yip from the north and wolves call at first light; Set responds with his authoritative voice.

On the following day Stone's party fords the Canadian River eight miles west of last night's camp and continues southwest. A couple of times they cross a profusion of pony tracks and twice the ruts of deeply cut trails caused by *caretas,* the rude, cumbersome, two-wheeled carts of Spanish settlers. They lead east and west, farther into the Plains and returning. Setpagoy explains that the caretas may belong either to Spanish villagers of the mountains out hunting buffalo or to *comancheros,* Spaniards who trade with Comanche bands for horses and prisoners the Comanches have taken in Spanish lands in the south.

Stone wonders why the Spaniards of this area trade for prisoners and horses the Comanches have taken from the Spanish in the south. Setpagoy has no answer; he just shrugs. These people are different from us, hard to understand.

They make camp for the night on a small lake on Carrizo Creek below Turkey Mountain. Due west lies the high, snowy rim of the

Sangre de Cristo range, with Trampas Peak reaching up to 12,175 feet, wondrous in the distance. Throughout the day they have seen no humans but herds of antelope, a few grizzlies, prairie dog towns, and a sky filled with formations of cranes and geese and ducks and their calls. They are glad to see grizzlies; in the mythology and the ancient stories of the three tribes, Kiowa, Gataka, Cheyenne, grizzlies feature prominently as benefactors, messengers of spirits, and spirits themselves.

But they see humans again on the next day. Twelve miles below their last night's camp, on the Mora River, they see a big camp in the distance. Earlier they met three outriders from the camp, who galloped away when they saw the norteños. They see a big camp with arbors and pens for mules and oxen and horses, caretas, people milling around after their riders come in. These must be the people from Cordova and Truchas who have come to hunt but have not found buffalo. They could ask Stone's party but don't ask and make no attempt for contact.

The party moves on, remembering what the Picuris told them, and once again they come into piñon and juniper woodland, the dark green, bushy trees dotting a hard, rocky ground covered with a thin veneer of scrawny grasses. Again the three Heviksnipahis Kit Foxes ride rear guard. Set is in constant motion, ringing the column and running ahead with the fleet, effortless gait of the wolf. When they come into mesa country, they follow a well-worn trail leading south and make camp for the night on the banks of the Gallinas River below Mesa Apache. Daha and Setpagoy agree that they are a half day's ride away from the genizaro town of San Miguel del Bado beyond the good spring of Bernal.

SIX
October 7, 1807

In the light-filled early afternoon, two women wash clothes in the Pecos River three stone throws south of San Miguel del Bado. They kneel in the swift, clear waters of the river, which ripples south from the snowy mountains of the Sangre de Cristos. One is a middle-aged woman, Teresa, the other a young girl, Maria, nineteen years old. Both are servants of the alcalde of the hamlet; both are genizaras, females of Indian origin once captured by hostile tribes and later ransomed by the Spanish at the Pecos Fair. Teresa is of Ute descent; Maria is a Hiaqui from Sonora. Like all the genizaros of San Miguel, they were never able to return to their people. They were Christianized by Spanish priests and stayed. The two women talk with each other while they soak and beat the clothes. Maria's little son, Manuel, three years old, plays in the water near his mother. He is startled when a kingfisher flits by, a blue and white jewel that skims over the river nearly touching its surface and disappears in the haze upstream. Suddenly the women hear new sounds from across the gentle, murmuring voices of the river, hooves on soft ground, a clanking on stones. They look up, and Maria reaches for Manuel. The women rise and stand, the river curling around their knees, as the party comes in sight.

Daha and Däveko ride point twenty paces ahead of Stone and Setpagoy. Behind them a column of riders comes into view. Maria looks along the line of fierce-looking men, at cased firearms, lances reaching up from the saddles of war horses, painted shield covers, and quivers with bows and arrows slung over saddle horns. "Naciones del Norte," Maria whispers. Her experienced eyes recognize Gatakas and Kiowas by the residue of facial paints and details in clothing, but she is puzzled by the appearance of the majority of men as they come closer in single file. Who are they? To what nation do they belong? When she lived with the Comanches she saw persons from many factions of the southern Plains and the Cross Timbers, but never any like these.

Glancing along the warriors' file she distinguishes the leader from the others, a hard, serious man, a power within himself, lean, medium-sized, a typical headman, who measures her with a quick, penetrating look as the horses splash through the river twenty feet above her. Haughty, imperious men, she thinks, men she has known and suffered from. And the women riding up are like the men, arrogant, she thinks, insolent, strong-willed, self-assured. Two are Kiowas, two Gatakas, the others of the norteños she does not know. These women take no notice of her. They are drawn by the forward column and, it seems, by a larger purpose, and they climb up the west bank with their pack-horses and extra horses and move on without looking back.

When Maria thinks that she has seen all of them, three more riders appear, the rear guard, norteño warriors of the mystery nation, heavily armed, with war ponies by their knees, hard men again, one looking at Manuel as if he knows him. And then they are gone.

Maria looks at Teresa. The older woman makes the sign of the cross. Suddenly a red wolf bursts upon the scene and throws himself into the river, the waters not even reaching his powerful shoulders, and gets through, shakes his unusually colored coat and lopes away on the trail of the warrior party. The women look at each other. What was it that has passed? They wring the wet clothes and fill their baskets and walk toward the irregular clusters of adobe huts grouped around the stone church, past the fence of the wide corral for the *churra* sheep.

• • •

In the evening, when Maria and Teresa are in the *obraje,* the workshop in the alcalde's adobe house, processing wool by cleaning and carding, the alcalde walks in, calling on Maria to come with him. He is Severino Jaramillo, a mestizo. He and his family and about a dozen families of mestizo settlers, persons of mixed Spanish-Indian descent, are nevertheless regarded as Spanish locally and by authorities in Santa Fe and elsewhere. In addition to these, about thirty genizaro families, perhaps thirty genizaro servants in Spanish households, and a resident Franciscan priest, José Francisco Leyba, make up the population of San Miguel.

The alcalde and Maria walk through the narrow courtyard and into the plaza. In front of the church six riders sit horses ringed by Spaniards and genizaros, who have come to look and listen. The riders are Stone, Eaglenest, Daha, Setpagoy, and two of the Hovxnova men, Powderface and Porcupine. The warriors are unarmed. The Franciscan and a genizaro interpreter stand before the riders. The alcalde pushes Maria forward. They join the priest.

Maria recognizes the mounted strangers as belonging to the party of northerners she saw earlier. She becomes aware that the strangers study her thoroughly, their eyes running all over her. They see a thin, scared girl, barefoot, the black hair clipped short, wearing a short leather skirt and a cotton blouse. They also see an Indian face.

The Franciscan speaks rapidly in Spanish, with an angry voice, staring into the calm, stoical face of the headman above him. He gestures with his arms. He stops. Stone looks to the interpreter, a genizaro of Kiowa origin. The man understands enough Spanish to get some essential parts of the Franciscan's speech. He addresses Stone in Kiowa. "The Father, he does not want you to take the girl. He needs her in his church." He points. "She sings songs during mass. No one else here can sing in that language. They call it Latin." He shrugs.

Eaglenest translates to her husband in Cheyenne. Maria, who speaks Spanish and Kiowa fluently, has heard the priest and the interpreter. She knows that the interpreter has understood only part of the priest's harangue and has left much out, including a threat the priest has made. She realizes with a shock that she is the subject of the confrontation. What do they want of her? She winces, tries to back away, but the alcalde has his hand on her shoulder.

Eaglenest ends her translation. Stone speaks to her briefly in Cheyenne. Eaglenest relays his words to the genizaro. He speaks to the priest in broken Spanish, groping for words. Maria hears with a sinking feeling. "It is not you who owns the girl. It is this man." He points with the quirt to the alcalde. "He owns her. I am talking to him."

The priest responds with a barrage of angry words. The alcalde raises his hands. "This girl is valuable to me," he says in Spanish. "I bought her from a Comanche chief for a mule and twenty feet of cotton. I want to keep her."

Once again the complex process of translation from Spanish into Kiowa and Cheyenne is repeated. When it is finished, Stone raises a hand to end the conversation. He looks at the alcalde. "Yes. I understand. But I need the girl. I give you two good horses for her."

"She has a young boy," the alcalde says.

Stone is impatient. "I want her. The young boy is hers. We will take him too."

The alcalde dithers and answers with a flood of words. Perhaps he wants to strike a better bargain.

Stone interrupts. "Two horses. That is all." He is getting angry. He bends forward in the saddle, looking down at the alcalde. "Two horses. If you refuse, we will take her by force."

Maria has heard his words in the Kiowa translation. She feels lost, an object of barter. She has been that before. Her mind is flooded with bad memories. She looks at the headman and the warriors around him. She believes what he says. So do some of the onlookers who understand Kiowa. They are uneasy. There is a silence. The only sounds are from the horses scraping the ground with their hooves, tossing their heads, blowing through their nostrils. Maria feels the warmth of their bodies.

Now Eaglenest speaks directly to the girl in Kiowa. "We want you to come with us," she says gently. "We need you because you speak Spanish well." She makes a sign with her hand. "We will not harm you. We need you for something we have to do. When it is done, we let you go. You will have a horse. You can go wherever you want to go."

"I have a son," Maria says in a whisper.

"Yes. You bring him. We have children with us, too. You have seen them."

The alcalde speaks rapidly in Spanish to the Franciscan. He answers angrily and walks away. The alcalde looks over the townspeople around him, perhaps for support or to assess how they would

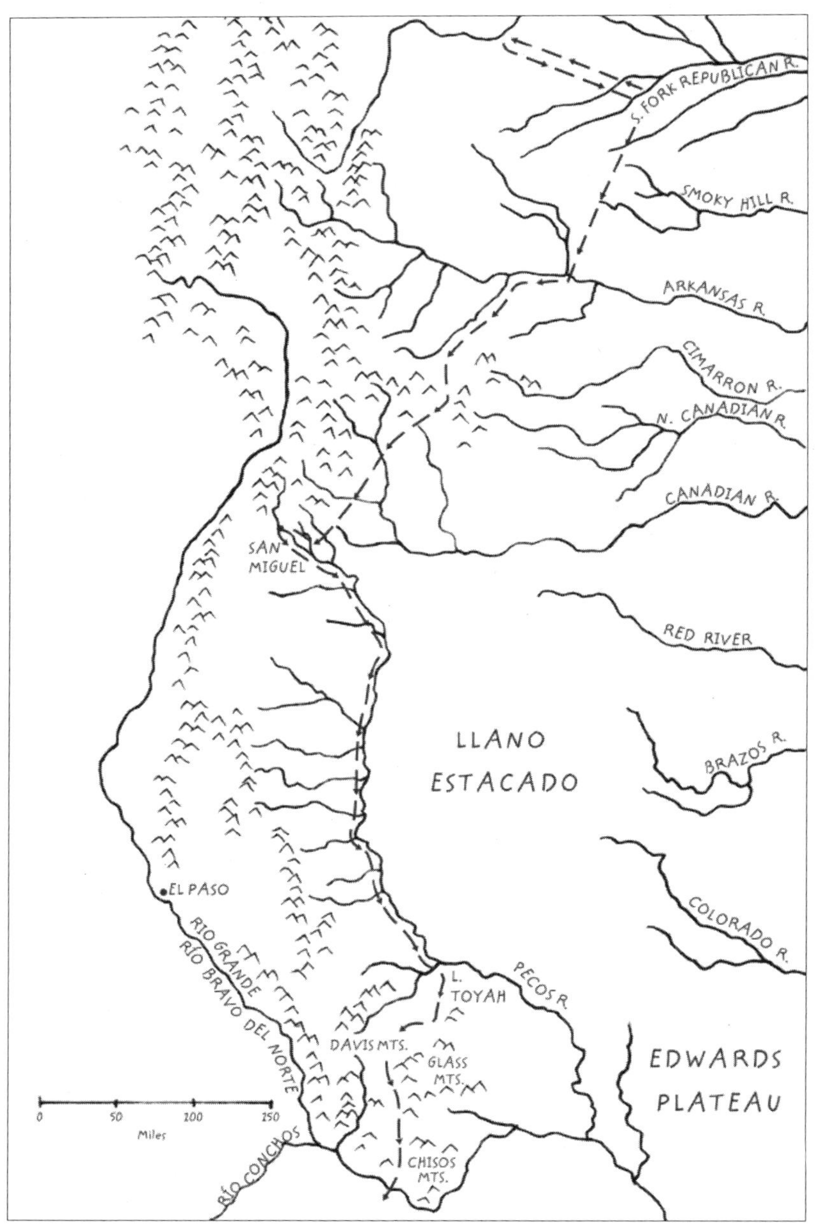

The trail of Stone's Party from the camp on the south Fork of the Republican River through the western Plains to the mouth of Terlingua Creek on the Rio Grande, September 17 to October 24, 1807.

react if he were to refuse the trade and the northerner would make good on his threat. He sees nothing to encourage him. Faces are blank or apprehensive. No one would raise a weapon in his defense. It is between him alone and the strangers. He shakes his head and speaks to Maria in Spanish. "Tell this man that I take the two horses. You will go with him."

Maria looks at Eaglenest and, in Kiowa, hears herself say, "He says he takes the horses." This is the second time that she has been sold.

Eaglenest nods and smiles. She turns to her husband. He listens and signals to Porcupine. The warrior backs his horse out of the ring of bystanders and turns it and rides away to bring the horses.

• • •

Set howls the morning song at first light, giving the signal to rise. The men and women of Stone's party wash themselves in the Pecos, the river the Kiowas call P'a E'dal Sän, Little Great River, and break camp. When they ride out, Daha and Setpagoy are forward as scouts. Stone has replaced Däveko with Setpagoy because he and Daha know the trail to the Spanish heartlands. Däveko has joined with Set'toni ahead of the women's contingent. Maria has attached herself to Eaglenest, riding next to her, with little Manuel sitting on the saddle blanket in front of her.

The three Heviksnipahis Kit Foxes remain as a rear guard. Although under the headman's command, they prefer to stay by themselves. They watch and immerse themselves in the features of the land they pass through, the trails and watering places, tracks and animal populations, burning the knowledge into their minds, storing it away for future use. Someday they expect to come back with a Heviksnipahis raiding party.

Maria is uneasy and tense. The women, with the exception of Eaglenest, ignore her, and from occasional glances she thinks she senses some hostility. The men pay no attention to her and the boy at all. She is a person without relations, without a tribe, a lone stranger everywhere, a young woman lost. She clutches Manuel and holds him to her body, the one thing that is her own, her life, her blood and soul. Her apprehensiveness is felt by the child who gazes at the cavalcade around it with huge eyes. It is Eaglenest who feels for her and encourages her to ride beside her and Sendehma, talking with her, giving her a friendly smile. They converse in Kiowa. Sendehma holds back, but little Gondaima, her daughter, is fascinated by Manuel.

The party follows a well-used trail near the west bank of the Pecos River. They are still in open juniper and piñon woodland. About ten miles south of San Miguel they pass the last of the genizaro towns on the Pecos, La Cuesta, a cluster of adobe huts bunched together on a hill. They are watched as they ride over fallow fields from which chile and beans and corn and squash have been harvested months ago. They turn their backs on the last outpost of New Mexico, leave the bend of the river, and ride up a low plateau, taking a direction toward the southeast. The trail between the genizaro towns has ended at La Cuesta, but the two scouts know their way. Fifteen miles farther they reach the Pecos again and, at midday, rest for a meal and for the horses. Twenty miles on they make camp for the night in a grove of cottonwoods below the bend of the river where Esteros Creek, its bed dry as a bone, falls into the Pecos. Twice they have crossed broad trails carved by caretas wheels leading east into the Plains and returning to somewhere in the west. The sky above is still filled with cranes and geese and ducks and the calls that keep their formations together.

In the gathering dark Eaglenest takes her husband aside. "I talked with the girl, Maria," she says. "She told me where she is from and what has happened to her."

Stone listens carefully, looking to where Maria sits by the fireplace among the women, quite alone.

"She is Hiaqui, from a people that lives far to the west. She was born in a town called Torim. The Hiaqui live in eight towns along the Hiaqui River. They have been fighting with the Spanish for a long time. There are a few Brown Robes among them, Franciscans she calls them. When her parents died, one of the Brown Robes took her and her brother in."

She pauses.

"When she was fourteen years old, the Brown Robe went east to teach tribes in the high mountains about his spirits. He asked her and her brother to go with him. She did not want to, but her brother wanted to go. They went together. First they stayed with the Tarahumara, a mountain tribe, then with people farther east called Concho, on a river."

Stone interrupts. "Where is the child from?"

Eaglenest shakes her head. "The Brown Robe, he was the father."

When Stone looks at her with a question in his eyes, Eaglenest explains. "There was an attack by Comanches. They killed the Brown Robe and her brother. They took her with them to their camp east of here." She points. "These Comanches are from the Kotsoteka band. The man who got her is a little chief of the Kotsotekas. His name is White Horse."

She pauses again.

"She had the child in the Kotsoteka camp. White Horse has two women in his tipi. Kiowas. They are sisters. They did not want the Hiaqui woman. They treated her badly. Sometimes they beat her. This went on. Finally the women talked their man into trading Maria to the Spanish."

Another pause. "Some Kotsotekas and some Nokoni Comanches went to the pueblo called Pecos. White Horse knew that the Spanish exchange prisoners taken in Spanish lands for goods. He had been there before."

She looks to where Maria sits with Manuel asleep in her lap. "They traded her." She waits. "That was one winter ago." Again she falls silent. Then, "She speaks Kiowa and Comanche and the Spanish tongue. She is gentle, scared. I think that she can help us."

Stone agrees. "Stay close to her. She knows more about the Spanish than any of us, more than Daha and Setpagoy. Learn from her what she knows. We need to know about the lands and the places and the peoples there if we are to find my brother." He pauses. "Be good to her. Make her understand that she is safe with us as long as she is truthful and does not deceive us. Tell her why we ride."

They look into each other's eyes. He touches lightly his wife's shoulder. A brief moment, a feeling, an expression of the bond between them, a remembrance. Nothing has to be said.

• • •

A sudden wailing breaks the stillness of the night, a series of high-pitched cries. Gondaima is teething. Set, who has lain near her, now stands over her, probing the child's face. Stone sees it in the last flickering light of the fire. Sendehma half rises and pulls a short piece of buffalo hide from her pack kept for this purpose. She places it in Gondaima's mouth for her to bite on. A few more muffled sounds. Quiet again. The tapping of hooves in the dark as the horses move around slowly, cropping grass. Two of the Hovxnova Kit Foxes, Yellow Eyes and Lame Bear, are on guard. No human enemies are expected, but the scent of a wandering grizzly or a puma, sleek killer of horses, could cause their mounts to panic.

They start on a cloudy day, and when it becomes light, migratory birds above them cruise sometimes so low that it seems they can be reached by an arrow shot from a good bow. At midmorning, twenty miles on, the wooded hills shrink back and before them opens the great span of the shortgrass Plains once again. They are at the edge of the Llano Estacado, which stretches east of the Pecos, a rolling range of low rises and wide, flat valleys that run on and on.

They see that they are not the only travelers. In the distance great numbers of buffalo move. Many have forded the river and drift west, while others mass in the river and along its eastern bank, drinking. These are pressured by new herds appearing on the hills to the east, the swell of a dark brown wave on a sea of yellow grass, pressing down. Wolf packs accompany the herds on the ground, flights of ravens shadow them from above.

The party has halted, watching. Stone turns in the saddle and waves to his wife to come to him. He asks, "How much food have we left?"

"Enough for today and tomorrow," Eaglenest says. "That is all. The women say it would be good to have three or four young cows. Maybe three would be enough. That would give us meat for ten days." She thinks for a moment. "We need two days to care for the meat."

Stone nods. Two days of rest would be good for the horses. He talks to the two brothers directly behind him, Porcupine and Powderface. He tells them that each should kill two young buffalo cows. The men know what to do. They dismount and get their war horses ready, removing saddles and weaponry. They undress to breechclouts and brace their bows by placing the tip under the left foot, bending the belly of the bow over their right knee, and slipping the bowstring over the nock. Each takes a few arrows in his bow hand and mounts, tucking the two reins of the bridle into his belt. Bareback, directing the horses with their thighs, they ride off, making a wide swing to the east.

The wind is from the south. The party watches as the hunters approach the walking herds. They ride hunched over their horses' backs, heads lying along the horses' necks. They advance slowly, using folds in the land's surface to get close, and then, when stragglers at the herd's edge recognize the danger, dash into the surprised mass of animals. As the buffalo attempt to break away to the south but are hampered by the many in front of them, the two riders cut a bunch from the stampeding mass and turn it in the opposite direction. Cows run faster than bulls, and the bulls fall back as the hunters pursue the cows, with some calves running beside them. As the chase gets closer to the party, the onlookers see the hunters approach their selected victims on the animals' right side and, about a bow length away from the target, bend over and release the arrows. The buffalo heart sits very low in its chest, below the lungs; a powerful bow is required for the arrow to penetrate the rib cage to either organ. Two more cows are hit and the hunters pull back. The watchers observe quietly as the animals that were shot slow down, stagger, drop. The remaining buffalo circle wildly and race south after the main herds.

Stone moves the party on to the river where a campsite is selected under the golden canopy of a stand of cottonwoods. There is enough firewood, good grass for the horses. The packhorses are relieved of their loads, and the women ride out with them to butcher the buffalo. Wolves have already congregated within bow range around the kills, sitting on their haunches, waiting for their share. To speed up the process of skinning and cutting, a few men join the women.

The lower legs up to the joints are cut off with hatchets and thrown away, as are the heads after the tongues are taken. The corpses are skinned by splitting the hides down the middle of the back and from the throat down to the tail. Guts and stomachs, preserved at other times, are rejected and discarded. Kidneys and livers will be eaten raw later. Hearts and lungs are discarded but for one buffalo heart Sendehma reserves for Set, who sits nearby with Gondaima, the girl and the dog viewing the bloody scene before them, the dog with growing excitement, the girl unruffled, indifferent. The sinew from the large tendon that lies along both sides of the buffalo's backbone and under the shoulder blade is removed and cleaned by scraping; the sinew will be used for sewing and for bowstrings. The ribs, with the meat attached, are packed on the green pieces of hides.

The work is finished after a few hours, and the loaded packhorses are led back to camp. There the women's work continues, preparing the meat for curing. Away on the kill sites, the wolves, joined by kit foxes and coyotes that have arrived out of nowhere, and the ravens fight noisily over what is left of four buffalo cows. The humans feast in the early evening too.

It is time to rest. The horses deserve it. But Stone sits glumly away by himself. Brother, he thinks aloud, I am coming, but how do I find you?

SEVEN

On the second day in camp, when most of the women's work is finished, Stone calls on Eaglenest to bring Maria for a talk. The three sit in the sparse grass under one of the cottonwoods outside the camp. Stone sits cross-legged, the women with their legs to one side. Maria has brought Manuel; he could not be left in camp without his mother. The boy sits on Maria's lap. Her arms tightly squeeze him as if she is afraid that someone might take him away. He is quiet, looking at Stone and Eaglenest with his keen black eyes.

Stone faces the river and the hills to the southeast, which now that the buffalo have passed, lie empty under the sun and a breezy north wind. Maria is edgy. She evades looking into the headman's face. They sit in silence. Stone is aware of the girl's uneasiness. "I want to know about *xamavostaneo* in the Spanish lands," he says, as friendly as he can. It is the Cheyenne word for Indians, meaning, "original people."

Eaglenest nods. She translates into Kiowa, speaking the Kiowa word for Indians, *gi'aguadalta'go,* "red people."

Maria looks at Eaglenest and answers her in Kiowa. She will not look at Stone. Indian women do not look directly into the face of a man who is a stranger; Stone is still a stranger to her.

"I do not know much about Indians over there," she says haltingly in Kiowa. "I know about my own people a little, Hiaquis." She pauses.

"Not much. I was fourteen when the Brown Robe took us away, me and my brother." She looks sadly down at Manuel in her lap. "Hiaqui country is near the salt water sea far west of here." She falls silent, listening to Eaglenest as she translates her words into Cheyenne.

Stone clears his throat. "You were moving around with the Brown Robe. What other Indians did you see?"

Maria sits thinking. "When Father José took us away from Torim, we went east through the country of the Mayos. We went into the high mountains."

"José is his name? He is the father of Manuel?"

"Yes." Her voice is barely audible.

There is a pause.

"Where did you go in the high mountains?"

"To Sisoguichi. This is a mission. We were there for some time. Then to San Felipe. This is a mission on the Conchos River."

Stone listens to Eaglenest's translation. Then, "What is a mission?"

"A church and an Indian village. Brown Robes and other priests teach Indians about their spirits, about a spirit they call god. They also call him Christ."

She pauses. "Indians who are taught about Christ are called Christians."

Stone looks at her curiously. "Are you a Christian?"

Maria is unsettled by the blunt question. Finally she says, "I don't know."

Eaglenest gives Stone a disapproving glance. He nods, agreeing with his wife. "These Indians at the missions, are they Christians? What tribe are they?"

Maria is glad that she is not the subject of the query. "The tribe is called Tarahumara," she says, more confidently. "Some are Christians, many are not." She thinks. "Those who are Christians still have their own spirits too. Father José was often angry about that. He said they did not need their old spirits anymore."

Stone is amused. "Why do the Brown Robes go around telling other peoples about their spirits?" He looks at his Gataka wife and makes a gesture toward the camp where Cheyenne, Gataka, and Kiowa women work together on the hides taken the day before. "We, we would never think to do that. We would be insulting each other."

Eaglenest has not translated the last sentences. Maria shrugs uneasily. "I don't know."

Stone changes the subject. "Where did you go from there?"

"Down the Río Conchos to the Mission San Pablo. The Indians there were called Concho."

"What kind of Indians are they?"

"They have fields of corn, frijoles, and chile. They have a few villages around missions. Most work for haciendados on large haciendas. The haciendados own these Indians."

"What is a hacienda and what means 'own'?"

"A hacienda is a large area with fields. On these they grow corn and chile peppers, and other plants: wheat, barley, cotton, tobacco. The hacienda belongs to the haciendado. He lives in a large house with his family. There are small houses in which the Indians live who work for the haciendado."

She pauses, waits for the translation. Then, "Owns—it means these Indians are the property of the haciendado. They can never leave that place. The haciendado can do with them as he wants. He can starve them, beat them, or kill these Indians if he wants to."

Stone is aware that Comanche, Gataka, and Kiowa raiders regard prisoners taken in New Spain as personal property. Maria herself was earlier the property of the Kotsoteka chief, then the property of the alcalde of San Miguel del Bado. Perhaps she was also the property of the Brown Robe. Stone realizes suddenly that she might think that she is his property because he paid two horses for her.

He frowns. "You are no one's property now," he says. "You are not my property. I wanted you for something I must do in the Spanish lands. When it is done, you are free to go wherever you want to go."

Maria listens to the translation with bowed head. She is not aware that her right hand strokes the hair on Manuel's head. The boy tries to look up at her, seeking her eyes.

"Who are these haciendados? They are white?" Stone continues.

"Some are." Maria smiles at her son and hugs him. "There are two kinds of whites. One is called *gachupines.* These were born in a country across the sea, most often in Spain. Father José was a gachupine. He came from Spain. There are just a few of them. The other whites are called *creoles.* These are whites born in the country. There are not many of them."

She waits for the translation. Then continues: "Some of these are haciendados and rancheros are mestizos." Again she waits.

"What is a mestizo?" Stone asks.

"Mestizos are part white, part Indian, mostly Indian. They were all born from an Indian woman." She pauses. "Mestizo haciendados and rancheros act as if they are white, but they are not. Every Indian there knows that."

Stone thinks about it. "Is Manuel a mestizo?" he asks.

Maria vigorously shakes her head. "No! He is Hiaqui. I teach him to be Hiaqui."

Stone approves. He smiles. "What other Indian tribes do you know about?"

"I have heard about some Indians on the big river, the Río Bravo del Norte." It is the Spanish name for the Rio Grande. "These Indians are called Yumanos. They used to hunt buffalo where the Comanches are now, but the Comanches drove them away. There are only a few of them now."

As an afterthought she adds: "East of the Sierra Madre and the Tarahumaras, very few Indians are left. They were killed off by the whites and the mestizos or were sent to work in the mines where they were forced to dig for silver. Many, most, died there."

She pauses, waiting for the translation.

"The only Indians left south of the Río Conchos, all the way to Durango, work on haciendas and ranchos. Father José told me there are some villages of poor mestizos in that country, but the Indians are all gone. There used to be a tribe called Toboso there. Not anymore. I have seen a little of that country myself. Those who live there are all afraid of the warriors from the Plains and the Apache."

There is a long silence. Finally Maria asks the question that has been on her mind. Eaglenest has already told her something, but Maria wants to hear it from the headman. "What do you want me for in that country?"

Stone takes time to answer. "Ask questions for me. That is all. You speak the language. My brother is somewhere down there. I think he is a prisoner, maybe on one of the haciendas you told us about. You help us to find him. After that you may ride wherever you want to."

Maria has heard. She can hardly believe it. I am to find his brother? I? This norteño chief must be crazy. I am only a girl. I know nothing. If I ask questions in the wrong places we will all get killed. She breathes heavily. But she is eager to please. "Yes," she says. She puts her head down. She suddenly remembers the day when the Comanches struck and killed Father José and her brother and three mestizo helpers and dragged her away, the long trail to the Kotsoteka camp, the way she was treated by those two pompous Kiowa women of White Horse. She thinks. Perhaps soon comes a time when I and Manuel can get away from this man, Stone, and the bunch with him.

• • •

On the following day they ride on through the flats along the Pecos, aiming slightly southeast, keeping a distance of half a mile from the river. Daha and Setpagoy are about five hundred paces in front. From there bits of traveling songs in Gataka and Kiowa drift occasionally back to the column. The sun rises on another cloudy day. The wind is again at their backs.

Stone rides with Powderface by his side. The man, the same age as the headman, is not a member of a soldier society. He left his two young wives and a baby son back in the Hovxnova camp, where they are cared for in his absence by relatives. His wives are sisters, cousins of Stone and Whirlwind; it is for this reason that Powderface and his brother, Porcupine, joined the expedition. Powderface is one of two ceremonial men on this journey; the other is Holy Singer of the Heviksnipahis.

Stone and Powderface talk while they look over the land. Their eyes can see far in every direction. The Pecos River is the only reliable source of water for many miles east and west, especially in the fall, when most of the creeks running into it have dried up. Animal populations and scarce human groups from all around depend on the river and do not move too far away from it. The buffalo herds have passed but will come back. The only large source of water farther west from where Stone's party is currently passing is the Laguna del Perro, eighty miles distant, below the slope of the Manzano Mountains, but it still does not hold enough for so many buffalo.

Stone and Powderface survey the profusion of animal tracks leading to the river and away from it. Fresh and old, the prints of bighorn sheep, deer, elk, and antelope are easily distinguished. Here and there bleached bones are nearly hidden among the grasses and flowers. Elk antlers, one branch lying flat, the other sticking up, reach over the waving tops of the yellow and green. The riders see bands of antelope and twice small bunches of desert bighorn. Residents of a couple of prairie dog towns watch them with fearless curiosity. Once they observe a grizzly feeding on a carcass surrounded by a circle of coyotes. Near midmorning there is a shout from the rear. White Wolf of the Heviksnipahis. He is pointing to the sky.

Stone halts the column and lifts his face upward. Behind and above, perhaps five hundred feet up, a funnel-shaped mass of hundreds of small forms of vivid red orange is drifting south, carried by the wind. Stone looks closer. "Maehoze," someone behind him says in awe. It is a great flock of red butterflies, monarchs, on their annual fall migration to somewhere in the Spanish lands. The riders watch in silence as the swerving funnel slowly passes over. Some of them have never seen this rare, soundless spectacle. Stone has seen it only twice, once near the Black Hills, once on the Platte. "Red messengers," Powderface says quietly. "They fly ahead of us. Perhaps they show us where we are supposed to go."

Stone's eyes focus on the disappearing little red cloud. His face is rigid as in a trance. He grabs Powderface's arm. "Talk to them. Ask them."

• • •

Powderface nods. He hands Stone the reins of the horse and dismounts. He pulls his pipe bag from the saddle bag and walks a dozen paces forward and sits down in the grass facing south. Stone sees only his back but knows that the man is placing the bowl on the pipestem and filling it with ceremonial tobacco. He hears Powderface clear his throat and begin to pray. Powderface sways from side to side. Way ahead Daha and Setpagoy have halted and look back. Behind Stone the column stands still; only a few horses shuffle or try to nibble on the grass. Finally Powderface lights the pipe from a tiny fire his brother, Porcupine, has quickly built, and offers it to the spirits of the directions. He finishes, cleans the bowl, and separates it from the stem, putting both back into the fringed rawhide bag. He looks at Stone when he gets to his horse and puts the bag away. He makes the sign for "good," and the headman thanks him. It is a good time to have the first meal of the day, and they choose a site by the river. This time it is Bear Doctor Woman of the Hovxnovas who speaks a prayer before they all eat, and then she goes to feed the spirits.

• • •

In the early afternoon the scouts turn straight south, bypassing the bend of the Pecos that juts out westward and then recoils back to the east and southeast. When they cross the deep, empty gash of Salado Creek they see smoke flags to the southeast and black dots circling low in the sky. Everyone knows the signs: vultures over a big kill of buffalo or antelope not far from a camp. Ahead, Daha and Setpagoy speed to investigate. They have mounted their war horses and leave the travel horses behind; the trained horses stay where they are and are gathered when the column comes up. A few miles farther, coming over a slight rise, Stone and the companions see the killing ground before them and the camp to the east, about four miles away, in the Bosque Redondo, an oxbow of the Pecos River marked by a half circle of cottonwoods. When Setpagoy joins up with the column later, Stone makes the signs for, "Where is Daha?"

Setpagoy pats the neck of his horse. His hands move quickly. "He is in that camp, talking." He points with his head.

Stone looks back and catches Sendehma's eyes. He waves her over, and she rides out and guides her horse to his side. Gondaima has been riding with Tasenma since the rest stop. Stone points with his chin to Setpagoy.

"Who are these people?" Stone asks. Sendehma translates.

"Kanzole'go," Setpagoy answers. "They speak a language close to Gataka. We know them. The Gatakas know them. They come to our camps to visit." He points northeast.

He waits for his sister to translate into Cheyenne.

"These people used to live north of here, way north. The Comanches drove them out. We were always at peace with them. They are called Carlana-Llaneros by the Spanish and by the Comanches." His tongue stumbles over the Spanish terms. Sendehma smiles as she searches for the Cheyenne words.

Setpagoy gazes toward the camp. "They are blood enemies of the Comanches. When they meet they fight."

A few tipis are visible through the cottonwoods. The camp is pitched in the crescent-shaped bend of the river. A couple of hundred horses graze widely scattered west of the bosque.

"They told us there is another camp of their people farther south," Setpagoy continues. "We know this band too. We call them Zebä-gianis, Long Arrows. We are friendly with them too.

He waits for Sendehma to speak.

"In the fall these people camp on the river. There is little water in Päsä'ngyä, and the buffalo come here." It is the Kiowa word for the Staked Plains. "In the spring they move east into Päsä'ngyä for buffalo. Then they often fight with Comanches. Two or three bands go together so there are more fighting men."

After Sendehma has explained in Cheyenne, Stone thanks them both. He has memorized what he has learned. "Let us ride on," he says. He knees his mount forward, and the column sets in motion again. Setpagoy stays back and collects his travel horse. He takes the lead again. They pass near the killing ground where the carcasses of buffalo are spread out far over the ground. Vultures whirl low above and walk between the carcasses, competing with coyotes for what little is left. Wolves and ravens are gone. Set lopes off to investigate but returns soon to rejoin the riders. Daha catches up with the column some time later and takes the lead again beside Setpagoy.

In late afternoon, fifteen miles farther south, they come near the camp of the Long Arrows, a sister band of the Kanzole'go Apaches. Hunters of the first camp had driven the buffalo south toward the second camp, and the Long Arrows had taken their share of the herds. Carcasses are everywhere, still picked over by wolves and ravens and foxes. The tipis of the camp are arranged on the east bank of the river beyond the horse herd, about two miles away in a location where the Pecos arches to the west, above Conejo Creek.

A group of riders dashes from the camp and circles around to the south and comes up in front of Stone's party. They watch them coming. Daha and Setpagoy have fallen back and sit their horses next to Stone. They are joined by four of the Hovxnova Kit Foxes and Powderface, who form a line on Stone's right. The other warriors remain in front of and behind the women and children.

It is a tense moment. The Long Arrows' men number eight and would have no chance in a fight, but this is their land and Stone and his group are the intruders. Stone wants no trouble with them. He signals to his wife to come to his side because she speaks the three languages perhaps needed in this encounter.

He looks over the Apaches before him. They wear moccasin boots that reach below the knee and are naked except for the breechclout. They are heavily armed with lances and bows, but only one carries a firearm. Their dark faces are impassive. One is a boy Big Bow's age, the others men in their twenties. He identifies the leader, a rather young man who sits his horse in the middle of the group. The man wears a beaded leather amulet on his chest. A single eagle feather attached to his loose hair lies horizontally over his left shoulder. A hard face and strong, probing eyes. Stone knows such faces; his own face is much the same. He raises his right arm, extending the open palm toward the Long Arrows' leader.

In sign language he says: "Stone I am, Tsistsistas, Cheyenne. My people live far to the north. Those with me are Cheyennes and Gatakas and Kiowas. We are passing through. We mean no harm. We want to travel in peace. We are on the way to the Spanish lands. But if we need to fight, we will fight."

The Long Arrows' leader has seen the signs but does not respond. He watches, perhaps calculating his chances. Perhaps he thinks it wise to stall and get more men from camp. Perhaps he ponders whether the strangers should be attacked later when they make camp. Perhaps not; perhaps he does not understand. His cool glance drifts over Stone and the hard-faced warriors beside him, the women, children, the horses and packhorses, especially the horses. Stone nods to Eaglenest, and she repeats the meaning of his signs in Gataka language.

The man turns his gaze upon the pretty young woman as she speaks. His dark face lights up a little, shows the hint of a smile. He seems to have understood some of what Eaglenest has said.

"Wolf Face I am." He speaks an Apache dialect different from Gataka, although the words are related. "You are Gataka?"

Eaglenest nods. "Yes." She points with her chin to Stone. "He is my husband."

"Tell him we don't want to fight with him." He pauses. "We know about Gatakas. We know about Kiowas." Again he pauses. "In my grandfather's time our people used to live where your people are now." His voice is brisk.

He listens intently as Eaglenest translates into Cheyenne. He continues: "I have heard about Cheyennes. The Spanish and the Comanches call them norteños. We have never met Cheyennes before. We have no reason to make war with them. Our enemy is the Comanche, sometimes the Spanish."

His eyes shift to Set who walks from the back around the warrior line and slowly starts circling the Long Arrows' riders, taking their scent, emitting a low growl from deep in his chest. The Long Arrows' horses eye the large red dog with unease, wide-eyed, and have to be held tightly. Their riders view him with fascination, with wonder. Set has completed his circle of inspection and sits down on his haunches, his eyes on the Long Arrows, watchful, alert.

Wolf Face squints and allows himself a rare smile. "A red wolf," he says. "Only one time have I seen one from far away. Over there." He makes a wide gesture toward the low Llano Estacado hills behind the Pecos. "Who does he belong to?"

Eaglenest has not caught his question and asks him to repeat it. He does and she tells Stone. "Gondaima," he says. "The daughter of my brother and Sendehma. She is back there with her mother."

Wolf Face sits thinking. "It is good to see a wolf like that. I am related to the wolf." He pauses. He looks strangely at Stone. "I think the two of us should pass the pipe so that when your people and mine meet they know that there is peace between them."

Stone listens to the translation. He looks at Wolf Face. "Yes," he says gravely. "It is good."

"Let us smoke my pipe," Wolf Face says. Stone agrees with a hand sign. He dismounts. Wolf Face dismounts and brings a beaded pipe bag from a pack behind the saddle of his horse. Stone gives a wink to Powderface. The man dismounts. Stone and Wolf Face sit down on the ground between the two groups of warriors.

Powderface kneels beside the leaders. From the bullet pouch on his belt he removes the fire-making utensils: the fire steel, a half-inch-wide band of steel bent into an oval form four inches in diameter, and a piece of flint, both obtained from English traders, and pieces of punk—fine, dry fibers of flammable tinder. He places the tinder on the ground between the two men. His brother has also dismounted and searches for dry grass and some dry splinters of wood. He kneels beside Powderface. Powderface makes a slicing blow with the fire steel against the flint that causes sparks to fly. The downward directed shower of sparks is caught by the tiny bed of punk. He repeats the action twice, a third time, and bends and blows, and the punk lights up and ignites. He quickly puts the dry grasses and thin splinters of wood over it and, still blowing, causes a little flame to leap up. Dry sticks are placed over the flame crosswise.

Wolf Face has loaded the bowl of the elbow pipe and bends low to bring its mouth close to the flame and pulls. The tobacco catches and starts to burn.

Thus they come to smoke together, each addressing the spirits in his own language, binding each other and their people, creating a bond, a pact, and a story, a story to be told around many campfires so that it will be known.

EIGHT

They spend the night by the river ten miles south of the Llanero camp. The country has changed. The shortgrass Plains has been replaced along the Pecos by a vegetation of saltbrush and greasewood in open stands with poor grass between them. Near midmorning, during the rest for first food, they enter a plain dominated by creosote bushes and tarbush and yucca and desert agave. They follow a faint trail south not far from the river that wanders through dense vegetation, where the view is restricted by rolling ground. Later they come to a broad trail leading east to the Llano Estacado. It is cut by the hoofprints of many horses and drag marks caused by tipi poles. Whoever went through here did so perhaps ten days ago, Stone and the men agree. From the drag marks they estimate a camp of forty to sixty tipis. Riding on they see no game, and the sky is empty. They make forty miles and camp again by the river.

Midmorning on the following day they have their first meal by a small lake half a mile west of the river, below Garcia Flat. The lake is covered with ducks and geese and a few cranes. Men and women watch in wonder and think that this may be a stopping place for the migratory birds whose flights have darkened the sky during the past weeks but have ended now.

Two fires burn brightly. In copper cooking vessels hung from provisional tripods over the flames a meaty broth is simmering. As on every day during this period, after a bath in the river and work done, husbands braid the long hair of their wives and are braided by them in return. Men without wives on this journey braid each other, often jokingly and with laughter. Sendehma's hair is done by her sister-in-law, Tasenma. When hair is combed and braided, men and women paint themselves for the new day. Maria alone does not paint, and her short hair does not need braids.

Stone is still working on Eaglenest's hair. Because men and women sleep in separate groups, these are the only moments every day when the two can be close, touching, feeling the other—a brief, cherished time together. The three children, Gondaima, Walking Last, and Manuel, are in a group thirty feet away, playing around a creosote bush that still bears a few yellow flowers.

A thunderous growl comes from where the children are, followed by a thumping sound. Eaglenest rises from her sitting position, and Stone behind her springs to his feet. In a flash they see Set rising high in the air and hurling something wide with a twist of his head, something long, limp, pendulous. A snake! The snake hits a piece of sandy ground fifteen feet away, while the dog, in a burst of red, breaks through a shrub to get there. The women run for the children as the man closest to the snake, Porcupine, reaches it. Injured by Set it slowly tries to escape. The dog stands, tense, ready to spring, snarling. Porcupine severs the snake's head with his hatchet.

They gather around the snake. It is a massasauga rattler, about forty inches long, with dark bars on top of its head, the body speckled with rounded dark brown blotches on the back and sides, the rattle at the tip of a stocky tail. It seems that it was lying under a creosote bush when the children's presence made it uneasy and, trying to get away, it moved in the direction of one of the children. Set saw the danger and jumped and gripped the snake in the middle of its body and flung it away. It happened so fast that the snake had no chance to turn its head and try to bite the dog. Sendehma searches Set's thick ruff but finds no bite marks. If one of the children had been bitten it certainly would have died from the poison. The children are too young to understand what happened so quickly. Gondaima cries a little because of the sudden commotion. Set has proven himself a warrior—a fellow traveler who can be relied on in dangerous situations.

Men and women eat their meals in a somber mood. The incident is within everyone's experience, but it reveals once again that death may strike unexpectedly, with the speed of lightning. On this occasion death was turned upon its messenger through Set's intervention. Perhaps the spirits worked through him. In thanks, Sendehma gives Set an extra portion of meat through Gondaima's little hands.

After they have eaten and the horses have foraged on the sparse grass, they saddle up and ride. Stone calls Big Bow to his side to ride with him. Although they sleep next to each other during the night, he feels that he has neglected his brother on this journey. Big Bow usually rides with Set'toni, Sendehma's youngest brother, or with Däveko, the younger brother of Eaglenest. He is comfortable with them. The three, separately, each trying to be unobtrusive, eye the young woman Maria with a mixture of curiosity and empathy, perhaps even with a degree of affection. None dares let the others know. Whether Maria notices their occasional, seemingly inadvertent glances, is not known. If she were to notice she might regard them as inept, laughable, even frivolous. She is generally treated by men and women indifferently, correctly, but as from a distance. Even Eaglenest's friendliness does not overcome Maria's conviction that she will always remain an outsider, that she is a victim of circumstances outside her control, a person estranged, without a life of her own, and with a little son who has no future either. She is grateful to the red wolf; Manuel could have been bitten.

The party nears Bitter Lake close to noon. From way off they see cranes and geese and ducks whirl and bank, and when they come into view of the lake they see it blanketed with thousands of birds. The column halts above a low rise west of the lake, a body of water a mile long west to east and nearly as wide north to south. The river runs through a wet plain half a mile to the east, below a high bank. It forms a series of large pools, all dotted with birds of different kinds. The travelers note the black ashes of old campfires and the stone circles of tipi rings. This seems to be a seasonal campground, but there is no sign of humans. Gaps in the reed belts mark places where hoofed animals and predators come to drink. There are tracks of deer and elk and bighorn sheep, and of wolf and coyote and, in wet earth, the tiny prints of foxes.

Later, five miles south of Bitter Lake, there is a shout from the scouts who ride ahead of the column. Stone and the others see Daha and Setpagoy ride toward a small cluster of black dots to the west. When the column halts, it appears that the black dots have stopped moving too. There seems to be a parley, and then the scouts and the strangers move together toward Stone's party. Eaglenest comes to Stone's side to serve as interpreter as the other group approaches.

They are three men, two women, and a boy of perhaps twelve. The men and women wear the high rawhide boots of the Apaches. The men are dressed in breechclouts of white calico and white calico shirts. Their long hair is held by red headbands. They are armed with bows, the boy too. The women wear blue calico gowns, with some silver conchos on their belts. The calico has been traded for at Spanish posts on the Rio Grande. The women lead five heavily loaded packhorses. The three men halt side by side in front of the women. The boy rides up from the back and sits his horse next to one of the men, perhaps his father. The man in the middle, a robust figure, raises his arm as Stone does the same, palm forward.

He speaks a few sentences in Apache. Eaglenest translates with some difficulty. "He is Llanero. He wants to know who we are."

Stone nods. "Tell him we have met two camps of his people farther north. We only ride through."

The man listens carefully to Eaglenest. He speaks again, this time using sign language too. "I have never met people of your tribe before. Where do you live?" His eyes take in the column before him, resting on the hemen on the Kit Foxes' chests, the red shield covers of the Red Shield soldiers, the muskets, the women and the packhorses, the weaponry displayed on the war horses.

Eaglenest answers and explains. Then Stone says: "Tell him that I smoked the pipe with Wolf Face the day before yesterday. There is friendship between our peoples."

The Apache leader talks with the men beside him. He turns to Stone again. "It is good. We know Wolf Face." He pauses. "Our camp is just across the river. We have picked up some things in the mountains." He points west toward the hazy, pale blue scarps of the Sacramento Mountains and the Capitan Mountains forty miles away. He turns again to Stone. "You are welcome in our camp. We will share our food with you." His eyes glance over Stone's party and come to focus on Set, who sits off to the side, watching, breathing through his open jaws. He nearly repeats Wolf Face's words. "You ride with a red wolf," he says and stops. He leaves something unsaid, perhaps a question inappropriate to ask, a bewilderment about something deeper.

Stone understands his perplexity regarding Set. It is reminiscent of Cheyenne religious lore about Xaenone, the red spirit wolf, servant of Thunder. He thinks about that. He feels that it is impolite to refuse the Llanero invitation, but he feels that he must.

He speaks slowly to Eaglenest, making signs with his hands. "I am grateful to them for inviting us to their camp. At any other time I would have accepted gladly." He pauses. "We come from afar. We are on a special mission and we must hurry on. Someone's life depends on it." He makes a gesture expressing regret.

The Apache listens. He too makes a gesture of regret. "Yes," he says. "We wish you a safe trail."

Stone nods. He raises his right arm again, and the Apache leader raises his.

Eighteen miles farther south, they camp for the night by the river across from the wide, white, empty depression of Buffalo Lake.

• • •

In the early afternoon of the following day, under a cloudy sky, with a soft south wind in their faces, the column meets with a group of hunters who have come out of the Seven Rivers Hills a few miles to the west. The scouts are talking with them by the time Stone and the party approach. Eaglenest once again takes the place at her husband's side as interpreter. The group before them comprises six men and two women. They are Apaches but dressed differently from the Apaches of the day before: these wear no trade cloth; instead, the women wear knee-length buckskin gowns and the men buckskin leggings and breechclouts. On their feet are partly decorated low Plains-style moccasins. Their hair is long and unbraided. Four of the men carry amulet pouches on bandolier cords on their naked chests. Painted bow-and-quiver cases are slung across the men's backs. The two groups scrutinize each other, as strangers do in this vast land, with experienced, observant eyes that miss nothing. These Apaches know Gatakas and

Kiowas and their enemies, Comanches, but have never met Cheyennes before. Eaglenest tries to explain in her Gataka Apachean language, despite the fact that the dialect of these people, although related, differs from hers. Still, many words are comparable, and with additional hand signs they make themselves understood.

"Guhlkaindes," Eaglenest tells Stone, a band of Mescaleros. "Their camp is east of here across the river."

There is a rapid exchange in Apachean between her and the Guhlkaindes as Eaglenest seems to inform them about the purpose of Stone's expedition. The impassive, cautious stance of the Apaches changes. They talk among themselves. Their speaker says some words with a friendly smile. "Ride in a good way," Eaglenest translates.

"Tell him the same," Stone says. He and the Apache leader nod to each other, making the sign for "good." The man clicks with his tongue and the horse moves, walking a dozen steps, then changing into a slow lope, followed by the others.

Stone lets them pass. The two women lead a small string of pack-horses. Two of them carry the dressed carcasses of desert bighorn sheep. "We could use some fresh meat," Eaglenest says quietly.

They have come into a shrub savanna dominated by tarbush and creosote bushes, with short grass between the shrubs. To the south and east the eye can roam wide, but to the west the view is checked by mesas and hills that run down from the heights of the Guadalupe Mountains, thirty-five miles away. They make camp early at the mouth of Cass Draw, empty of water like all the creekbeds emerging from canyons to the west. As all along, there is good grass for the horses by the river. A hunting party rides out with Stone. The men have taken their trained war horses and left the travel mounts to graze and rest. They look for mule deer. Because the river is the only source of water for many miles around, deer and other animals must come here to drink. The party breaks up and rides a wide circle to the west before turning back toward the river. Jackrabbits and a herd of peccaries, perhaps twenty squealing animals, are caught in the drive. Both species are ignored. Peccaries are said to eat snakes, and therefore their flesh is regarded as unfit as food. Finally about a dozen deer are stirred up, and while most double back through the gaps between the hunters, bowstrings twang and five animals are shot.

Later, around two blazing fires, under a night sky lit by a low yellow moon and the brilliance of myriad stars, with full stomachs, the people are happy, listening to the chorus of coyotes around the camp that wait for their share of the kill. Stone lies on his back looking into the sky. His gaze follows the broad, mysterious swath of Seàmeo, the Milky Way, said by some to be a hanging road between earth and sky over which the spirits of the dead travel away from the living. He thinks, Are you up there, brother, or are you still on this earth? Tell me. But no voice answers.

• • •

Another morning and they break camp at first light after Set has ended his morning song. Riding on, riding, riding toward the southern horizon under an endless sky. But they are used to this endless sky and vast open spaces. It is their world; they know no other. They were born into it and they live out their lives in it. They think nothing of traveling far. Distances mean little, and they know how to breach them; they are experts at it. Still, each day brings something new, something not seen before. Their eyes are open, and they absorb the beauty around them without calling it by its name.

At noon they pass another Apache camp. This one is on the west bank of the river; a few men ride out, alerted by the horse guards. They are dressed like the Mescaleros the day before, and they hold their weapons ready. Daha and Setpagoy have fallen back to Stone, leading the column. Again Eaglenest is the interpreter.

It turns out that theirs is a Lipan tribal camp. The middle-aged man, who is the speaker of the five, calls the name of his people, Nadish Dené, after Eaglenest tells him who Stone and the companions are. The Lipan speaks an Apachean dialect different from that of both the Llaneros and the Mescaleros, one more closely related to Gataka Apachean. They have heard of three raiding parties coming this way and heading for the Spanish, and have seen two others themselves, the Lipan says, one of them Gataka, the other Kiowa. When? Two moons ago. The man shrugs. Because none have come back yet, they must still be down there. He points with his elkhorn quirt. When asked if they have seen Comanches, the man's face darkens. No. They will be down there too, raiding for horses. But they do not come along this river.

They know better. Comanche camps are way over there. He shakes his quirt east toward the Llano Estacado. "They use a trail farther south when they come and go. Sometimes we ambush one of their parties when they come back and take their horses and their scalps." Now the man grins broadly, and his companions chuckle.

They part amiably, but when Stone looks back later he sees that the five Lipans still sit their horses in the same place, staring after them, perhaps wondering about the encounter and the strange norteños.

They meet the first of the returning raiding parties the next day, after leaving Sand Lake where they stopped for first food in mid-morning. Ahead, Daha and Setpagoy have halted, looking east. There is a low, rolling sound when two riders appear on a ridge far to the left of the scouts, moving fast, outriders. Then the sound slowly increases and becomes a constant drumming, a rumbling as from thunder, and the point riders come over the ridge and behind them as a flood, a wild stream—horses, horses with waving manes above shining bodies and the pounding rumble of a thousand hooves. Horsemen along the sides of the avalanche yell, waving things high over their heads, holding the animals together. In a cloud of dust the host passes on, driven forward mercilessly, and then the drag riders come into view, barely seen in the swirling dust, pushing the herd hard.

Stone's party has halted, watching the scene half a mile away, as the long surge of horses, perhaps three hundred animals strong, rolls on and the sounds of their transit slowly fades. The raised dust lingers. Three riders, apparently a rear guard, materialize about a mile back, riding swiftly. Daha and Setpagoy ride out to intercept them, and Stone's party watches as they meet and slow down and come to a halt. They talk for a while, and then the rear guard continues and the two scouts ride back to wait for their column to reach them.

Eaglenest translates as Daha speaks with satisfaction. "Gatakas," he says, "from Little Raven's band on the Cimarron. They are hurrying home." He pauses. "They took the horses from a big ranch south of the Nazas River. They were followed by vaqueros and had a fight. That was all. They beat them back and took a few scalps. They lost no one. Crane Shield is the leader of the party."

They spend the night on Toyah Lake, a body of water on the southern edge of a large playa whose dry surface shimmers white from concentrated salt deposits. The lake, well west of the Pecos, is near the gate of the mountains and the trail that leads through them to the Rio Grande.

• • •

During that night Stone asks Setpagoy about the trail. Sendehma translates. "Six days we ride," he says. Our sixth camp should be on the P'a E'dal, the Great River." He refers to the Rio Grande, which the Spanish call the Río Bravo del Norte. "It is a rough trail; we always lose horses on it. This is a Kiowa and Gataka trail, the trail we take most often. On the third day we come to a high plateau with water and good grass. There are a few springs there too. Parties going south or coming back often make a rest there." He pauses. "The Spanish used to have a fort there with soldiers. They are gone. Now there are only ruins, a few walls standing. One of the Mescalero bands, Tsilinainde, visits there sometimes. They see this as their land."

"How far from the Great River to the place where Magpie was killed?" Stone asks.

Setpagoy thinks for a moment. "Nine days, maybe ten." He makes the number sign with his hands. He nods to his sister, listening to her translation. He looks at Stone, who sits motionless, thinking. Finally the headman says, "It is good. We sleep now." The dying fires barely light the bundled-up forms of sleepers in the two parts of the camp, men's and women's. No guard is out; the people have come to trust Set's nose and ears. As on every evening lately, the horses' forelegs have been hobbled with broad strips of rawhide, the forefeet bound about fifteen inches apart so that the animals cannot run but only walk slowly, one foot at a time.

After they break camp in the morning they head straight south, riding on high ground along Barrilla Creek. After ten miles they meet with the deep trail carved the day before by the Gataka raiders and the remuda of stolen horses. The scouts take the trail and the column follows. The mountains rise before them, ridge upon ridge, emblazoned by the rising sun, the first of upward shifting slopes now less than ten miles away. The savanna vanishes, and on the first bend of Barrilla Creek they come into a prairie of blue grama and coarse tobosa grasses. But soon the mountains close in on both sides, and the trail meanders through a valley strewn with large boulders. By afternoon, clouds roll in from the south. The sky darkens and it starts to rain. Covered with buffalo robes, the riders pass two sites where wolves feed on horse kills, apparently lame animals left behind by the Gataka party. They spend a wet night in crude shelters built from hides above a water tank in the dry creekbed. Despite the steady rain, they manage to make four small fires, more for self-assurance than for practical purposes, because they eat cold, chewing jerky. The rains end early in the morning, and in the gray dawn they ride on, continuing upstream, passing below the Barrilla Mountains on a hard, slippery trail that turns west toward the Davis Mountains, which soar to nearly eight thousand feet.

They ride slowly to save the horses. Again and again they see pallid, scattered bone deposits, mostly of horses, occasionally of cattle—animals disabled on the trail that were left by raiders and became the prey of wolf or puma. At times, when the trail crosses and recrosses the creekbed, by now gushing with a foam-capped surge owing to the rains, they observe in soft sands the prints of the animals of these mountains but see nothing alive throughout the day but small birds and once a golden eagle circling high, regarded by all as a good sign. The mountains around them carry open forests of juniper and oak. The trail rises steadily, and they camp for the night between Black Mountain to the west and Major Peak to the east, eating silently to the chorus of a wolf pack singing outside the camp.

The trail continues southwest, and in the afternoon they reach the high plateau Setpagoy has mentioned. They make camp beside a creek that runs out of the Cuesta del Burro Mountains and turns south toward the Rio Grande. There is plenty of firewood and good grass for the horses, blue grama and tobosa. But they have lost one horse on the last stretch of the trail before reaching the plateau. It is Yellow Eyes's traveling horse; it goes lame and must be left behind. Sendehma has given the man one of her extra horses. Stone decides to let the horses have a rest, and the party stays for a day and hunts for game.

Before sunrise on the following day the men start two sweeps to the northwest and southeast across the broken ground of the plateau, and by midmorning they have killed eight mule deer and four elk cows with arrows, the meat to be added to the shrunken supply of buffalo jerky. It is hoped that their provisions now will last them to the end of the Bolsón de Mapimí, when they reach one of the cattle ranches near the Nazas River. They have a good, happy camp in the great stillness of the plateau, where familiar night sounds, the yipping of coyotes, the singing of wolves, the sighing of horses, and the tapping of hooves in the grass, accompany them into sleep.

On the following day the column continues southeast and reenters the mountains on the headwaters of Terlingua Creek south of Cathedral Mountain. When they make camp that evening, they are two more days away from the Rio Grande.

Again it is a very rough trail south along the creek, and on the next day, after thirty miles of slow riding, they make camp west of Nine Point Mesa. All are eager to reach the river. Reaching and crossing it seems to be a marker, more symbolic than real, for the long ride of this expedition, although no one knows what lies ahead beyond the river and what distances still must be overcome.

Another day dark and gloomy and with some rain, and they ride down, down, past Agua Fria Mountain and the Chalk Mountains, and below the Christmas Mountains the heights recede and the country opens wide, and ridges upon ridges tumble down toward the river. Since leaving the Hovxnova camp on the Republican River, Stone and his companions have ridden eight hundred miles as the raven flies, perhaps twelve hundred miles on the ground.

NINE
October 24, 1807

The sinking sun in their eyes, they line up on a bench above the river east of the mouth of Terlingua Creek, sitting their horses side by side. Below them the floodplain of the Rio Grande runs southeast, a quarter of a mile wide. Within it the brown waters roll slowly through three narrow channels, around exposed sandbanks and islands overgrown with brush and tall grasses. On the opposite shore the waters lap on slowly rising ground with huge cottonwoods whose golden-leafed canopies shimmer in the sun. Beyond, pale blue in the distance, the ragged crests of the Sierra Grande rise into the sky. A few sandhill cranes and a flock of ducks take flight from the closest of the islands, wary of the intruders.

"You call this the Great River?" Stone, surprised, says mockingly. Eaglenest translates. A few laugh. "Our rivers in the north are much bigger than this." He names in Cheyenne the Missouri, the Platte, and the Arkansas.

"This is the biggest river in the Spanish lands we know of," Set-pagoy says, making a gesture with his hands almost in apology.

They sit, looking. There is a silence.

Maria speaks up for the first time. "The river that runs by my home is bigger too." She pauses. "The Río Hiaqui. That river runs into an ocean, a great sea that seems to have no end. It lies far to the west. I have seen it." She stops, surprised by herself, suddenly aware that she has made a comment and that these people might not approve of her intrusion.

But Stone bends forward and looks at her where she sits her horse at the end of the line, the boy in her arms. He listens to Eaglenest's translation. He solemnly nods to Maria, perhaps approvingly. He turns back and clicks his tongue and his horse moves and the others follow one by one, and they ride down into the first channel, where the slow-moving waters reach just over the fetlocks of the horses. They cross the sandbars and splash through two more channels and gain the opposite bank. They make camp under the trees less than a mile downstream.

• • •

Stone wakes up shortly after midnight. He comes out of a dream he does not remember. He does not know what woke him. The night is clear and bright and still. There is no sound but the low rustling of dry leaves as a gentle wind from the south moves the cottonwoods above. Something has stirred him, perhaps a nudge by someone in his dream. He suddenly feels that there is something he must do. He sits up and looks around. Dark bundles around the fires, quiet breathing. Beyond, shadowy forms of horses, heads down, moving ever so slowly. He unwraps himself from the robe that covers him, careful not to touch his young brother, who, in sleep, has rolled up against him. His motion, noiseless to his ears, nevertheless brings an investigator. Set has materialized out of nowhere and stands at the man's feet, probing his face. When Stone gets up, the dog backs a few steps away but keeps watching him, curious. Stone searches the pack behind the folded robe that serves as pillow. He removes the pipe bag. Kneeling by one of the fireplaces, he stirs the ashes with the short wooden prayer stick until he finds a coal still glowing. He lifts it out with his fingers and places it in his drinking cup. When he walks away toward a rise a bowshot away, Set follows him a dozen paces but then stops, stretches out and yawns, and disappears into the night.

Stone sits down, crossing his legs, facing southwest toward the Spanish heartland. He slowly opens the pipe bag and removes bowl and stem, putting them together. He loads the bowl with tobacco and places the pipe in front of his knees. He bends, and, with his thumb, draws the circular Cheyenne earth sign in the sandy soil. He places the coal behind the drawing. He clears his throat. He waits, gathering his thoughts. Finally he speaks with a clear voice. After identifying himself, he addresses the spirits, calling them by their ceremonial names. He explains once again the purpose of his quest and asks protection for those with him, protection for his brother, and a successful journey to find and free him. He pledges gifts to Mahoz, the sacred arrows, if a safe return is granted.

When he is finished, he lifts the pipe and grabs the coal with his fingers, placing it gently on top of the bowl. He sucks the air in and the tobacco starts to burn. He removes the coal and draws a few times to keep the tobacco lit. Now he makes the four ritual puffs and offers the mouthpiece of the pipe to Maheo, the creator, who resides in the blue sky above, to the Nevestanevoo, the four guardians in the four corners of the universe, and to the ground below where Esceheman, the Old Woman, the earth spirit, lives, and where Maakootanovosans, Badger, serves as her messenger. Thus sealing a contract, he finishes smoking and empties the ashes on the earth drawing and wipes both away. He disconnects pipe bowl and stem and puts them away in the buckskin bag.

He sits motionless as a sculpture, overwhelmed with emotion. He sits while slowly around him the night comes to an end and the gray dawn begins to spread out from the east. A bird sings, and across the river a wolf pack starts its morning song, answered by Set from the campsite. Stone gets up slowly and walks back to where the companions are already up, shaking out their sleeping robes. They see him come, the pipe bag held diagonally across his chest, his face serene, a faraway look in his eyes. They pretend not to see, but they know.

• • •

They march twenty miles along the Rio Grande, pausing at midmorning to eat and let the horses graze. They fill water bags with precious water and saddle up and ride south into what the Spanish call the Tierra Despoblado, the Empty Land, on the northeastern corner of their New World empire. That part of the Despoblado that Stone and the companions are entering is called the Bolsón de Mapimí, a pocket of high desert roughly 120 miles wide and 250 miles deep, surrounded by sierras that converge near the bottom of the Bolsón upon the Laguna de Tagualita, a large swampy lake fed by the Nazas River and summer rains.

The surface of the land lying before Stone's party is similar to the trans-Pecos shrub savanna through which they have come: the ground is dotted with creosote bush and tarbush, with short grasses between the shrubs. Here and there stand tall palmlike soaptree yucca, rising to a height of seventeen feet, some still crowned with white flower stalks reaching up another five feet. And there are cacti on the ground and lechuguilla agave rosettes whose whitish gray stalks stand vertical like lances someone has stuck into the earth as a warning.

As always, Daha and Setpagoy ride a few hundred paces ahead of the column, and the three Heviksnipahis Kit Foxes bring up the rear. The scouts follow a broad, much used trail near an empty bed of a stream that, during the rainy season, runs out of the sierras to the west and east and merges with the Rio Grande in the north. The country is a wide, open basin surrounded by mountain ranges brown and naked and sparsely flecked with the long, graceful stems of ocotillo, the lancets of sotol, clusters of agave. The eye can see far across the basin and into the blue haze to the south. Twice, small bunches of antelope are spotted in the distance. The trail is crossed occasionally by other trails going west and east, the hoofprints in them mostly old, some quite fresh, perhaps made two days ago. When they camp for the night in the bed of the nameless creek, Stone has questions for Daha and Setpagoy. Eaglenest translates.

"This trail we are on, who uses it?"

"Parties like this one," Daha says. "Parties that raid for horses and captives, mostly women. Gatakas, Kiowas. There are a couple of trails. They go south and north." Setpagoy nods in agreement.

"There are trails that go this way too," Stone says. He points east and west. "Who made them?"

"Perhaps the people who live here." Daha shrugs. "Mescaleros and Lipans. Some of their bands have taken this country away from the Spanish." He pauses and waits for Eaglenest's translation. "There are no Spanish until we come to the Nazas River. From there, west and east, the Spanish have ranchos and haciendas." He smiles. "That's where we go."

Setpagoy raises his right hand. "There is one Spanish town far southwest of here. Mapimí. The Spanish there are no trouble. The Mescaleros have run off horses and mules there many times. Sometime they make trade with them." He pauses. "Apaches have been attacking Spanish places long before we came, Kiowas, Gatakas, Comanches." He looks at Stone. "And now you, Cheyennes."

After the translation Stone asks, "Were there no xamavostaneo here, Indians, before the Apaches came?"

Setpagoy nods. "Yes, the Apaches say that there were Indians here. But the Spanish killed them or dragged them off to work on their haciendas or in places in the mountains where they dig in the earth."

Sunrise finds the party continuing south on the main trail on a slowly rising ground. From the foot of a sierra to the west, perhaps fifteen miles away, smoke rises from unseen fires. The thin curls stand high in the still air, announcing the presence of a camp over a great distance. Near midday the riders pass an antelope trap where wolves and coyotes still feed on carcasses. Turkey vultures draw circles in the sky. The corral into which the antelope had been driven seems about fifty paces in diameter, built from a circle of brush reinforced by a system of horizontal and vertical poles. The wings of the drive lanes that converge upon the narrow opening of the corral are made of brush and extend out for a couple of hundred paces, making clever use of natural features of the terrain. The riders halt for a moment, observing the arrangement before them with knowledgeable eyes. Later they see dust clouds below the barren flanks of a low range of mountains to the east. They halt once again and watch.

They see, ten miles away, a raiding party heading north toward the Rio Grande. A few point riders are easily distinguished. Behind them follows a long string of horses, perhaps three hundred, four hundred or more, with a few riders along the sides of the remuda, two drag riders in the back. Then follows a group of riders and packhorses, perhaps camp women with captives. Far back, a small screen of horsemen, the rear guard. The raiders move at a low canter. They do not seem to be in a hurry; once in the Bolsón they know that a Spanish force, military or militia, only rarely dares to follow. There is no telling who the raiders are.

That night Stone's party camps on a low ridge west of the northern edge of a playa that extends for forty miles southward through the center of the basin. The women have gathered firewood from stands of honey mesquite that ring the shores along with white-dusted Apache plume. In parts up to eight miles wide, the playa is a lake formed by springs, the runoffs of precipitation from the surrounding mountains, and monsoon rains. Its water has receded into the deepest depressions, leaving wide areas dry, the salt deposits shining white in the glare of the setting sun.

When they rest at midmorning of the following day, it is White River who calls out and points up into the deep blue sky. "Maehoze," Stone says aloud, in wonder. The red messenger. A few hundred feet above them circles a flock of monarch butterflies, red and orange in the fierce light of the sun, hundreds, with outstretched wings like so many birds, making use of the uplift of an air current that carries them higher. Slowly, still circling, they drift away. All eyes from the ground follow them as they climb until they become a cluster of tiny dots, and then the flock turns south and is gone.

"This is the right trail," Eaglenest says quietly, but everyone has heard.

The vegetation of the basin has become more open, with better grass between scattered creosote bushes, the lancets of lechuguilla, the occasional soaptree yucca, lone giants. All day long they pass along the playa, taking note of the many horse tracks and the prints of mule deer, desert bighorn, fox, coyote, wolf. Once, before they camp ten miles south of the lower end of the playa, the scouts ahead have halted and dismounted, searching something on the ground. When Stone comes up with the column, he notices the pug marks of a large cat that has just crossed the trail ahead of them. "Puma," Stone says.

Setpagoy shakes his head. He places his right hand over one pug mark, fingers spread out. "This is a different cat, one more dangerous than puma. They call it jaguar. We have to watch over our horses tonight."

They select a campsite with the jaguar in mind, trusting Set to raise the alarm, but the night is quiet except for the usual night sounds, the tapping of hooves, the sighing sound made by horse, bird calls, Set's midnight song, answering calls from a wolf pack miles away.

At sunrise next morning, after they have traveled ten miles, they have company. A group of riders comes from the Sierra Mojada to the west, whose brown, craggy peaks rise to a height of over eight thousand feet. They have probably watched Stone's party for some time and recognized that they were not Comanches, whatever they might be. Eight horsemen suddenly emerge from a fold in the terrain and advance at a leisurely pace. Daha and Setpagoy have fallen back in the column when Stone calls for a halt. The unknown horsemen form a line about a hundred paces away. They are not stripped for a fight. Stone views them with the eye of an expert. Three are middle-aged men and five are younger warriors. They wear moccasin boots that reach to below the knee, breechclouts, and leather vests. All have bow-and-arrow cases slung across their backs and hold painted shields on the left arm, feathered lances tipped with long metal blades in the right hand. A few have medicine pouches on bandoliers strapped over their chests. They look like serious opponents if one were to engage them in combat.

One of the older men rides forward and raises his right arm. His is a roundish face with high cheekbones, a hard mouth, a strong chin. The hair hangs loose over his shoulders, held in front by a red headband across the forehead. The first to greet him is Set, who runs a circle around the leader. The horse nickers and stomps and tries to back away but is held tightly. Stone rides out to meet him with Eaglenest at his side. Sendehma calls Set, and he bounds away with the swift, floating, effortless movements of the wolf.

The Mescalero taps his chest and gives the name of his band. "Tuetinini." Then his personal name, "Chinonero." Eaglenest is unable to translate it.

Stone speaks his tribe's name, "Tsistsistas," and his personal name. Although Eaglenest speaks in the Gataka dialect, the Mescalero seems to understand.

"Norteño." He nods. In the conversation that follows, Eaglenest tells him the truth, who they are and where they are going and why. The man listens attentively. His glittering eyes move along the file of riders before him, scanning the warriors, war horses and weapons, the women and the packhorses. Briefly his eyes follow Set's movements. He knows war and is a good judge of men.

"I have a brother," he says slowly. "If he were lost I would follow his tracks and bring him home." He waits for Eaglenest's translation. "Tuetininis," he continues, "we have no trouble with you." He stands up in the stirrups. "A little way down there," he points slightly southwest, "is a good campsite, a spring surrounded by trees. You cannot miss it. You are welcome to camp there. We call it the Place of Rock Squirrels." He pauses. "I wish you find your brother."

He slowly backs his horse away and raises his right hand in greeting. Stone does the same, thanking him. "Aho." He watches as the Mescalero joins his men. They turn their horses and ride west without looking back. The spring is not difficult to find—the trees give it away. A steady trickle of water runs down from a yellow outcrop of rock connected with an arm of the Sierra Mojada, forming a small pool beneath it. Sands around the pool hold the prints of animals like a book easy to read, and they include the pug marks of another jaguar.

Another day of riding south through the heart of the Bolsón. Again they pass an antelope trap and twice empty stockades built to hold captured horses. They also ride by two campsites occupied in the past, marked with the ashes of campfires, stone circles where tipis had stood, bleached bones and strips of tattered skin. They ride and familiarize themselves with the country, its watering places and animal populations, scarce in this desert. They meet no other people but once see smoke from a camp in the distance to the east. They move by small salt lakes white and forlorn in the yellow and brown desert. Their fifth night camp after leaving the Rio Grande is a dry camp. They find no water and share the water of their water bags with the horses. Both Daha and Setpagoy agree that they are getting close to the place they want to see. On the following day, after a short ride of twenty miles, they reach the southwestern shore of Laguna de Tagualita. For miles they had seen great swarms of birds to the south, rising, turning, and floating down, disappearing.

They sit their horses above the shore of the laguna. Except for Daha and Setpagoy, they were unprepared for this wondrous mystery of the Bolsón, a real lake, a huge lake. In this, its southern part, it is wider west to east than the eye can see. Coming out of the desert they gaze in wonder. The lake is surrounded by marshes and vast belts of reeds, yellow and green, and stands of willow and mesquite. Behind this unexpected burst of vegetation the shimmering waters seem to reach to the horizon. Thousands of birds wheel above the lake, geese and ducks and species unknown to the riders. Farther to the southeast, from where the Nazas River runs into the lake, its waters extend northward for about fifty-five miles between two mountain ranges, the Sierra de Tagualita on the east, and the Sierra de la Campagna to the west. When the party stopped for their fifth night camp below the Sierra de la Campagna, and continued south on this, the sixth day, they were unaware that the northern arm of the laguna was just across the mountain belt to their left.

While the riders view the marvel before them in awe, Daha and Setpagoy smile. They have seen it before and were equally stunned the first time. "We will cross the Nazas tomorrow," Setpagoy says. "From there to the place we were ambushed is only a little ways."

They ride on. The trail forks. One branch turns west toward the distant Spanish ranches, haciendas, and mining towns above the big bend of the Nazas River; the other branch continues south along the western shore of the laguna. They remain on this trail, and twenty-five miles farther make camp below the south shore. In this camp they are only thirteen miles away from the mining town of Mapimí, although they see no sign of its existence.

At sunrise on the following day, having ridden fifteen miles, they come to a trail that runs west and east. Among the hoofprints of horses and mules are ruts caused by the heavy wheels of caretas, and, for the first time in many days, human footprints. This seems to be more a road than a trail, traveled in both directions and in use perhaps a long time, if infrequently. Stone dismounts and walks along it, checking the human footprints. They seem to be of males, a very few those of women, some children's. Most are barefoot, others show the imprints of sandals.

He turns to Setpagoy. "Where does this trail come from and where does it go to?" he asks.

"It comes from Mapimí and farther west. It goes to a ranch on the east bank of the Nazas that way." He points east. "From there it runs to a town called Parras and on to other towns. I have crossed it once on the other side of the river. I have not seen Parras but was told by Kiowas who have seen it."

They ride on in a slightly southeastern direction, while the Nazas on its way to lose itself in the laguna runs north in a slightly northeastern direction. They have long left the former trail and aim for one of the bends of the river, arriving there in late afternoon. Brush and trees line the banks. Setpagoy edges the horse next to Stone. "This is where we crossed after Magpie was killed," he says. Stone searches for Eaglenest. She knows and rides over to translate. Setpagoy repeats what he said. Stone looks across the river, thinks: I am almost there, brother. Tomorrow I will be at the place where it happened to you.

Aloud he says, "Let's cross and camp on the other side." He knees his horse forward and into the current, the swift, clear, cold water reaching as high as the stirrups, and they make camp by a cluster of willows. They find tracks of horses and cattle, nothing suspicious. Scouts go out and check the area but find nothing. They wait until darkness to build a fire so that no smoke can be seen to betray them. That night, and from then on every night, they have a guard out, a pair of human eyes and ears to complement Set's keen senses.

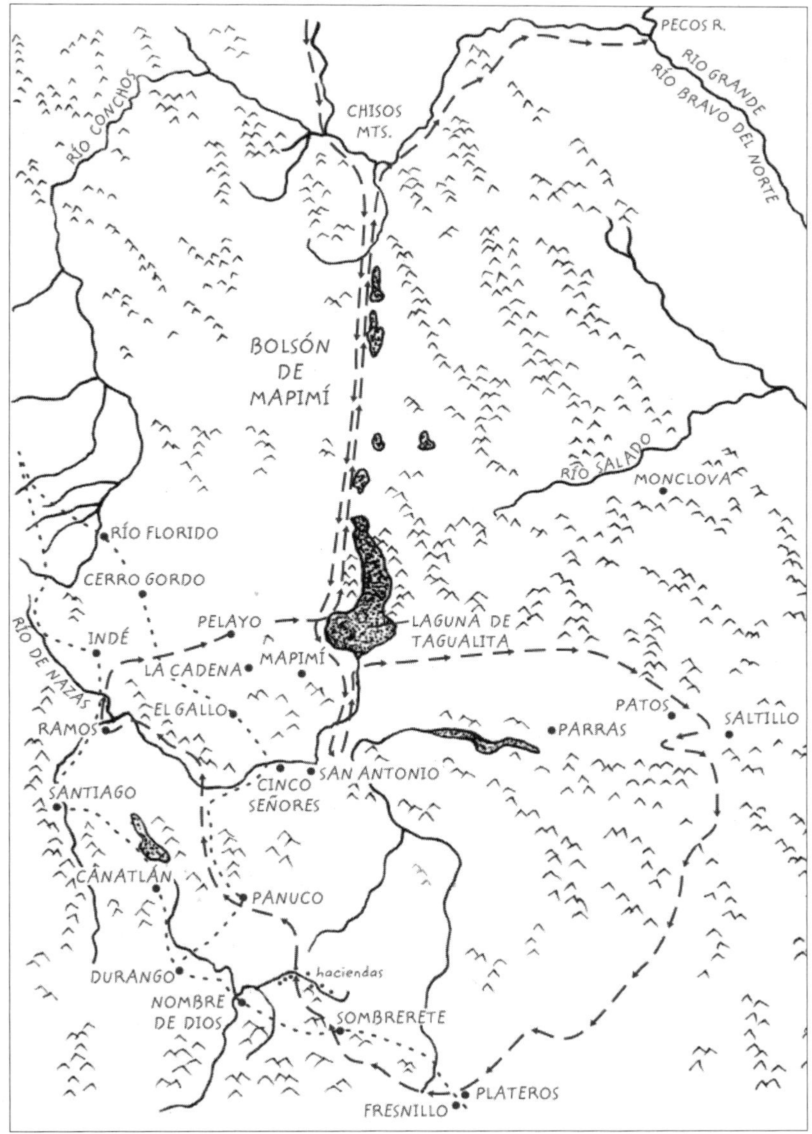

The trail of Stone's Party from the Rio Grande through northeastern New Spain and back to the Rio Grande to the mouth of the Pecos River, October 24, 1807, to April 14, 1808. The Camino Real, with two branches from Durango to Parral, is indicated by dots. (Based on the 1805 map by Juan Pedro Walker.)

TEN

They rise at first light as on every morning. But on this morning, after packing their sleeping gear away, they have a cold meal before they get the horses ready. The men check the hooves and, where edges are splayed, pare back the hoof walls with knives. They saddle the war horses and examine their weapons. The eight men who possess North West trade guns unsheathe the muskets and inspect the locks and the flints embedded in leather caps. Stone tightens the screw on top of the lock and tests the bevel of the light yellow flint with his index finger. He is satisfied with the fit. The muskets remain unloaded but ready for use. There might be a need for them yet. The smoothbores are efficient in shocking an enemy from rather close by, useless beyond a distance of over a hundred yards. For longer range, bows perform better. One by one the men sheathe them again and attach them to the horns of saddles. They string bows, remove shield covers, and hitch shields to saddles, easy to reach. Some warriors loop lances across their backs, while others fasten them with rawhide thongs to saddle and stirrup, the weapon then standing vertically behind its owner. Men and women paint their faces as on every morning; for the warriors it is not yet the time to paint for war in their personal colors and designs and those of their societies. When they move out, the warriors' travel horses are brought along by the women, each woman, including Maria, leading a string.

Daha and Setpagoy ride ahead as usual. Stone leads the column about three hundred paces behind the scouts. They go slowly, weapons ready. The farther south they get, the greater the chance that they will run into enemies. They let the horses pick the trail, careful to make as little sound as possible. Ten miles south of the Nazas bend they come into hill country with a covering of desert shrubs and yucca, and after a few miles they enter a long valley surrounded by steep, rocky ridges trending south. They come by a lone knoll, and two miles farther the valley narrows to a pass in the rocks that is two horses broad in places and opens into a rolling grassland about a mile deep.

The scouts have halted. When Stone comes up, he sees why. Before them are hundreds of Spanish churra sheep, their heads to the grass, their bodies white, brown, and black in the green foliage, between mesquite trees. And from a ravine issues smoke, drifting low due to a gusty wind from the west. Three saddled horses are tied to a shrub above the ravine. A camp of three men. Stone turns and beckons to two of the Hovxnova men behind him, Powderface and Porcupine, to join him. In sign language he signals that they need captives, that they must take someone over there alive.

The column remains behind when the five men ride out slowly, bring up bows, and notch arrows. They fan out in a half circle, Stone in the center. They move through sheep that silently give ground and approach the ravine. The horses tied up above the ravine notice them. They raise their heads and look toward the riders. One snorts. Stone and the men get quickly to the rim and look down. Three men sit around the fire and get up, startled. Two try to scamper away, but bowstrings twang and they fall. The third man stands stock-still, arms hanging limp. He is looking at death, but death passes him by. Stone rides down close to the man and covers him with his horse. He gestures that he is safe, but the man does not comprehend; he stands as if frozen into place. Stone dismounts and grabs his arm. He leads him out of the ravine to where the three horses stand, pulling his war horse after him. He forces the man to mount and mounts himself, taking the reins of the prisoner's horse. As he moves, letting the horse walk, the dead in the ravine are scalped and their belongings rifled.

The column has begun moving. When Stone meets with it, he looks for Eaglenest. "Bring Maria," he calls. He dismounts and makes the prisoner do the same. He hands the reins to Big Bow. The men and women of the party dismount and form a circle around the two, who are joined by Eaglenest and Maria. The Hiaqui girl has brought Manuel with her.

Now the four warriors ride up, the two captured horses on loose reins. Daha waves one scalp in the air, Porcupine the other. Blood is still dripping from the flesh part under the hair. Short hair. Stone asks Setpagoy, "How far from here to the place where Magpie was killed?"

"Just over there."

"You and Daha ride and search that place." The two listen and swing their horses around.

Stone sits down and gestures to the prisoner. The two men and two women sit in a circle.

Stone looks the man over. He is about thirty years old, short, square-chested, with a sharp, brown face and shoulder-length black hair. He is dressed in white cotton, long pants, and a shirt open at the throat. He wears high leather moccasins. He is still in shock, staring down. Stone reaches out and removes a long knife from the prisoner's belt and lays it aside.

He looks at Eaglenest. "Tell Maria to ask him who he is." Eaglenest speaks and Maria nods. She asks in Spanish, but the prisoner does not respond. Stone touches his knee, and the man slowly comes to as if out of a trance. He looks around at the many faces. He is still fearful, but the faces of the strangers seem curious, inquisitive, not hostile. Maria repeats the question.

The man swallows and finally speaks his name. "Juan."

Stone asks, "Is he xamavostan, Indian?"

So begins the intricate, sometimes confused process of translating from Cheyenne into Kiowa, then into Spanish, from Spanish back into Kiowa, ending in Cheyenne.

"Toboso," the man says. He is a Toboso Indian.

"Where is he from?"

"Tagualito, a rancho." He points south.

"How far?"

"Not far." Stone recognizes that while Maria speaks Spanish fluently, the prisoner speaks it only poorly. It will do, he thinks.

"What were he and the other men doing here?"

"Guarding the sheep."

"Were they his and the other men's sheep?"

"No, they belong to the ranchero."

"Who is this ranchero?"

"The Marquis de San Miguel." The prisoner has difficulty in pronouncing title and name. He speaks it three times.

"Where does the ranchero live? In Tagualito?"

"No. Tagualito is a small place. Tagualito belongs to a large rancho on Río de Nazas."

"How far?"

"Three hours of riding, four hours." The prisoner shrugs. He looks around, still fearful.

"Tell him that we will not harm him." Maria seems to tell him twice before he understands. Slowly his face lights up.

"Does the ranchero live in that large rancho by the river?"

"Sometimes. Not now. He has many ranchos everywhere. He lives in the rancho Patos. It is far away there." He points northeast.

"How far away?"

"Five days of riding. Maybe six."

"What is the name of that large rancho by the river?"

"San Antonio."

"How many men in these ranchos, Tagualito and San Antonio?"

The man thinks. "Fourteen at Tagualito. Many more at San Antonio. I do not know how many." It is not clear whether he includes his two dead companions in the count or whether he is even aware that they are dead.

"These two ranchos, they have only sheep?"

"No. Tagualito has sheep, some horses and cattle. San Antonio has horses and mules and cattle. Many horses."

"Tell him," Stone says, addressing Maria, "that I want him to take us where the horses are. After that we will let him go. But if he lies to us or tries to get away, we will kill him. Tell him. Make sure that he understands."

The Toboso seems to comprehend the message. He nods eagerly, trying to please. But his dark eyes are shaded. There is no way of telling whether he trusts the words of the stranger. That makes two of them,

Stone thinks. There is no telling either whether Maria truly believes what I promised her.

• • •

The place where Magpie was killed is only two miles farther south. Daha and Setpagoy are waiting there. When the column arrives, Stone sends two of his Kit Foxes to scout ahead so they will not be surprised by someone from the ranches. He looks at the setting, so undistinguished from any other. A grayish rocky ground strewn with some shrubs, a few trees. Prints of horses and cattle and their dried dung. Still, this is the place. Setpagoy points to scattered horse bones, a remainder of the ambush. A pile of rocks hidden in brush, Magpie's burial site. Under the rocks lie only his bones, his spirit has traveled on. Little Bird, a cousin of Magpie, sits by the grave and smokes the long-stemmed pipe and prays. The others stand behind him in silence.

The sound of voices carry from where the horses are held and where Bear Tooth watches over the prisoner. When Little Bird's short ceremony is over, Bear Tooth pushes the Toboso and Maria toward Stone. "The woman says this man knows something," he says.

Stone views the prisoner. He looks disheveled, his hands are tied behind his back. His face is tense, apprehensive. Eaglenest stands next to Stone.

"Juan knows what has happened here," Maria says. Stone listens as Eaglenest translates.

"What does he know?"

"He knows that soldiers had a fight here with Indians from the north."

"Was he here when this happened?"

"No, soldiers told him."

"Where were the soldiers from?"

"Some were from Tagualito, most from the rancho San Antonio."

"Where are they now?"

"In Tagualito and San Antonio. And in other ranchos that belong to the marquis. They are his soldiers."

There is a pause. The Toboso is terrified, breathing hard, trying to avoid Stone's cold stare.

"What does he know? What happened here?"

Maria herself is tense, trying hard to make the prisoner understand the questions.

"The soldiers killed one man and wounded the other."

Perhaps this is the moment, Stone thinks. Perhaps now I will know the truth. "What did they do with the wounded man?"

The man stammers, groping for words. "They brought him to Tagualito. They whipped him and tied him to a pole."

"And then?" Stone's voice is almost a whisper.

"They tortured him."

"What then?"

The man speaks haltingly, then rapidly in the Toboso language. Maria asks again in Spanish. The man tries to answer, shaking his head.

"The soldiers sold him to someone," Eaglenest learns from Maria.

"Sold?"

"Someone paid the soldiers money for him." Maria shrugs uncertainly as Eaglenest translates.

"Who paid money for him?"

There is a flurry of quick exchanges between the prisoner and Maria. Finally she says, "They sold him to a man from a *circo*."

As Stone raises his eyebrows, Maria tries quickly to explain. "A circo." She stops, shaking her head. How to explain this? "A circo is a group of people who travel through the country. They travel from town to town, from rancho to rancho. They have musicians and dancers, persons who make people laugh. They do this for money. I have seen a circo once. They have always animals with them in cages, a wolf, a jaguar, monkeys, colorful birds. They travel with caretas."

"Where is the circo now?"

The Toboso shrugs. "The circo traveled east when it left Tagualito. To Parras. Maybe to Monclova. East."

"And the wounded man went with them?"

"Yes."

There is a long silence. Stone is looking at the ground between his feet. He is somewhere else, traveling unknown roads. You are alive, brother.

Finally he looks up fiercely into the Toboso's eyes. "You know these places in the east; you have been there?"

The man nods reluctantly. "Yes."

Stone measures him. "You lead us there. I need you." His eyes search for Sendehma. She is standing there, Gondaima in her arms. A tall, strong woman, she is crying. "You have heard, sister-in-law," Stone says gently. "Your husband is alive." He pauses. "We will bring him home. For you, for him."

• • •

It is early afternoon, and they ride to Tagualito.

Before they left Magpie's grave site, two meetings were held. In one, Stone talked with Juan again. He demanded that the Toboso help him to track the traveling circus. The man accepted reluctantly but asked that his wife and young son, both at the rancho, be allowed to come with him. To that Stone agreed. He had Juan draw a map of Tagualito in the sand and mark the soldiers' hut among the buildings.

The second meeting had been with the companions. Stone stood in the center of the circle, a slim, intense figure. The men sat tightly packed before him. The women sat behind the men. He said that something had to be done first before they went after the circus. He laid out his plans and answered questions. He received eager approval.

A few miles north of Tagualito they come into rolling grassland again, with groves of mesquite in the draws, tall yuccas standing as silent sentinels in the yellowing grass. They ride through red-colored cattle with broad, curved horns, which feed peacefully and reluctantly give way. Stone is in front with Powderface. The prisoner rides between them. The warriors have fanned out, and the women follow with the packhorses and the strings of travel horses. Sendehma leads Set on a rope and holds the dog close to her horse. Outriders cover both flanks a distance away from the main body. Before they come to a ridge above the rancho, the outriders on the west bring in two vaqueros who had been riding the perimeter of the cattle herd, two frightened Toboso men. They have been disarmed. They have surrendered their machetes, their only weapons, without resistance. Their eyes wander to Juan, who sits his horse unharmed among the strangers. He makes a hand sign to tell them not to be afraid. At a wink from Stone, Big Bow takes the reins of their horses as the raiders proceed.

They line up on the rim of the ridge looking down. A hollow with a grove of mesquite trees near a pond, nine small huts for vaqueros and peons and their families, a wooden hut, two pole corrals, five horses in one, three in the other, a blacksmith workplace, three sheds, a barn, two caretas by a broken-down cabin, garden plots, an old stone house—the cookhouse, smoke curling from a chimney. Clotheslines with laundry strung behind two of the adobe huts. According to Juan's drawing, the wooden hut is the home of the five soldiers. None of them is in the open, but their horses are in one of the corrals. A few children play around the adobe huts. Two women work outside the stone house. South beyond the rancho, horses can be seen grazing on low ridges.

Stone calls out and the men ride down upon the rancho. They have formed a wide half circle and ride slowly to give the soldiers time to get to their horses. They are noticed. Dogs emerge from out of nowhere and bark hysterically. The women by the stone house disappear, and the children scurry to safety. The soldiers, partly dressed in white uniforms, burst from their hut and duck into the corral. They hurriedly mount, and the first rider opens the gate and they clear out, heading south. Now a dozen warriors give chase. They race through the open spaces between the buildings, and when the soldiers' horses slow down climbing the slope out of the hollow, three soldiers fall to arrows. The other two, as was intended, get away. Two of the soldiers on the ground still live. They are finished off and three scalps are taken. Their horses, bucking and careening on the slope, are rounded up.

Stone and Powderface sit their horses outside Juan's adobe hut as he drags his weeping wife and the boy into the open. Stone signals to Big Bow, and he lets the two prisoners go. When Juan has gathered a few belongings, his wife is mounted on one of the vaqueros' horses, and Juan mounts up with his son in his arms. The women of the party ride down from the ridge from where they watched the attack. The horses in the second corral are hazed out, and the column forms up again and they ride south, driving the captured horses before them. Once Stone looks back and sees women and children and the two vaqueros standing there, motionless, their faces pale and rigid, staring after them as if they are seeing ghosts.

In the grasslands south of the rancho the warriors split up and round up a horse herd of perhaps two hundred animals. They have no use for so many horses at this time, but Stone wants to draw the soldiers from San Antonio after them, letting them think they are dealing with a horse-raiding expedition of Indians from the north. That is the plan.

These are spirited, unbroken horses, difficult to get under control. But every man of the party has experience in running mustangs in the High Plains. At last they are brought together, and with two point riders and riders along the flanks, the stream of animals is pushed north, past the rancho and past Magpie's burial place toward the pass at the mouth of the long valley. They ride in and two miles farther stop for the evening camp at the foot of the lone knoll they had noticed on the way in. The broad trail they have left behind is easy to follow. Two scouts are placed miles back to watch over the trail. Given the distance to the large rancho by the river, Stone expects the pursuit from there to arrive at the pass during the morning hours. The women have butchered a few sheep, and the fires burn bright that night under a brooding sky.

The men who have taken scalps sit outside the camp by a small fire. For the short ceremony, each scalp should have been placed on a buffalo chip. Because there are none available, each man cuts a small piece of sweetgrass from the twist each carries in his bow case, puts it on the earth, and places the scalp upon it. Pipes are readied, and each man prays to the spirits in the unseen world, tries to propitiate the spirit of the slain man and asks for forgiveness. Then pipes are smoked and the ashes emptied on the sweetgrass. Flesh particles are shaved from the scalps and placed on the ashes. Each scalp, in size a little larger than a silver dollar, is stretched inside a hoop made from a soft twig and is tied to it. Later the scalp hoops are attached, without ceremony, to the bridles of the men's war horses. The tiny curls of sweetgrass with the pipe ashes and flesh particles are left in place on the ground for the elements to dissolve.

ELEVEN

They wait in ambush position on both sides of the pass.

Stone has split his little force. Setpagoy has been sent north through the valley to scout toward the bend of the Nazas River and watch for enemies. Daha and two warriors, his brother and Set'toni, are with the women, the Toboso prisoners, and the captured horses behind the knoll. Daha is armed with a musket and is to fire it in an emergency. Stone knows that Daha sits in cover halfway up the knoll, watching. He is to take the women to safety if the enemy force should get through the pass. Two warriors hold the war mounts out of sight where the pass broadens into the valley. Besides Stone, six men with him are armed with North West trade muskets.

At first light on this morning, before they rode to the pass, the men had prepared themselves for battle. Dressed only in moccasins and breechclouts, they had painted themselves in the manner of their societies. The Kit Fox men's bodies and upper parts of arms and legs were painted yellow, the lower halves of arms and legs from the knee down, black. Each Kit Fox wears the black crescent of the hemen on his chest. The Red Shield men painted red stripes over their bodies and wear a broad, fringed belt over the top of the breechclouts, painted red. As head adornments, the Kit Foxes wear two eagle feathers standing vertically above the head, while the Red Shields wear buffalo horn bonnets, the horns painted red. Each Red Shield soldier carries the red-painted shield with a buffalo tail attached, for which the society is named.

The sun has risen, and the scouts have not yet come in. The sun is warming up the sands and the rocks behind which the warriors are positioned. Stone checks his loaded musket for the second time. His hand caresses the smooth wooden stock, and he looks at the date and the maker's name on the right side of the lock plate: Barnett, 1804. He slightly turns the weapon and inspects the ornament on the left side of the lock plate, the long, curved body of a dragon with its head turned back. Three screws secure the dragon's body to the plate. He tests them; they are tight. He places the musket across his knees and waits. He has placed on the rocky surface next to him a .54-caliber ball encased in a thin leather patch and a piece of hollowed bone with the measured load of powder for the pan and the barrel. This is for a second shot. Within reach are bow and the arrow case.

He waits. Slowly the sun climbs higher into the sky. Stone sits in a crevice twenty feet above the floor of the pass. He sits at the northern end of the gap from where it winds south for a hundred paces or more to its opening toward the grasslands where some white dots of sheep are still visible between brush and mesquite. In the rocks across from him he sees Little Bird, the Red Shield soldier, fearsome in his appearance, the red-striped face and the buffalo horn headdress, and he knows that eight more men hide on both sides of the pass farther down. When he turns his head he sees the knoll in the middle of the valley that shelters the women and the captured horses, invisible to his eyes. When he stands up he can see south across the mouth of the pass into the grasslands.

He waits. Time passes slowly. Then a low whistle. When he peers over the ledge he sees two riders galloping up through scurrying sheep. The scouts. They are Lame Bear and Necklace, both Kit Foxes. During the night they have dressed for battle and painted themselves. They shake shields and lances over their heads, and when they ride into the gap Lame Bear shouts, "They come. Men dressed in white." He makes the signs for many, forty, fifty. Stone stands and points to where the horses are hidden and tells them to stand back, out of sight, and to cut down any enemy who might come through. High above in the blue sky buzzards circle, watching. Then there is a faint sound in the distance that grows slowly into a rolling thunder, the hooves of many horses running fast. Stone moves a few steps down, covered by the rock wall, and holds the musket in a half-ready position, and sees Little Bird across from him do the same. The riders close the distance fast, but when they come to the mouth of the pass they must slow down. The sounds of flapping stirrups, creaking leather, horses pounding the ground, a command in Spanish as the horses bunch up and the riders change into single file and surge into the gap. Suddenly the clamor of hooves is quelled by the bone-chilling war cries of Cheyenne warriors and the booming reports of two muskets, three, four, five, magnified by the close space.

The first enemy Stone sees is a white-clad soldier with a saber, red shoulder straps, a wide open mouth, yelling. He hits him in the chest with the heavy bullet and bends to reload. Little Bird has fired too, and already powder smoke hangs heavy in the air. Stone jerks the ramrod from beneath the barrel, pours the powder charge into the barrel, and rams the ball home. He cocks the hammer, opens the battery, and pours the rest of the powder into the pan. He steps forward and looks for another target. Below him one horseman passes, but behind, a bucking, crippled horse has blocked the passage. The warriors stand lined up on both sides, silent now, and send arrow after arrow into the melee of squealing, frightened horses and desperate men below. Stone sees one soldier, high in the saddle, trying frantically to turn the horse around, and he kills him from a distance of fifty paces. He drops the musket and grabs the bow. He gets off four arrows, shooting at soldiers on the ground trying to hide. Then it is over. The soldiers outside the pass are on the run, galloping away. Warriors jump into the gap and finish off the wounded. Stone walks down. He sees the one soldier who passed him lying a distance away, run through by Lame Bear. In the gap he counts fifteen soldiers in blood-smeared white uniforms, including the officer with the red shoulder straps. He watches scalps taken from the dead. Eight of the horses are uninjured and are caught and loaded with the equipment of the dead. Riding gear, lassos and blankets, and weapons: lances and machetes. No firearm is found; the soldiers were poorly armed.

They leave the dead where they lie and move out to their horses and mount up and ride away. These soldiers are the same lancers who killed Magpie and tortured Whirlwind. Stone thinks of the promise he made to Magpie's widow in the Ka'ta camp. It is fulfilled.

• • •

They pass the knoll and get to the campsite where the women have readied the travel and packhorses. The captured herd is spread out two miles farther north in the valley, guarded by Däveko and Set'toni. The women are waiting anxiously for the warriors to return. Daha is standing with them. The nine men who fought alongside Stone have tied the fresh scalps to their lances below the point. Lame Bear, who killed the one soldier who got through the fusillade, has done the same. They shriek and wave lances triumphantly above their heads. The women have noticed that none of their husbands is injured and break into high-pitched songs as the riders come to a halt in a swirl of dust. Set joins the chorus with his wolf howl. Maria watches the scene quietly; she has seen this before. The Toboso family beholds the spectacle with wide eyes, uncertain whether to be afraid or pleased. Eaglenest shyly approaches Stone, who sits the dun war horse in silence and without emotion. She looks up and touches his knee, smiling. "You are back safe," she says. "We heard the gunfire." He nods and his eyes smile at her but his lips do not move. She steps back and joins the women standing in a line, singing the Cheyenne victory song. To'giai, Daha's wife, and the two Kiowa women, Sendehma and Tasenma, stand with the others but do not sing. They wait until the Cheyenne song is over, then sing their own victory song, a song that Kiowas and Gatakas have in common. They sing for the action of the day before. Eaglenest joins them, singing this time for her brothers. It is not even midmorning. The sun still stands low in the infinite blueness of the sky.

Stone lets the last song be finished. He calls to move out, and the impromptu celebration comes to an end. The women and the Toboso family mount up and ride off. One bunch of warriors rides ahead to get the herd moving. Stone stays behind with another bunch as a rear guard. The remuda moves out at a good traveling speed, and they reach the bend of the Nazas, fifteen miles to the north, at noon. Setpagoy waits for them there and reports to Stone that all is clear. Powderface, who is riding point, takes the herd into the river, and wild-eyed, with manes flying, the surge of horses slashes across and breaks through the brush on the west bank and gains the flat ground beyond. The women follow with the baggage train without incident, and the rear guard crosses last. Now Stone takes the lead with Juan, who knows the country farther up on the east bank, and with Maria and Eaglenest as interpreters. So they ride once again into the Bolsón de Mapimí, the Empty Quarter of Spanish Mexico. Once, twenty miles farther, Juan points out that a large sheep and cattle ranch, the Hacienda de la Laguna, sits across from them on the east bank, not visible from where they are. It is another property of the Marquis de San Miguel. He has more such large ranchos to the east, all at the edge of the Bolsón, ranchos such as San Lorenzo, Cienega Grande, and Patos. The marquis has his own soldiers stationed at all of them, many soldiers. This is where the circo has gone, Juan believes. When asked if he knows these places, Juan says yes.

They make camp ten miles south of the mouth of the Nazas and the Laguna de Tagualita. The warriors wash off their war paint in the river. At dusk two scouts who covered the back trail ride in and report that no one is following. The women wait until dark to build fires and cook the first meal of the day, mutton. Before they eat, Stone gives a short talk, thanking the warriors for their prowess, their closely following agreed-to plans. He reminds them that the herd was taken to deceive the Spanish, and that the horses will be abandoned on the next day when the party crosses the river and rides east on the circus's trail. There is some muttering among the men, but no complaint is spoken. After they have eaten, he sees Setpagoy and Daha talk to Eaglenest. She comes to her husband with a worried face and tells him that the Kiowa and Gataka men want a meeting, that they have something to say to all of them.

They sit in a tight circle, the women behind the men. Stone sits amid his Kit Foxes, with Eaglenest beside him as interpreter. There is silence among them. An owl calls from across the river. The night wind gently brushes their faces. The women are wrapped in robes, the children in their laps. It is Daha who speaks first.

"We talked among us. We are going home. We don't want to leave the horses we have captured." His face is set, serious. He does not evade Stone's eyes, but it is apparent he is uncomfortable. He waits for his sister's translation.

"Who is we?" Stone asks.

"Me and Däveko, Setpagoy and Set'toni."

There is silence Everyone feels the tension. Most stare at the ground in front of them.

"We will get more horses later," Stone says.

Now Setpagoy speaks. "I have done what you asked me to do. I have taken you to the place where your brother was captured. You don't need me anymore."

He points to Maria, and to Juan, who sits with his wife and son among the women. "You have a woman who speaks the Spanish tongue. You have a man who knows the country."

A pause. "You know now how to find him," he continues. "We have kept what we promised you. You don't need us anymore."

Some angry motion stirs among the Cheyennes. "You didn't take the horses by yourselves. We were there too. They are ours too." This is Powderface. Others agree.

"That is true," Setpagoy says. "But you can't take them with you when you hunt for Whirlwind. Why leave them here? Whoever wants to come with us gets his share."

Stone nods. "I can't hold you. If you want to leave, you have a right to do that."

He looks along the row of Cheyennes. "Whoever wants to ride with them is free to leave. There is truth in what these men say." He points with his chin to the two Kiowas and two Gatakas.

There is a long silence.

Powderface speaks. "I stay with you. I want to get your brother back. I say let them take the horses."

Silence again.

"I say the same," says Porcupine, Powderface's brother. "We have not finished what we came for. Let them take the horses."

One of the Heviksnipahis speaks up, White Wolf. "We came with you to help you find your brother. We came also to see this country for ourselves, learn about it. We are not through yet. We will stay." He looks to the two Heviksnipahis next to him. They grunt in agreement.

"I speak for the Red Shields," Little Bird says. "We are Hovxnovas. We stay with you. I understand them." He points to the Kiowas and

Gatakas with a little stick in his right hand. "I say let them have the horses. They have done good for us. Let there be no bad feeling between us."

One by one the Cheyenne men who have not yet spoken, speak up. All support Little Bird's statement. One, Red Bird, says something most are thinking. "We made you rich, cousins. Remember that when you come to us in the spring and bring us these same horses to trade for you to the English." There is friendly laughter.

Stone speaks the last words. "It is good," he says, making the sign with his right hand. "Pewe. I thank all of you. I thank Setpagoy, Set'toni, Daha, and Däveko for taking us to this place, to where we made the soldiers bleed for Magpie." He pauses. "I wish you a safe ride from here."

At sunrise in the morning the two groups separate after the horses have been watered and the travel horses of Stone's party, worn from the long ride, have been exchanged for fresh mounts from among those captured. Kiowas and Gatakas leave first. The good-bye is brief. Setpagoy takes the point, Set'toni and Däveko ride the flanks when Daha rides drag, and the stream of horses moves out, Tasenma and To'giai following, each woman leading two packhorses with equipment, weapons, and provisions. Stone's eyes follow them as the many hooves stir the desert surface and raise a dust cloud that lingers behind them for a while until it subsides. Four men and two women and all those horses, he muses, and dangers ahead. He watches as the remuda slowly disappears, then calls out, and the party, already waiting, sets off once more across the Nazas for the push into the unknown east.

• • •

On the east bank the party turns north. After a mile they reach the east-west road that runs below the laguna. Some days earlier they crossed it farther west when they came down from the north. Juan has told Stone that the road, a narrow dirt track, after passing along the mountain chain he calls the Sierra de la Payta, swerves north toward Monclova. He is confident that the road is well beyond the grassland grazing grounds of the marquis's ranches. It is rarely traveled, and only by larger parties, because of the ever-present danger of attacks by

Apaches and norteños. Tracks and the ruts of caretas confirm Juan's words; they are weeks old. Stone is unconcerned about raiders from these tribes but does not want his party spotted by Spanish eyes.

When they take the road east, Stone rides ahead of the column with Eaglenest and Maria, Juan between them as guide. Juan's wife, Lucia, and their four-year-old son, Pedro, ride with the women. Powderface and Porcupine scout ahead within sight. The three Heviksnipahis, as always, bring up the rear behind the women and the packhorses.

The track leads through a shrub savanna they are already familiar with. The terrain is sprinkled with tarbush and creosote bush, yucca and prickly pear, and stands of mariola, a pungent-leaved shrub. Looking toward the south the eyes scan the vast plain to the low, pale line of mountain ranges thirty miles away. To the north, the bland, dust-colored slopes of the Sierra de la Payta, less than a dozen miles away, pile up to a height of six thousand feet. Stone is eager to learn about ranches and haciendas and settlements, which will come up before them soon.

To get this information from Juan is difficult. His Spanish is poor, and Maria has to rephrase questions again and again to receive some answer that she can explain to Eaglenest in Kiowa, who translates its essence into Cheyenne for her husband. It is a frustrating exercise for all involved, but Stone forces himself to be patient. The information obtained may be crucial for the journey and the success of the quest. By the time they camp for the night by a muddy pool with water barely fit for the horses, after an easy ride of forty-five miles, Stone knows something about Spanish outposts and settlements between their present location and the town of Saltillo east and the town of Monclova north. He is trying to work out in his mind how to get from these places the information he needs on the movements of the circus.

After they settle down in camp, before nightfall, Stone lets Juan draw another map in the sand, marking places and distances. A curious circle of onlookers watches Juan, and inquisitive eyes follow the Toboso's hand as he deftly scratches with a twig.

"San Lorenzo," he says. He marks the rancho with a cross. "Parras," he says. He makes a circle. "Ciudad." He looks at Maria to translate. Stone watches as the girl gropes for words. Then, with a torrent, she tries to explain to Eaglenest. Eaglenest listens carefully, asks a question, and nods after Maria responds with another deluge of words. Eaglenest glances at Stone. "Ciudad is a place where many people live all the time, a place like the one where we bought Maria, but larger, much larger." She looks into Stone's eyes to see whether he understands. He nods and smiles. He nods to Juan and makes a sign to continue.

"Cienega Grande," Juan says. "Rancho." He makes a cross. "Patos." He makes a cross east of Cienega Grande. "Rancho." He makes the sign for large. He repeats the sign. This is a very large rancho. He makes another circle southeast of Patos. "Saltillo," and he says again, "ciudad."

"Monclova?" Stone asks. Juan draws another circle well north of Saltillo.

"How far from here," Stone points to the ground, meaning the campsite, "to there?" He points to the cross that marks Cienega Grande. Eaglenest gives the question to Maria, who speaks to Juan. The Toboso listens, thinks, shrugs, lifts two fingers.

"Two days," Maria says.

"How far from there to Patos?" Again words go back and forth. "One day." Juan nods confidently.

"How far from there, Patos, to this ciudad and this one?" Stone points to Saltillo and Monclova. Juan thinks. "One day to Saltillo. Three days to Monclova."

Stone sits thinking. "Ask where he thinks the circo went. East to here," he points to Saltillo, "or there?" He points to Monclova.

There is a long silence after Maria explains the question. Finally the Toboso looks at Stone, a frown on his face. He says something in his language, then says reluctantly, "Saltillo."

Stone nods. Now he addresses Eaglenest. "This is important. Ask him whether people in these places know him, might recognize him."

The Toboso listens as Maria asks in Spanish. He thinks, scratches his head. He points to San Lorenzo, Cienega Grande, and Patos. He searches for Spanish words. He speaks to Maria. The answer comes back. "He has been to San Lorenzo, Cienega Grande, Patos. He drove horse there for the marquis. Some there have seen him. In the towns,

Saltillo, Monclova, no one knows him."

There is a silence. But then Juan has something important to say. After a lengthy exchange in three languages, Stone learns this: that the road they are on turns north toward Monclova after it is met by a road that comes up from Cienega Grande. In that rancho people should know whether the circo went north or east. If it went east, it went on another road that runs from Cienega Grande through Patos to Saltillo. The first place where they should ask is Cienega Grande. If the circo went east, they should make straight for Saltillo.

Stone and the others perched around Juan and the earth drawing have understood. Stone gets up and thanks the man. "Pewe. Thank you." He knows now what to do.

TWELVE

On the following day they continue until they meet with the road coming up from Cienega Grande. They have ridden nearly fifty miles but have seen nothing of the Spanish, nothing but desert, animal tracks, once a band of antelope far away, a golden eagle, circling, a good sign. They look south down the Cienega Grande road. It lies dead; nothing moves on it. Nothing has moved over it for a long time. Stone gazes down it as far as can be seen before it disappears in a fold of the terrain, a jumble of tarbush and mesquite. He calls out, and they ride back from the road juncture for about five miles to where they had taken good water from a pool beside the road. There is grass for the horses, and they make camp for the night.

After midnight, in the dark under a waxing moon, everyone is awakened by the mating call of a female puma, a high scream, repeated, sounding much like the shrill, desperate cry of a woman terrified. Perhaps the camp by the pool interferes with the cat's searching for a mate. The agitated horses strain against their hobbles. The men walk among them and touch and stroke bodies and talk to calm them. The puma's screams continue for a while, then fade as the cat walks away. The horses are nervous for the rest of the night, although two guards are posted with them.

At first light, after a quick cold meal, Maria mounts up. She is wearing a plain dress from Juan's wife's small bag of clothes, cotton skirt and cotton blouse, a mantilla thrown over her shoulders. The horse has been packed with blankets and saddlebags holding gear and dry food, the appearance of necessities for a long ride. Everyone knows that she will be judged and observed closely at the rancho. She must tell a believable story about why she has to find the circus. Stone has left the details to her. Her experiences as a traveling companion to a Franciscan will help her know what to say, how to act. Her excellent Spanish sets her apart from regular Indian women and will help to strengthen her story.

The three Heviksnipahis Kit Foxes mount up with her. They will escort her to the Cienega Grande road and stay until she returns, watching over both roads. Stone raises his arm, and Maria and the three warriors ride off. She looks back once, searching for her son who is nestled comfortably in Sendehma's arm. She holds him in one arm, Gondaima in the other.

Two of the Hovxnova Kit Foxes, Lame Bear and Yellow Eyes, are sent back west for ten miles to cover the road in that direction until evening. The camp stays by the water, giving the horses a rest. Men and women do repair work on gear and, when this is done, sit around talking, waiting. Stone tries not to think about what kind of information Maria might bring back, but he can't help thinking, wondering.

It is a long wait. The sun rolls slowly toward noon and toward evening. When the brilliant red ball dips toward the horizon, a clatter of hooves nears from the east. Maria and the three warriors ride up. Her face is tired, flushed, but self-assured. When she dismounts, she stretches and reaches for Manuel. She lifts him up and hugs him and walks to where Stone is waiting. The two are quickly surrounded. She looks at Stone when she speaks in Kiowa. Eaglenest translates.

"I went there, to that rancho," she says simply. "I talked with the mayor de edad. I told him why I am after the circo. He did not believe me. I told him a long story, a sad story." She laughs. "Finally he believed me. I lied good." She pauses.

"The circo came through Cienega Grande a long time ago. It gave a performance on one evening. From there it went east toward Saltillo."

"Did you find anything out about my brother?" Stone asks.

Maria nods. "Yes. But I had to be careful. I asked about the persons who perform in the circo. I said that I wanted to be sure that it is the circo I am searching for. I asked about the man who runs the circo. He described him to me. I said yes, this is the one."

"What about my brother?"

Manuel moves in Maria's arms. He wants down. She sets him on the sand and turns once again to Stone. "Yes. The mayor de edad said the circo travels with a jaguar in a cage, a wolf in a cage, and a norteño in a cage. The norteño man's right hand is injured. People who want to see the jaguar, the wolf, and the norteño have to pay one tlaco to see them in their cages." Her voice is steady, but there is sorrow in it.

There is a silence.

"What is a tlaco?" Stone asks quietly.

"A copper coin, a piece of copper money." She pauses. "Coins come in silver and gold. I have seen silver coins myself. Copper is the lowest kind of money. A tlaco is the smallest coin."

Stone swallows. His face has hardened. "How does he live?"

Maria shakes her head. "He did not say. He does not know. But your brother lives. They must feed him like they feed the wolf and the jaguar. He is alive. That is what you wanted to know."

Another silence.

"I had to be cautious," Maria continues. "I made sure that the mayor did not see me ride north from the rancho. He expected me to ride east. The peons did not understand us speaking Spanish, so they did not matter." And as an afterthought, "No one followed me."

Into a heavy silence, Stone says, "Saltillo."

• • •

At daybreak they water the horses, fill water bags, and move out on the road. When they come to the place where the Cienega Grande road merges with the Monclova road and turns north, they leave the road and continue east toward the dark shoulder of the Sierra de la Palma, which reaches to a height of almost eight thousand feet. Stone plans to cut across the desert to the first rises of the Sierra, twenty miles away, and follow them south and southeast to the southernmost edge above a grassy plain. There the plain, part of the horse and cattle range of the rancho of Patos, is only a narrow strip fifteen miles wide, bounded on the southeast by another high sierra within which lies the town of Saltillo. Stone acts upon information from Juan. He thinks that they might cross the plain at night and slip into the mountains and get near Saltillo while it is still dark.

They ride through a typical desert land of low ridges, with shallow dry basins and sandy ravines between them, a sparse growth of tarbush and cacti and shrubs. Nineteen miles east of their last campsite they climb to the four-thousand-foot terrace and follow it southeast along the bottom of the naked, brooding mountain above them. Marching in the order of the days before, Stone sees that Powderface and Porcupine, a short distance in front of him, have halted and dismounted, studying something on the ground. They squat, touching the earth with their hands.

When Stone gets close, the two point to the ground. Stone raises his arm and the column behind him stops. He dismounts and walks forward. Hoofprints have cut into the sand, coming from the north, going south. Porcupine has loose sand in his hand, removed from one of the tracks. "This morning," he says. "They have come through this morning or just before we came."

Stone bends and looks at the tracks. He straightens up. He looks along the trail, north, south. "These horses walked," he says. He checks the tracks again. "How many? Thirty? Some more?"

"Yes," Porcupine says. They look and think.

The men have dismounted and gather around. They look and spread out and walk slowly along the tracks in both directions. Set has been there before them. He romps right over the tracks, pauses and sniffs, his nose to the ground, runs on. Sendehma calls him, but the dog pays no attention. A low whistle. Necklace has found something and holds it up. A tattered moccasin. They all stand close when Necklace hands it to Stone who passes it to Eaglenest.

Eaglenest turns it in her hand. A worn two-piece moccasin without a tongue. A sole thin from wear with a hole in it. The top a narrow field with a design made of black and white quills in a diagonal pattern. It is a moccasin for a woman's foot.

Eaglenest looks puzzled. "I don't know. I don't think it is Gataka. Could be Kiowa or Comanche."

She hands it to Sendehma. The Kiowa woman inspects it with a quizzical look, turns it around, traces the quillwork with a finger.

"Could be Kiowa. Could be Comanche. These colors set against each other—Comanche women like that."

The moccasin goes to Maria. The girl tests the thickness of the buckskin with her fingers, scrutinizes the quillwork. "I am not sure, but I think this is Comanche." She looks at Stone and turns the piece over to him. Absentmindedly he hands it back to Necklace.

He looks at the women, then at the men around him. "I think this is a horse-raiding party from up north. Probably Comanche. They have women with them." He pauses.

"We know they came through here before we arrived. I think they are after horses from that big rancho, Patos." Once again he pauses.

"We better move on to where we wanted to go. These warriors here might attack at first light. That's what I would do. Should that happen we will know what to do."

A murmur of agreement from the men. They ride on, careful to stay within the desert fringe above the grasslands, and make another twenty miles to a ravine below the barren face of the Sierra de la Palma. From the rim of the ravine they notice a road a few miles away that runs northeast. Juan explains that the road comes from Patos and the pueblo of La Florida, which lies a little ways north of the rancho. They cannot see either locality, but according to Juan's uncertain ramblings they may be only ten and twelve miles away. South in the grasslands they see dark dots in the yellow grass: grazing cattle and horses. Once they see a group of riders, perhaps soldiers on a patrol.

Nowhere have they found water. The use the water they have brought with them for the horses and themselves. There is some grass. But their own food supply is almost gone; they chew on the last flakes of jerky. That night they do not build a fire.

At daybreak, the Comanches strike. The first indication is a brief flurry of gunfire to the southwest, from the direction of Patos and La Florida. Men and women hasten from the camp to the rim of the ravine and lie flat, looking over. For a while they see nothing, but then a column of smoke unfurls in the distance, slowly growing into a black cloud that stretches out and climbs into the early sky.

Nothing more happens for some time, but then a clatter of hooves is heard to the northeast, advancing rapidly. When the riders come into view they are soldiers in the white uniforms of the marquis's private cavalry, lancers, perhaps fifty of them. They gallop on the road toward the great balls of smoke. They pass rapidly and after a mile or more disappear in the terrain.

A short wait. Nothing more happens. Stone stands up. "This is good," he says. "The Comanches be blessed. Now we ride."

They mount up and follow the bottom of the ravine south. They ride out and come to the road and cross into a different world, a world of grass, similar to a world they know from back home. They ride happily, feeling at ease, comfortable in these surroundings. The horses feel it too and are energized. Before them opens a plain with low, rolling hills covered in grass, stands of mesquite in the breaks, dwarfed, knotted, dark of bark, but graceful. And a few yuccas, crowned with a shock of green bayonets, silently stand watch. They pass a pond but keep on to get farther away from the dusty track of a road that has disappeared behind them. Before them looms the high sierra that hides the town where they want to go. They pass through red-colored cattle and ride at a walk so not to frighten them into a run. They bridge the short distance from their last campsite to the brown slopes of the sierra shortly after midmorning and search for water. A pond is found, and they stop to rest.

A small party goes back for meat: four warriors, Powderface, Lame Bear, Yellow Eyes, and Necklace, and the women, excluding the Toboso woman. Three steers are lanced and cleaned out and chopped up and brought to camp, where the meat is processed. Livers and lungs are eaten raw. The horses are given time to rest and graze on the good grass. To the northwest the smoke cloud still hangs in the sky, undiminished. The party wonders what the Comanches have done. Did some of them attack one place, Patos, or the other, La Florida, as a feint, pulling defenders to the wrong place while the others did what they had come a long way to do, raid the horse herds? This they come to agree on.

While the party is still resting, Stone rides out with his brother to look for an entrance into the sierra. It takes some time before they come to a trail that leads into a canyon twisting south, with hoofprints of horses and mules on it. At the mouth of the canyon sits a wooden cabin with a pole corral, both empty but recently in use. Perhaps a guard post serving the marquis's herds. Stone walks in while Big Bow sits the horse outside. He looks the cabin over. A big fireplace, rolled-up blankets on the floor. A rough table. Some clothing on pegs on the wall. A battered, smudged sombrero. Stone takes the hat and two dirty, frayed serapes hanging by the door, a pair of sandals from a corner. Outside he thoroughly shakes the serapes and the hat. Before they reach the camp he slips a serape over his head and dons the sombrero, and they ride in to the laughter of the warriors.

In the early afternoon they ride into the canyon toward Saltillo, past the cabin. Stone and Powderface have taken the lead. The warriors ride their war mounts, fully armed. Red and gray rock walls streaked with vertical lines in white, a rough, stony trail along a thin, rushing creek. The trail climbs steadily, winding through an empty desert of sheer stone rarely softened by the intrusion of shrubs that have gained a foothold in a crevice or on a ledge. At the top of the canyon, when the party reaches the watershed, side canyons open up. They have seen no one.

Stone halts and thinks. The town should be near, somewhere down there. He believes that they are close enough. He follows the headwater of the creek into one of the side canyons. After searching the area thoroughly, they make camp. That night they build a fire and roast meat and feast. "Tonight we eat until we pass out," Big Bow remarks. They won't, but all laugh cheerfully.

THIRTEEN
November 9, 1807

Guards have been posted around the camp. Spaniards who might stumble upon them have to be killed. Stone cannot let it get around that a norteño party is hiding in these mountains. At daylight, after a first meal of cold meat, leftovers from the roasts of the evening before, three riders leave camp and make for the trail in the main canyon.

The three are Stone, Eaglenest, and Maria. Their saddles have been exchanged for blankets tied to the backs of horses. Eaglenest and Maria are barefoot. They wear simple cotton blouses, skirts, and rebozos, or head scarves, from the Toboso woman's limited array of garments. Stone wears one of Juan's short cotton pants and the pieces he took from the cabin: sandals, serape, and sombrero. On his belt under the serape, out of sight, he carries knife and hatchet. The three have loosened their braids and let their hair fall naturally, as is the custom of Indians and mestizos of the region.

Under a cloudy sky they reach the canyon trail and turn south. The trail hugs a rock wall on the left that sometimes forms an overhang over the trail. On the right a precipitous gorge has opened in front of the canyon wall. The trail's rocky surface is uneven and in many places only wide enough for one horse or mule. The horses, unaccustomed to such restricted space between rock and gorge, are nervous, and the riders try to soothe their anxiety by talking and holding the reins tightly. After about two miles they notice that a pack train has halted farther down to let them pass, in a spot where the trail is wide enough for two animals. When he gets close, Stone measures the mestizo at the head of the mule train with a searching look but tries to appear friendly. The man, with a lined brown face under a wide-brimmed sombrero, his black hair tied in the back, and piercing eyes, touches the rim of the sombrero and says a greeting in Spanish. Stone parrots the gesture and rides by without a word. When Maria comes up she says something in Spanish, and the man responds with a relaxed laugh. Stone counts twelve mules with heavily loaded pack frames. The drag rider, a surly looking older man, says nothing, but his eyes follow them after they have passed.

They ride another three miles, and the trail dips down into the gorge where it flattens out. The first isolated ranchos appear, small stone houses with low stone walls to keep animals out of cornfields now lying fallow. Dogs bark as the three ride by. A woman works in the open; a few men stand together at another place. When they round the shoulder of the mountain, the sun breaks through the clouds and shines upon Saltillo below them.

Stone halts and gazes at the view. The town is a maze of one-story gray stone buildings with a few adobe huts mixed in. Its center is dominated by the high spires of the Cathedral de Santiago. A system of narrow streets seems to converge on the cathedral and the plaza in front of it. A blue veil hangs over the town, the smoke from wood fires arising from many roofs. Saltillo lies in a pocket surrounded by mountains on all but the northeastern side, mountains that rise to ten thousand feet in the east and to more than twelve thousand in the southeast.

The two women have halted beside Stone. Only Maria has seen a town of similar or even larger size, Chihuahua. Stone's and Eaglenest's experiences with large gatherings of people have been with Arikara and Hidatsa earth lodge villages and with tribal gatherings for special purposes, the annual ceremonial camps of Cheyennes, Arapahos, Gatakas, Kiowas, and Lakotas, where up to five thousand people come together. Saltillo seems to have a population of twice that number.

But Stone and Eaglenest are not impressed. They cannot imagine living in a permanent settlement where people stay most or even all of the year. The Arikaras and other peoples on the Missouri River whom they know, Mandans and Hidatsas, and even Skiri Pawnees, corn growers all, live in villages only part of the year during planting and harvesting, but spend months in tipi camps in the Plains hunting buffalo and other game.

Stone points toward the cathedral and asks what it is. Maria explains and Eaglenest tells him. "A place of worship. A place where people go to pray."

Stone nods. A place where people pray—he understands that. He clicks with his tongue and the horse moves. They ride down into the first street, which is rutted from the wheels of caretas and wagons, the hooves of horse and mules and burros. On both sides small houses with the dark openings of doors, many without windows. No woman is in sight. Children, some half naked, run in the street, and men sit by doors wrapped in serapes, watching the three riders without interest. A few empty areas between houses are closed with low stone walls. Behind are an occasional careta, a flock of chickens, a pig or two, mules, burros, or a horse. They pass a *pulqueria,* a tavern where men have gathered. "Leperos," Maria says in disdain. Eaglenest asks and Maria says curtly, "No-good Indians who hang around towns." A street-corner stand with a table and an iron plate over an open fire where two women pat out tortillas, a pan of chile peppers. Three times they pass *leñeros,* sellers of firewood, who course streets with burros heavily loaded with wood, looking for buyers. Another side-street pulqueria and they come to the cathedral and the plaza.

The plaza, quadratic and 150 yards wide, is surrounded by trees. Horses, mules, and burros stand tied up among caretas and a few wagons with spiked wheels. A fountain with a stone water basin is located on the edge of the plaza. Stone and the women dismount and water the horses, drink themselves, and fill water bags. They talk briefly, and Maria walks to the plaza while Stone and Eaglenest retreat with the horses to a corner near the cathedral. They have a good view from this spot.

The plaza is filled with food stands and liquor stands and stands where sellers display wares from apparel to utensils of all kinds, new and used, and food items from garden products to selected specimens of livestock, piglets, chickens, turkeys. One hears singing and music made with fiddles and mandolins and small Indian drums. Stone and Eaglenest watch the colorful scene and remember trading days in the

Arikara villages, Indian camps and horse herds, intertribal feasts, the caravans of bearded North West Company white men, horse races and martial displays by soldier societies. They have seen Maria disappear into the crowd of Indians and mestizos milling around and know that she will talk with people and ask questions. They look away and examine the architecture of the cathedral. It is the largest building they have ever seen. Set against the front of the cathedral are columns of elaborately carved pale gray stone. On a ledge at the top of the dome is a human figure in stone.

"Who is the man up there?" Stone wonders aloud. "Is he the keeper of the house?" A flock of pigeons with flapping wings whirls around the towers and circles and settles in a row below the ledge with the figurine. "He is a bird man," Eaglenest says. They look at each other, so different in their poor Spanish Indian garb from the way they usually look, and they burst out laughing.

They look around. They have not drawn attention to themselves. Most of the people they see are dressed as they are. Only their horses could give them away to an astute observer; they are of higher quality than the horses they have seen so far.

A careta drawn by two oxen creeps past, the big, raw wheels creaking. Eaglenest nudges her husband. A wealthy ranchero rides by. He is dressed in leather trousers and jerkin, a jacket of cloth gaudily embroidered, a serape over his shoulder, a wide-brimmed and silver-corded sombrero on his head. The heels of his boots are armed with spurs whose three-inch rowels gleam like the blades of daggers. His bridle is made of solid silver. A sword is strapped to the saddle inlaid with silver. At his side rides a young woman, perhaps his daughter. She wears a fancy blue hat with curled red feathers, gloves that reach above the elbows, white blouse and velvet vest, a multicolored long skirt, a lace mantilla over the shoulders. Both ride purebred horses and seem oblivious to the bustle around the plaza. They look straight ahead, out of place in this drab town, in a world by themselves, arrogant and self-assured. Eaglenest notices that the woman is smoking. She holds a *cigarrito* delicately poised in her right hand, a cigarette rolled in a cornhusk.

"Look at the woman," she says excitedly. "She smokes something she holds in her hand."

"Yes." Stone regards them coldly and watches them closely, especially the man, as if spotting the exact place to put an arrow or a bullet. "It's not a pipe. It looks like a tiny stick. Maria knows what it is." His eyes take in their whole appearance, their horses. "They have fine horses. Perhaps these are the people who own the horses we all come down here to take away, Kiowas, Gatakas, Apaches, Comanches. Now us too."

They watch as the ranchero and the woman disappear among the common folk who fill the street. They let their eyes wander, trying to see and remember everything. After some time Maria returns, a smile on her young face.

"I found out about the circo. The circo has been here twice."

She pauses and waits for Eaglenest to translate.

"After the first visit the circo went east to the town called Monterrey, not far from here. Then it came back and was here for a few more days. From here it went south. I was told the circo went toward Fresnillo. That is a town five days' ride away if one takes the road."

Stone listens to Eaglenest speaking in Cheyenne. "Did you learn anything about my brother?"

"Yes. What I was told is good. There is a norteño who throws knives at a woman on a wheel, a Toboso woman. People have to pay money to see the animals and the things the circo does. One of these is the norteño throwing knives. I was told that he is very good at this."

There is a pause. So he is healthy again, Stone thinks. Then, "How do we get to Fresnillo?"

"There is a road from this town to Fresnillo. It starts at the plaza and goes through the mountains."

Stone hears. He thinks, shakes his head. "Too many people here, too many eyes and ears. Someone would see us, hear us, even if we ride through at night." He pauses. "We have to find another way to get to that town."

He pauses again.

"Try to find out whether there is another trail, one that goes around this town, maybe around these mountains."

Maria nods. "I will find out." She goes once more to the plaza and mingles with the people.

• • •

Early afternoon. On level ground by the camp men and women sit in a tight circle. Stone sits on the west side, facing east. The guards have been brought in because the party will leave soon. Everyone looks at Stone.

"We went to that town Saltillo," he says. "We found out about the circo. It went south from that town to another town, Fresnillo."

He pauses.

"We also found out about my brother. He seems to be well again. He does something special in the circo. He throws knives. He throws knives at a woman on a wooden wheel that turns. It goes round and round. That is what Maria was told by some who have seen him." He nods to Maria, who sits on his right.

There is movement around the circle. Sounds of surprise. Cheerful sounds.

"He was always good with knives," Little Bird says with a short laugh. "I know. What happens if he hits the woman?"

Stone nods. He raises his eyebrows. "I hope he doesn't. I pray he doesn't."

"Who is the woman?" Powderface asks.

"We were told she is a Toboso woman. She must have been the one who cared for him when he was sick."

Some faces turn toward Sendehma. The Kiowa woman's face is without expression. It is impossible to know what she thinks. It is her husband they talk about. She has come a long way to get him back. She gently holds Gondaima against her body. Perhaps she is glad that someone did something good for Whirlwind.

"What will we do now?" Red Bird asks.

"We follow the circo to that other town, Fresnillo."

"How far is it?"

"Esiensz nohona. Five days." Stone shrugs. "Maybe less. We will use a road but we must travel at night. At night the roads in this country are empty. No one travels in the dark. Bandidos. They are called bandidos. They are men who rob people, often kill people. They are the only ones on the roads at night, looking for people to rob."

He points to Juan. "Ask him." He looks at Eaglenest, who sits on his left. Eaglenest translates to Maria, who addresses Juan who sits behind the circle with his wife and child. There is a brief flurry of words in Spanish, and then Juan nods emphatically and repeats twice, "Sí, bandidos."

"We must stay hidden during the day so that no one sees us. We ride at night," Stone continues. "There will be more people when we get near that town Fresnillo. We must be careful. If someone sees us, the Spanish will bring all their soldiers down on us. Then we'll never get my brother."

A silence. Faces are thoughtful.

Finally Holy Singer asks, "Where is the road that goes to Fresnillo?"

"There is a road that goes south from the town we have seen, Saltillo. But to get to it we have to ride through Saltillo. That will not do. Too many people. Even in the dark someone will hear us, see us." Stone pauses. "There is another road we have learned of. It goes around this mountain here and leads us to the road we want. We have to ride half of the circle."

Again there is silence.

"We have to avoid people during the day. We have to kill whoever sees us. If we meet riders on the road in the dark, they are bandits. They are bad men. No one misses them when we kill them. They might try to ambush us." He pauses again. "From now on we take no more scalps." He looks into warriors' faces. He repeats forcefully, "We take no more scalps! If they find people scalped they will know who we are. We don't want them to know. We ride like mista, ghosts. If we kill bandidos, no one will come after us."

Again there is a silence. Farther down the canyon a bird screams once, twice. The canyon walls throw the echo back.

"What is the town like that you saw?" Holy Singer asks. "Is it like Hidatsa and Arikara villages?"

"No." Stone shakes his head. "It is very different. It's like the Spanish place where we got Maria but much larger. Ten times the size."

He pauses.

"Little stone and mud huts, many of them, many, cramped close together, sitting in rows shoulder to shoulder. There are narrow spaces between the rows, streets, for wagons, walking, riding. There is a foul stench of too many people, smoke from too many fires, few dogs, some donkeys and oxen, hardly any horses. We saw a huge stone house, a place of worship where people pray. No one was praying that we saw. In front of the huge stone house is an open place. Trading was going on there. No trade as we know it from the Arikara villages. No white traders. No horses. We saw nothing we would trade for." He pauses.

"Strange all this. Lots of people sitting around, men and women, standing, drinking, talking. We heard one drum, a few people singing. We saw no skins, no fur, no animal hide. No one was wearing skin clothing. They were wearing cloth, dry goods. Those Spanish don't look good. But we saw one horseman and his woman who were dressed in a fancy way. Maria told us he was a ranchero or a hacien-dado, one who has many people work for him. These were different from all the others. They had good horses too. The woman was smoking as they rode by."

"Smoking?" Someone finds it hard to believe.

"Yes," Stone insists. "Maria told us she smoked a cigarrito, tobacco rolled in a leaf. It looks like a small stick. This woman held it in her right hand." He pauses.

"This is not a place for us. We could not live in a town like that. The people seem to have nothing, do nothing. They live on top of each other. They live in a desert they made themselves, a desert of little huts of rough stone and mud. No grass anywhere, nothing green, just a few trees on that open place where they were trading. No air to breathe. A bad smell everywhere. Litter everywhere. That town is nothing but a big cage without bars."

A long silence after he has ended.

Then, "Yes. That is what it is. The Indians we saw looked like prisoners. This is a dead place."

He looks along the faces around him. "This is settled," he says slowly. "Let us get the horses ready and ride."

The meeting breaks up. They fill water bags in the creek. When they ride out on the same trail on which they had come up the day before, Stone leads, with the best bowmen behind him, Porcupine, Powderface, and Yellow Eyes of the Hovxnova Kit Foxes. If there must be killing on the trail, it has to be noiseless and swift. As on the day before, the men ride their war mounts. The three Heviksnipahis warriors act as rear guard behind the women, who lead packhorses and most of the men's travel horses. The trail lies empty before them.

As so often, Set runs ahead, testing the wind, and waits up somewhere to let the remuda pass. After reassuring himself that Gondaima is still where he expects her to be, the red-coated spook frolics around Sendehma's horse and the child in the woman's arms and sprints ahead again to explore.

After riding eleven miles, they come to the cabin at the mouth of the canyon. The pole corral is empty and the cabin door is flung open wide as Stone had left it the day before. Once again they gaze into the Patos plain, a sea of grass with low, rolling hills that stretch to the northeast as far as the eye can see.

Stone halts and scans its expanse thoroughly but sees nothing to worry about. So they ride on, Stone waiting for a road that is supposed to come across the plain from the northeast and pass into the mountains to their left. That is what Maria was told in Saltillo. They ride along the northern foothills of the sierra without incident and, fourteen miles farther on, reach the road and follow it southeast into a gap that cuts into the sierra. From there it angles toward the Saltillo-Fresnillo road. The only signs of life are the black wings of turkey buzzards drawing a wide circle beneath the blue tent of the sky. The ruts of caretas and hoofprints on the rough dirt track that serves as a road are many days old. When the mountain walls widen to a narrow basin, the waters of a small lake glisten through reeds and groups of mesquite and willows like an invitation to a rest. Stone whistles softly and points, and he and the three men behind him ride forward and fan out and circle the lake and come together on the opposite shore. He waves the column over and they camp for a few hours. Stone announces that they will wait there until dark, then cook and eat and move on to the Fresnillo road. Guards are placed to cover both directions until daylight fades.

• • •

They have watered and hobbled the horses. Maria and Juan's wife, Lucia, have gathered firewood. When night falls, the two have built a fire in a depression deep enough that no trace of light can be seen from a distance. The smell of smoke could give them away if any stranger were near enough to notice, but there is no one. The four women from the Plains—Eaglenest, Sendehma, Bear Doctor Woman, and She-Wolf—have cooked meat and distributed it. All are eating when a waxing half-moon climbs over the pinnacles of the Sierra Madre Oriental to the east. When Stone is finished, he puts the empty plate on the ground beside his left knee. He says something to Eaglenest, and she calls to Maria to come over and sit with them. Maria is still feeding Manuel small pieces of roasted beef, but she walks over and sits down, the boy on her lap, the plate in her left hand, the knife in her right. She keeps slicing meat as Manuel munches, his huge dark eyes on the headman.

"I want to know about the circo," Stone says. "Why did the circo go to Saltillo, why to Fresnillo now?"

Maria listens to Eaglenest's translation. "I don't know," she answers. "I do not know why the circo chose this particular route." She pauses, holding out a piece of meat to Manuel. "A circo goes from town to town but stops at every rancho and hacienda on the way. At each of these places the circo gives a performance for money if people can pay for it. At a rancho or hacienda the circo stops for one or two days and performs on one evening. If it is a big rancho, perhaps it gives two evening performances. Then the circo moves on to the next place."

She pauses, waiting for Eaglenest to translate.

"In towns the circo may stay for a week or longer and perform on three or four evenings—or more if people still pay to see it."

Again she waits.

"From Saltillo the circo went first to Monterrey, another town, then came back and went to Fresnillo. I don't know why. It could have gone north. Where it goes from Fresnillo no one knows. It could go south or north. The man who owns the circo decides that."

Stone listens attentively. "How does the circo move?" he asks.

"With caretas or wagons, perhaps wagons, because caretas are very slow. They take too much time to go from place to place. They probably use mules to pull the wagons. They may have a few horses."

There is a pause. Stone looks absentmindedly at Manuel, who is playing with the food on Maria's plate. Finally he asks, "If all goes well and we make good time on the road—how long does it take the circo to cover the distance we cover in one night?"

It is a difficult question, and Maria has no concise answer. She shrugs. "It depends on how often they stop at a rancho or hacienda or at a colonia. These places are often half a day's or a day's ride apart, or even more." She frowns. "We are still in a high desert here, and there are not many places where people live." She thinks hard. She looks at Eaglenest while she talks to Stone. "Perhaps." She stops. Then, "Perhaps a day's ride or a night's ride for us takes six days or more for them."

She waits again.

"Also, the circo stops at every place where there are more than a few people, but we don't stop there. We ride around these places." She shrugs. "It is hard to figure out."

As an afterthought she adds, "If I remember what the Brown Robe told me, once we are out of the desert we come into country where there are more settlements and haciendas, more people. Then the circo travels even more slowly, stopping everywhere."

Stone listens as his wife explains what Maria has said. He nods. And now he asks the question that concerns him the most. "What does Maria think: how many days of our riding is the circo ahead of us?"

Maria exhales heavily, blowing through her pursed lips. She looks at Stone and shakes her head. "I don't know."

Stone tries to encourage her. "Think about it. Make a guess."

Maria nods. "Yes." She counts on her fingers. Again. "Thirty days maybe?" She sighs. "It depends on how fast we ride. If we get into fights . . ." Her voice trails off.

"Yes," Stone says. "Aho. Thank you." He makes the proper gesture with his right hand. "Pewe. It is good. I think you could be right."

People sitting close by have either finished eating or have stopped to listen. Their faces are turned toward Stone, Eaglenest, and Maria. They have overheard the conversation. "Have you heard?" Stone asks, meaning no one in particular.

Powderface clears his throat. "Yes, we have heard. This is good to know. Did she say thirty days?"

"Yes, it's a guess." Stone looks back at Maria. The girl cringes. She is apprehensive. What if she is wrong?

Stone notices. "It is good," he repeats. "No one knows for certain. We will find out soon enough."

"We have come far," Holy Singer says. "We will do the rest of it too."

There is a murmur of support among the warriors. This ends the talk.

They finish the meal, clean up, extinguish the fire with sand, fill water bags, water the horses, and saddle up. There is enough moonlight to mark the contour of the road. When they move out they ride close together in three groups. Stone leads the first group consisting of six warriors and his brother, Big Bow. He wants the boy by his side. Seven warriors make up the last group. Wedged between the two groups of soldiers are the women with the packhorses and the Toboso hostages. Stone and three men of the first group, Powderface, Bear Tooth, and Yellow Eyes, have laid loaded muskets across the saddles. Three men of the rear group also ride with muskets ready: Little Bird, Standing, and White Wolf. Should they run into bandits on the road, Stone expects that they might be attacked from the front and back simultaneously. In an ambush Cheyenne firepower should prove superior to the bandits' weapons. Musket fire on the road at night would cause no concern to anyone but the bandits.

They ride at a walk, listening into the silence of the night. Set is their best ear for near and distant sounds. He runs ahead, stops and sniffs the ground, and runs on. The moon throws a pale light over the land, creating silvery patches and objects, shadows and black pits. A night bird calls. A shy wind from the south brushes body and hair as with silky hands. The sound of hooves meeting soft ground, the creaking of a saddle, as the dirt trail snakes through hollows and around sudden outcrops and rises. Occasionally a clump of desert brush. No trees. After twenty miles they reach the Saltillo-Fresnillo road, another dirt track, and turn south on it. Ten more miles and they pass the colonia Agua Nueva, sleeping soundlessly by the road, and come into the pass between two high mountain massifs of the Sierra Madre Oriental, the gate to the vast plateau that stretches south to the Sierra Madre Occidental and to the town of Fresnillo that sits before it. The moon is slowly sinking toward the west when they leave the pass behind. Before first light creeps across the eastern sky, Stone calls an end to the march, and they leave the road and turn east and away into the foothills of the sierra where they make camp in a fold of the terrain with some grass for the horses but without water, six miles off the road. When Set howls his morning song no wolves answer, but a few coyotes yip and bark miles away to the southeast.

FOURTEEN

Stone wakes up at noon. He looks around. Men and women are wrapped in their robes, still asleep. Set has curled up next to Gondaima, his back against the girl. She is wedged between the dog and her mother. The midday sun is hidden by a dark cloud layer that has swept in from the south. Stone gets up and shakes out his sleeping robe, looking out for scorpions. Set has heard him and raises his massive head, blinks his yellow eyes, and goes back to sleep. Noiselessly, Stone walks from the camp through the hobbled horses and urinates behind a tarbush. Then he makes a call on Porcupine, who has sat as guard below the rim of the hollow, scanning the distance. Nothing seems to move.

"Seen anything?" he asks.

"A mule train came through some time ago, going north," Porcupine answers. "Two riders with some cattle, also going north. That's all."

Stone nods. "You get some sleep. I'll stay here."

Porcupine grunts and edges away. Stone gazes at the spread of the land before him. To the northwest the Sierra de Parras stretches on and on, an unbroken mass of naked, treeless ridges and snags and pinnacles, rising to a height of almost thirteen thousand feet. To the southwest and south lies a rolling, treeless plateau on the six-thousand-foot level in desert brown and gray, surrounded here and there by the bulging backs of rock formations that jut out to ten thousand feet. The dirt track of the road is visible only in a few places where it drops from higher to lower terrain. For most of its course it must be imagined, although whatever moves on it can be seen from where Stone sits.

He is mulling over worrisome thoughts in his mind. How many night rides can we make without being detected and reported to someone who can bring a small army upon us? He is not afraid of a fight. He trusts himself and his men. Bandits at night are no real danger. But once we are seen and soldiers come looking for us, their scouts will find our tracks and lead the enemy to the camp. He is confident that they could break through any force thrown against them, but then they would have to retreat into empty desert country. What about the circus then? How would we know where the circus went? How would we get to the circus when everyone is looking for us?

He is not aware that Eaglenest has sneaked up behind him. She sits down next to him. "What are you thinking?" she asks softly.

For a while Stone does not answer. He keeps looking across the plateau. "I am thinking about where we are and how we will get to know what we need to know."

"Yes," Eaglenest says. "But our visit to Saltillo went well. We found out what we wanted to know. We'll do the same in Fresnillo."

Stone does not respond. Eaglenest sighs. "Turn toward me," she says. "I want to braid our hair."

Reluctantly, Stone turns around. Eaglenest parts and brushes his hair quickly, with adept, experienced hands. He looks into her serious face, the eager, intense eyes. He can't help smiling. She deftly finishes one braid, then the other, and ties them with yellow cloth near the ends. She nods and lets her hands fall into her lap. She says the obvious. "We need water."

"Yes. There must be water along this road for all who travel it. Water for men and animals. We'll find some tonight."

Eaglenest nods. "I want to talk about something. Sendehma. She misses her brothers. I think she is unhappy with us. She feels left out." She pauses. "It is her husband we want to bring home. You should involve her more. Instead of me, let her interpret for you. You know that she can do it. It would give her a purpose. I think she feels all alone. That's not good."

Stone keeps looking into his wife's dark eyes. He still smiles. "Good," he says. "You are right. We'll do it that way." He pauses. "Now you keep still. I'll braid your hair now."

Eaglenest hands him the brush and lowers her head as he starts working on her, sifting the shiny black hair with the bluish tint through his calloused hands. How he would like to embrace her! How she would like to embrace him! But this is a warring expedition, and as long as it is one, they cannot indulge in something personal, intimate, affectionate. They have to wait until this is over.

When Stone is finished, they are joined by the two brothers, Little Bird and Red Bird. "What do we see?" Little Bird asks, his gaze on the horizon. But Stone's eyes follow Eaglenest as she backs away, follow her lithe figure in the antelope skin dress as, head held high, she strides back to camp.

• • •

After dark, in a cloudy, moonless night, they break camp and move to the road and turn south. They had a cold meal before they left and shared the last of the water with the horses. The road before the advance guard is more to be imagined than actually seen. The column has spread apart somewhat so that the women with the packhorses do not run into the lead group and the rear guard does not run into the packhorses. Set is the one who scouts ahead; he is gifted with extensions of the senses humans have never had, living by smells and voices humans can never experience. For him the road is alive with signals he can identify, and any presence that would concern him and the people he is a guardian of, he would communicate to them.

Lucia and her son ride with the women, but Juan is surrounded by the men of the rear guard. They cannot allow the Tobosos to use the dark to escape. As the column moves, a feeling takes hold that spirits are depressed, weighed down by passively enduring a ride into blackness and the unknown. Even Stone, in the lead with Powderface and Big Bow, has the sensation of riding into a black hole. Only the steady shifting of the horse's body under him, and the horse's breathing, give him a sense of something solid, even though the eyes find nothing to hold on to.

Farther behind a child whimpers and starts crying. Who? A soft voice sings a lullaby in a strange language, trying to calm the child. It is Lucia, singing a Toboso song. Perhaps little Pedro is afraid of the dark and the strange persons who surround him. Lucia's voice is low and soothing and does not reach beyond the confines of the column, but it has a positive effect as something human, an expression of faith in an empty, ghostly world. By the time the song ends, the child has become quiet. But now Sendehma picks it up. First is a Kiowa lullaby, sung for Gondaima, and then she sings a Kiowa strong heart song, a song of encouragement for warriors before they ride into battle. She sings defiantly against the dark, the silence. Stone feels spirits lift along the column. Even the horses seem to move with new energy. And so it goes on. When Sendehma has ended, She-Wolf sings a Cheyenne lullaby and then breaks into a powerful song from the Oxheheom ceremony addressed to the thunder spirit, Nonoma, bringer of rain and new life, who lights up the sky with the arrows of lightning. Then it is Bear Doctor Woman's turn. She first also sings a Cheyenne lullaby, then follows it with a couple of wolf songs, songs of scouts traveling in enemy territory. At last Eaglenest's voice is heard. She sings Gataka strong heart songs. Maria is too shy to sing.

So they move on, self-contained, eager to get to Fresnillo. Twice they smell smoke but see no fires. After fifteen miles they come to three dilapidated huts by a well at the place where the road makes a turn in a southwestern direction. The opening of the well shaft is sealed with wooden planks, the windlass made of a cottonwood log. A wooden trough next to the well contains some water. The earth around it is trampled to dust by the hooves of animals. Stone dismounts and tastes the water, drinking from the cup of his hand while Set is lapping beside him. The water is no spring water but usable. Quickly men remove the planks; the large leather bag attached to a rope is dropped down and then lifted with the windlass from about twenty-five feet below the surface, part of an underground seep. The trough is replenished with water until the horses' needs have been satisfied, and then the people are served and water bags are filled up. It is slow going and takes time; all counted there are forty-seven horses in the column.

When they are finished and have covered the well and move on, the clouds withdraw and a yellow moon appears and stands above them, casting a precious brightness over the road and the land. Ten miles on they reach a jumble of huts and two pole corrals full with sheep. Stone holds the column for a few moments. When the women bring up packhorses, men of the rear guard slip into one of the corrals and swiftly kill a number of animals and lift the bodies over the fence. They are placed on the packhorses and the column moves, leaving an angry chorus of sheep dogs behind. The huts have been watched, but no one has come out to investigate. Fear of bandits is obvious. Travelers using the road and those who live by it seem willing to pay a small levy rather than lose more in a confrontation with the lawless.

For another fifteen miles they change gaits often to cover ground without draining the horses, and just before first light they pass a sleeping colonia at the foot of a mountain over ten thousand feet high. They ride another ten miles and leave the road and take shelter for the day at the mouth of a dead-end canyon. There is some grass for the horses but no water. The women dress the sheep carcasses and hang the meat on lines of rawhide rope to dry.

A guard keeps watch as the others sleep. Stone replaces him at noon and is joined by Eaglenest and Sendehma. The mountain at their back, they look across the high desert plateau to the east and southeast where isolated humps of barren mountains rise. They see the red dots of some cattle in the distance. A yellow bank to their right prevents a view southward, where they will go, but the road is clear in their sight. There is some traffic on it. Once a large flock of sheep is slowly driven south, twice small herds of cattle in the same direction, a mule train going north, oxen-drawn caretas, a few horsemen. When a group of people appears, men, women, and children walking south, over a hundred strong, with a few donkeys piled high with packs, Stone calls for Maria.

She peers intently from cover and has a quick answer. "Los peregrinos." She explains to Sendehma, who finds no exact word for it in either Kiowa or Cheyenne. When Maria tries to interpret the Spanish word with a flurry of words in Kiowa, Sendehma nods. She turns to Stone. "These people walk in a sacred way. They will visit a holy place, a shrine."

Maria speaks again. Stone hears "Santuario de Plateros," "Fresnillo," and "El Santo Niño de Atocha." Sendehma thinks for a moment and describes what Maria has said. "Not far from Fresnillo there is a holy place the Spanish call Santuario de Plateros. There is a shrine for a boy named Jesus, whom the Spanish call the Son of God. The Spanish pray to him there. El Santo Niño, Maria says, is the holy child. Many people go there to pray, people from all over, many from far away."

Stone looks from Sendehma to Maria. "We don't know that Maheo had a son," he says. "I have never heard that before. Where did this son come from?"

Sendehma and Maria talk in Kiowa. Maria shrugs. "The Brown Robe told her," Sendehma says. "Those churches we have seen, many others, are built for the holy child. The Brown Robes and Spanish priests serve him."

She pauses.

"The holy child is not from this country. He was born at the edge of the world in another country. That was a long time ago."

"Why are they praying to him here?" Stone asks.

There is silence.

Maria speaks again, shyly. "The Spanish believe in him. They brought him with them from across the ocean. Now many Indians believe in him too."

"They brought the child here?" Stone asks.

"No. The Spanish say that the boy lives in the sky with his father."

Stone looks once again at the line of walking pilgrims. "Strange, what the Spanish believe. We know who lives in the blue sky. Maheo lives there, the creator. We do not know of a son." He pauses. "We do not respect the Spanish, but we respect those who walk a long way to a sacred place. Sometimes we do the same in our country."

He leaves it at that.

• • •

Early that night the women cook mutton. All eat their fill, clean up, pack the horses, and move back to the road. They ride in moonlight, in the established order. Set scouts ahead as always. The road, the land, lie silent, peaceful. Far away a pack of coyotes barks and yip-howls and carries on for a while. Silence again. There is only the low thud of hooves on soft ground, an occasional creaking of leather. Stone is dreaming, wondering about what brought him here with the warriors. Whirlwind. The twin who is part of him in flesh and mind, inseparable yet separated. The one with the easy laugh, reckless, dazzling, impulsive. And seductive, charming. All of these. The brother so different from Big Bow next to him, a wild-eyed, reliable, attentive youngster who adores him. He glances at him as he rides quietly on his left, absorbing the sights of the unfamiliar country before him.

And then Stone thinks back to that other time and place three years ago. There had been a bloody battle with Skiri Pawnees on White River in early spring. One of the Kit Fox headmen had been killed in the battle, Wolf Lying Down, of the Hoohksitan band of the Wotapios. With his death, the two bands of the Wotapios, Hovxnovas and Hoohksitans, had Kit Fox soldiers but no headman. Some time after the battle four Kit Fox headmen came to visit Stone. They were from three of the six Cheyenne divisions: Heviksnipahis, Hevhaitaneo, and Masikota. It was a formal visit. They asked him to accept a headman position for the Wotapio Kit Foxes. His parents and his brothers were present when the offer was made. Because of the stringent duties imposed on a headman, the candidate's family has a say in the matter. He told the visitors that he wanted a day to think about it. They stayed in the Hovxnova camp for the night under the care of the band's Kit Fox soldiers.

Stone had joined the society when he was twenty years old. As a Kit Fox he had been in a number of raids, skirmishes, and battles with such opponents as Crows, Nez Perces, Utes, and Kitkahaki Pawnees. He carried the scars to prove it: scars from an arrow wound in his right thigh, from a lance thrust in his upper right chest that missed the lung, and from an arrow wound on his torso above the right hip. He had gained a reputation for bravery, clear-headedness in dangerous situations, dependability, and for not losing sight of the larger picture in the shifting details of individual mounted combat.

He had confirmed it once again in the Skiri battle. In one phase of the battle a massed force of Skiri warriors threatened to break through Cheyenne ranks. They were led by a chief on a white charger waving a curved, feathered lance. Stone, all alone, rode against him and pierced him through with his lance. When the Skiris saw their leader fall, they pulled back in horror and, dispirited, were driven off the field by a concerted Cheyenne charge.

When Stone dismounted and approached the dead man, he recognized that he was a Skiri of prominence. About forty-five years old, he wore an otter collar; the skin of the animal was split in the middle so that the man could put his head through it. The head of the otter was at the back. On his right shoulder he wore a swift hawk, and a decorated leather bundle was tied above his left shoulder. On his breast he wore two flint arrowheads, each embedded in a ring of sweetgrass. One eagle feather was tied to his scalplock. A buffalo hair rope was attached to his belt. The shaft of the crooked lance was wrapped with swan skin; pendants were eagle feathers, and the iron point was nested in owl and eagle feathers. This was clearly a special society lance. The man had no other weapons.

Although it was expected that he would scalp him, Stone did not. Because he had killed him, it was for him to do what he thought was right. He did not touch anything on the body. He stuck the Pawnee society lance in the ground next to the corpse and walked away. The man's white horse, painted with blue lightning trails, he led away and later gave to the widow of the Kit Fox headman who had died in the battle.

When he and his family talked about the offer to be a headman, his parents and Whirlwind were against it; Big Bow was too young yet to understand. Headmen of Cheyenne soldier societies were expected to lead in battle and therefore die young. Stone felt that he could not refuse. His mother cried when he told the visitors that he accepted. He was inducted as headman in a ceremony following the Massaum ceremony at Bear Butte in the summer of 1804. This was two years before he met Eaglenest and she became his wife.

A sudden, throaty growl ahead on the road, a hundred paces away. Set. It brings Stone back to where he is. Two lean shadows jump across the road from the left to the right and disappear. Deer? It would be the first they have encountered for many days. The land seems to have been stripped of original animals; they have been replaced with domesticated animals for use or slaughter.

The night ride is uneventful. Twice they pass small settlements by the road. Wherever there is a settlement there is water; no settlement in this high desert can exist without it. At the second settlement they water the horses at a pond and take water for themselves. When the road climbs through another mountain range, they slip into a side canyon for the day, after a ride of forty miles.

FIFTEEN

Near midmorning Stone is awakened by Holy Singer, who has stood guard. He follows him to a place in the jumbled rocks from which they have a view of a good section of the road, less than half a mile away. After one quick look Stone tells Holy Singer to bring Maria and Eaglenest. When they come up behind him, he turns to Maria and asks, "Who are they?"

Together they fasten their eyes on the road. Riding in twos is a column of about eighty to a hundred dragoons dressed in blue jackets and yellow trousers, with white carbine belts across their chests, wearing blue helmets. Ahead of the column ride two officers sporting elaborate blue and gold helmets with horse hair plumes. Besides the carbines the men are armed with sabers. Behind the officers, in front of the ranks, ride a flag bearer, with the regimental colors in yellow and red, and a trumpeter. The ranks are followed by six canvas-covered supply wagons drawn by horse teams. The column is briskly moving north.

Maria talks excitedly to Eaglenest, her eyes seeking Stone. Eaglenest explains. "Soldiers of the king of Spain. Maria has seen soldiers like these only once before."

"Where are they going?"

Maria listens and shrugs. "North there are some presidios, forts. Monclova. San Juan Bautista on the Río Bravo del Norte. San Antonio de Bexar in Texas. They could be going there."

"How does she know about these places?" Stone asks.

Another exchange in Kiowa. "Maria was shown a map of the Spanish country in the north by the Brown Robe. He had a map on which presidios and towns were marked." She pauses. "But Maria says these are not presidio soldiers. Presidio soldiers fight Indians on the border. They are not armed well and do not fight well. Most of them are Indians themselves. They have been forced by the Spanish whites to serve as presidio soldiers as a punishment. These blue soldiers are probably mestizos, but the two headmen are whites."

Eaglenest questions Maria again and continues. "These headmen are either gachupines, whites from Spain, or creoles, whites born in this country. These soldiers are trained to fight whites."

"Whites? What whites?"

Another exchange between Eaglenest and Maria. "There are people east of Texas, by a great river, east of the Spanish lands, who are white also. They are called French. They also have a king across the ocean, and they sometimes fight with the Spanish."

Stone measures the Spanish dragoons with the eyes of an expert. These men are well armed and ride large horses, horses perhaps too large to be useful in Plains combat. They ride well and are disciplined. In his mind he compares them with the fighting skills of Cheyenne soldiers, his Kit Foxes and others. It would be impossible to withstand the blue soldiers were they to make a massed charge. But he would never allow the Kit Foxes to stand against such a charge. He would split his force and let the dragoons charge into empty space while his men would circle them on the flanks and in the rear on more nimble horses and shower them with arrows. Once their formation was broken up, the Kit Foxes would move in for individual combat. In this type of fighting the dragoons would be at a disadvantage. Still, he muses, it's good that we did not meet them in the present situation; it could have been disastrous.

They watch until the long column of soldiers and supply wagons have disappeared from sight and return to the camp.

No more Spanish soldiers come over the road that day, and after nightfall, under a moon almost full, they break camp and move out. After a few miles the road dips down to a level plain and the column marches at a good pace. After twenty more miles another dark hump of a mountain looms before them as fires suddenly appear to their left, near the road. Then they hear hoofbeats, voices, muffled sounds in the dark. Stone passes the word to be ready. This may be the ambush he has anticipated.

They ride on; every warrior knows what to do. Nothing happens for a few hundred paces. Everyone is tense, waiting. Then Set, ten paces in front of Stone, stands stock-still. Stone sees the dog's hackles lift, and a threat takes form deep in his throat and comes through snarling teeth as an aggressive growl. From behind cover on the left, riders sling onto the road and form a line across it. They are eight.

The distance to Stone is about seventy paces. He does not stop but rides on. He and Powderface next to him hold their muskets low on their right side. From behind, Bear Tooth and Yellow Eyes, both with muskets, ride up and join Powderface on the right and Big Bow on the left. One of the bandits shouts in Spanish. Stone knees his mount into a lope and the others follow. They quickly cut the distance. Stone raises the musket and fires, hitting a heavy-set man in the middle of the bandit line. As the man is thrown from his horse by the impact of the heavy ball, the muskets of the warriors around him let loose with thunderous noise. Two musket shots come from the bandits. Stone's horse collides with a horse in front of him, and he swings the musket by the barrel and hits someone on the side of the head with the butt. A sickening sound. He looks down at the fallen form and firmly brings his frenzied mount under control. Then he notices Big Bow at his side, lifting the shield over his head. Bowstrings twang, and it seems over.

From the rear of the column come screams and the blasts of muskets, the sound of galloping horses, calls from the women holding the strings of packhorses and travel horses with difficulty. The noise slowly abates, a final scream from a horse, and a deadly silence follows. The warriors dismount and inspect the places of carnage. In front of Stone and the men of the advance guard lie eight bodies. Set walks between them with teeth bared. Six men, two women. All wear wide-brimmed hats. The one Stone killed with the musket butt is a woman. She lies on the trampled ground spread-eagled, her wide, white skirt puffed up all around her, looking in the moonlight like a bizarre, giant doll. Stone feels regret, but then he sees the saber, half covered by her body.

They look at the men. Bearded, sun-burned faces. Their clothes are stained with grease, tobacco juice, and sweat. Two still breathe but are badly wounded. Porcupine and Necklace bend and quickly finish them. The bandits have three muskets between them, but only two were discharged. All had sabers or machetes, including the second dead woman.

From the back of the column comes the wailing of a woman. Stone quickly walks there. When he passes the women he notices that Bear Doctor Woman is steadying She-Wolf, who was grazed by a musket ball. She looks pale but tries a brave smile while Bear Doctor Woman is pressing a leather piece on her right thigh. "Nothing," She-Wolf says. "A flesh wound. A scratch." And Bear Doctor Woman nods. Stone's eyes seek Eaglenest and Sendehma and Maria. Eaglenest sees him and waves him on.

There are four dead bandits on the ground behind the rear guard. One more was shot down some distance away, trying to escape. But dead also is Juan, lying in a pool of blood, his wife sitting by him, holding his head, crying.

"What happened?" Stone asks.

"He rode toward the bandits, shouting, and they shot him," Little Bird says. "There was nothing we could do. I don't know what he shouted at them."

Stone nods. "How many escaped?"

"One," Little Bird says, leaning on his musket. "Two rode away. We went after them and got one; the other disappeared. He might have been wounded."

Stone looks at the Toboso woman. Tears stream down her face. Sobbing, Juan's head in her lap, she rocks back and forth. From behind, where the women have held him back, Pedro runs to his mother and starts crying.

"Did we lose anyone?" Stone asks.

"No. Lame Coyote got a light wound on his right side." He points to White River, who is bending over the body of his horse. "The horse took a ball in the chest."

"You did well," Stone says. He looks at the ground, thinking. "The bandits did not expect us to take the fight to them. They expected us to stand and talk. They didn't know that we have muskets."

There are four dead horses on the ground. They cannot be moved. Two more of the bandit's horses have been crippled and are left where they are. Four of the bandits' horses are rounded up, but the others have run away too far. Stone sends out scouts to the west and east to search for an arroyo where the bodies can be hidden. They find one nearly a mile to the east. From those bandits and horses shot with arrows the arrows are removed so that the party cannot be identified as norteños when someone finds the dead. They strip the bandits of their weapons and parts of their clothing; their clothes could be helpful in the future. The bodies are packed on their horses and taken to the arroyo and dumped unceremoniously. There they are out of sight until the vultures find them and do the rest. The six muskets taken from the bandits may come in handy sometime. These and the other weapons, sabers and machetes, are divided among the men who want them.

Stone and his party come away from the skirmish with little loss and some gain. Three were slightly wounded: She-Wolf, Lame Coyote, and Big Bow. It turns out that Stone's brother had lanced one of the bandits and was hit with a saber cut across his right shoulder, the rim of his shield taking the full impact of the downward swing of the blade, preventing a serious injury.

In the bandits' saddlebags they have found a small treasure of coins. All counted it amounts to a handful of gold coins, forty silver pesos, about a hundred reales and medio reales in silver, and pouches with copper coins, quartillos, and tlacos. Maria has briefly explained their value. Money means nothing to the Cheyennes, although coins are sometimes used for adornment, as in a woman's necklace or a hair piece. While in New Spain, this money might be helpful. On his next visit to a town Stone will be able to buy food or other items on the plaza market. For the time being he has placed the coins in Sendehma's custody.

When they leave the place of the clash, they take Juan's body with them for burial. He was not one of theirs, but he had helped them along the way. The column follows the dirt track of the Fresnillo road for another eighteen miles and find a hiding place to the west before the moon pales and the gray curtain of first light opens on the eastern horizon. Before they rest, Bear Doctor Woman, a healer, dresses the wounds of the three injured, and Stone and two men help Lucia to bury her husband. She is the only one who knows Toboso burial practices, so Stone lets her take charge. She searches for a cave or a crevice and finds a low rock overhang. Stone carries the body in and places it against the back wall, head to the east, as Lucia wants it. They leave the woman and child alone with the dead, and later, after she has finished the ritual required by her culture, they help to block the opening with rocks.

• • •

Guards watch the road all day, but nothing unusual is reported. With darkness the women cook the last of the mutton. Everyone gets a little but not enough. Before they leave, Stone addresses the group. They stand by their horses. "Someone has found the dead horses, perhaps the dead bandidos too." He uses the Spanish word. Cheyenne language does not have a word for bandit; there are no bandits in Cheyenne country. "They will wonder who did this." He pauses. "It would be good if they thought that the blue horse soldiers we saw did this." He grins. "I don't think that we left anything behind that can be traced to us."

He pauses again, searching for their faces in the moonlight. "We need to find a place with grass for the horses or we will lose them. We need food for ourselves. We need a place where we can rest for a while."

There is silence. The only sounds are the breathing and sighing of horses. "We must be close to that town Fresnillo," he continues. "We must find a good campsite. You wait for me there. I take Eaglenest and Maria and find the town and ask about the circo."

He looks along their faces. "Agreed?" He hears a murmur of support, but no one speaks.

Once on the road they form up in three groups as before and turn south. They pass one hacienda on the east side, and after thirty-three miles they come to a dip in the road through which a rivulet runs from west to east. Stone at the head of the column halts. This is the first running water they have seen for some time. Its source must be on high ground somewhere to the west. He is thinking. Perhaps they could find a place there to camp for a few days. He knees the dun forward and rides from the road into the brush west along the creekbed. The warriors follow in single file. The women, each with a string of four or five horses, have some difficulty at first forming the animals into a file to get through the brush; patience and experience win out.

After eleven miles Stone halts the column below the shoulder of a mountain at a spring that feeds the rivulet. There is a small water-filled basin in a hollow surrounded by mesquite and desert willows. And good grass all around. He calls out, and men and women dismount and let the horses drink. They do not remove saddles and packs. They have seen no cattle or sheep and no sign of human occupation. Strange, Stone thinks. This is a spot rarely encountered, with water, trees and grass. Why is no one living here? What is behind the mountain?

First light is coming, and he sends Lame Bear and Yellow Eyes to investigate. The party settles down and waits, and when first light lies brightly over the land the scouts return. Stone stands before them when they dismount.

"We circled around this side of the mountain," Lame Bear says. "There is another spring on the other side. A creek runs into a wide valley that goes north. In the valley is a small ranch, four or five houses, two corrals, and sheep are everywhere."

"How far is the ranch?"

"Half the distance from the road to here."

"Did you see people, riders?" Stone asks.

"No. They still sleep." Yellow Eyes laughs.

"Did you see anything else?"

"No. Only sheep and the ranch."

Stone thinks. Then, "We cannot stay in this place. People from the ranch, someone, will see us, see our smoke and come to look." He pauses. "We take the ranch and camp there . . . Yes."

He speaks to the men who surround him and the scouts. "We take the ranch and make all who are there captives. We don't want to kill anyone unless we must. But we don't let anyone escape. We stay there for a few days. We don't want to hurt anyone. Agreed?"

The men nod. He motions to six warriors, including the scouts. "You ride with me." He motions to his brother to come along. "The others follow. Don't hurry."

Stone and the seven with him exchange their mounts for fresh horses and saddle up. They ride off with the two scouts in front. When they come into the valley of the sheep they fan out and make straight for the ranch. They ride at an easy lope on both sides of the slow, winding creek through churra sheep that scatter before them. They get closer to the ranch and Stone views the spread: a one-story stone house near the creek with a wooden veranda in front, three small adobe huts near it, off to the side, two hornos, adobe ovens, a small blacksmith workplace, a shed, a large wooden barn, two pole corrals, one with five horses in it, the other empty. A wagon next to the barn, a large garden farther down the creek. Stone signals, and the flank riders speed up and swing wide to the left and right to circle the ranch and come up behind the buildings. Three black furry dogs run out and start barking, but Stone and the five men with him ride on. When they are about fifty paces from the stone house he signals and points, and bowstrings hum and the dogs fall quiet with arrows in their chests. Men scramble from the huts and the stone house, four in all, and stand frozen with blank faces when they make out mounted men who have brought their horses to a halt and sit, six abreast, muskets lowered at them.

Stone makes signs to the Spanish, pointing to the empty corral, and pushes his horse forward to brush against the man from the stone house, the ranchero. Looking up with raised arms he shows that he understands and slowly makes his way to the corral, the others, Indians or mestizos, following. While two of the warriors take up positions by the corral, eyeing the captives, Stone and the others dismount and search the houses.

Stone and Big Bow walk up the steps of the veranda and into the stone house. Stone holds the firearm lightly in a forward position, the hammer cocked. The front room is dimly lit from the door opening and a glass window in the left wall. Furniture is sparse and consists of a table, four chairs, two wooden storage boxes on one wall, and piles of sheep skins on the floor by the other wall. A door in the back leads to another room, the kitchen. Stone enters slowly. A window opening in the right wall covered with a blanket, a wide fireplace on the ground in the back wall with glowing coals in the chamber, a table, a few shelves on the left wall, a grain chest. To his left, pressed against the wall, stand two women, one elderly, with a young child in her arms, next to her a younger woman. Their faces are white with fear. Stone shakes his head and tries a smile to comfort them. He lowers the musket. He speaks to them in Cheyenne, making room for them at the door and gestures that the women leave the room. They obey slowly, uncertain of what is intended for them, the older woman going first, the child staring at Stone with huge dark eyes. Mestizos, their black hair is long, touching their shoulder blades under the thin calico dresses.

When they reach the veranda, the young woman screams as she sees her husband and the other men in the corral and sees women and children marched there from the adobe huts. Now all the women start wailing as the corral gate is closed behind them. Families bunch together like sheep waiting to be slaughtered. The two warriors who had covered the rear of the ranch building ride in and signal that no one got away.

Stone waits impatiently for the column to arrive so he can speak to the captives through Maria. When it finally comes, Set leading the way, Stone tells Maria to assure them that they will not be harmed. She dismounts and steps quickly into the corral, her son in her arms. She stands among the captives and talks, and finally the sounds of lament let up and an uneasy quiet settles. The men of the rear guard have already killed a few sheep before coming in, and the women begin to dress the animals and to build a big fire. Set sniffs at the dead dogs briefly, then lopes away to comb the ranch grounds to familiarize himself with the place.

• • •

Stone has brought the ranchero from the corral. They sit on the ground in a small circle: Stone, Maria, Sendehma, and the ranchero. The two children, Gondaima and Manuel, frolic with Set nearby. The sun stands near midmorning. The ranchero, a mestizo perhaps forty years old, looks pale despite his brown skin. He has a sharp, expressive face, short black hair, bushy eyebrows, and a mustache the ends of which sag around the corners of his mouth. He is dressed in leather trousers, leather boots, and a calico shirt. He sits rigid, tense, staring at the headman as the master of life and death. Stone has not known such fear but understands the man's distress. "Let him know that we mean no trouble for him or his people," he says to Sendehma. "We stay here for a few days, that is all."

Sendehma talks in Kiowa to Maria, who relates the message in Spanish. The ranchero listens, but his expression says that he does not believe it.

"No one of his people is allowed to leave the ranch. Whoever tries will be killed."

The ranchero nods. Such language he expects.

"Ask him whether he knows who we are."

Another exchange in two languages. The ranchero answers in a barely audible voice. "Norteños."

Stone nods. "Tsistsistas. Cheyennes. We are Cheyennes. Tell him."

The ranchero listens, but the definition makes no difference to him. Norteños are all alike, he has heard, thieves and murderers.

Stone points with his chin to the children playing with the monster dog. "We have children and women with us. We mean no harm to his people and this place."

The ranchero looks toward the children, then again at the women. One of them Indian, the other Indian or mestizo, he thinks. They do not seem unfriendly. What do they want from him? Why did they come to this ranch?

Stone seems to grasp the man's thoughts. "We have come here to rest and rest the horses. We take some of his sheep for food. We give him four horses in trade." The bandits' horses.

The man relaxes a little. Perhaps this is not so bad after all.

"During the day he and his people stay in the corral. During the night all stay in the stone house. There will be two guards. He must tell his people."

The ranchero looks from Stone to Sendehma, to Maria. He nods a couple of times. "We need food too," he says meekly.

"Two of the women are allowed to leave the corral to cook food. Two." Stone raises two fingers.

"I have a question for him," Stone says. "That road east of here—how far is it to Fresnillo?"

There is a fast exchange between the ranchero and Maria. Stone hears Fresnillo and another word, "Zacatecas."

Maria explains through Sendehma. "The road east of here does not go to Fresnillo, he says. It goes to Zacatecas, a town south of Fresnillo, a town bigger than Fresnillo."

Stone, Sendehma, and Maria look at each other. Stone is the first to get control of himself. "Ask him how he gets to Fresnillo."

The ranchero is getting animated. He points in two directions. Maria listens carefully and turns to Sendehma. She nods and tells Stone. "The man says Zacatecas is almost straight south. Fresnillo is southwest from here. There is a trail. It goes from the ranch to Fresnillo."

"Fresnillo—how far from here?"

The man thinks. "Ten *leguas.*"

Stone frowns. He asks Maria. "How far is that?"

Maria shrugs. "A legua is two miles and a half. The Brown Robe told me." She pauses, thinking. "Maybe twenty-five miles to Fresnillo." She pauses again. "A ride from sunup to midday. Or less."

Stone's face lights up. "That's not much." He is thinking. "Ask him whether there are other ranchos like this near here."

The man nods eagerly. He points north and west. "Many ranchos."

Stone views him coldly. "I want the truth. If he lies to me, he and his people will be punished."

Maria delivers the message and the threat convincingly. The tone of her voice, gentle at other times, is gruff.

The man trembles, stutters. He avoids looking at Stone. "No. No. One ranch north." He points with his arm.

"How far away?"

"Twenty leguas."

A whole day's ride," Maria suggests.

"Why not more ranchos or colonias?"

The man only confirms what they have experienced. "No water. Only this creek. The next creek is far away." He points west.

SIXTEEN

Stone, Eaglenest, and Maria leave before sunrise. Eaglenest leads a packhorse with water bags, food, and blankets. Before they left, Stone told the men and women staying behind that he planned to be back the next day or the day after. Should he not be back then, they are to wait no more than five days, then ride north. He stressed that the Toboso woman not be allowed to talk to people of the rancho; she might pass information harmful to them. Maria has taken some of the captured coins along; she plans to buy pinole, cornmeal, and frijoles, beans to make tortillas—a food the Cheyennes have yet to experience. Manuel made no fuss when his mother left; he preferred playing with the other children to riding again.

When the three riders take the trail to Fresnillo they are dressed in clothing taken from the bandits. Eaglenest and Maria wear *enaguas,* petticoats of flannel, Eaglenest one in blue, Maria one in scarlet. The enaguas are belted around the waist over a loose white chemise. Rebozos, scarves, seven feet in length, slung over the upper parts of their bodies, and sandals, complete the apparel. Stone is dressed in leather leggings, botas, a white calico shirt, a *chaqueta,* or jacket of cloth, and a serape, or slitted blanket. For footwear he has kept his moccasins. A simple palm-leaf sombrero, a *sombrero de petate,* covers his head. The three leave their hair loose, unbraided. Stone and Eaglenest feel weird in their costumes and hope that they cause no attention, but Maria has insisted they will not. All three carry belt knives; Stone has two hatchets hidden in saddlebags.

They ride over a dusty trail with wagon tracks and hoofprints weeks old. Stone looks out for animal prints, but only once they come to a spot where two coyotes have crossed. All morning long he watches, but there is no trace of deer or antelope; it seems they have either left the country or been killed off. The land around them is still high desert, sparsely flecked with tarbush and cacti, unfriendly even to Spanish sheep. Brown humps of low mountains lie to the north and south. They see a few small birds and the ever vigilant turkey buzzards cruising in the blue sky. They see no humans.

Before noon they pause for a meal and to rest the horses. Stone has chosen a rise that allows a good look around so they cannot be surprised by someone. The horses are hobbled below, out of sight. He has checked in all directions and now watches Eaglenest and Maria, who have taken food and water bags from the horse and are coming up to where he sits. They walk gracefully, their long black hair wafting over the scarves. As they come closer his eyes focus on Eaglenest. It would be unbecoming for him to look closely at a woman other than his wife. The Cheyenne law pains him not; he has eyes only for his wife anyway. So his gaze embraces Eaglenest as she approaches. Through the crazy costume that hides her figure he sees or imagines every part of the body he knows so well, better than his own. He can see her still as he saw her for the first time. His thoughts trail to another time, a better place, a place where spirits still roam, not this lifeless country.

Eaglenest stepped into his life in early May 1806, shortly before the Hovxnovas went north for the annual ceremonies by the Black Hills and the Arikara trading. She had come with a small delegation of Gatakas and Kiowas who brought horses for the Cheyennes to trade for them up north. With her were her two brothers, Daha and Däveko. Eaglenest had accompanied them for the short journey from camps on the Arkansas River to the North Fork of the Republican River, where the Hovxnovas had spent winter and spring. She had not been the only female among the Gatakas and Kiowas, and Stone had paid no attention to any of them. It would have been improper, even insulting, for him or any strange male to do so. On the third day of the visitors' presence in the Hovxnova camp, Stone and Eaglenest passed each other on a trail to the river. The girl had filled a water jar, while Stone was just walking with nothing special in mind. Each had stopped politely for a moment, looking at the other. Their eyes met, gazing deep, losing themselves in the other's eyes, falling in, falling. For what seemed a long time their gaze held, then Eaglenest bashfully bowed her head and quickly walked away, while Stone stood, stunned, his eyes following the lithe figure until she vanished in the chokecherry shrubs.

For him and for her, as he later learned, it had been the same unexpected, unique experience: the complete, unquestioned recognition of the other's being. The Cheyenne word for love is *mehosanistoz*, a word rarely ever spoken because the people are shy in expressing deep emotional feelings. But this was what Stone felt. From then on, every chance he got he watched the girl as she quietly and efficiently worked among Gatakas, doing women's chores. He learned her name, translated as Nizevós in Cheyenne, Eaglenest, and her age, twenty-one. Before the visitors left, he talked with her brothers and told them that he wanted to marry their sister.

It was the older brother, Daha, as was the custom among the tribes, who would decide the issue more than the parents, if the sister agreed to marry the man who asked for her. Stone remembers the meeting; a man of his band fluent in Gataka had translated for him. Daha responded that he had to talk first with his sister. He said that he was honored by Stone's asking. He knew that Stone was a headman and widely respected among the Cheyennes, with a good reputation among Gatakas and Kiowas too. But he was worried over Stone's role as headman: the first into a fight, the last to withdraw. "Are you going to make my sister a widow next year?" he had asked bluntly.

Stone remembers that he had smiled and said it was up to the spirits whether to protect him or take him away. He had also said that he would never leave her and never take another woman. If Eaglenest wanted him for her husband and he, Daha, consented, he would come for her in the fall after the Hovxnovas returned from the Missouri River.

On the day when Gatakas and Kiowas broke camp, Daha rode over and told Stone that he was welcome to visit their camp in the fall. That was all that was necessary to say. When the Gatakas rode away, Eaglenest cast one last look into Stone's eyes. Not a word had been exchanged between them, and they had not been alone again for a moment, but both were eager for fall.

In September, after the battle with the Kitkahaki Pawnees, Stone rode south, alone. Custom requires that a prospective son-in-law make gifts to the girl's parents to show his appreciation. For a yet undistinguished young man the expense of the gifts expected could be challenging, ranging from four to a dozen horses or something of equivalent value. For a man of Stone's stature, gifts were considered a matter of minor importance. Nevertheless, on the war horse he led on a rope, beside his weapons, were tied two muskets, packages with powder and lead and tobacco, dry goods, trade beads, and a copper kettle.

He looked first for the Ka'ta camp of Kiowas and found it on Fountain Creek at the foot of the Rocky Mountains. In his brother's and Sendehma's tipi he had admired their baby girl, Gondaima, and later explained the purpose of his journey and asked them to mediate for him. They rode to the camp of the Guantekana band of Gatakas, fifteen miles to the southeast on the upper Arkansas River. Unknown sources had already signaled their coming. When they got to Daha's tipi, they were expected. First they ate together, then Daha took them to his parents' lodge. They went in: Daha, Stone, Whirlwind, Sendehma with the baby. Sendehma translated from Cheyenne into Gataka. Stone explained himself and asked for Eaglenest. Goñkõn, Eaglenest's father, and Tsach, her mother, both appearing reserved, then sympathetic, consented. Daha and Whirlwind went outside and brought Stone's gifts in and placed them next to the fireplace. They were looked at but not touched. Daha went back out and brought Eaglenest into the tipi.

Stone remembers, cherishes, the moment. The pretty face framed with braids that reach nearly to the belt, wrapped with streamers in red cloth. The fringed white buckskin dress worked with delicate quillwork designs on shoulders, breasts, and sleeves in red, green, and blue. White moccasin boots, the tops quilled in a diagonal pattern in green and red. A broad buckskin belt with a blue lightning design in quillwork. Eyes blinking at him, then shyly lowered, she stood there as if she were all alone.

There was a brief ceremony that evening, and then the couple retired to a tipi set up for them. There the two finally came together. After a feast on the day following, Stone and his wife rode west into the mountains toward the headwaters of the Arkansas to where the aspens, their leaves turned, stood in golden splendor.

Stone looks at her now. She has spread a blanket and is cutting meat. He feels the same for her as he did during those weeks in the aspens a year ago, and he thinks that he always will. She looks up and sees him looking at her and she smiles. Perhaps she knows what he is thinking.

The first Spanish place they come to is the Santuario de Plateros. The church is in the middle of a cluster of adobe huts and can barely be seen. Streets leading to the church are lined with stalls selling religious artifacts, especially the gaudily painted figure of a small child. Pilgrims are everywhere; many are camping and sit around fires on which food is prepared. Some horses and mules are tied up around tents. The people Stone sees are mostly Indian and poor. As they slowly ride by, an Indian passes with the boy figure of Jesus in his hand. Stone points and Maria asks him. He answers in broken Spanish and holds the figure up. It is the image of an infant holding a staff and basket and wearing a pilgrim's feathered hat. Stone looks at the wrinkled face under the straw hat as the man speaks the name of the figure, "El Santo Niño de Atocha." Stone nods to him. Maria thanks him, and as he walks away with his treasure she explains to Eaglenest.

"This is the place Maria told us about," Eaglenest says. "The Santuario, the holy shrine. The church over there is the shrine. The figure the man showed us depicts the holy child, El Santo Niño, Jesus. But it was not the real figure. The real figure is on a table in the church."

"If this is a boy, why does he have a basket and a staff and wear a girl's dress?" Stone asks.

Eaglenest passes the question to Maria. Maria shrugs; she does not know. Stone wonders about the figure these people pray to but keeps his thoughts to himself.

The Santuario and Fresnillo are situated on a wide plain. As they ride the two miles to Fresnillo they meet groups of pilgrims on the road, walking, some singing. To the west lies the dark shadow of the Sierra Madre Occidental, running north to south, reminding Stone of the Rocky Mountains as seen from the headwaters of the Republican River. Fresnillo is a grimy mining town. It lies at the foot of the isolated knoll of Proaño, pocked with the black holes and yellow tailing heaps of mines, most no longer worked. Before they reach the town they pass fruit orchards and large cornfields covered with dead whitish stalks. They ride into the main street, a narrow track with adobe huts and wooden shacks on both sides, similar to what they have seen in Saltillo. But the street is empty, and when they get to the main plaza, with the church of Nuestra Señora de la Purificación on its north side, the market is closed. They have arrived at the wrong time. Merchandise on stalls is covered with cloth. Vendors lie behind their booths asleep or resting, or sit, two or three together, talking. Stone does not understand what is going on.

Maria explains through Eaglenest. "It is custom that every day after the midday meal people in Spanish towns and villages rest, sleep. It is called siesta. All shops, all buildings are closed during this time. No work is done. Siesta lasts for two hours."

Maria shrugs. This has to be endured. They dismount on the edge of the plaza and water the horses from a duct of running water. They sit down in the shade of a tree. They look like so many others. Stone is impatient. Finally he asks Maria to walk around and ask questions.

He and Eaglenest watch as Maria proceeds among the stalls, approaching groups of persons who sit idle, talking, some smoking. She walks slowly, stopping, talking, moving on. It takes a while until she comes back. She is beaming.

"The circo has been here," she says. "First it went from here to Zacatecas, then came back and went north. I was told that it went to Sombrerete, a town north of here."

She pauses, waiting for Eaglenest to translate.

"I know the name of the circo. It is called El Circo de Parral. The man who owns the circo is Don Lorenzo de Avila. He is a creole, a white man born in this country." And now she smiles broadly. "The norteño who throws the knives is still with the circo."

Stone listens to the translation. His face shows no emotion. He nods. He has understood. Another town, he thinks, and then another. How many more until the warriors want to quit?

"How far is the circo ahead of us?" he asks.

Maria shakes her head. "No one could tell me exactly when the circo was here. Some say three moons ago. Some say two." She thinks about Stone's question. "I think the distance from here to Saltillo and some more. But the good thing is that the circo is going north, maybe back to Parral, and not south. On its way north we catch it."

Stone listens. "Parral?"

"A town north, maybe eight days' ride if we could ride on the road openly. But we will catch the circo before it reaches Parral."

Stone nods glumly. He thinks about the next town they have to see, Sombrerete. Another of these places in a dead land. They all look alike. He looks at the two women.

"Shall we wait and buy some pinole for food?" Maria asks.

"Pewe." So they sit and let time pass like everyone else on the plaza, and when the market opens again Maria buys two bags of pinole and they ride out of Fresnillo and past the Santuario and take the trail back. The moon is hidden by a blanket of clouds, and they camp for the night near the trail. It is a dark camp without the cheerful sparkle of a fire.

• • •

When they reach the ranch near midmorning, they arrive at the end of a funeral. On the slope behind the stone house the ranchero and two of his men shovel earth into a grave pit. A wailing woman and a child kneel in front of the grave. Lame Bear and Yellow Eyes sit their horses nearby, watching. As Stone, Eaglenest, and Maria ride into the compound, Stone makes for Necklace, who is perched on a wooden plank atop the corral in which the prisoners are held. Women and children in the corral stand stiffly on the side of the corral facing the burial. Some are crying. On the slope the work is finished, and the ranchero stands a rough wooden cross at the head of the low mound.

"What happened?" Stone asks Necklace.

"Last night one man crept from the stone house to the horse corral. He was shot when he was getting on a horse."

"Who shot him?"

"Red Bird."

Stone nods. He watches as the two Cheyennes drive the burial party from the grave and toward the corral. The woman resists; Lame

Bear uses his horse to force her away. The men drop the shovels as they pass the stone house. The woman, clutching her child, is still crying, and the men look distressed when they file into the corral. Necklace closes the gate behind them.

"We have to have a meeting," Stone says.

They sit in a circle by the creek with a view of the prisoners' corral, the women behind the men. Stone has informed them about the visit to Fresnillo. "The circo has gone north," he concludes. "The next town we have to see is called Sombrerete. The circo is from the town of Parral, farther north. We believe that the circo is going there."

"How far away are we from the circo?" Holy Singer asks.

Stone shrugs. "I don't know. Maybe half a moon."

"Are you saying that we meet with the circo in half a moon?" Sendehma asks. She sits behind to his right, beside Eaglenest.

Stone turns and looks into her bright, wide open eyes. He nods. "I think so, sister. That is not so long now. If the spirits are good to us, we will get my brother soon." He pauses. "And then we go for Spanish horses, lots of them, and we ride home the way we came in, through what the Spanish call the Bolsón." He grins.

"We don't like to ride at night," Little Bird says. "What are we afraid of?"

"We are not afraid of anything," Stone says brusquely. "But we don't want to announce that we are coming, where we are going. Have patience. Our night rides will be over soon."

He pauses, looking at the sand in front of his knees, then looking at faces before him. "We stay in this place today and for three more days." He pauses. "We kill enough sheep for food to last us ten days. When we leave here, we leave before sundown and get past Fresnillo by sunrise, close to that other town, Sombrerete."

He looks from face to face. "Agreed?" There is a murmur of support.

The meeting breaks up. A few warriors ride down and drive about forty ewes to the ranch and into the barn. The prisoners look on as the sheep are brought out two at a time and are slaughtered by the creek and dressed out by the women. Men help with the cutting, and thinly sliced strips of meat are hung to dry on lines stretched between trees. It takes most of the day to finish the work. For the evening meal Maria and Lucia have a surprise. They discovered an iron plate in the shed and have built an open-air kitchen. They rest two edges on stones and keep a good fire going under the plate. From the cornmeal Maria bought in Fresnillo the two women pat out tortillas and prepare burritos filled with roasted mutton. Skeptical Cheyennes try the strange food. When Maria spices the burritos with chile taken from the stone house, Cheyenne men and the women cautiously have a taste but reject this dish; the red powder is too hot for their liking.

In the afternoon of the last day they break camp and get the horses ready. On the packhorses, along with the supply of mutton, ride bags of tortillas Maria and Lucia have prepared for the journey. Stone tells Lame Bear to bring the ranchero over to him.

They sit by the creek—Stone, Sendehma, and Maria. Stone gestures to the ranchero to sit with them. The man seats himself slowly, reluctantly. His face shows that he is worried. He has seen that the norteños are preparing to leave but wonders what they will do before they leave.

Stone recognizes the man's apprehension. He bends and places three gold coins from the bandits' hoard in front of him. "Tell him that this is for the sheep we took from him." Sendehma translates to Maria, and Maria explains to the ranchero in Spanish.

The man looks at the coins, at Stone, at the two women. He cannot believe it. His face relaxes. He shakes his head. He speaks rapidly to Maria in Spanish. Maria translates and Sendehma says, "He does not want that money."

"He has to take it," Stone says. "We are not bandidos. Tell him that."

The man listens. He strokes his mustache, thinking. He spreads his hands in a gesture indicating that he complies.

Stone nods. "Tell him that we need something from him. We need him to be our guide. He has to take us where we need to go. We don't know the country. We need to know what he knows. He will not be harmed. When we have what we are looking for, I will let him go."

When Sendehma speaks to Maria, the ranchero is watching, puzzled. When Maria is halfway through the Spanish he seems to come apart. His face sags. He tries to say something, but no word comes from his lips.

"Tell him again," Stone says. "We need him as a guide. He has to take us somewhere. Then we let him go."

Maria talks slowly and patiently to the man. His glittering eyes under the bushy brows watch Stone. It is not hard to imagine what the ranchero thinks. How can I refuse? These norteños already killed one of my men; if I say no they might kill me and all of us. He looks helplessly to the ground, at the coins. How could I get into this? What have I done to justify this? He breathes hard. He looks up and nods. He tells Maria that he will do it.

Stone listens. "Pewe. Now tell him that he will be the first to die if he leads us into trouble! He must tell his people that he will be away for some time, that they must not inform anyone about this. If they do, and if soldiers come after us, he will die."

When Maria has ended, the man agrees quickly, trying to please. Stone makes a gesture of dismissal. When he gets up he leaves the coins lying on the ground. Stone picks them up and tosses them to him, one after the other. The man catches them. Before he walks away, Stone tells him to get ready, to pack and saddle his horse.

They let the prisoners out before they leave. The ranchero's wife holds on to her husband's saddle, crying. Powderface pulls her off, and the column sets in motion. They ride in the formation adopted earlier: eight men in front, seven men in the rear, the women with the packhorses between them. Stone takes the trail southwest toward Plateros that he had traveled with Eaglenest and Maria. As they ride in single file, the ranchero is behind Stone and in front of Powderface. To the west the sun is sinking toward the crest of the Sierra Madre Occidental, but it will be light for a while longer. Set, as always, explores the trail ahead, his nose to the ground.

Riding, they see high desert vegetation but no animals. Tarbush, yucca, and cacti, the occasional mesquite, seem lost and forlorn in this their land as if its spirit is gone. Even the chatter of birds is rare, as if they are afraid to disturb the silence. There is a light wind from the south. They see nothing of humans. When the sun drops behind the Sierra Madre, Stone halts the column. As the riders tighten the girths of their horses, Stone and Powderface tie the ranchero's hands behind his back. Stone slips the sling of a reata over the man's head and wraps the lower end around the horn of his saddle; there is no way the captive can escape in the dark. When they ride on, Stone lets the ranchero take the lead. Thus they continue for about four hours before halting to give the horses a rest. Stone takes the noose from around the captive's neck and helps him from the saddle. They stand and sit for a while, then mount up and ride on, the ranchero first, as before. It is not yet first light when they get near Plateros.

Stone halts the column. He calls for Maria and Sendehma. He asks the ranchero, "Where is the road to Sombrerete?" Under a waning moon they sit their horses close together. "Half a legua west of here," the man says. His hands are bound, so he points with his chin.

"Take us there," Stone says.

They ride around Plateros, a quiet place at night, and take the side road that angles northwest and connects with the main road. They arrive and halt. Stone asks, "Is this the road that goes to Sombrerete?"

"Yes," the ranchero says. "It is called El Camino Real. It goes all the way north to Nuevo Mexico and Santa Fe, south to Mexico City. But two leguas north of here there is a fork. A road goes north to Rancho Grande and Cuencamé and the Río de Nazas, but El Camino Real goes northwest to Sombrerete."

"How far from here to Sombrerete?"

It is some time before the ranchero answers. "Twenty leguas. Perhaps less."

"Fifty miles," Maria says.

Stone nods at her.

"About a good day's ride."

Stone is thinking. "Have you been to those places, Sombrerete, that other place, Cuencamé?" he asks the man.

"Yes. El Camino Real makes a wide swing west, north of the fork toward Sombrerete and Durango. I have been on that part of the road."

Stone is wondering. "If the road goes west, north of here, could we ride west and north from here and get close to Sombrerete that way? We need a good place to stay out of sight. Do you know any?"

He listens as Sendehma and Maria translate his question. After they are through, there is a long silence. Finally the man says: "Yes, we can ride west across the river and north to a little lake in the mountains. Indians used to live there. They were called los Tepehuanes. They are gone now. I know the place."

Stone waits. "How far to the lake?"

The man looks east where first light has not yet shown. "Three hours, four hours."

Stone has made up his mind. "Take us there."

He lifts the reata noose from around the man's neck, and the column gets in motion again. They cross the Camino Real and make for the fast little stream the Spanish call the Rio Grande and cross and take a trail that leads northwest. This is hilly country, stony ground. They are in the foothills of the Sierra Madre. They see no one except once some cattle to the south, a curl of smoke far away, and when the trail snakes westward the ranchero leads them straight north. They come to a small creek, an outlet of the lake that carries water to the river they have crossed earlier, and follow it and get to the small lake framed by a horseshoe of mountains fifteen miles southeast of Sombrerete as the raven flies. The risen sun stands low in the sky. Around the lake grows a belt of reeds with willows and mesquite, and on the slopes stand ocotillos and a sprinkle of pines, the first they have seen for what seems a long time. Stone sends Necklace around the lake. When he returns, he reports deer tracks and some remains of old huts, but no recent evidence of humans. They make camp above the reeds on the eastern shore.

• • •

It is midafternoon, and the men and women are awake. Some inspect the horses; others toy with equipment or sit together, talking. Stone has decided to tell the prisoner the purpose of their journey. He thinks it better to ask for his cooperation than to have him along as a silent enemy. He has called for a meeting. White River, who has been on guard for the last three hours, comes down from his post up on the slope where he has watched the opening of the horseshoe and the area to the south. Men and women have gathered on level ground and, as always, form a tight circle so that everyone can take part. The prisoner, his hands freed, is placed near the center of the circle. He is tense, edgy, afraid of what might happen next. Sendehma and Maria sit at Stone's right.

First Stone tells the man again that they do not wish to harm him, that he will be let go after they have accomplished what they are after. Then he explains that they track a circus that holds his brother prisoner. After his brother is freed, they will let the ranchero return to his family—but only then. If he wants to see his family again, he must help them find the circus.

The man has listened to Maria's translation with an intent expression, absorbing every word. After Maria has ended, he sits motionless at first, thinking, then seems to loosen up. He looks at Stone, expecting to be questioned. But he has a question of his own. He seems no longer as afraid. "What is the name of the circo?" he asks.

Maria answers directly. "El Circo de Parral. Have you seen it?"

The man shakes his head. "No. I have never heard of it."

Maria speaks to Sendehma, who translates for all present. "He knows nothing about the circo."

Stone nods. "Tell him we have tracked the circo from Saltillo to Fresnillo. In Fresnillo we heard that the circo has gone to Sombrerete." Both he and Sendehma have difficulties pronouncing the names of the towns, but Maria speaks the names perfectly in the Castilian Spanish that she was taught by the Franciscan.

"We know that the circo is going north, we think back to where it came from, Parral," Stone continues. "How does the circo go there from Sombrerete?"

The man swallows, his face earnest. He gets up, looking over the ground, apparently searching for a twig or something. Little Bird tosses him his knife. He picks it up and steps back. He looks for two small rocks. He places them on the ground two paces apart. He points to the first one. "Sombrerete." He looks around and repeats the name. He points to the second rock. "Durango." He draws two lines in the sand with the knife, starting at the first rock, ending at the second one. "Two roads to Durango. One goes northwest from Sombrerete to Durango through Mateo Gomez and Conception."

He waits for the translation. Everyone in the circle is engrossed in the map being drawn in the sand. "The other road goes straight west from Sombrerete, then northwest," the man continues. "It goes through Calabazal and Nombre de Dios and meets with the other road."

He waits again, looks around the circle, then at Stone.

When Sendehma has ended the translation, Stone asks, "How far from Sombrerete to Durango?"

The ranchero strokes his mustache. He spreads his hands. "Twenty-five leguas."

Maria counts quickly. "Sixty-five miles." She pauses. "One and a half day ride."

All listen quietly to Sendehma's rewording in Cheyenne.

"Where is Parral from Durango?" Stone asks.

The man listens to Sendehma and to Maria repeating the question. He scratches his head and walks beyond the Durango rock to the edge of the circle. He stabs the knife in the ground. "Parral," he says.

There is a groan from Necklace. So far—how far do we still have to ride? A murmur around the circle. The warriors think the same.

"How does the circo go from Durango to Parral?" Stone asks, unmoved.

The man pulls the knife from the ground and walks back to the Durango rock. "There are two roads." He waits. He cuts a line from Durango northwest. "The circo could take either one. This one goes through Canatlán and Santiago and across the Río de Nazas." He waits again for the translation. He bends and marks a line from Durango straight north. "This one goes through Choro and Panuco to the Río de Nazas." He looks at Maria and Sendehma and listens to Sendehma's Cheyenne words.

A thoughtful silence. Stone breaks it. He addresses his men. He grins. "We know that the circo is going north on one road or the other. That's where we want it to go. That's where we take horses after we have captured the circo." He pauses. "That river, Nazas, we have been there. Both roads go there. We know how to get home from there. It won't be long now."

He looks around. He can read through the impassive faces of his warriors, restrained faces, masks. He knows that some are doubtful, that most are tired of the journey, but he knows that they still trust him, that he can rely on them.

He has two more questions of the ranchero. "How do I get from here to Sombrerete?"

The man points to the western crags of the horseshoe of mountains surrounding the lake. "Around that mountain, jefe. Behind that mountain you turn north. There is a trail, I believe. It goes to Sombrerete or to the Camino Real that goes to Sombrerete."

"Sombrerete, how far from here?"

The ranchero shrugs. "Not far, five leguas."

"An easy morning ride," Maria tells Sendehma.

Now Little Bird speaks up. He is a Red Shield soldier, not a Kit Fox. He is not bound to Stone as his headman. He and his brother, Red Bird, have given their loyalty freely as cousins of Magpie, killed when Whirlwind was captured. They both took the pipe with Stone to avenge Magpie and free their boyhood companion, Whirlwind. Now Little Bird looks straight at Stone. He speaks with a quiet, straightforward voice. "Brother, we have come a long way together. We still have a long way before us. We grow restless. We want this to be over soon. We ache to get back to our own country, our people. We ask you to think about that when you ride to that Spanish town tomorrow."

Powderface has the last word. He says what everyone knows. "The horses are worn out. They need a rest and plenty of food. The way they are now we could not escape an enemy if we had to. They still walk, that's all. If we get into a fight we cannot depend on them anymore. We need new horses, fresh horses. If we don't get them, we'll have to go on foot. We won't get the circo that way."

All eyes seek Stone. He sits thinking. Powderface is right. I have been obsessed with the circo and neglected everything else. We have to get fresh horses or we will not make it. I have failed in my responsibility.

He nods and looks along the faces before him. "Yes. This is my fault. I should have known. We will get the horses we need. Pewe." He makes the gesture with his hand. "Give me a few more days, then we'll go after horses. Agreed?" There is a murmur of support. The band has agreed to a few more days.

SEVENTEEN

Stone leaves at first light. With him are Eaglenest, Maria, and Big Bow. His brother begged to go with them. After he showed that his light shoulder wound was healing well, and that he has full use of his right arm, Stone relented. He suddenly becomes aware once again that he has neglected Big Bow, expressing concern only for his lost twin. He thinks this is how Big Bow might feel. He pledges to himself that he will bring him closer, involve him more. Both men carry concealed bow-and-arrow cases on their horses, wrapped inconspicuously in cloth. The two women and the brothers are dressed in costumes taken from the bandits.

Before they left, Stone stressed that the ranchero be guarded at all times and tied up at night. And he reminded his men to take all necessary precautions usual on a raid and that, if he was not back in five days, they should quit and head north to the Nazas River and home.

Stone and his three companions leave camp without looking back. In the Cheyenne way of thinking, as it is with Gatakas and Kiowas, to look back betrays a premonition that one might not return, or, worse yet, might produce that result. They pass along the reeds on the eastern shore and below the lower end of the lake cross the creek and follow the swerve of the mountain, first south, then west, and ride on and come to a trail that bends northwest, and take it. They ride through high stony ridges, mountains on both sides rising to over nine thousand feet. Behind, to the west, lies the dark mass of the Sierra Madre. The trail seems to be in regular if sparse use; most recent tracks of mules and some sandal footprints are at least a week old. They ride at a brisk clip and see no one until the trail melts into the Camino Real. Before them, to the west, lies the mountain called Sombreretillo, "little hat," because of a rock formation on top that resembles a sombrero. At the foot of the mountain sits the mining town of Sombrerete.

There is not much traffic on the king's road. They pass a group of Indian men, walking with packs on their backs, two oxen-drawn caretas with squeaking wheels, and, coming toward them, a Brown Robe with a young Indian woman servant, both on mules, and a coach drawn by four fine horses with two heavily armed, stone-faced coachmen high on the box. Maria glares at the Brown Robe with disdain; it is as if an unpleasant part of her past has come alive. They come to the main street into town, a gaping hole between old stone houses, and they ride in and clatter up on a narrowing street. There are few people around. In the entrance of a massive old stone building they see a Brown Robe talk to an old woman covered with a rebozo. This is the Franciscan convent of San Mateo, but they pay it no heed and ride on and get to the plaza in front of the Templo de Santo Domingo.

The plaza shows the typical arrangement of stalls and carts and animals, of criers praising their wares. Loudest are the incessant shouts of "Pulque! Pulque dulce! Pulque bueno!" Even Stone, hostile to everything Spanish, especially Spanish settlements and towns, realizes that the flavor of this town is different from that of Saltillo and Fresnillo, more intimate, subtle, cleaner. But he has come to this place for one reason only—to find out about the circus. So he leads his little group to an empty spot near the *templo,* and they dismount and he sends Maria off to ask questions.

Stone, Eaglenest, and Big Bow sit and wait. Big Bow, who is seeing a Spanish town for the first time, surveys the strange sights, the bustle of people, the stone architecture, with wide open eyes. He listens to sounds he has never heard before. He watches with the eyes of a hunter, always, unconsciously calculating movement and distance. He is somewhat impressed with what he sees, yet not sure what to make of it. What he sees is big but confined. Houses seem to fall into one another. Except for the plaza, there is no open space as in the

Arikara and Mandan towns on the Missouri River, no air, no open sky. These Spanish in front of him are either loud and boisterous or seem sullen, subdued, shriveled within themselves. He is a complete outsider thrust into an alien way of life. He feels his brother's eyes on the back of his head. He turns and shrugs and shakes his head, his gestures saying, I don't know what to say. Stone nods, knowingly, and again scans the throng in the plaza into which Maria has disappeared.

They do not have to wait long. Maria returns, walking fast, beaming. She speaks rapidly in Kiowa to Eaglenest, who translates for the brothers. "Yes, the circo has been here. People said that it went to Durango after two evening performances in this plaza. They were not sure on what road. It could be that they took the road northwest to Mateo Gomez. There are seven or eight haciendas on that road. The circo probably visited all of them."

"My brother is still with the circo?" Stone asks.

"Yes. Throwing knives at a woman on a wheel. They said that."

Stone ponders the situation. "How far from here to that place, Gomez?"

"I asked," Maria says. "Perhaps six leguas." Quickly she adds, "We could make that hacienda by midday."

"Pewe," Stone says. "Let's ride there."

They leave Sombrerete in the opposite direction from their entry, past the plaza, Maria leading, and at the western edge of town once again get to the Camino Real. They take it to a fork a short distance away where the king's road arches west and a smaller road angles to the northeast. "This must be the one to Mateo Gomez," Maria says, pointing to the smaller one, and they switch to it.

An empty road. Much traveled during harvest time, connecting the haciendas farther up with Sombrerete and Durango, the road presently seems not much in use. Tracks on it are at least a few days old. Ruts are carved into the sand by caretas and wagon wheels, perhaps including some made by the carts of the circus. Stone looks them over but sees no distinguishing features that could be remembered. Under a full sun they ride through high desert country with sand flats and rock-strewn ridges, with mesquites in low places and yuccas reaching up on the heights. After about six miles they see strange rock formations to the west, a series of fantastic hogbacks that run north for twenty miles. Ahead, the road edges toward this unusual sierra, and as they get closer they see a jumble of dark canyon lands, some heights with white bands and steep, broken, hard mountains and on some of their peaks tall pillars of stone standing side by side.

Stone signals a halt, and they sit their horses and look. "Good places to hide in," he says and points with his chin. They gaze and ride on along the front of the magic mountains and make the hacienda at midday as Maria has said they would. Mateo Gomez lies by a small stream that runs in from a mountain range to the southeast and curves north to west until it drops into the Río Mesquital southeast of Durango. Along the course of the stream are eight more haciendas, using the fertile valley for growing crops of chile, beans, corn, tobacco, and barley. Mateo Gomez is surrounded by fields on both sides of the stream. They now lie fallow. The main structure of the hacienda is a wide, white stone building with windows and balconies, a broad staircase leading up to a portal behind a terrace roofed over with wooden beams. Three horses are tied up next to the staircase. A chapel with a bell tower sits next to the main house on the right. Large wooden stone houses stand in a row to the left. Beyond the chapel are horse barns and, partly hidden, rows of huts for the laborers of the estate and their families. Few people can be seen. At the foot of the staircase three women wrapped in rebozos sit with two small children between them. Stone sends Maria to them while he and his wife and Big Bow stay back.

They watch as Maria approaches the women and dismounts gracefully. There is a brief conversation and then she mounts and rides back. "The circo was here," she says. "The women have seen it."

Stone waits. Then, "How long ago?"

"Less than one moon ago," Maria says. "That is all they could say."

Stone nods. "Aho." He smiles at his companions. "Now let us get back to the lake."

They ride into camp in early evening.

• • •

As the sun sinks behind the Sierra Madre, men and women sit once again together. Stone has told what he has learned. He has answered a few questions, and now he thinks about the mountain range northwest of Sombrerete. His eyes search for the ranchero. He sits behind Powderface. Stone waves him over and points to a place within the circle. He gets up and walks through between Powderface and Porcupine and sits down. This time Eaglenest, and Maria, are ready to translate.

"We took the trail from Sombrerete to Gomez," Stone says, addressing the ranchero. "Northwest of that town Sombrerete we saw mountains that look special. What are they?"

The man listens to Maria's Spanish. "Yes." He nods eagerly; his head bobs up and down. "The Sierra de Organos."

"Who lives there?" Stone asks.

The ranchero shrugs. "No one." He thinks for a moment. "Bandidos sometimes. Indians sometimes; Indians who have run away from haciendas or the mines." He pauses. "I don't know anyone who has ever been there. People say it is dangerous."

Stone nods. "Aho." He dismisses the ranchero with a movement of his hand. As the man trudges away, Stone speaks to his band. "We went by these mountains. I think they are a good place to hide in for a few days. There must be water in there somewhere." He pauses. "You stay there when I ride to Durango to find out which road north the circo has taken."

He looks over his men. This is the moment to speak up, but no one does. He sees that some nod in agreement; others just sit and look at him.

"Pewe," he says. "We leave here after midnight and get to these mountains at first light. We look for a good campsite on the west side of the mountains, not far from the road."

The meeting breaks up. After nightfall the four women from the Plains build fires and prepare mutton while Maria and Lucia make tortillas using heated stones as cooking surfaces. Earlier they have watered the horses and filled water bags. The leave under a waning moon. They ride in the proven three-group formation. Stone and Big Bow, who know the trail, lead. They reach the Camino Real without incident, circle north of Sombrerete, and take the Mateo Gomez trail. At first light they have the Sierra de Organos before them, continue for eight more miles, and ride into a canyon that takes them northwest within the mountain chain.

They ride slowly, looking around. Under a brilliant blue sky the naked mountain tops are purplish gray. The higher slopes are dotted with creosote bushes, lechuguilla agave, and cacti in many different forms. Lower slopes, in addition to the ever-present cacti, have tarbush with creosote bushes, the spindly arms of ocotillos, giant soaptree yuccas, coarse tobosa grass. The riders have seen similar country before. They look for tracks but see few, mostly of deer and coyote, once the pug marks of a big cat, either puma or jaguar. Later, hoofprints of horses, coming from the right, going into a narrow canyon to the left, weeks old. Later still, the scattered remains of a few crude shelters of brush, ashes, barely visible, from a camp an unknown time ago. The bed of a rivulet on the canyon floor, running with water during other seasons, is dry. After a few miles Stone takes an opening to the west. Slowly the Organos change their appearance. White and yellow and red sands, boulders strewn over the bottom of the canyon, steep white and yellow and red cliffs and heights that stand yellow against the blue sky. They ride into a wonderland of color and bizarre rock formations.

The Cheyennes present as well as Eaglenest and Sendehma have seen places like these: the multicolored broken country southeast of the Black Hills. And some have seen the breaks of the Missouri River or the mysterious yellow and red rock formations near the head of Fountain Creek inside the edge of the Rocky Mountains, a few miles north of Cheyenne Mountain—places of awe and inspiration, places where one feels the presence of spirits most intensely, places where it appears natural to worship. They ride on, and when they come to an open place from where the canyons lead west and north, Stone calls for a halt. He dismounts and so do the others. He calls on Powderface, who is not only a powerful warrior but a *zemaheonevsz,* a man who serves the sacred, to speak to the spirits of this place and ask for protection and a successful journey.

The men and women of the party have formed a half circle behind Powderface, who has turned to the east. They stand with bowed heads looking to the ground. Sendehma and Bear Doctor Woman hold their girls before them. As Maria and Lucia, their children, and the ranchero look on, Powderface first prays in a quiet voice, then sings a somber, plain song addressed to the spirits. He ends crying. Stone says "Aho," and the others join in.

They move into the shade below a vertical red rock wall to rest the horses and wait. Stone sends out two scouts to explore the canyon that leads west and two to follow the canyon that twists north. He tells them to look for water and a good campsite. The scouts who went north return after an hour. They have found a permanent pool of clear water at the base of two sandstone rock faces, and have ridden a few miles farther but seen no traces of humans. The scouts who went west take longer to return. They went as far as the end of the canyon where it opens to desert flats. There, to the southwest, they have seen smoke from a few huts surrounded by holding pens. They have found no water.

When Stone asks the ranchero about the settlement, he calls it by its name, "Corales," a place where cattle and sheep and horses, which roam widely dispersed throughout the year, are corralled every fall. Stone decides to make camp near the pool. The sands around it are like a book containing tracks of all animals in the area. Most conspicuous are pug marks of two big cats, perhaps a male and a female puma or jaguar. Camp is made around a rock slide out of sight of the pool, about two hundred paces away to let animals have access to water. They are under the protection of the spirits of these mountains. The pool's water, under a rock overhang not reached by the sun, is clear and cool. The horses are confined to a brushy area with some tobosa grass and hobbled. In Cheyenne the puma is called *nanoseham,* the "leaper" or "pouncer," and is considered a horse killer. Guards climb to overlooks. The women prepare a cold meal. After they have eaten, they sit for a while and talk, inspired by the magic of the place. When they finally get to sleep, it is late afternoon.

EIGHTEEN

Stone remembers seeing him like this before. Whirlwind. He rides a spotted horse, its mane flying like Whirlwind's hair, a black swirl behind his head. He rides bareback, barefoot, even his breechclout lifting in the wind. He rides fast and splashes through a shallow river, the water a glittering vapor around the horse. Behind is a dark, green wall of cottonwoods beneath a deep blue sky. He is a boy, impetuous, tempestuous. The world is fresh, new, offering itself like a gift, a promise. And then Whirlwind stands looking at him. He is old. No, he is not, but he looks different. His face is drawn, haggard, his eyes burning like coals from a glowing fire. He wears a white shirt and white trousers. His hair is carefully braided. By his side a woman, young, with long black hair, dressed like the Toboso women he has seen, like Lucia. Whirlwind holds her by the hand. They both look at him, the woman with huge, dark eyes, confident but shy. She is pregnant. Whirlwind speaks to him, but he cannot understand a word. Whirlwind seems to speak louder and louder and then bends forward, his face coming close to Stone's face. There is no anger in the face, perhaps a passionate appeal to be heard, to be understood. And then Whirlwind steps back and from out of nowhere the woman hands him a dozen knives with wooden handles, the blades shining. Now Whirlwind smiles and points. Behind him a solid wooden wheel of dark wood with holds for hands and feet. What is it? Whirlwind points again and starts to turn—then there is a sudden noise and Stone wakes up.

He looks around. It is dark, and he feels more than sees the sleepers bundled around him. He hears. It is Set howling his midnight song outside the camp. Wolf sounds, rising and falling, melodious. And then comes an answer floating in from the north. One wolf answers, two, a whole pack sings.

Stone sits, still dreaming. Whirlwind was so close he could have touched his face had he tried. Did he try but does not remember? What was it that he saw? Did his brother try to tell him something? Did he want to show him the woman at his side? Stone stares into the dark. Whirlwind is alive and a woman is with him bearing a child. His child?

Stone lies awake for a long time looking up at Seàmeo, the Milky Way, the Hanging Road. A cool wind brushes his face. Not yet; we are not traveling there yet, you and I.

Sendehma. Sendehma, what will you say?

• • •

At first light they ride again, Stone and Big Bow, Eaglenest and Maria. Before they left Stone told his men to have a little more patience, that their days of inactivity were coming to an end. He is convinced of this. His dream he keeps to himself, however. When the four ride out, the two Cheyenne women, She-Wolf and Bear Doctor Woman, stand at the edge of camp and sing a Cheyenne wolf song, an encouragement for scouts departing for enemy country.

Honehena	Wolf I am
aenonevhaneo	in darkness
evepananoeva	in light
nohast'sa nanoxzeva	wherever I search
nohast'sa naameneoxz	wherever I run
nohast'sa nanhe	wherever I stand
nitaovae	everything
zepeva	will be good
. . . . . .	. . . .
. . . . . .	. . . .

They ride with the song in their minds and hearts. Set runs with them until they pass the pool. Three does are drinking there, and Set cannot resist chasing them until they climb a cliff. He is only toying with them, though; the chase is in his blood. They ride the short distance to where the canyon they had explored the day before opens on the west side, and enter it. For over an hour they ride on the sands on the bottom of the canyon, around massive boulders that have fallen in from the red and yellow walls. When they reach the opening they come once again into broken high desert country, with cacti and tobosa grass between rocks, yucca, and sotol, rare soaptree yuccas standing as lonely guardians. They see the smoke of Corales and turn northwest toward the Mateo Gomez road where it curves south and continues northwest to join the Camino Real. Occasionally they see red-colored cattle, single animals foraging in a harsh land, and after a hard twelve miles they reach the road at the hacienda Conception. They halt for a while, giving the horses a rest, and view the white stone building, storehouses, and huts partly hidden by great cottonwoods, surrounded by fallow fields.

They take the road that dips to the southwest past two more haciendas, and then the road angles northwest across the creek that waters the fertile valley of the haciendas. Now the road runs along a jagged volcanic flow that extends north and northwest as far as the eye can see. Black and red lava rocks and lava tubes form a wild jumble. Between the lava, grass and shrubs have found holds. Isolated parks of trees ringed by concentrations of lava are visible in the distance. Stone calls for a halt, and he and the others gaze at the phenomenon of the quiet, eerie landscape, such as they have never seen before. "What is it?" Stone asks.

"El malpais," Maria says, then translates the Spanish designation as "evil land," a term Eaglenest cannot explain. In the Kiowa, Gataka, or Cheyenne languages there is no word for it; there is no "evil land" in the perception of these peoples. Land that mestizos or whites see as evil, Indians may see as wondrous, powerful, mysterious. Thus Eaglenest translates it to *havsevomao,* "bad land," a term that does not include the Spanish concept of evil and leaves open the question of why this land is supposed to be bad. Eaglenest shrugs, and they leave it at that. "Malpais." Stone repeats the word and tries to remember it.

For another ten miles they pass along the malpais until they ford the Río Mesquital and, two miles farther, meet with the Camino Real at the little town of Punta. The malpais is still to the north, a desert of a different kind, perhaps empty of humans but not empty of life—plants and greens and animals of many kinds.

There is some movement on the king's road. They pass a train of four-wheeled wagons, each pulled by six mules, a mule train, a herd of cattle driven north, some riders passing south, scanning Stone and his companions with hard, penetrating eyes, perhaps wondering about their good horses. Then, again, a group of Indians on foot, carrying loads.

They ride on, but when they pass through the hamlet of San Lorenzo, clusters of huts around a plaza and a white-washed church, the sun sinks below the Sierra Madre. They are only eight miles east of Durango, but there is nothing that they could achieve in that town at night. So Stone decides to camp for the night in the malpais away from the road. They turn north and recross the river. In Arenal, where little houses and huts group around a plaza dominated by a church, they water the horses and walk toward the malpais north beyond the edge of the hamlet. They find a rough trail and follow it to a small open place between twisted lava blocks that holds a single mesquite and even some grass. They munch on a meal of cold meat and tortillas and wash it down with water from the water bags, and sit and talk for a while as the night blankets the malpais.

Near midnight Stone awakes to the hooting of an owl. He counts the hoots: . . . five, six. And again. Perhaps a great horned owl. Owls are called *mista* in Cheyenne and are regarded as spooks, even feared as carriers of witchcraft. Stone thinks about this. Perhaps a bad sign; perhaps it is nothing but the hunting call of a real owl searching for rodents and small mammals. He cannot think of anyone trying to bewitch him or anyone with him. He brushes his thoughts off and goes back to sleep with the faraway yipping and barking of coyotes.

They wait until the sun rises and retrace their steps to Arenal, cross the river and enter San Lorenzo once again. As in Arenal, chimneys belch smoke, but there are few people in the open, none of whom pays them any attention. Beyond San Lorenzo the Camino

Real proceeds north, but a side road leads southwest into Durango. The town lies in a level plain, surrounded on every side by low mountains, some pocked with the filthy tailing heaps of mines. Wood smoke lies over the town like a thin dark cloud.

As Stone and the companions ride in, they notice open aqueducts with running water in the streets, the water fed from a spring outside of town. Despite the aqueducts, *aguadores,* sellers of water, offer clear water directly siphoned from the spring, carried into town in barrels by burros. They call through the streets, praising their commodity. Their voices match the shouts of the leñeros, trying to sell firewood brought in from the mountains on overloaded burros. A few people walk the street, women covered with rebozos, men with sombreros and dressed in serapes. Riders move to the main plaza with pack animals. Stone follows them. When they arrive near the plaza, stalls are being set up, wagons with goods are brought close and are unloaded. The first cries, "Pulque, Pulque dulce," ring out. Facing the plaza's north side is the Catedral Basilica Menor, an imposing structure. Stone ignores it and focuses on the market as it sets up. He leads the group to a corner near an aqueduct where they dismount. The water is filthy, with offal in it. As he, Eaglenest, and Big Bow sit down on a low stone parapet, Maria merges with the crowd on the plaza.

They do not have to wait long. But when she comes back she looks worried. Her face is serious, thoughtful. "The circo was here and is gone," she says. It left less than half a moon ago."

Stone watches her as Eaglenest translates. This is good news, but he recognizes that something bothers the young woman. "What is it?" he asks.

Maria shakes her head. "The circo went northwest on the Camino Real toward Canatlán and Santiago. This means a longer ride for us. The circo could have taken the other spur of the Camino Real, the one that leads northeast to Panuco and the Nazas River. That would have been much easier for us." She stops, with disappointment in her voice.

After she has translated, Eaglenest looks troubled too. "What does it mean?" she asks Stone.

Stone shrugs. His face is stern. He is thinking. "It is as Maria says. It means a longer ride."

"You still think that we will reach the circo?" There is some doubt in her voice.

"Yes," Stone says. "Let's ride." They mount up and ride out the same way they came in. But the new information lies like a rock on his shoulders. He knows that the warriors have tired of chasing something they have a hard time imagining, something unreal, that slips constantly away from them, something unseen, a distant rumor. What do I tell them now? The truth? But how will they handle it? How can I keep them together? There is a limit to their willingness to continue. Should I set them free, release them from their pledge sealed by having smoked the pipe with me? They cannot break it without doing harm to themselves, but I can unbind them as the holder of the pipe.

They ride on, Stone ahead, but much concerned with his conflicting duties. Eaglenest and Maria are behind him, Big Bow bringing up the rear. They pass people walking and some riders. Among these is a group of four men who have scanned the horses of Stone's party first and then discovered the two pretty women followed by a boy. Four Indians, they think, only one man among them, exceptionally good horses. Maria has felt the eyes of the men on her face and all over her body as if they were undressing her, violating her. Eaglenest has not noticed the insolent stares; neither has Big Bow. They are not accustomed to such behavior; Maria is.

She dares to look back after they have covered a hundred paces or more. The four men have halted and gaze her way. The men look dangerous. When they passed, Maria caught only a glimpse of them, but she remembers hard faces, gaudy clothes, sombreros, serapes, and horse trappings, pistols and swords. Bandidos, she thinks. She quickly turns around, knowing that the men have seen her looking at them. She feels very uneasy. She wonders what the men will do, whether they will ride away or come after them. She says nothing to Eaglenest and waits until they ride out of Durango. She looks back again and sees the men she thinks are bandidos following from a distance.

Now she tells Eaglenest. "I think we are in trouble. Don't turn around! There are four men, bandidos, coming after us," she says hastily.

Eaglenest looks at her, raising her eyebrows. "How do you know?"

"I saw them when they passed us in Durango. They were riding to the plaza, but after they saw us they stopped. Now they are following us." She pauses. "It is me and you they want, I think. I have seen men like them. They think we are Spanish Indians, easy to take. They don't know we are norteños. Tell your husband and Big Bow! But don't look back."

Eaglenest speaks in Cheyenne, unruffled. Perhaps Maria is mistaken. Big Bow waits for his brother to say something, but Stone does not react. They ride in silence for some time. When the side road from Durango merges with the Camino Real and they turn southeast on it, Stone finally speaks. "Maria, take a look back. See if they still follow us."

Maria does as he asks. "Yes, they are following."

"How far away?"

"Four hundred paces, five hundred."

There is traffic on the king's road coming their way. Before them lies San Lorenzo, and they ride in and out to the barking of dogs. They have not changed the gait of their horses, but Stone looks for a place where he can deal with these men, bandidos or not. They ride by a rocky hillside and Stone asks again. "Are they behind us? How far away?"

Maria takes another look. "Same distance as before." It seems the bandidos are keeping pace.

There is a fold in the hillside to their right, a narrow grove surrounded by steep slopes, with a rocky outcrop that juts out to the right of the opening. Stone quickly, grimly, rides in. As the others follow, he dismounts, ripping the bundled bow-and-arrow cases from the horse. He shouts, "Stay with the horses, act as if we are resting! Brother, stay with the horses; get your bow ready but don't let them see it!"

He hurries to a nook behind the jutting rock, hidden from sight, unwraps the weapons and braces the bow. He takes four arrows out and slings the quiver over his shoulder. He holds three arrows in his bow hand, points down, feathers up. He notches the fourth arrow. For a moment he looks down at it: a small iron point, four shallow grooves along the shaft in a zigzag from point to feathers, a fletching of three striped turkey wing feathers. Fly straight for me if I need you, he asks the arrow in his mind. He looks to where the women busy themselves with the horses, adjusting saddlebags, rummaging for food. Big Bow stands behind his horse. He has strung his bow but holds it so that it cannot be seen.

With a clatter of hooves the men ride in. Stone, behind the rock, cannot see them yet. He hears one man laugh, then another. Shouts in Spanish he does not understand. He sees Eaglenest and Maria standing stiffly by the horses, facing the men. Again laughter and Spanish phrases. Two of the men have dismounted and walk toward the women, talking in Spanish, acting friendly. Now they walk into Stone's view. Two men on horses edge forward to the left and right of the men on foot, encircling the party. The ones on foot slowly approach Eaglenest and Maria. Eaglenest's right hand grips the handle of her belt knife. One of the walking men draws a pistol from his belt. Stone steps forward and lifts the bow and releases the arrow. He sees the arrow strike the ribs under the man's right arm and as the pistol drops from his hand Stone hits the farthest horseman in the throat with the second arrow, the arrow almost passing clear through his neck. He tumbles from the saddle, a gurgling sound coming from his throat, and the panicked horse drags him away.

Big Bow has shot the other man from twenty feet away, but the rider nearest to Stone has turned his horse and races away. Stone tries to hit him before he gets out of sight but misses. He rushes down and finishes off the two bandits on the ground. He and Big Bow retrieve their arrows, and Stone turns to the women. Both still stand in the same spot they were in when the bandits walked up to them. Maria's face is pale. Eaglenest looks at her husband and shakes her head. "Bandidos," Stone says. "You were right." He looks at Maria. He nods. He is relieved. He and Big Bow take the swords in their scabbards and three pistols from the dead and small pouches with powder and ball from their belts. They hide the weapons along with the bow-and-arrow cases. "Pewe," Stone says. "Let's ride." They mount up. They gather the two horses of the bandits, drop the saddles, but leave the men where they fell. Back on the Camino Real they let their horses run a little to get away from the place of death. Almost an hour later they pass through Punta and turn away from the king's road and take the side road to the haciendas on which they had come in. After crossing the Río Mesquital they rest for some time on the east bank. They watch, but no one follows them. They continue without incident and at nightfall camp east of the hacienda Conception. The rugged desert country west of the Organos is too difficult to cross after dark. They ride into their camp in the mountains around noon of the following day.

• • •

"You told me about the two roads that go from Durango to Parral," Stone says. "Tell me again."

He sits with the ranchero, Eaglenest, and Maria. Sendehma joins them as he talks. Eaglenest and Maria have put the question to the ranchero. He nods. "The Camino Real," he says. "Yes. There are two routes now. The old one goes northwest through Canatlán, Santiago, Ramos, Indé, Sestin. That's the first Camino Real."

He waits, listens to the translations.

"The other spur goes first northeast to Panuco, then north to the Río de Nazas. At the bend of the river it turns east and goes along the river to Cinco Señores. There it crosses the river and goes northwest to El Gallo, Peñoles, La Zarca, Cerro Gordo, Río Florido."

Stone listens to Maria and Eaglenest. He watches the ranchero's face, studying it, wondering whether he tells the truth. What reason would the man have to lie? The place-names do not mean much to Stone, but the directions the two routes take are important to him.

"You know these places?"

The man nods emphatically. "I have worked as a *caporal* at Ramos and at La Zarca," he says proudly. "That was before I got my own little rancho. I have only three thousand sheep. At Ramos we had forty thousand sheep. At La Zarca we had two hundred thousand sheep, forty thousand mules and horses."

"What is he saying?" Stone asks.

"He has worked at two of these places, Ramos and Zarca," Eaglenest says. She shakes her head. "He has given numbers for sheep at Ramos and sheep and horses and mules at Zarca. We know he says that there were very many but we cannot translate how many."

Maria repeats the numbers in Spanish: "Forty thousand, two hundred thousand." She shakes her head in frustration. "I cannot say this in Kiowa." She looks to Sendehma, but she also shakes her head. She has an idea. She looks around for stones. None are near. She sees a twig and gets up and picks it up. She sits down again. She breaks the twig into pieces. She knows the Kiowa word for one hundred. She puts one piece in front of her and points. "One hundred."

Eaglenest translates into Cheyenne. "Matòtnoe." One hundred.

"Ten times one hundred," Maria says.

Eaglenest says it in Cheyenne. "Matòtoa matòtnoe."

"Ten times that," Maria says.

Eaglenest nods. "Matòtoa matòtoa matòtnoe." Ten times ten hundreds.

"Four times that number," Maria says. She does not really know where she is going.

Eaglenest sits thinking. "Nivá matòtoa matòtoa matòtnoe." Four times ten times ten hundreds.

Maria claps her hands. They have done it, it seems. She repeats in Spanish: forty thousand sheep in Ramos, forty thousand horses and mules in Zarca.

Stone has watched the two. He is amused at how they have figured out how to convey astounding numbers. A Hiaqui girl and a Gataka girl have arrived at a rarely used number in the Cheyenne numerical system. He is surprised and proud of them. He looks at them, at Sendehma too. Everyone smiles. Only the ranchero, left out of a discussion he does not comprehend, is puzzled. Stone repeats the number. "Nivá matòtoa matòtoa matòtnoe." Horses, mules, that many. That place, Zarca. Sheep do not concern him. "Aho," he says. "Pewe."

He thinks. Then, "Ask the ranchero whether he knows the two roads well, the ones he has mentioned."

Eaglenest passes the question to him. It seems that he is eager to tell. "Yes," he says, thinking about a stage in his life he seems to feel happy about. "I went all over these places. We drove sheep to Parral and to Durango and Zacatecas; sometimes we drove horses. I have been on both branches of the Camino Real."

Stone hears what he says. He thinks it best to inform him about the road the circo took. "The circo took the western road," he says slowly. He watches the ranchero, waiting for his reaction. Much depends on what the man knows and is willing to tell. He has been to all of these places. Stone feels like a blind man searching for something to hold on to. He is very much concerned but cannot show it.

The man is not perturbed. He has no reason to be. "Yes," he says simply, "I understand why the circo went that way."

"Why?" Stone asks.

"There are haciendas and colonias and towns on that route where the circo can stop on the way."

"There are these on the other route too."

"Yes, but you told me that the circo went from the Nazas to Saltillo. The circo has been on that route coming from Parral."

Stone thinks for a while. The man is right. That's the reason why the circo took the other route. "Tell me about the road the circo has taken. How can I get to it?"

The ranchero contemplates the question. "You can follow that road from Durango or you can get to it another way."

"How?"

"You can take the other road and go north to the Río de Nazas, and when you get to it you follow it upstream. Then you come to the place where the other road crosses the river."

Stone lets the information sink in. "Where is that?"

"At Ramos." But then the ranchero asks, "When did the circo leave Durango?"

Stone, Eaglenest, and Maria look at each other. "Tell him," Stone says.

"Less than half a moon ago," Maria says. "That's what they told me in Durango."

The ranchero's eyes light up. He strokes his mustache. Perhaps he has made the case of the norteños his own. At least, as soon as they accomplish what they are after he will be free again. That is what the jefe said. But he wants assurance now.

"If I help you to get to the circo, do you let me go?" he asks. "You promised me that."

Stone considers the question a moment. "Yes. I said so."

The man nods excitedly. Maybe this will be over more quickly than he had hoped. "I can take you to Ramos probably before the circo arrives there. You want that?"

Stone nods solemnly. "Yes." He repeats it. "Yes. How many days from here to Ramos?"

"Four days."

Stone looks to the ground. He looks to the sky. White clouds drift by. Could it be that this is coming to an end? "How do we get there?"

"There is a trail that runs north from San Estevan, a hacienda east of Conception. You have been to Conception. San Estevan is just a little to the east. The trail that goes north goes to the little town of Sausillo. It's a dead town—no one lives there anymore. From Sausillo we cut northwest to the Camino Real and Panuco, then follow the road north to the Río de Nazas. Upstream on the river we get to Ramos."

Stone nods. He thinks about Whirlwind and the woman. But already he thinks about Zarca and the forty thousand horses and mules the man has seen with his own eyes. He owes it to his men to let them have some of these horses.

He gets up. This talk is over. He calls for a gathering of the band. He explains what he knows. Faces before him brighten. Men and women feel reassured, no longer troubled, content. How easy they are to please, Stone thinks, how trustful they are. It does not relieve the burden he feels. His heart goes out to them. I have pledged them my life; I give it gladly for them if I must.

Before they make Zarca they have to make Ramos. In order to get to Ramos in four days, or at all, they must have fresh horses. Tomorrow, he has promised them . . .

NINETEEN
November 24, 1807

They move out at first light, riding in the proven fashion of advance guard and rear guard, the women with the packhorses in the middle. The men are fully armed. Of the fifteen men, including Big Bow, only two are without muskets: Big Bow and Necklace. The six muskets taken from the bandits have added to the party's armament. Muskets are carried loaded and primed. The ranchero rides with the women; for what is to come he is of no use. Stone and Big Bow sit the horses they captured on the Camino Real. The twelve miles to Conception are covered before sunrise.

While Stone and a few men surround the main building of the hacienda on three sides, the other men continue to the corrals back of the great house. They must find trained saddle stock; there is not time to deal with unbroken animals. Two of the corrals hold horses they want. Expert horsemen, with the skillful use of hand and voice they slip the Plains Indian two-rein bridle over horses they have selected. Because these horses are used to metal bits, it takes some patience to fit the bridles: the middle of the lariat is carried back of the horse's ears, then both ends are passed over and around the lower jaw and pulled back. This simple and effective device, much more horse-friendly than Spanish tackle, takes a little to get used to for an animal trained differently. They take twenty-nine horses out, more than enough to provide everyone of the party with a fresh mount. With much regret they leave the same number of their travel-weary animals behind. They need at least another dozen so that each rider has a spare mount and the packhorses are replaced. The new stock is obviously corn-fed; the sleek bodies are shiny and healthy looking. They expect to find what they need at the next hacienda, San Estevan. No one at Conception offered resistance. A few women looked out from windows, and once a man, perhaps the haciendado, stepped from the portal but quickly, wisely, withdrew as he saw a musket leveled at him. From the peons' huts shabbily dressed people looked on in silence.

They continue northeast on the Mateo Gomez road and cross the creek and get to San Estevan after a brisk ride of four miles. Without opposition they take another fifteen horses and leave behind all the remaining mounts from the long ride. The men are especially sorry to part with their war and buffalo horses. Bags with corn have been found in a stable, and three of the pack animals are loaded with them for horse feed and human consumption. The ranchero guides them to the Sausillo trail leading north, and they take it as the early morning sun bathes the land in light. The horses step out eagerly after their confinement in corrals, and the column moves at a quick pace. North of the agricultural valley they once again enter dry country. The trail, barely visible and unused, winds north five miles to the east of the edge of the vast, cratered malpais, and after twelve miles it climbs up to the spur of the sierra that stands to the east. This mountain range, with barren, dust-colored heights, rises to nine thousand feet. At midday, after coming down again to lower ground, they rest by a trickle of water, the first water they have seen since they started from San Estevan. Later, eight miles farther, they approach the colonia of Sausillo, a collection of deserted houses lying in ruin. Stone halts and calls for the ranchero to come to his side. "What happened here?" he asks. He looks for Maria and Eaglenest, and they ride forward.

"This place was burned down about twenty years ago," the ranchero says.

"Burned down?"

The ranchero shrugs. "Los Apaches," he says laconically as if no other explanation is necessary.

Stone is curious. "Why?" He thinks of a Cheyenne trading expedition to one of the Hidatsa villages on the Missouri River. A Crow delegation was visiting, enemies of the Cheyennes. There were arguments and bad feelings, and the Cheyennes left with anger, but they did not think of burning the Hidatsa village.

The ranchero shifts uneasily in his saddle. "There is a story," he says reluctantly. "The Apaches used to steal horses east of here but never touched Sausillo. They had a peace with this place. The people were afraid of them, but they traded with them, especially for buffalo robes from the grasslands in the north."

He pauses, listening to the translation.

"But the people of the ranchos east of here were mad and bitter. Herders were killed and horses taken, cattle and sheep butchered by the Apaches for food. Only the people of Sausillo were safe, no one else. So it was decided to get rid of the Apaches, and Sausillo was forced to participate."

Again he pauses.

"The next time the Apaches came, riders were sent to the ranchos. Sausillo gave a big fiesta and invited the Apaches into the town to stay. There were musicians, dances, much food, much pulque. Everyone seemed to be happy. But after dark, when many of the Apaches were drunk, the vaqueros rode in. Most of the Apache men were killed. The few women with them were spared and distributed among the ranchos. They were made slaves. Only a few men escaped."

Another pause. He watches as Maria and Eaglenest translate.

"A short time later the Apaches came back. They killed everyone in Sausillo but the young women and some of the children. These they took away. They burned every house. No one has lived here since. It is a place of ghosts. Some say that the spirits of those murdered here roam at night. We learned from the prisoners that these Apaches are called los Mescaleros."

Stone has listened in silence. "Did you take part in this?" he asks.

The ranchero shakes his head. "No. At that time I was running sheep for the hacienda Ramos."

Stone nods. "Pewe." He dismounts and tightens the saddle strap; others of the party do the same. He remounts, and the column gets back in motion. Stone keeps the ranchero next to him. They ride through the little town that was, looking at desolation, wrecked adobe houses and burned shacks and stalls, wooden storehouses where only fragments of walls stand, debris everywhere. An empty creekbed runs through the middle of the main street as if the water had died along with the people. After they are through, Stone asks, "What direction now?"

The ranchero points northwest. "Toward Panuco."

"Take us there," Stone says.

They ride into a rolling plain with desert vegetation and little grass. After eight miles they pass the flank of a lone mountain, and after another four miles they reach the northern edge of the vast malpais that Stone, Eaglenest, and Maria have already seen in the south, on the road to Durango. The others stare at this natural spectacle with wonder. They are amazed by clusters of weird shapes, knife-edged towers and spires fashioned from coal-black and red lava, with mesquite and green shrubs growing from crevasses and isolated parks in the great jumble. They ride slowly around the northern border of the volcanic labyrinth and make camp where the last tongue of the malpais recedes southwest. They have not found water and take water for the horses and themselves from the bags carried on packhorses.

The sun sinks. They wait until darkness before building a fire. They have made fifty miles that day and covered one-fourth of the distance to Ramos. Since leaving the haciendas they have seen tracks of small animals, birds, a few jackrabbits that Set chased, and the ever-present buzzards in the sky, but no humans.

• • •

The camp awakes to Set's morning call. No voices answer. As men and women shake out their sleeping robes, Bear Doctor Woman points to the northeast. Now they all see it: a cloud of smoke from a huge fire rises straight into the still air. There is no cause for concern; whatever is burning is about twenty miles away, perhaps more. Stone turns to the ranchero. "Los Apaches?" he asks mockingly. The ranchero stares at the distant smoke. He shrugs. "Los Apaches. Los Cumanches. Los Norteños." He looks gravely at Stone.

Stone nods. Could be any of them. "When do we get water?"

"Six leguas from here. We will come to a river that runs north into the Río de Nazas." The ranchero is firm in his knowledge of the country. "The river comes out of the mountains near Panuco, the mining town."

"Fifteen miles to there," Maria suggests, and Eaglenest gives the Cheyenne rendering, "Ematotxeo enohoneo taeoneva estazeso."

They break camp and ready the horses and move out, continuing northwest. In front of them loom two mountain massifs, both rising to ten thousand feet, with a gap eight miles wide between them. This is where the ranchero is guiding them. When they cross the Camino Real after a ride of seven miles, the sun has not yet risen. At that early hour the road is empty, but tracks on it indicate that it is well traveled. As the road curves north toward Panuco, Stone's party moves parallel to it three miles away to the west. They march on rolling ground and up onto the 6,500-feet level between the two massifs. A few miles due west of Panuco they pass by one of the craters that exploded outward to the south and southeast, ejecting the material that created the malpais. The crater's center is hidden in a wide, circular mound of ash and cinders several hundred feet high. The early morning sun strikes the crater's slope. Iron has colored lava so intensely red in some patches that it seems to still glow with heat. Two miles beyond, they reach the river the ranchero has promised. They have a glimpse of a long mule train coming south from the mining town that is hidden in a break in the mountains. As the Camino Real continues north on the west bank of the river, the column crosses the road and the river and marches in cover along the east bank. Near midday, after having passed the colonia Sauz de Arriba, they rest in a hollow invisible from the road. Men and women, separately, bathe in the river, and the men, naked, ride the horses in and splash them with water. Set stands on the river's bank and tests the air with quick lifting motions of his muzzle, assembling and sorting out a picture of what is within the range of his senses.

Later, marching north again, they come to a wolf kill where a heifer has been run down. The animal lies on its side, eyes glazed over and tongue out. It seems that a small pack has started feeding on it between its rear legs, dragged the intestines out and eaten meat from the inside of the thighs. The heifer is not yet stiff. The riders seem to have disturbed the wolves, who must be close by. Set takes a special interest but gallops after the party as it moves on. They make camp near the river in a depression and below a rocky outcrop that allows the guard to watch the Camino Real across the river, four miles away.

Again they build a fire after dark. After they have eaten, Stone and Eaglenest sit together a little back from the others. Eaglenest touches her husband's shoulder. "Do you see what Maria is doing?"

Stone follows the direction of her eyes. "Maria is making moccasins," she says.

Stone sees nothing special in that, but Eaglenest informs him with a smile. "She is making them for Yellow Eyes."

As Stone raises his eyebrows, Eaglenest continues. "Yellow Eyes has taken a liking to Maria and Manuel. You have not noticed, but we have. Whenever he can, he plays with the boy and teaches him Cheyenne. He does not talk to Maria, but he helps her with the horses when he can.

"And Maria?" Stone asks.

"She is shy. Both are shy, but she does not reject him. I think they are attracted to each other."

"Pewe," Stone says. "It is good." He smiles at Eaglenest. "She makes a good wife." He looks to where Lucia sits by herself, lost among strangers. Her little son, Pedro, plays with Manuel. "What about the Toboso woman?"

Eaglenest shakes her head. "She still mourns for her husband. She does not want anyone to look at her."

They leave it at that, but Stone tells himself that he should watch more closely what happens around him.

That night, at Set's midnight song, wolves answer from the south.

• • •

On this, the third day on their quest for Ramos, they move again at first light and continue north through rugged country east of the river. After nine miles they pass the settlement of Palmito, which sits on the Camino Real surrounded by fallow fields. From a distance they see no life. Here the mountains recede on all sides and leave a wide, irregular basin of lowland into which the Nazas River runs from the north before it turns straight east. Well before sunrise Stone's party crosses the little river near where it merges with the Nazas and crosses the Camino Real, which switches direction and follows the shore of the Nazas east. "What is east of the Río de Nazas?" Stone asks the ranchero.

"Three haciendas, the town of Cinco Señores, and the big rancho San Antonio."

Stone nods. He knows of the rancho San Antonio. They had a fight with the marquis's soldiers from that place when they took revenge for Magpie. "Where does the Camino Real go?"

"It goes to Cinco Señores, then crosses the river and goes northwest toward Parral through El Gallo, La Zarca, Cerro Gordo, Río Florido."

As they continue north, they come to another little river. It runs in from the west, and they cross it near its mouth. Now they move through the floodplain of the Nazas, above its west bank. Both banks of the river have a covering of shrubbery. The floodplain is of uneven width, ranging from three miles to nine miles across, and becomes a narrow strip farther upstream. It is surrounded on both sides by barren mountains, those on the west rising to ten thousand feet. They have come into cattle country, and the ranchero warns of the rancho San Salvador, which stands behind the river's east bank ahead of them. Some red-colored cattle graze on the light grass cover and eye the riders nervously as they pass. Stone takes the column to the western edge of the floodplain, riding along the serrated mountain slope to keep out of sight of the rancho. They are confident that they have not been noticed. But later, where the floodplain narrows to a slim channel, they see three riders on a bluff to the east who sit their horses, watching. Nothing can be done about it, but it gives Stone's mission a degree of urgency. Perhaps the watchers will inform someone of their presence. Perhaps not. Stone knows that he must continue to do what is necessary, and whatever happens must be accepted and dealt with.

They make camp twenty-two miles southeast of Ramos as the raven flies, though they do not know yet that they are that close. Before settling for the evening, the men kill three heifers with lances, and men and women work into the night, dressing the animals and treating the meat taken from the carcasses. Wolves will see to the remains. In a secluded location they build a fire and feast on the abundant meat. Most of it is preserved for the coming days.

On the following morning they ride nineteen miles upstream to the bend of the Nazas. They get there at sunrise. The river, coming from mountains in the north, is forced here into an erratic bend nine miles long from east to west. Into its western corner, from the southwest, runs the Río Santiago, named after the town, a major Spanish post on the western Camino Real. And ten miles southwest of the mouth of the Santiago River is the site of the sheep ranch, Ramos. This the ranchero tells Stone as the column halts at the eastern corner of the Nazas bend.

"Where is the Camino Real?" he asks the ranchero.

"This one goes through Ramos and north after crossing the Río Santiago."

"Ramos, how far from here?"

The ranchero thinks for a moment, using fingers in counting. "Seven leguas."

"Eighteen miles," Maria says.

Stone is all smiles. He addresses the band. "We are eighteen miles from Ramos now. Ramos is over there." He points west. "We could be there at midday if we tried." He pauses. "But we will not, not yet. I have to find out whether the circo has been there or is still on its way to Ramos."

He looks into the faces of the men and women of the band. They seem bored, listless. Now, when the purpose of the long ride is near a final resolution, they seem to have become detached, indifferent. Are they simply worn-out? Has he driven them too hard? Did he expect too much? Has he stretched their loyalty to the breaking point now, when the end is within reach? He looks at the women. At Eaglenest. She looks as drawn as the others. How could he expect them to share his passion? An insane passion? Suddenly he feels sad, unsure of himself. Then he thinks, why crumble now?

When he speaks to them, they seem to perceive his distress. He has taken the short, unadorned prayer stick from his belt and fingers it. He looks up into the sky, to the ground. "We are at the end," he says quietly. "Ramos is over there." He points with the stick. "The circo will be under our arrows tomorrow or the day after. We will turn home after that. We will be finished here."

They have heard him. They remain silent.

TWENTY

Near midday Stone finds a secure campsite just east of the mouth of the Río Santiago. He posts a guard and has the horses unpacked. The women prepare a meal, and after they have eaten, Stone, Eaglenest, and Maria ride again. In camp the women work curing the meat from the kill of the day before. The men have nothing to do besides check the horses, cleaning out and paring down hooves when necessary. They might check their weapons again. After that they wait. Riding and waiting, that's what their life has been for too long. They are restless.

Stone and the two women once again dress in mixed Spanish garb. As before, when they visited the towns, they agree that in case they are stopped by someone and asked who they were, Maria will do the talking. She will say that they are Hiaquis from the north, and that her two companions do not speak Spanish. They ride the eleven miles from their camp to Ramos at a leisurely pace, changing from a slow lope to a walk. The ranchero has described the layout of the buildings to them. They cross two small rivers that run into the Santiago from the south, from the great horseshoe of high mountains that dominate this direction. They pass through grassland cropped short by Spanish churra sheep, of which they see large numbers way to the south and southwest. Near Ramos they pass by two herders, Indians on good horses who look them over and raise a hand in greeting as they pass. Maria says something in Spanish to them, but they only laugh in a friendly way; they do not understand her. Half a mile from the cluster of buildings, Stone halts. He sends Maria on alone while he and Eaglenest dismount and sit down. Waiting as so often before.

They see Maria disappear between sprawling pole corrals and storehouses. The sun stands above them in a hazy sky where the light filters through a thin layer of clouds. Buzzards circle up high, and a hawk drifts lazily with outstretched wings on a soft wind breathing from the west. It does not take long for Maria to return. She is smiling. Her pretty face, still innocent despite the wretched circumstances that preyed on her young life, is aglow with good news.

"The circo is not here yet," she says as she dismounts.

"Where is it?" Stone asks. He is relieved.

"The circo is at a colonia ten miles south of here. Word is that it will be here tomorrow and will put up a show in the evening."

There is silence. "We could catch the circo on the road midday tomorrow," Eaglenest suggests.

Stone nods. "Yes. But I want to see with my own eyes what that circo is and what my brother does there." He nods again. "Yes. I want to see him doing what he does." He pauses. "We catch the circo the day after."

He looks up to the hawk floating effortlessly across the sky. "Tomorrow night I will see him. I will not let him see me."

Back in camp he tells the band. There is a response this time, expressions of satisfaction that this is almost over, a weight lifted, a feeling that they finished what they had set out to do.

"What happens after we get Whirlwind?" Powderface asks. A staunch supporter of Stone's quest for his brother, he has become tired lately, even cynical. Some of the men look up to him to speak out for them.

"Zarca," Stone says. "Forty thousand horses and mules we were told. We take what we can handle." He glances at the ranchero who sits impassively, not knowing what is being said, wondering, fretting. Stone looks at the faces of his people. They seem uplifted, more at ease than before.

A long night is coming up, and Stone is awake for most of it. Brother, we are here, finally. What about you?

• • •

This time they ride at dusk—Stone, Eaglenest, and Maria. Maria carries a handful of copper coins in a handkerchief attached to the belt. Stone wears a wide-brimmed sombrero and a serape that covers his upper body. The women ride with rebozos slung over their shoulders to be drawn over their heads once they arrive at the rancho. The dying moon is a thin sickle in the sky, but the blazing stars illuminate the trail on a cloudless night. At first the only sounds in the stillness are the familiar sounds of the hoofbeat of their horses and the creaking of saddle leather, but later, still a mile away, they hear music and the sounds of singing. These sounds intensify as they get closer. When they arrive at the sheep corrals they find them empty. Saddled horses are tied up in a long line along one side of the corral nearest to the main group of buildings, belonging to visitors who have ridden in from all around to see the circus. The three dismount and lash the reins to poles of the fence. It seems that many people have passed before them as they walk toward the long-walled compound. They have come late; the show is already in progress. Ahead the music and the singing end, followed by applause. Oil lamps on the ground on both sides of the stone archway light the entrance as Maria, ahead of Stone and Eaglenest, steps into the portal. A man dressed in black comes forward and Maria hands him her copper coins. The gatekeeper thanks her and drops the coins into a bucket on the ground next to him. They pass through.

The compound opens wide. The white main building stands in the back, lit by torches. On both sides circus wagons have been drawn up, creating a lane that leads visitors to where the circus performs. As they go through they notice iron cages exhibited on three of the wagons. In one cage, black rosettes on a golden fleece, a jaguar paces back and forth in the confined space. In another a sleek light yellow form, resting, a puma. And in the last one, crumpled in sleep, a bundle of gray and light fur, a wolf. The eyes of the jaguar and the puma, burning bright in the lights of the oil lamps, follow them as they move on. They move slowly, their heads turned back, their eyes gazing into the unremitting fire of the cat's eyes. A chill runs down Eaglenest's spine, while Stone is angry that such creatures, spirits of the original land, have been imprisoned so that the Spanish may gawk, taunt, and harass them in safety, protected from their fury by iron stakes. There is no telling what Maria thinks.

The loud voice of an announcer bellows as they step into the circus lights. Oil lamps stand in a semicircle on the ground, and more lamps hang from a rope stretched overhead around an open piece of ground serving as arena. In front of it the crowd sits quietly on the ground, tightly packed, families with children, men in groups, a bunch of girls to one side. Stone and the two women sit down behind the last row. Men have kept their sombreros on, so the three slide to a section with more women and children in front of them than men. But they still have to look around heads to see part of the show. At the edge of the ground stage, still under the lights, sit three musicians, one player with a harp, two with guitars. They wear jackets gaudily embroidered, pantaloons trimmed with tinsel lace, red sashes drawn around their bodies, and black bandannas wrapped around their heads.

The harpist nods to his fellow musicians, and they play a fandango, the harpist singing with a tenor voice. From behind a canvas screen on the left come two dancers, girls dressed in wide white gowns. They hold up the hems of their gowns, baring high-heeled shoes. They stomp the ground with quick feet to the rhythm of the tune, twisting and turning, pushing forward and pulling back, hammering the earth with the staccato of their feet. Their hair is combed up, held by glittering barrettes that form the hair into little black towers topped with silken cloth. Broad red sashes of cloth encircle their waists. Both are young. They could be sisters. One looks to Stone to be sixteen, the other perhaps three years older. The older one is a little full in the middle of her body—perhaps she is pregnant. Stone suddenly remembers his dream in which Whirlwind pointed to a woman beside him who appeared to be pregnant. Could this be the woman of the dream? The dancers move vivaciously, gracefully, gowns spread out with raised arms, fluttering across the earthen stage like butterflies. The song comes to an end, and the dancers bow to applause, and again, again, and then retreat to the screen.

Out comes a clown dressed in rags, the face painted white. A tiny monkey with a chain around its neck perches on his right arm. It wears a doll's dress and a plumed hat tied under the chin.

"What kind of animal is this?" Stone asks Eaglenest.

She whispers to Maria and turns back to Stone. "Mono, she says." She whispers again to Maria and listens to her. She tells Stone, "There is no word for this animal in Kiowa. Maria says this animal lives on trees far south of here. She has never seen one before. But she has heard that there are different tribes of them. Some are like little people, doll people, some are half as big as humans. They live in green dense forests with trees taller than cottonwoods."

Stone watches, fascinated, as the monkey scurries up and down the clown's arm, sits on his shoulder, then on his head, then perches on his hand, stretches a tiny hand toward people sitting in the first row. Then it grimaces and climbs again. The antics of the monkey are independent of the pranks of the clown, who tells jokes in Spanish with a booming voice and goes through a routine that earns him resounding laughter from the crowd, sometimes embarrassed laughter from a few, silence from many.

Stone and Eaglenest have seen clowns in the Cheyenne Massaum ceremony, when they enact a behavior contrary to normal, play irreverent fools, making people laugh, in actions and costume representing the opposite of the sacred to which they make obeisance at the end. Stone and Eaglenest look at each other. They see no deeper meaning in the Spanish clown's frolic; he represents only himself. The monkey is more entrancing than the white-painted man.

They wait. Finally the clown finishes and bows to applause and departs to the canvas screen and returns and bows again, under applause, and disappears.

There is no telling what Maria is thinking, and she is not asked, but Stone and Eaglenest observe with interest everything around them: the performers, the alien people, the arena and the lamps, the arrangement of the compound. They will remember what they see and add it to all the new sights and places they have encountered and to what they have learned on this journey into unknown lands.

Once again the band plays a tune, and a woman comes around the screen and steps into the middle of the arena and faces the audience. She is middle-aged, rather heavyset, dressed in a loose, flowering gown that reaches to the ground. Her fleshy face is daubed with makeup: powder, rouge, and black eyeliner. Her hair is bound up like that of the dancers earlier. She wears much jewelry, necklaces, rings on most fingers, bracelets on her bare arms. She turns to the harpist. He stops the tune and starts a fresh one, the guitar players joining in.

The woman begins to sing with a strong soprano voice. This seems to be a song known to most present, and people hum along. There is wild clapping of hands when it ends, and the prima donna smiles and bows graciously. She sings two more songs, both received joyously by the audience. For her last number she chooses a ballad that seems to have lost love as its theme. She sings with great feeling, almost crying at the end. There is no applause. The crowd sits in silence. Some women cry.

The prima donna bows into the silence, and as she moves away the crowd erupts into a tumultuous applause. Four times she moves away and four times she comes back to receive another ovation. Smiling, she accepts the approbation as her due and walks off the arena even though handclapping continues.

There is a pause, and then the band plays again. From behind the screen three men walk into the arena carrying wooden beams. They take them to the left side, below the hanging lights, and connect them on the ground to form a rectangular base with two beams running through the center. As people watch, a solid wooden post is brought in and fitted vertically between the two center beams. An iron knob protrudes from the middle of the post, almost five feet off the ground.

Stone watches with rising interest but sees few of the details because of the people in front of him. The large wooden wheel, a solid piece that is rolled in, he can see clearly. As it is fixed to the post, its very center clamped over the knob, Stone feels tense, anxious. Is this device prepared for Whirlwind? He looks to Eaglenest and Maria next to him. Both wonder as he does, and Maria nods with raised eyebrows. Eaglenest puts her arm around Stone's arm.

In the arena a footstool is put below the wheel, and a table is set up opposite the wheel about twenty feet away. Some objects are carried in and placed on the table. The workers finish and walk away. The band has played throughout the time it has taken to set the stage. Now it stops as a heavyset man dressed in a black suit emerges from behind the canvas screen. He stops in front of the audience, bows, and delivers a speech in a sonorous voice. Stone and Eaglenest do not understand his Spanish, but Maria whispers that this man is Don Lorenzo de Avila, the owner and director of the circo, and that he introduces the norteño knife artist. "He calls your brother Mario," Maria whispers.

Mario? Stone wonders. Is Whirlwind Mario, or is this a different man and not Whirlwind at all? Has he been mistaken all this time? Stone feels as if a heavy hand grips his throat. In the arena the director bows smartly and withdraws as the norteño comes around the screen. Stone breathes out. It is Whirlwind. Two females accompany him, the same girls who danced the fandango earlier in the show. This time they are dressed in tight-fitting blouses and leather trousers and boots. Whirlwind wears an open cotton shirt, leather trousers, and moccasins. His braided hair hangs over his chest. As a concession to the norteño image, he has a yellow face painting. This is not a Cheyenne but an Apache design: a yellow line drawn across the cheekbones and the bridge of the nose. Stone smiles at the subtle deception. His brother looks fit, although weird to him in Spanish clothes. He appears composed, impassive.

The three in the arena bow, and then the younger of the girls walks lightly, almost as if floating on the air, to the wheel, steps on the footstool and onto a foothold on the wheel. She spreads her legs out. With her hands she slaps two leather straps for a hold, her arms apart. As she stands against the wheel, the older girl takes two knives from the table and hands them to Whirlwind. He moves his left leg slightly forward and throws both knives in quick succession. A gasp runs through the crowd as the knives hit to the left and right of the girl's waist, close to the body. He turns and receives two more knives and throws, this time the knives framing the thighs. The next knives stick along the lower legs, and then he edges them along both sides of her torso. The next to last knife he throws between her legs below the knees, and the last knife he throws toward the head, where the blade stands quivering ten inches above the girl's hair.

As he bows to furious handclapping, the older girl walks to the wheel and pulls the knives out one by one. She holds them up in a bundle, showing them to the crowd. They have short wooden grips, and the blades, shiny and sharp, are about ten inches long. She places them back on the table and returns to the wheel and sets it in motion, pulling with both arms. As the wheel and the girl on it rotate, she steps back to the table and hands Whirlwind the first two knives for the next act.

Whirlwind makes a few steps forward. He waits, judging the speed of the motion, and throws the first knife as the audience seems to hold its breath. The knife hits near the right side of the girl's waist at the moment when her body is upside down. Whirlwind continues to string knives along the body, framing the target when the girl is in the upside-down position on the slowly turning wheel. The last two knives, as before, strike the wood between the girl's legs and above her head.

When it is over, the crowd sits in a stunned silence, then erupts into furious applause. In the arena Whirlwind stops the wheel and the second assistant removes the knives. Hand in hand the three walk to the middle of the arena, Whirlwind in the middle, a girl on each side. They bow to the applause once, twice, then walk off as the band starts with another jig.

As the workers return and disassemble the wheel, the show continues. Out from the back comes the clown again, this time as a juggler, bouncing four colored balls in the air, moving around slowly.

Stone has seen enough. He nudges Eaglenest, who nudges Maria. They get up and walk away, past the wagons and the cages to their horses. Untying them, they mount up and ride away. In the stillness of the night the sounds of music from the circus follow them a long way.

They are eagerly awaited in camp. Stone tells what he has seen. There is a general, although imperceptible, sigh of relief. Tomorrow, everyone thinks.

TWENTY-ONE

They break camp at first light, pack the horses, saddle up, and move out. They cross the Santiago River, the water reaching no higher than the horses' fetlocks. They ride slowly northwest, fully armed, and reach the Camino Real, a rutted dirt track, after ten miles. Ramos is almost due south, about eight miles away beyond a series of low yellow hills and the river. Stone looks north over the road toward Indé, twenty-two miles away as the raven flies. There is no sign of travelers from that direction yet, none from the south. He takes the companions into the mouth of a broad ravine where they dismount. He dismounts outside and positions himself on the slope high enough for a clear view to the north and south. Now they have to wait. In the east, the red rim of the sun peers over the mountaintops.

Time passes, and the sun slowly moves higher into the sky. A light breeze brushes in from the southwest. First he sees thin swirls of dust in the south, and then a wagon train comes over the first of the yellow hills, following the road, less than a mile away. Stone watches as it approaches. Banners in blue and gold hang limp from poles on both sides of the box of the first wagon. Pennants in the same colors are draped on the wagons following. Stone has seen enough. He walks down to his horse and mounts. He checks the musket. He rides into the mouth of the ravine and gives the signal. The band mounts. Everyone knows what to do. When the lead wagon is about four hundred paces away, he calls. As the warriors ride out, Necklace turns north to scout the road in this direction. The others swoop down on the caravan and surround it on every side.

There are nine gaudy little wagons altogether, each drawn by a two-mule team, the wagons covered with pennants, the mules fitted with gay bands of cloth and tinsel. They are nice to look at. Stone halts a dozen paces in front of the first wagon. Beside him are Sendehma, Maria, and Big Bow. Set explores the train and discovers the cages on their wagons near the end. As the warriors sit their horses, their muskets aimed at the circus personnel, the women and the ranchero emerge from the ravine and bunch the packhorses and spare horses on the road.

The caravan comes to a quick halt. Although the warriors haven't painted and stripped for battle, they appear fierce and terrifying to the Spanish as they control restless horses in a threatening silence, cold, aloof, the impassive faces framed by braids, with eagle feathers jutting out upward and sideways. Men and women on drive boxes of the wagons sit stiffly erect, numb, too frightened to move, their faces stricken. Stone is prepared to have Maria call for the director of the circus, but it is not necessary. Lame Coyote shouts words in Cheyenne from near the fifth wagon in the caravan. Whirlwind has climbed down from the seat and walks slowly to where his brothers and his wife wait. A few more words as he passes Yellow Eyes, who laughs. It breaks the tension. Now the circus people dare to watch, although they cannot imagine what is going on.

Stone watches as Whirlwind comes near. A white cotton shirt and black cotton trousers, the feet shuffling in worn moccasins, the hair loose, the face pallid.

Whirlwind's eyes scan the riders before him. On the left an Indian girl with long hair, next Sendehma, then his brothers. His gaze shifts again to Sendehma: tall, pretty, strong, the hair neatly braided. She smiles. Gondaima on the saddle in front of her: quiet, a serious little face, huge eyes looking at him. Stone: stiff, solemn, a hard man who cracks a thin smile. And Big Bow, older than he remembered him, raising his right hand, a joyous face.

Now he stands before them, the horses shuffling, jerking their heads. Dust. How does one greet another after a separation of a thousand miles and more, different lives lived in different places, remembering much of the old but also remembering some of the new? A blank. What to say? This moment struggled for, this moment feared.

"Vahé, brother!" Stone's voice.

Whirlwind looks at him. The face more lined than in his memory. He nods. "Vahé!"

The warriors drift away from their positions along the caravan and sit their horses in a semicircle around the group. The circus people crane their necks trying to catch every gesture, every moment, of the surprising event unfolding before them.

"I was afraid you would come for me." Whirlwind looks into his brother's eyes, sees his face harden.

A silence suddenly heavy with uneasiness.

"Afraid that I would come?" Stone's voice has a tinge of incredulity. "Why?"

Whirlwind shrugs. "I have a new life now."

He looks at Sendehma, at his little daughter. Sendehma's face has turned cold. She is furious but hides her anger behind a mask.

Another silence. Set has recognized Whirlwind and strides up to him, but when Whirlwind puts out his hand to touch him on the head, the dog lopes away.

"What life?" Stone demands. "Throwing knives in a circo?"

"You can't understand," Whirlwind says slowly. Among the warriors no one stirs. They stare at the man they thought they knew, knew well enough to risk everything for. Their faces too have become masks.

"You have a wife and a daughter," Stone says. "They are here."

Whirlwind nods, sadly. "I have another wife. She carries my child."

He turns around and calls in Spanish. From one of the wagons a girl steps down, then another. As they approach, bravely but hesitantly, Stone recognizes them as the two dancers of the show. The older of the two is the one he has seen in his dream. It is coming true, what he was afraid of. They walk slowly into the semicircle of warriors and step to Whirlwind's side, heads bowed, afraid to look up.

"This is Inez," Whirlwind says, touching the shoulder of the older girl. "This is her sister, Ada."

Stone looks them over. Drab cotton dresses, bare feet, black hair down to the middle of the back. Spanish Indians, he thinks.

"They are both your wives?"

Whirlwind shakes his head. "No. Inez is my wife. Ada lives with us. Their parents and relatives are dead. She has no one else."

Whirlwind pauses. He knows, the girls know, that everyone stares at them. "Inez saved my life after I was captured. Without her I would not be here."

Slowly the girls look up into the impassive faces around them and sense the hostility hidden in them.

There is an awkward silence.

"You already have a wife," Stone finally says. "You can leave that one behind."

"Inez is with my child," Whirlwind says. "I will not leave her behind."

Now Sendehma breaks the silence. "I am your wife and this is your daughter." She pats Gondaima. She pauses. "You can bring these two with you. They can live with us in the Ka'ta camp or in the Hovxnova camp. If I can say that, you can agree to that too." She pauses. "We have come a long way for you. Did we come for nothing?"

Whirlwind nods. "I am grateful for what you say. You are a good woman. But I can't do that. I do not want to go back. I have another life here. I want to stay." He speaks with sadness.

A strong murmur comes from among the warriors, the angry voice of Powderface. "I left my two wives and my two children in the Hovxnova camp to come for you. We thought you needed to be rescued. Now I see that you have joined the enemy."

Little Bird speaks next. "You have a good woman and a beautiful child. Sendehma says that she would take this Inez woman in and her sister. Why is that not good enough for you?"

Another awkward silence.

"Our parents want you back," Big Bow says. "Why are you so selfish?" Anger and disappointment rise in his voice. "They want to see you again."

The two girls do not understand a word of the exchange but grasp its substance. Inez clasps her hand over Whirlwind's arm.

"You do not hear me," Whirlwind says stubbornly. "I do not want to go back with you." He looks into Stone's eyes. "Let me be."

A long silence. Then Stone nods. "It is as you say. You decide." He pauses. "Should you think differently after we go, you know where to find us."

Silence again.

"Where do you go from here?" Whirlwind asks, although he seems to ask without real concern.

"To Zarca." Stone half turns in the saddle and points to the northeast. "We were told that there are thousands of horses there. We take some and make for our own country."

He nods to his brother and calls out, and the half ring of warriors breaks up and moves up the road to where the women wait. No one looks back, not even Sendehma, to where Whirlwind and the two girls are left standing in the dust.

Stone has one more thing on his mind, one problem easy to solve. He hands the musket to Powderface and rides along the wagons looking for the cages. The circus people still sit in a stunned silence, their eyes following him as he passes. On the sixth wagon he finds the caged wolf, the metal crate half covered with a tarp. He brings the horse close and bends and unplugs the bolt and opens the cage door. The wolf springs out and runs. He goes on to open the cage of the puma on the next wagon and that of the jaguar on the next. He pulls the horse away and, to the recoiling and shrieking of the mules, watches as the cats bound away.

He turns the horse with the reins and slowly passes the caravan and Whirlwind and the two sisters. He does not see them now. He looks straight ahead.

• • •

Stone moves off on a slow lope, the band following, forming into the three-group column of march. Stone wants to get away from the circus and from his brother, not thinking about anything else, not even aware that he takes the Camino Real north. Behind him Sendehma has informed the women: Eaglenest, She-Wolf, and Bear Doctor Woman. No one talks now. The band rides in a glum silence. Everyone feels pity for Stone. After half a mile, when the circus is out of sight, they let the horses walk. A dot ahead turns out to be Necklace, who lets the column come up and reports that the road is clear. He looks around in surprise, expecting Whirlwind to be with them, then becomes aware of the mood of the band. He does not ask and Stone explains nothing. He joins the warrior group behind the headman. Someone there will tell him with words or in sign language.

They ride on, Stone still anxious to put distance between him and the place of disappointment back there. A coming together that should have had a joyful ending has turned into something odd, incomprehensible. So much effort, sacrifice wasted. Those who have come with him freely have left parts of their lives behind for this one mission. Has he betrayed them? He is ashamed. He feels responsible. How can he do good for them? He feels a bitter anger rise, but then he realizes that they are marching north aimlessly.

He abruptly halts the horse, and the band behind him also comes to a halt. He calls for Maria and Sendehma and the ranchero to come forward. As they edge their horses next to him, he asks, "Zarca, how do we get there?" His voice is brusque.

The man listens. He points east and speaks rapidly in Spanish. Sendehma translates from Maria's version in Kiowa. "See that mountain?" He points to a range with craggy heights rising above seven thousand feet. The range is about twenty-five miles away, east of the Nazas River. The range is a long rise, stretching northwest to southeast. In its southern half are two saddles that allow passage through it. The ranchero points to the saddle slightly northeast from where they are. "Beyond that opening in the mountains is the rancho La Zarca."

"How far behind the opening?"

The ranchero shrugs. "Five leguas."

"Thirteen miles," Maria says.

The ranchero coughs, nervous but determined. "Jefe," he says meekly, "I have done what you wanted me to do. I took you to Ramos. I have taken you close to La Zarca." He pauses briefly. "I have been a help to you. You promised to let me go." He pauses again. "I have a wife and a child. I have people who depend on me. When will you let me go?" He looks into the headman's eyes. He searches for a sign of understanding, for compassion.

Stone listens to the translation. He ignores the ranchero's plea. "We must decide something else," he says. "You told us that Zarca is a very large rancho. Horses, cattle, sheep. Where are the horses? You know that we want horses. Where are they held? Are they all over the rancho?"

The ranchero answers eagerly. Perhaps this little bit more and he is free? "There is a range for sheep, a range for cattle, and the horse and mule range. The horse and mule range is north of the rancho, east to Pelayo." Soldiers are stationed at Pelayo to protect the horse herd against Indian attacks out of the Bolsón de Mapimí, but that he does not tell Stone. Let him find out by himself.

Stone sits thinking it over. "You take us close to the horse range today. We camp there for the night. Tomorrow I let you go. Now let's ride!"

The ranchero is disappointed and angry. He is also afraid. If the La Zarca people find out that he led the norteños to their horse herd, what will they do to him? As he moves his horse next to Stone's and the column sets in motion, he ponders what he should do. He decides that it is best that he takes them where the headman wants to go. When they set him free, he is going to put as many miles between La Zarca and himself as the horse permits. But what about the Toboso woman, Lucia? Will she talk when she is let go? She has been to his rancho; she knows where he lives.

They continue a few more miles on the Camino Real, and then the ranchero leads the column east toward the Nazas River and they cross near the mouth of a small river that runs in from the colonia Indé and farther north. A tributary of this river originates in the long mountain range east of the Nazas, near the upper saddle. They climb up along the tributary toward the peaks and reach the head in early afternoon, a spring with good, clear water. They have not seen any humans but noticed that the slopes farther to the southeast are dotted with churra sheep.

After a guard is posted northward to watch toward the saddle, and the band settles down, Stone calls for a meeting and orders the ranchero into the middle of the circle. "Make a map," he says. "Show us what is north, south, and east of Zarca. Tell us what you know. Tell us the truth."

The ranchero knows what is expected of him. He has done it before. He nods. He picks up a number of rocks. He puts one down. "La Zarca," he says.

"How far from here?"

"Six leguas." Maria explains, "Fifteen miles."

The ranchero puts a second rock on the ground, a distance southeast of La Zarca. "Peñoles."

"How far from Zarca?"

The ranchero shrugs. "Five leguas, six."

"Fifteen miles," Maria says.

The ranchero nods. He bends and sets another rock northwest of La Zarca. "Cerro Gordo." This is a presidio with soldiers, but he does not tell. He gives an estimate of the distance between Cerro Gordo and the rancho before being asked. "Ten leguas."

"Twenty-six miles," Maria says.

Stone nods. "What is east of Zarca?"

"Two places. Only a few houses in each. La Cadena. Almost straight east." He places a rock. "Fifteen leguas from La Zarca."

"Forty miles." Maria's voice. Sendehma's voice.

The ranchero puts another rock down northwest of La Cadena. "Pelayo," he says. "A short way from La Cadena. Three leguas."

After Maria has given the distance between both places, seven miles, Stone asks, "Where is the horse range of Zarca on your map?"

The man makes a few scratches on the ground from north of the rancho toward Pelayo.

Stone nods. "How far from here to Pelayo?"

The ranchero counts with his fingers, speaking words referring to landmarks no one here knows. After a while he has figured it out. "Twenty leguas."

"Fifty miles." Maria again.

There is a silence.

"What is east of those places, Pelayo, La Cadena?"

The ranchero raises his eyebrows. Everyone knows that. "No more colonias and ranchos. La Tierra Despoblado. The Bolsón." He pauses. "Los Indios. Los Apaches. Los Cumanches. Los Norteños."

Now Stone cracks a smile. He nods. "Los Norteños." Serious again. "There is water in Pelayo and La Cadena?"

"Yes. Good water in La Cadena, poor water in Pelayo."

Stone listens to the translations. He sits for a while, thinking. Then he dismisses the ranchero with a gesture. "Aho. Thank you!"

He looks at the arrangement of stones on the ground. "We must memorize this map," he says. "When we leave here tomorrow we have to keep straight east or a little to the northeast, but not much. We have to come out at either of these two places, Pelayo or La Cadena." He looks along the attentive faces in the circle. Eyes are focused on the stone map. "Pewe?" he says.

"Pewe," he is answered.

He has not forgotten what happened earlier, his great disappointment, but the pain of it has somewhat lifted.

His eyes search for Sendehma. She sits aside, not part of the circle. She sits alone. Gondaima plays with the other children. Stone half turns and looks into Eaglenest's eyes. He motions with his head. Eaglenest understands and gets up as Stone gets up. She walks around the circle and gets on her knees next to the Kiowa woman. Stone walks to a spot away from the others and sits down and waits.

As Eaglenest and Sendehma come up to him, he motions to them to sit. They do, women's fashion, legs sideways. Sendehma's face is drawn, distant, as if she is far away, somewhere unreachable.

Stone waits. He understands. Finally he speaks. He holds the prayer stick in his right hand. He speaks slowly, trying to make the words reach a woman devastated by what has transpired. "I know how you feel. I feel as bad as you do." He pauses. "It seems we came in vain." He pauses again. "I want you to know that I feel I lost a brother. I think you feel you lost a husband, a father to your daughter." Again he pauses. This is hard, not fashioned for a headman to resolve. There are others, *maheonhetaneo,* more qualified to deal with something like this. But it is he who must say something. "You are my brother's wife. You will always be that. Look at me."

Reluctantly, slowly, Sendehma raises her head and looks at him. "You belong to us," Stone says. "You belong to Eaglenest and me. We are your family." He pauses. "You have a family in the Ka'ta camp, your parents, brothers, relations. That you have. You also have us. We ask you to live with Eaglenest and me, in our lodge, Gondaima growing up with children we will have. I will care for you and your daughter as I care for Eaglenest. We will be one."

Sendehma looks into the headman's eyes. She looks away. She is hurt. She is thinking. Perhaps. That is one way. She looks up again. "Aho," she says. "I must think about it."

As the women get up, he gestures to Sendehma to stay. He asks Eaglenest to bring Maria and the Toboso woman. They come and Stone points to the ground. They sit down. Lucia has brought Pedro with her and clutches him, unaware of what she is doing. She transmits her fear to the boy. He looks startled.

"Tell Lucia that she can leave in the morning when we ride away from here." He addresses Sendehma, who, after some hesitation, explains it to Maria. Maria speaks to Lucia in Spanish. Lucia speaks only broken Spanish, and Maria has to repeat her words. Now Lucia comprehends and her face lights up. Her eyes brim with tears as she clutches the headman's hand. He gently withdraws his hand and tries a smile.

"You take the horse you have been riding," he says. "Eaglenest will give you some food for your journey." He pauses, waiting for the translations to run their course. "Sendehma will give you some coins we took from the bandits."

Lucia looks from Stone to Sendehma and Maria. It seems she cannot believe what she hears. She bends forward and cries, while Pedro watches with huge eyes, not knowing whether he should cry too.

Sendehma tries to calm her. "Where are you riding from here?" Stone asks to change the situation.

Lucia wipes the tears from her cheeks and tries to pull herself together. "Back to Tagualito. I have a sister there. A brother of my husband is there too." Suddenly she thinks again of her husband killed by the bandits. Again her eyes fill with tears.

Stone wants to end it. "Go now," he says firmly, "make ready for tomorrow."

When she gets up and leaves, Stone gestures to Sendehma and Maria to stay. Now he looks at Maria, who may know what is coming. "I have to talk to you," he says. He waits, letting Sendehma translate. "You have been of great service to me, to all of us," he continues. "Without you we would not be here. That my brother decided to stay with the circo no one could know. I did not."

Again he waits.

"I am grateful for what you did. I promised you after we got you from that town, San Miguel, that you could go wherever you wanted after this was over."

He waits. Maria looks at him with a smile.

"It is over now," he says. "Take some of the coins. Perhaps you can get back to your people by the big river in the north, bigger than the Río Bravo." He smiles. He remembers her saying that when they reached the Rio Grande and looked it over. It seems a very long time ago.

Maria shakes her head. "I still have to take you places," she says. She is not fooled by the headman. She knows that this hard man has a soft heart. "There are towns you have not seen yet." It is all in jest.

Stone understands and smiles a little and waits for the real answer.

Now she is serious. "One of your men has asked me to be his wife. Yellow Eyes. I said yes to him. I will become his wife when we get to your camp in the Plains. He is good to my little boy and he is good to me."

Stone has expected this since Eaglenest showed him Maria making moccasins for Yellow Eyes. He is genuinely pleased and shows it. "You made a good choice," he says. "Yellow Eyes is a Kit Fox, one of my best. My wife and I will help you when we are back in the Hovxnova camp." This is a very fortunate turn. To have a reliable and competent Spanish speaker around has been a blessing and will be an asset in the future. "I am glad for you and Yellow Eyes and your son." He means it, and it shows.

A few warriors stand a short distance away, waiting to talk with the headman. Sendehma notices and informs Maria with a remark in Kiowa. When the women get up and leave, the warriors let them pass. Stone points to the ground, and they sit down with crossed legs. They are Powderface, Porcupine, Little Bird, Lame Coyote, Holy Singer, and White Wolf. Stony faces. They are serious. Powderface speaks.

"I am a maheonhetan. I am also a warrior. I am not a member of a soldier society. I was asked to speak for all, for Hovxnova Kit Foxes and Red Shields and for the Heviksnipahis Kit Foxes. And I speak for the women too. They wanted me to say that."

He pauses.

"They want me to tell you that they have come on this ride for you and your brother. They say that they think that we did good and that we got where we wanted to go. We found your brother. We could not know that he has changed. He was free to choose. He chose to stay."

Again he pauses.

"It is all right. He must do what he wants to do. We respect that. We have not come for nothing. We have seen much. We have learned much. We have seen another country different from ours. A country dead in many ways. No game left. Only tame animals—sheep, cattle, mules, horses. Horses we like." He chuckles. "No one of us was killed or even badly hurt."

Another pause.

"Some things we did not see because we were riding at night so often." He chuckles again.

"You did well for us. Don't blame yourself for Whirlwind. This is up to him. We are grateful to you, although sometimes we bickered and were impatient. It was a long ride. Now we are ready to turn home."

Another pause.

"This is what I have to say for all of us."

Stone has listened, eyes to the ground. The prayer stick is motionless in his hand. Now he looks up. "Aho," he says.

"Aho," they all answer.

The warriors get up, one by one, Powderface first. They extend the open palm of their right hand toward Stone's right hand without touching. They look into each other's eyes. It is done. It has been said. They stand together for a moment, and then the warriors walk away.

After nightfall, for the evening meal, a fire is made that is invisible from farther than three hundred paces away.

TWENTY-TWO

November 28, 1807

Set's morning song is the last Lucia will hear from Stone's party. At first light, when men and women wriggle from their sleeping robes, the Toboso woman has already packed and saddled her horse and is mounted. Her eyes look for Stone, and when she sees him standing among the first warriors getting up, she raises her right arm. He does the same. Pedro sits behind her, holding on to her belt, his eyes taking in the scene of the waking camp. Perhaps he searches for the children with whom he has shared food, play, and endless hours on horseback. His mother slowly guides the horse around the edge of the camp, and then, with a clatter of hooves on the rocky ground, they are gone.

The ranchero has watched them leave. Now he comes walking toward Stone. The headman makes signs, letting the ranchero know that he may leave, and he hurries back to put his gear together. He takes his pack and the saddle to where the horses are bunched and leads his mount out from among the others and saddles up. He moves quickly. When he mounts up he does not bother with a last look but rides off, eager to get away.

When the hoofbeat fades away, Stone calls on Lame Bear. He tells him to follow the ranchero a short distance to see what direction he takes. It is expected that he will make for the Nazas and Ramos and the Camino Real, but Stone wants to be sure that he does not take another route and try to warn La Zarca of the Cheyennes.

When Lame Bear is gone the others break camp. It takes a little more than half an hour until the party is ready. They are standing by their horses when Lame Bear returns. His face is grim.

"The Spanish man has killed the woman and the boy," he says bluntly, looking at Stone.

A groan. Maria. She is the only one who could communicate a little with Lucia. She has worked with Lucia making tortillas, cooking food. Pedro was Manuel's playmate. A sad but good woman.

The others are stunned. "How did it happen?" Stone asks with a harsh voice.

"I rode a ways to a point from where I could see much of the trail down. The Spanish man overtook the woman. They rode side by side, and then he knocked her and the boy down. He dismounted and killed both with a knife. He took the woman's horse by the reins and rode off, fast." He pauses. "They were too far away. I could not do anything."

Stone nods. "Yes." He stands looking at the ground. A bad, cold-hearted act, this. He has seen how the Spanish treat Indians in their country. It is something to remember.

He looks over the rigid faces around him and turns back to Lame Bear. "Which way did the man ride after that?"

"He stayed on the trail we came up on yesterday."

He makes for the Nazas, Stone thinks. "Pewe," he says. And after a moment, "Let us ride."

They ride parallel to the crest of the ridge and reach the saddle, a gate in the mountains, after four miles. They let the horses walk to save their stamina for what is to come. Each member of the party rides a fresh horse, one not ridden on the uphill trail the day before. This time the warriors follow Stone in single file. Each of the five women leads a string of packhorses and reserve horses behind the men. From the summit of the saddle they have a wide view of the country to the east. They halt and form a ragged line, looking out.

They see a high grassy plateau, cut by some northeast-trending arroyos and topped by a few smooth, low hills and one mountain far away. The land is like a flat plain. From where they are on the seven-thousand-foot level, the land descends gradually to five thousand feet fifty miles away, where they believe the two places the ranchero marked on his ground map, La Cadena and Pelayo, to be. They notice to the southeast, about fifteen miles away, some smoke coming from behind a hill: this should be La Zarca. For about ten miles below them the land lies empty. Beyond, east and southeast, for a few miles, they see the tiny whites and blacks and browns of churra sheep, grazing, hardly moving. Miles farther, rust-colored cattle, and even farther, not yet visible in the predawn light, the horse range, or where it should be. They imprint the lay of the land upon their minds and match it with what they have heard from the ranchero. They have seen enough. Stone calls out and they ride down, slowly, to protect the horses.

They ride in a loose formation, the women bringing up the rear. They ride straight east, and after ten miles they ride into the rising sun. Where the plateau drops to six thousand feet, they pass a quarry and negotiate a steep slope and come in among the churra. The sheep are widely scattered, and the party moves through without causing a scare. But two mounted herders, protecting the sheep from wolves, have seen them and both gallop away toward La Zarca.

From now on everything depends on speed. The party switches to a slow lope. Stone figures that it may take upward of two hours before the vaqueros from the ranch begin trailing them or, believing that the raiders are after horses, try to pass them on the south and circle to cut them off before they reach either La Cadena or Pelayo.

They pass through the churra herd and miles farther come upon the cattle. These are robust, half-wild animals that give ground reluctantly. But they are spread thinly over a large area, and the party moves through without hindrance. An arroyo opens up before them, cut two dozen feet deep into the level plain, its sides eroded in places where cattle and sheep walk down to drink. The riders follow the sharp edge of the arroyo wall until they come to the broken slope above a watering place where they guide the horses down and up the other side. There is a seep of water on the bottom of the arroyo, marred by cattle tracks. Again they let the horses walk for most of a mile before they let them run on another slow lope. Soon they pass through an empty stretch of land, overgrazed and barren, where only cacti and some creosote bush and a few yucca hold on to the dry soil. The cacti slow them down, as they let the horses find their way around clusters of low-growing cacti to avoid injury from their needle-sharp spines.

Looking back, Stone sees nothing of a pursuit yet. The sun rises steadily in a clear blue sky. After they get through the barrens they come to another arroyo with water in it, and after they have crossed they have reached the horse and mule range. They have covered about thirty-five miles since riding down from the gate in the mountains and are eighteen miles northeast of La Zarca as the raven flies.

Stone halts the column, and they gaze over the land. In the southeast, in the direction of La Cadena, rises a lone mountain from the plain, and in the northeast, in front of Pelayo, sixteen miles away, lies a batch of low hills that mask the hamlet somewhere behind it. The whole plain before them, as far as the eye can see, is dotted with hundreds and hundreds, thousands, of animals, the dark red humps of mules, horses in black and white, skins in roan, bay, and pinto. No one of the party has seen that many horses in one place. They watch, absorbed, until Stone rides forward and they move out.

They ride close together into the scattered herds, changing often from a walk to a lope, so not to disturb the animals and to save their own. Stone has taken the course toward Pelayo. He wants to draw away from a possible ambush attempt by an enemy coming from the south before La Cadena. He plans to get near Pelayo before cutting out a couple of hundred animals and then drive the captured herd through the hills and through Pelayo. As they ride on, mules and horses give way, keeping a distance. The animals, as wild as mustangs, are used to vaqueros and see no danger in these riders. Only a few stallions, protecting small family herds, show defiance, facing the column with angry roars and stomping hooves.

White Wolf shouts and points east. They see them now: three vaqueros, about two miles away, sit their horses, watching. As the column proceeds, they whirl their horses around and ride off. One takes the direction of Pelayo, the others make for La Cadena. They will raise the alarm.

As the party makes its way toward the hills in front of Pelayo, the men from La Zarca finally show themselves. They have come out of the long Arroyo de las Cadena and ridden north in the cover of the lone mountain and emerge in swirling dust around the mountain's east shoulder. Sendehma, in the rear, has seen them first. After eyeing them for a while, Stone guesses their number to be between forty and fifty. They are headed straight north and may be ten to twelve miles away.

The race has started. The rushing band of vaqueros creates some panic among the herds to the south, but this takes place too far away to stir the animals in front of Stone's party. He sends seven warriors and Big Bow ahead to round up a couple of hundred horses toward the gap in the hills. As this group speeds up, followed by the women with their strings of animals, Stone and the remaining six warriors do not change their pace. He keeps measuring the speed of the vaquero advance against the speed of the roundup.

The vaqueros, excellent riders on good horses, as Stone observes, are gaining ground but not as fast as feared. They must have ridden at least thirty miles or more and not spared their horses much. Their mounts seem to slow down. As they push forward, they are no longer in a compact group. Their formation becomes drawn out; riders have fallen back.

Four miles ahead of Stone, the roundup has started. Yelling and yipping, some singing in high-pitched voices, the men of the advance party have fanned out and encircled a large number of animals and are beginning to drive them toward the hills. There is no time to separate horses from mules, and from the mass of animals gathered, small bunches branch off and escape, slipping by the few herders. To bring so many animals together takes some time, but then one warrior takes the point and flank riders urge the animals forward, and with the women and their strings in the drag position, the stream of horses sets in motion. Slow at first, the stream quickly gains speed with a powerful churning of hooves.

For the remuda the distance to the gap in the hills is about three miles, but these horses are rested and willing to run. The enemies' horses are tiring. Now about two miles behind the rear guard, the vaqueros are too late to catch them, but they keep coming. Stone's group speeds up more. Their horses are tiring too. They ride on, the first bunch of vaqueros slowly gaining on Stone. Ahead, the wave of horses has thinned out and surges into the gap. The vaqueros use quirts and spurs to force their mounts to give their last to catch at least the rear guard, but after a run of another mile and a half the Cheyennes reach the gap a few hundred paces before the enemy.

The seven Cheyennes ride into the gap, a passage between bulging slopes, and bring their foam-covered, exhausted horses to a halt. They check their muskets and straighten bow-and-arrow cases on their backs. As the rumble of hooves draws near, they ride out and form a line across the mouth of the gap. In front of them, a short distance away, the front riders of the vaqueros bring their horses to a sudden halt, creating a melee as more riders drive in from behind, colliding with horses and men in front of them. The Cheyennes raise their muskets and fire. The salvo has a shattering effect. Men and horses have been hit. Screams, shrieks, as horses tumble or break away. The Cheyennes reload their muskets and fire another crashing salvo, and then only a few crippled horses and a few men dead or wounded remain before them; the vaqueros in the rear are in full flight. Again the warriors reload, but there is no target left. They shout the war cry of the Kit Foxes, raising their weapons in their fists, turn their horses, and ride slowly into the passage on the fresh trail cut by thousands of hooves. They give their horses a little rest and ride on.

They come out to Pelayo, a station for a handful of soldiers, surrounded by hills. Two warm springs are in that place, and the smell of sulfur taints the air. Soldiers stand between the two major buildings looking east to where the remuda has disappeared. They seem to have offered no resistance when the remuda came through, and they offer none now when the rear guard rides by. Instead, they hasten to their lodgings, and Stone and his men ride on without a shot being fired. A mile out on the trail the women wait with the strings of extra horses. The men change mounts and they all ride on, following in the dust of the remuda trail. A few miles farther, the men riding herd have turned the mass of animals upon itself, waiting. As the rear guard and the women come up, Stone takes the lead as point rider and the remuda is set in motion again, turned east toward the great laguna, where they have been once before.

• • •

They are back in the Bolsón, the Empty Quarter of northeastern New Spain. The camp is by the southwestern bulge of the Laguna de Tagualita, thirty-five miles due east of Pelayo, eighteen miles northeast of the former presidio and mission of Mapimí, now a small, grimy mining town. The captured herd is spread out in front of the broad reed belt of the laguna, where the grass is good. The animals have been counted. One count arrived at 427 horses and 43 mules, another at 439 horses and 43 mules. No matter, it is a good catch. Although Cheyennes have no use for mules as riding and pack animals, they can trade them on the Missouri River to the English traders.

Maria has shown the camp another use for mules. When she lived with the Comanches, she saw horses and mules slaughtered for food in times of need. When she told Sendehma, who translated this to a skeptical audience, the Cheyennes frowned on killing horses for food and rejected the idea outright. But the long march north to the Plains had to be considered, and the facts were that there are no cattle stations on the way and game is scarce. Finally, without enthusiasm, a mule was butchered and the meat tested. It was found unappealing but acceptable under the circumstances. As a consequence, on the second day in camp, strips of meat from six butchered mules were hung to dry on a net of lariats stretched between mesquites and willows near the shore. Firewood is plentiful, and fires burn bright at night. They intend to stay for a third day before taking the trail north. Through the day they have two scouts some miles back on the trail. During the night, guards ride herd on the horses, watching out for pumas or jaguars.

On the third night, an hour after sundown, after they have eaten, men and women, sitting apart in groups, congregate around the fire. Some quietly talk with others; some sit in silence, looking into the flames. An occasional muffled laugh. Set, who carries on with a bone in the dark outside the circle, suddenly stops and, with a howl, charges into the night. The women rise, men grab their weapons. They hear the hoofbeats of two horses as men who guard the herd converge on the location where Set snarls ferociously. He has detected something strange or dangerous or someone who does not belong, and he has brought to bay whoever they are or whatever it is. Then, away in the dark, voices speak in Cheyenne, a brief flurry, unintelligible, and riders move toward the camp despite Set's remonstrations. Because the guards have not called a warning, men and women by the fire stand, not knowing what to anticipate.

A Cheyenne voice again, trying to calm the dog. Dull hoofbeat. They come into the light of the fire: the guards on their horses and between them, still followed by the suspicious Set, one rider, two—no, one rider and two riding double. Mules. The guards hold their horses back, and the mules stop. The single rider dismounts and steps closer into the brightness. A white shirt, the hair carefully braided. The face . . .

It is Whirlwind. He stands and searches faces turned toward him. A horse nickers, a hoof is lifted and set back on the ground. Still no sound from the men and women. Whirlwind stands. Like a shadow someone moves through the cluster of men and slowly approaches him.

"Vahé." It is Stone's voice. He sees a tired face, the eyes glinting in the shine of the fire.

Whirlwind does not answer. He stretches out his hands toward his brother, who does the same, palms almost touching. Thus they stand for a long moment, then let their arms drop to their sides.

"You couldn't stay away," Stone says.

Whirlwind nods but says nothing.

"I have waited for this for a long time," Stone says.

"I know," Whirlwind says. Then, after a pause, "So have I."

A pause. Still no one else speaks. Men and women stand motionless as if tied to the ground.

"How did you find us?"

Whirlwind shrugs. The flicker of a smile. "I followed your tracks." A pause. "I could not miss them."

Finally a movement by the fire. Men open a path as Sendehma walks toward the brothers. Stone steps to the side. Wife and husband face each other. They look into each other's eyes. Thus they stand for a long moment. No word is said. Then Whirlwind reaches out and pulls Sendehma to him, hugging her. Stone sees tears glisten in her eyes, but she controls her emotions. A strong, sensitive woman, she will not cry.

Whirlwind releases her and puts his face close to hers. "I have brought Inez. You have seen her. She will live with us." He looks deep into Sendehma's eyes. So they stand. After a few moments that seem like an eternity, Sendehma nods. "Pewé."

Whirlwind hugs her once again. He releases her and half turns. "Inez, Ada," he calls.

The two girls dismount and slowly come forward. They wear long cotton dresses and rebozos over their upper bodies, Spanish style.

The black hair is loose and long. Light brown skin, high cheekbones. They stand shyly next to Whirlwind, looking down, knowing that all eyes are on them.

Sendehma breaks the silence. She makes a step forward. "I am Sendehma," she says in Cheyenne. She takes Inez's hand. Now the girl looks up.

Inez answers in Cheyenne. "Nanehov Inez—I am Inez."

Sendehma is surprised. "Vahé," she says.

Whirlwind prods Ada. The sixteen-year-old also calls her name in Cheyenne. "Nanehov Ada."

A soft, lighthearted laughter runs through the men. "I see you are teaching them our language," Stone says. Then, "Come in, sit down."

As they move to the fire, Whirlwind is mobbed by men whom he has known since childhood. Sendehma takes the girls to the women. Near them the children lie bundled up, asleep. The great red dog settles behind the robe that covers Gondaima, vigilant as ever. Friendly faces everywhere.

EPILOGUE

The story of the twins and the raid into New Spain in 1807 does not end at the great laguna. At the time of their reunion, December 1, 1807, winter storms were howling through the front range of the Rocky Mountains below the Platte, through the Panhandle and the Plains of Nuevo Mexico. The snow cover was deep in many areas, and the bare, frozen ground in others gave little sustenance to buffalo and other game and to horses from what remained of short grasses such as blue grama and buffalo grass. In the typical winter of the shortgrass Plains, animals suffered, while in the tipi camps people made do with the few resources available. Killing buffalo in snow drifts or starving elk were unexpected gratuities ensuring human survival; horses were sometimes kept alive on cottonwood bark alone.

Stone, who carried the burden of responsibility for the survival of the band and the captured herd, knew this too well. To drive the herd north into the winter Plains would have been disastrous. So he listened when Inez proposed a different strategy. She and her sister were not Tobosos, as had been thought, but members of the Cacaxtes, a tribe whose ancient homeland was below the Big Bend of the Rio Grande. Reduced in numbers by epidemics of European diseases, their last little bands had been driven south by Lipan Apache arrivals and Comanche raiders. Neither Inez nor Ada had ever seen the country of their ancestors but remembered old stories told when they were refugees on ranches near Parras. The stories described green valleys from below the Chisos Mountains in the west to the mouth of the Pecos River in the east. Why not wait out the winter there and take the herd north in spring when the new grass was coming out all over the Plains? Perhaps Inez was also thinking of the new life growing within her, soon to come into this world.

So it was done. They took the herd through the Bolsón to the Rio Grande and slowly followed the river east, moving from one valley to another. Across from the mouth of San Francisco Creek they found herds of buffalo that ended their food quest. There was one skirmish with a Lipan party, but afterward they were left alone. In early April a healthy baby boy was born to Inez, a joy for the whole band. In the middle of April they crossed the Rio Grande on the march to their home range, arriving in early June.

They lost no more than two dozen horses, and none of the surviving mules, since leaving the great laguna and before arrival at the headwaters of the Republican River. They had been given up for lost by the Ka'ta camp and the Hovxnova and Heviksnipahis camps and received a raucous welcome. They were just in time for the Cheyenne divisions' trek north for the annual ceremonies held near the Black Hills.

Whirlwind moved with his family—Sendehma, Inez, the children, and Ada—into the Hovxnova camp where his tipi would stand next to Stone's, with Eaglenest and their two children, as long as they lived. About later exploits of Stone and Whirlwind and the companions the storytellers have been silent. It is certain that the raid of 1807–8 was not their last into New Spain. It is recorded in history that Cheyenne parties, like parties of other tribes from the Buffalo Plains, continued to raid beyond the Bolsón into the 1850s, after Mexican independence from Spain and the Mexican-American War.

SOURCES & FURTHER READING

Archer, Christian I. *The Army in Bourbon Mexico, 1760–1810.* Albuquerque: University of New Mexico Press, 1977.

Bannon, John Francis. *Spanish Borderlands Frontier, 1513–1821.* Albuquerque: University of New Mexico Press, 1974.

Eguilaz de Prado, Isabel. *Los Indios del nordeste de Mexico en el siglo XVIII.* Seminario de Anthropologia Americana. Publicaciones 7. Seville, Spain, 1965.

Faulk, Odie B. *The Leather Jacket Soldier: Spanish Military Equipment and Institutions of the Late 18th Century.* Pasadena, CA: Socio-Technical Publications, 1971.

Foster, Morris W., and Martha McCullough. "Plains Apache." In *Plains.* Vol. 13 of *Handbook of North American Indians.* Edited by Raymond J. DeMallie. Washington, DC: Smithsonian Institution, 2001.

Gregg, Josiah. *Commerce of the Prairies.* Edited by Max L. Moorhead. Norman: University of Oklahoma Press, 1954.

Griffen, William B. *Culture Change and Shifting Populations in Central Northern Mexico.* Anthropological Papers of the University of Arizona, no. 13. Tucson: University of Arizona Press, 1969.

———. "Southern Periphery: East." In *Southwest*. Vol. 10 of *Handbook of North American Indians.* Edited by Alfonso Ortiz. Washington, DC: Smithsonian Institution, 1983.

Hardy, Robert W. H. *Travels in the Interior of Mexico in 1825, 1826, 1827, and 1828.* London: H. Colburn and R. Bentley, 1829. Reprint, Glorieta, NM: Rio Grande Press, 1977.

Kavanagh, Thomas W. "Comanche." In *Plains.* Vol. 13 of *Handbook of North American Indians.* Edited by Raymond J. DeMallie. Washington, DC: Smithsonian Institution, 2001.

Kenner, Charles L. *The Comanchero Frontier.* Norman: University of Oklahoma Press, 1974.

Levy, Jerrold E. "Kiowa." In *Plains.* Vol. 13 of *Handbook of North American Indians.* Edited by Raymond J. DeMallie. Washington, DC: Smithsonian Institution, 2001.

Mayer, Brantz. *Mexico, Aztec, Spanish, and Republican: A Historical, Geographical, Political, Statistical, and Social Account of that Country from the Period of the Invasion of the Spaniards to the Present Time; with a View of the Ancient Aztec Empire and Civilization; a Historical Sketch of the Late War; and Notices of New Mexico and California.* Hartford, CT: S. Drake, 1851.

McAlister, Lyle N. *The "Fuero Militar" in New Spain, 1764–1800.* Gainesville: University of Florida Press, 1957.

McAllister, J. Gilbert. "Kiowa Apache Social Organization." In *Social Anthropology of North American Tribes,* edited by Fred Eggan, 99–169. Chicago: University of Chicago Press, 1955.

Mooney, James. *Calendar History of the Kiowa Indians.* Pt. 1 of Seventeenth Annual Report of the Bureau of American Ethnology (for) 1895–96, 129–468. Washington, DC: Smithsonian Institution, 1898.

Moore, John H. "The Ornithology of Cheyenne Traditionalists." *Plains Anthropologist* 31:177–92, 1986.

———. *The Cheyenne Nation.* Lincoln: University of Nebraska Press, 1987.

Moorhead, Max L. *The Apache Frontier: Jacobo Ugarte and Spanish-Indian Relations in Northern New Spain, 1769–1791.* Norman: University of Oklahoma Press, 1968.

———. *The Presidio: Bastion of the Spanish Borderlands.* Norman: University of Oklahoma Press, 1975.

Murie, James R. *Ceremonies of the Pawnee.* Edited by Douglas R. Parks. Lincoln: University of Nebraska Press, 1981.

Noyes, Stanley. *Los Comanches: The Horse People, 1751–1845.* Albuquerque: University of New Mexico Press, 1993.

Opler, Morris E. "Mescalero Apache." In *Southwest.* Vol. 10 of *Handbook of North American Indians.* Edited by Alfonso Ortiz. Washington, DC: Smithsonian Institution, 1983.

———. "Lipan Apache." In *Plains.* Vol. 13 of *Handbook of North American Indians.* Edited by Raymond L. DeMallie. Washington, DC: Smithsonian Institution, 2001.

Parsons, Elsie Clews. *Kiowa Tales.* New York: G. E. Stechert, 1929.

Pike, Zebulon Montgomery. *The Journals of Zebulon Montgomery Pike with Letters and Related Documents.* Edited and annotated by Donald Jackson. 2 vols. Norman: University of Oklahoma Press, 1966.

Sauer, Carl. *Aboriginal Population of Northwestern Mexico.* Berkeley: University of California Press, 1935.

Schlesier, Karl H. "Rethinking the Dismal River Aspect and the Plains Athapaskans, A.D. 1692–1768." *Plains Anthropologist* 17:101–33, 1972.

———. *The Wolves of Heaven: Cheyenne Shamanism, Ceremonies, and Prehistoric Origins.* Norman: University of Oklahoma Press, 1987.

———. "Rethinking the Midewiwin and the Plains Ceremonial called the Sun Dance." *Plains Anthropologist* 35:1–27, 1990.

———. "Commentary: A History of Ethnic Groups in the Great Plains A.D. 150–1550." In *Plains Indians, A.D. 500–1500,* edited by Karl H. Schlesier, 308–81. Norman: University of Oklahoma Press, 1994.

Schroeder, Albert A. *A Study of the Apache Indians,* pt. 1–5. American Indian Ethnohistory: Indians of the Southwest: Apache Indians I. Edited and compiled by David Agee Horr. New York: Garland, 1974.

Weber, David J., ed. *New Spain's Far Northern Frontier: Essays on Spain in the American West, 1540–1821.* Albuquerque: University of New Mexico Press, 1979.

———. *The Mexican Frontier, 1821–1846: The American Southwest under Mexico.* Albuquerque: University of New Mexico Press, 1982.

Weltfish, Gene. *The Lost Universe: Pawnee Life and Culture.* Lincoln: University of Nebraska Press, 1965.